Healing Hearts

New Hope Falls: Book #6

By

KIMBERLY RAE
JORDAN

THREE**STRAND**
P R E S S

A CORD OF THREE STRANDS IS NOT EASILY BROKEN.

A man, a woman & their God.
Three Strand Press publishes Christian Romance stories
that intertwine love, faith and family. Always clean.
Always heartwarming. Always uplifting.

HEALING HEARTS/ Kimberly Rae Jordan. -- 1st ed.
ISBN-13: 978-1-988409-44-3

There is no fear in love;
but perfect love casts out fear,
because fear involves torment.
But he who fears
has not been made perfect in love.

I John 4:18 NKJV

CHAPTER ONE

Sophia Haldorson shut off the car's engine, then turned to look at her almost-five-year-old son who sat in his car seat behind her. "Ready to go see Nana?"

He nodded, his unruly curls dancing with the movement of his head. "I can color there, right?"

"Yep. You know Nana has crayons and coloring books for you." She smiled at him. "You can undo your buckle now."

"Thanks, Momma."

She pulled the keys from the ignition and dropped them in her purse before getting out of the car. When she opened the back door, Bryson climbed out holding a small bag and immediately took her hand.

Together, they hurried toward the entrance of the personal care home where her grandmother now lived. Small puddles from the rain earlier in the day dotted the asphalt of the parking lot, but unlike many kids his age, Bryson wasn't drawn to them. Despite Sophia's best efforts encouraging him to indulge in things like puddle jumping, he wasn't having any of it.

Hoping that the rain was over for the time being, Sophia looked up. She was happy to see that the sun was peeking out from behind the clouds that were streaked across the sky like a diaphanous white veil.

Your steadfast love, O Lord, extends to the heavens, your faithfulness to the clouds.

The verse flitted through her mind, catching her a bit off-guard. It had happened a lot over the years she'd been away. Something would trigger a verse or a song, always things she had memorized growing up. Somehow, she thought that it would be a less frequent occurrence now that she and Bryson were back home.

She didn't have time to dwell on that thought right then, however, as Bryson practically dragged her to the doors leading into the building. As they walked through the foyer of the care home, the nurse behind the receptionist desk smiled at them.

"Hiya, Bryson. How's it going?"

Bryson pressed closer to Sophia as he looked at the matronly nurse who greeted him. "Good."

Sophia was glad that he responded, except she knew that it was an automatic response, born out of a fear of repercussions. Not from her. Never from her. But they were both still having to relearn their responses and reactions.

"I'm glad to hear that." She gave Bryson a wink. "I know Nana is looking forward to your visit."

Bryson nodded, then looked up at Sophia.

"Yep, and we're looking forward to seeing her too," Sophia said. "We brought her a treat."

When Bryson lifted the bag, the nurse said, "Well, I won't keep you because I know Nana loves treats."

They said goodbye and made their way to Nana's room. It was a corner room at the end of a long hallway, and on sunny days, it was flooded with light.

"My sunshines!" Nana greeted them with a broad smile and held out her arms.

With only the briefest of hesitations, Bryson moved to where she sat in her wheelchair and gave her a hug. Sophia wanted to weep with relief at seeing how Nana's love was drawing him out of his reserved shell, even if it was just a tiny bit at a time.

"Look at you, my handsome boy." Nana cupped his face in her hands and kissed his forehead, then looked up at Sophia. "And look at you, my beautiful girl."

Sophia bent to kiss her cheek. "You look very nice. Did you get your hair cut?"

"I did." Nana fluffed her white curls, then held her hands out. "And I got my nails done too."

"That's a very lovely color for spring," Sophia said, admiring the bright shade of pink on her grandma's nails.

Bryson climbed up on the chair he always used at the small table that sat next to the window. He leaned over and put the bag on the table in front of Nana. "We brought you cookies."

"Oooh." Nana picked up the bag and opened it, inhaling as she did. "Snickerdoodles? My favorite."

"I helped Momma," Bryson told her as Sophia settled into the other chair at the table.

Nana took a cookie out of the bag and bit into it. "I can taste your help, Bryson. This is a super yummy cookie."

Bryson beamed at her words, and Sophia couldn't help but smile as well. If there was one thing that her grandma excelled at, it was at loving. Sophia knew that firsthand.

"Here." Nana held out a cookie to Bryson. "I think your help deserves a cookie."

"Thank you, Nana." Bryson took the cookie and settled back in his chair.

Nana turned her soft blue gaze to Sophia. "How was dinner?"

Sophia leaned back in her chair and sighed. "A little bit of everything."

"Tell me all about it," Nana said, then lifted her hand, palm out. "Except if your mother's pregnant. I don't want to hear that."

With a laugh, Sophia shook her head. "Nope. Not Mom."

Nana's eyes widened. "There *was* a pregnancy announcement?"

Sophia nodded. "Oh boy, I'm not sure I want to know."

"Well, it wasn't Madelyn."

"I should hope not. That girl's not even out of high school yet."

"Let's just say that the announcement led to another epic argument."

"Chloe then."

"Yep. Baby number five on the way."

"Let me guess," Nana said. "Natalie lectured her on all the reasons why she shouldn't keep having kids."

"Yep. But I think Chloe was spoiling for a fight because if she hadn't been, she would have announced her pregnancy last week when Natalie and Anthony weren't there for dinner."

"What did your mom say?"

Sophia sighed. "Well, as to be expected, she took Chloe's side. I mean, you know how Mom is about babies. The more, the merrier."

"I would imagine that even with your mom and Chloe against her, Natalie still held her own."

"Of course," Sophia said as she got the coloring books and crayons Nana kept for Bryson and gave them to him. "She knows how to hold her own and can out-talk us all when it comes to something she's passionate about. Natalie had news of her own, though no one reacted quite like they did to Chloe's."

"Not a pregnancy announcement, obviously."

"Obviously," Sophia agreed with a nod. "Something she was working on with her team was approved. She didn't give many details because most of us don't quite grasp what she actually does."

Natalie, the second oldest of her sisters, worked in marketing as a brand manager for some big company in Seattle. Her husband was a business consultant, and though married for four years, they had no children, and from the sounds of it, they didn't ever plan to. Her oldest sister, Chloe, was happy to be a stay-at-home mom with lots of kids while her husband worked as a manager at a grocery store in Everett.

The two sisters butted heads on a regular basis, and inevitably, the others in the family jumped in with their opinions, making for raucous discussions. It was way too much for her and Bryson to deal with, so they usually made their escape as soon as the meal was over. Thankfully, Sophia was pretty sure that none of them had noticed when they'd slipped away earlier.

"Everything okay at the house?" Nana asked.

"It's perfect. No issues."

"And the car?"

"Also doing just fine."

When she and Bryson had come back to New Hope, they'd stayed with her parents for the first couple of weeks, but the noisy chaos of the house had been untenable for her and Bryson. Plus, she didn't think her brothers had been happy about having to share a room so that she and Bryson could have one to themselves.

Thankfully, even though Nana had decided to move into the care home permanently because she'd fallen twice, breaking and then rebreaking the same hip, she hadn't sold her house and car. The older woman had been quick to offer both to Sophia. There had been protests by some in the family, but thankfully, her dad had shut them down.

"Are you sure you don't want to move back home with me?" Sophia asked.

Nana gave her an indulgent look. "Sweetheart, you know that would never work. The house isn't set up for wheelchair access. Plus, I kind of like this place. I've made friends here, and being able to hang out with them easily is a real blessing. The house is yours and Bryson's. I just want you to tell me if anything goes wrong with it so I can make arrangements for repairs."

"Let me pay rent." Sophia made the offer on a regular basis, even though she wasn't sure how she'd swing it. But if it made things financially easier for Nana, she'd figure out a way.

"Nope." Nana leaned forward, resting her elbows on the arms of the wheelchair. "I am more than happy to be able to do this for you."

Sophia was closer to Nana than any of her other siblings were, but that was mainly because Nana had taken over Sophia's care from the time she'd been six months old.

Her mom had already had Chloe, a five-year-old, and Natalie, a three-year-old, when Sophia had been born. Within two months of Sophia's birth, her mom was pregnant again with Christopher. Her pregnancy with him had been a hard one, leading to her being put on bed rest at five months, followed by a premature delivery at thirty-two weeks.

Her grandma on her mom's side had moved in to help out. She took over the care of Chloe and Natalie as well as her daughter and the house. Because she was older, it had been decided that three young children were too much for her to handle, so Nana and Papa had taken Sophia home to care for her. Even after things had settled down and returned to normal—so to speak—Nana had continued to look after Sophia most days and frequently, at night as well.

Looking back, Sophia felt that she had been somewhat overlooked from the very start, with the next child in the family—the first boy—having been born so soon after her. By the time she was three, another baby had arrived, and she had just never really found her place in the family, especially since even as children, Chloe and Natalie had butted heads, often demanding attention through their fights. And Chris had been a rambunctious child who kept her parents on their toes.

In Nana's home, Sophia always felt like she was important, and she was forever grateful that her grandmother had been willing to care for her the way she had.

"Are you sure you can afford for me not to pay you rent?" Sophia asked.

"I'm very sure," Nana said. "And it's what your grandfather would have wanted as well."

Her grandfather had passed away ten years earlier, and it had been a devastating time for the whole family. He had been such a stalwart support for everyone, but especially for Sophia. The love and devotion he'd had for Nana had spilled over to Sophia as if she'd been his own daughter instead of a granddaughter.

"I just don't want you to be put in a difficult financial situation."

"Don't worry about that, sweetheart." Nana reached out to pat her hand. "As you know, your grandfather was in finance, and during his career, he worked in various parts of the industry, some that were very lucrative. Over the years, he made investments that paid off quite well for us. But even with that, we decided that we wouldn't live lavishly."

"You really didn't live lavishly," Sophia agreed. "Papa's car was older than me, I think."

Nana laughed and nodded. "Yes, it was. He made sure that I had a car that ran well, but neither of our vehicles were very splashy. Aside from the house, our largest outlay of money was when we adopted your dad. We just didn't need to spend more on a bigger house or fancier cars. Those things weren't important to us. All we wanted was to have money available for our future and also to help others who might need it."

Sophia thought of the home she now shared with Bryson, and though it had been quite cute in its day, it was beginning to show signs of wear. Thankfully, it was still sturdy and had more than enough space for the two of them.

"Anyway, when your grandfather got sick, he made sure everything was in order for my future. He understood that might involve a care home like this, so he wanted to be sure I was free to make whatever decisions I needed to without any financial concerns."

"So even though you have to pay to stay here, you're okay financially?"

"I'm more than okay, sunshine, which is why I don't need you to pay me rent. The house is paid off, so there's no mortgage to cover."

"If you're sure..."

"I am positive," Nana said firmly. "I know that it's important for you to stay home with Bryson right now, but I also know that you're not making a lot of money babysitting. You should keep that money for your needs."

"Thank you, Nana."

The older woman reached out and gripped Sophia's hand with surprising strength for her age. "I wish that you and Bryson hadn't gone through what you did. And whatever I can do to help you, that's what I'm going to do. I'm just glad that you're both home again. Safe."

Sophia blinked back tears as she nodded. "I'm glad to be home too."

If only her bad decisions hadn't led her to that horrible place to begin with. Except...if she hadn't gone with Ezekiel, she wouldn't have Bryson. And for all that the past five years had been a nightmare, having Bryson in her life was worth it. She just wished they weren't both dealing with continuing issues from that time with Ezekiel.

More than anything, Sophia wanted to provide Bryson with what he needed to become the person he was supposed to be. Not the person his father had tried to mold him into.

"Now, if you want to pay me in snickerdoodles, I won't object." Nana gave Sophia's hand another squeeze before releasing it.

"I think we can do that," Sophia said with a smile that didn't feel as bright as she wanted it to be. "Bryson loves helping me in the kitchen, especially when he knows we're bringing treats for you. Right, Bry?"

Bryson looked up from the picture he was coloring. "Yep. Momma lets me measure the flour and stuff."

"And he's my official taster." Sophia reached out to ruffle his curls. "So he gets to try the first cookie."

"You're a great team." Nana's smile was warm and loving.

"You're part of our team, too, Nana," Bryson said, a serious look on his face.

His words were a big part of the reason she loved bringing him to visit Nana. He never spoke much around anyone else, certainly not her parents, who were usually surrounded by chaos. He'd been an early talker, but the environment they'd been in hadn't encouraged him to speak. Free from that now, she could tell how comfortable he was with someone by how much he spoke around them.

"I'm glad to hear that, Bry. I love being part of your team."

Sophia's heart clenched as Bryson smiled. Like Chloe, all Sophia had ever wanted was to be a wife and a mother—although not to quite as many children as her sister had. Now, though, it was just her and Bryson. The idea of the family she would have wanted them to be part of was long gone.

These days, all she hoped was that she could give this precious little boy a safe environment in which to grow and thrive.

~*~

Ryker Bennet took the stairs that led to the front door of his parents' home two at a time. If she saw him, his mother would no doubt scold him for his less than dignified approach, but he hadn't been doing dignified for a few years now.

He opened the door and stepped into the house. Warmth and delicious aromas greeted him as he closed the door. After he toed off his boots and hung up his jacket, he headed in the direction of the kitchen.

Judging from the vehicles in the driveway, he knew he was the last to arrive, but thankfully, he wasn't late.

"Uncle Ryker!" The sound of his nephew's voice brought him to a halt before he got too far, and he turned to see the child approaching from the family room at the back of the house.

"Hey there, Jonah." Ryker lifted his hand for a high five as the ten-year-old approached him. "How's life?"

Even as he smacked Ryker's hand, Jonah wrinkled his nose, which made his glasses shift up a little. "I got grounded from my Xbox, so I haven't been able to play Fortnite all week."

"Yikes. What did you do?"

"It's what he didn't do."

Ryker looked over to see his older brother, Silas, strolling toward them, then turned his attention back to Jonah. "And what was that?"

Jonah lifted his narrow shoulders in a shrug. "I was supposed to practice piano for thirty minutes, but I played on my Xbox instead."

Though he'd never say it out loud, Ryker would definitely have preferred to play video games than practice the piano. "Guess you probably should have put in the time, huh? Thirty minutes off the Xbox versus a week? I think you're smart enough to do that math."

Looking despondent, Jonah nodded. He definitely could do that math. The kid was smart as a whip, as was his younger sister, Emery. But it was really no surprise given who their parents were. Silas was one of the top trauma surgeons in the state, while Donna, his wife, was a math professor at the University of Washington. Ryker was no slouch himself when it came to brains, but Silas and Donna took it to genius levels, and apparently, their children took after them.

"You need a haircut." This pronouncement came from his younger sister, Callie, as she joined them. "And a shave. You're looking shaggy."

"So are you," Ryker said as he reached out to tug a strand of her hair.

She kept her dark blonde hair short since she said it was easier to deal with at her job in a lab where she was a researcher. Silas and Jonah had similar hairstyles with faded sides and back and slightly longer on the top. It was a style that Ryker had favored once upon a time. Now he went for something less refined simply because he didn't feel like going for a haircut every month.

"Grandma says it's time to stop talking and sit at the table," Emery announced, reaching out to grab her dad's hand.

They migrated from the hallway to the dining room where Donna was helping put food on the table.

"Hi, Ryker," she said with a warm smile. "Good to see you again."

"You too." He gave her a one-arm hug, then turned to greet his parents as they came into the dining room from the kitchen. "Hi, Mom."

"Hello, darling. I'm glad you could make it."

Ryker bent to press a kiss to her cheek. "I said I'd be here."

"That you did, son," his dad said as he clapped him on his shoulder. "And we're happy to see you."

Though he didn't enjoy parts of the family dinner, Ryker always tried to join them. Out of all of the family members, he was the one with the least demanding schedule. His Sunday evenings were never booked up. The rest of the family tended to have other stuff going on, so they only managed to get together once or twice a month. It was usually dependant on Silas's schedule.

"Why don't we sit down?" his mom said, gesturing to the table.

They had done this often enough that everyone knew where they were supposed to sit. He waited for his mom to take her seat, then settled onto the chair beside her with Jonah on his other side. At one time, someone different had sat by his side, but not anymore.

"Let's pray," his dad said, and Ryker bowed his head, listening as he said a prayer of thanks for the food.

As soon as he said amen, the conversation around the table picked up. His mom talked with Callie and Donna who were seated across the table from her, while Ryker focused on Jonah.

Silas, who sat at the opposite end of the table from their dad, occasionally interjected, shifting his attention between Jonah and Emery.

"Nick asked me the other day how you were doing." Ryker's mom's words were accompanied by her hand resting on his arm, enough to grab his attention if what she'd said hadn't.

"Mom," Ryker said, resisting the urge to roll his eyes. "Is that how you and Nick get around confidentiality issues?"

"He's just concerned about you." She squeezed his arm gently before releasing it and turning her attention back to her food. "When did you last see him?"

Ryker sighed, almost wishing that he'd never agreed to see Nick St. James for counseling in the first place. Along with a third partner, the two of them had one of the most successful psychiatric practices in Seattle.

"It was about a year or so ago." More like two years, but he wasn't going to tell her that.

"Ryker." Disappointment practically dripped from the word. "You should still be checking in with him."

"I'm doing fine," Ryker said.

"Sure you are," Callie scoffed. "You look like you haven't slept in years."

Tension built in his shoulders at her words. "Not sleeping has been a way of life since I was eighteen."

"Silas has gone through medical school, had sleepless nights with two babies, and has a stressful career, and I think he's still getting more sleep than you," Callie said.

"Don't drag me into this," Silas remarked from the other end of the table.

"We're just worried about you, darling," his mother said.

"I'm fine."

"Maybe if you had a life, we'd believe you," Callie said.

"What is your problem?" Ryker scowled at his sister. "I have a life. Just because it doesn't meet your standards doesn't mean it doesn't qualify as a life."

"You're wasting your time and talents working with mud and sticks."

"That's enough, Calista," his father said, his tone firm. "We don't need to argue over this right now."

Ryker was grateful to his dad for stepping in. Still, the reality was, his dad didn't exactly support the decisions he'd made over the past few years either. The man had already had plenty to say on the subject and would likely still have more to say in the future. He just didn't like to have arguments at the table while he was trying to enjoy his dinner.

Callie let out a sigh but didn't say anything further on that subject. Instead, she picked yet another subject that Ryker wasn't interested in discussing.

"By the way, Lydia asked about you the other day."

Ryker sighed and took a bite of roast beef so that he didn't have to respond.

"Whose Lydia?" Emery asked as she looked at her mom, then at her dad.

"She's an old friend," Donna said. "You're too young to remember her."

"I could tell she was disappointed when I told her you still weren't practicing."

"Is she dating anyone?" his mother asked.

Ryker kept his attention on his food, not really interested in hearing about his ex-fiancée. It wasn't that it would hurt him to hear that she'd moved on. He hadn't taken much time to dwell on the demise of his relationship with Lydia in the last year.

Back when everything had fallen apart, the breakup had seemed like the least traumatic thing that had happened. They were both alive. They would both go on with their lives. Not everyone could say that after that awful day.

He knew that his family wondered how Lydia had managed to move forward after what had happened, picking up her plans for the future with only the briefest of breaks. The truth was, Ryker also wondered why he'd been impacted so much more than Lydia appeared to have been.

Was he just weak? Emotionally fragile where Lydia had been strong?

During his residency, he'd always been sympathetic to the children he'd worked with, along with their families. But he'd been able to deliver bad news without feeling like he was going to break down in tears at the sight of the parents' distress. He'd been able to comfort them without allowing their grief to overwhelm him.

But the horror of that day and the ones that followed, along with his feeling of helplessness, had blown apart that ability, leaving him too vulnerable to be able to deal with patients' emotions or those of their parents. So while maybe he hadn't been weak before that day, he sure felt weak afterward.

And Ryker was so weary of thinking about it—being forced to think about it—every time he was around his family.

It was why he was so thankful for the job he had now where no one knew who he'd been before and what had happened to him. He wasn't Doctor Ryker Bennet, survivor of the bombing of a Syrian refugee camp. He was just Ryker Bennet, right-hand man to Michael Reed at Reed Landscaping.

The job was physical, which usually wore him out enough that his body overruled his brain when it came time to sleep. He needed to be physically exhausted enough that his nightmares weren't able to drag him up to wakefulness.

"Jonah, why don't you tell everyone about the project you've been working on?" Donna suggested.

Ryker shot his sister-in-law a grateful look. She gave him a small smile in return, and he was once again reminded of how thankful he was for Silas' wife. Her presence was always calming in a way that Callie's wasn't.

More than anything, he just wanted to escape the house. But he stuck it out because he knew that fleeing the gathering would just be one more thing his parents would be disappointed over and would give Callie more to rag on him about. He just needed to keep it together, and everything would be okay.

Once he got back to his apartment, he'd work out for awhile to make up for the lack of physical exertion that day. While his family might think his job was nothing special, it still required him to be focused and physically able to work. And though they might not understand, he gained a certain amount of satisfaction in the work he did with Michael.

For now, it was enough.

CHAPTER TWO

Ryker pulled his truck to a stop at the curb, checking the bronze numbers on the post of the porch that stretched across the front of the small house. He ran his gaze over the property, taking in the towering trees and the scraggly bushes along the front of the yard.

Gripping the steering wheel, he shifted his gaze to stare out the windshield of his truck. He took a minute to remind himself that he was doing this to help out someone he considered one of his best friends. Unfortunately, that didn't necessarily make it any easier.

Just pick up the baby and take her to Michael.

He could do that. It wasn't like he hadn't already had small interactions with her.

With a sigh, Ryker opened the door of his truck and climbed out. It didn't take long to get to the front door, where he pressed the doorbell, stepping back as it rang faintly in the distance.

As he waited for someone to answer the door, he looked around again, taking in the overgrown grass of the yard, some of it poking up through cracks in the sidewalk that led to the steps of the porch. The paint around the trim of the windows and the porch railing was faded and peeling in spots.

He was a bit surprised at the state of the property where the babysitter lived. Michael must not have a problem with it, though, because he hadn't mentioned anything about the house when he'd given Ryker the address.

The door creaked open, and Ryker turned to see a slender woman standing there with baby Vivianne cradled in her arms. Her blonde hair lay in a braid over her shoulder, and her light aquamarine-colored eyes regarded him warily.

"Sophia?" At her nod, he said, "I'm Ryker."

After the briefest of hesitations, she took the hand he held out and gave it a shake. "Please come in."

She moved back from the door, allowing Ryker to step into the house's small foyer area. There was a closet to his right while to his left, he had a clear view of the living room. For all that the outside of the home appeared to need some work, the inside was a different story.

It was nicely decorated, and it smelled clean with just a hint of an aroma of baking in the air. As his gaze roamed the room, it landed on a small boy with tousled blond curls. He was sitting in the corner of the couch with a pile of books next to him. His brows were drawn together as he stared at Ryker with a frown.

"I'm sorry that Vivianne isn't ready to go," Sophia said as she moved to where the car seat sat on the couch beside the little boy. "She decided to have a poop, so I had to change her."

"It's no problem," Ryker assured her.

The little boy shifted his gaze from Ryker to Sophia, and he whispered something to her.

Sophia reached out and ran her hand over his curls. "Vivi will be fine, Bryson."

Bryson shot Ryker a look that held a wealth of fear. Ryker tried to drag his gaze away from the little boy because that fear was pushing buttons in him that he hadn't experienced in a while.

"Ryker is Michael's friend," Sophia said. "Remember I told you that Michael got hurt?"

Bryson looked at Sophia again and nodded.

"Michael needs help, so Ryker will be coming to pick Vivi up every day."

"What about the lady?" Bryson asked.

"Lani will bring Vivi back in the morning. You don't have to worry."

Bryson regarded him again before saying, "Okay."

Sophia picked up the car seat and carried it over to where Ryker waited to set it on the floor. "Sorry about that. He's become rather protective of Vivi."

Ryker turned his attention back to Sophia. He hadn't been sure if Bryson was another child she was babysitting or her son, but now that he looked at her more closely, he could see the resemblance between them. The boy had the same eyes and blonde hair that Sophia had, and they both had slender faces and builds.

He couldn't help but wonder if there was a father in the picture. The way Bryson had looked at him with fear concerned him. He understood children being wary of strangers—especially strange men—but Bryson's reaction to him seemed to be more than that.

"That's okay," Ryker assured Sophia. "It's a good quality for him to have."

Though it might be concerning as to *why* he was so protective of a baby.

Sophia smiled as she glanced at Bryson. "He's always so disappointed when Vivi gets picked up. I think he'd like to keep her."

Ryker almost made a comment about Bryson needing a brother or sister, but he held his tongue. That wasn't appropriate, especially when he'd just met Sophia.

"I'm afraid that Michael might object to that. He's gotten rather attached to her."

"That's what I told him."

"Speaking of, I'd better get going. Michael is waiting for me to get back with Vivianne and some food." Ryker took the diaper bag that Sophia held out.

"Oh, also, she might be due for a bottle in a little bit."

"Okay. I'll let Michael know." He picked up the car seat. "I'll see you tomorrow."

She held the door as he stepped back out onto the porch. With a final glance at Sophia and Bryson, who was now standing next to his mother, his hand in hers, Ryker headed to his truck. It took him a couple of minutes to get the car seat all strapped in safely, but thankfully, Vivianne didn't put up a fuss.

Once he got to Michael's, he carried Vivianne and the food into the house. He wasn't surprised to see that Michael was asleep in the recliner. No doubt he hadn't gotten much rest in the hospital.

As Ryker set everything on the table, Michael stirred and opened his eyes. Ryker picked the car seat back up and carried it closer to the recliner.

"Look who's home, Vivianne." He tilted the car seat a bit so Michael could see her. "Do you want to hold her?"

"Yes," Michael replied quickly.

Setting the car seat on the floor, Ryker crouched down and made quick work of the straps. He hesitated a moment before sliding his hands under her head and her bum. With easy movements, he lifted her out and straightened back up to hand her to Michael.

"Sophia said she might be hungry soon. Do you want to eat first or feed her first?"

"Let me feed her first."

"Sounds good," Ryker said as he headed to get the bottle stuff in the kitchen. "I'll heat your food up when you're ready for it."

Once he had the bottle warmed, he gave it to Michael and watched as the man started to feed the baby. For all that he was a brand-new dad—and an unexpected one at that—he was doing really well with Vivianne. Though Ryker was glad he could help his friend and boss out, the situation presented a set of circumstances he'd rather not have had to deal with.

At one point in his life, the future he'd planned for himself had included lots and lots of children. Not all his, of course. But as a pediatrician, he'd anticipated spending a large portion of each day interacting with children.

Unfortunately, his trip as part of a medical mission to Syria had changed the trajectory of his life. What was supposed to have been the bridge between finishing his residency and starting his own pediatric practice had, instead, become a nightmare.

The first week the team had spent at the camp had been eye-opening and heartbreaking. Though Ryker was glad that he had the opportunity to give medical care to the children in the camp, the experience had also left him feeling hopeless at times. There was only so much he could do with the limited resources they had in the camp, and it had felt like it wasn't nearly enough.

The hopelessness...the helplessness...had already settled deep in his soul before the day that had changed everything for him. In the years since, he'd done his best to avoid children—especially younger ones—since interacting with them evoked emotions and memories that were hard to deal with.

Being able to help Michael with Vivianne had been difficult at first, but the routine was getting a bit easier. He just had to remind himself that the baby was safe in a place where she could get medical help if she needed it. She had a doctor of her own, which meant that Ryker was able to separate his care for her from the care he would have provided had she been one of his patients.

Still, he preferred to keep his interactions with her to a minimum, which was why he didn't offer to do more in helping Michael with her. As long as Michael could safely care for her, there was no reason Ryker had to step in.

Once Vivianne was done with her bottle, Ryker took it from Michael then started heating up the food he'd picked up from *Norma's*. Though he usually just went home to his apartment to eat by himself once he was done work for the day, that wouldn't be the case for the next little while.

Michael's broken leg had meant that the inexperienced father needed someone around to help him with other parts of the baby's

HEALING HEARTS · 25

care. And in addition to that, Ryker had needed to step up and take care of the business side of things for Michael as well.

To that end, as they ate, he and Michael talked about the week ahead, discussing the various jobs that were now Ryker's responsibility. Usually, he only oversaw a few of the jobs, but with Michael out of commission for the foreseeable future, he was picking up the slack. He just hoped he didn't let Michael down.

Around eight, Lani—an employee and friend of Michael's—arrived to take over the care of the baby. She would be taking Vivianne back to her place for the night. He knew it wasn't an ideal situation for Michael, but it was the best they could come up with.

"I'll see you two tomorrow," Ryker said as he prepared to leave.

"Thanks for picking her up for me," Michael said from where he sat in his recliner.

"You're welcome. It wasn't a problem at all."

Okay, so maybe that wasn't entirely true. He had a feeling that Bryson's fearful gaze was going to haunt him through the night in a way Vivianne's unexpected arrival in his life hadn't.

Thankfully, he'd had a busy day, so he hoped that would be enough to keep him asleep through the night. He'd do a workout, however, to exhaust himself even further. If he was going to see Bryson nearly every day, he would have to find a way to cope with it.

Hopefully if he could just get through that first night, he'd be okay.

The earth shook as explosions rent the air, shredding the tent around them. He froze, uncertain what was happening. His ears rang, robbing him of sound. Then the earth shook again, knocking him from the stool he'd been seated on.

On his hands and knees, the ground was rough beneath his palms. His head hung down as he tried to figure out what was going on.

Hands closed around his arm, tugging him up. He staggered to his feet, his equilibrium shot. He looked at the person beside him, the one who was urging him to move. Blood slid down the side of the face of a fellow doctor, a cut on the top of his bald head being the source.

He wanted to ask the doctor what was going on, but the ringing in his ears had deafened him. Instead, he moved with the man, his gaze darting around, horror growing at the sight that greeted him.

Around them...everywhere around them for as far as he could see...was destruction. Where once had stood tents and buildings, there was now rubble.

His feet became weighed down, and he didn't have the strength to move them. His arms hung useless at his sides. He pinched his lips closed, afraid that if he opened his mouth, he'd begin to scream out his horror.

The ringing in his ears began to fade away, and as it did, other sounds began to filter in—the screams of fear and pain...the wailing of grief. Shivers raced down his spine. The sounds were unlike anything he'd ever heard before.

"Run, man." This time he could hear the doctor who'd pulled him away from the tent where they'd been meeting to discuss the patients. Again, the other man grabbed his arm and pulled him forward, propelling him into action.

He lurched over the uneven ground, broken up by whatever it was that had wreaked havoc on the camp.

Lydia... Where was Lydia?

They'd eaten breakfast together, but then she'd gone to a different area of the camp to work with the women. Where was she now?

He tried to figure out the direction of the tent where she'd been headed, but nothing looked familiar.

As he looked around, his attention was drawn to a woman who was holding a child and wailing as she sat amid dust and rubble.

He stumbled toward her, but immediately, he could see it was too late for the child she held.

And then it was too late for another one.

And another one.

When he finally found a child he could help, his mind was already fractured. Part of him mourned the immense losses while the other part struggled to focus on helping the child in front of him.

The child had gazed at him with pain and fear, her dark eyes wide. He wanted to save her in a way he hadn't yet been able to save any of the others. He wasn't sure that he could handle one more loss.

And yet, even though that little girl hadn't been a loss, there had been more losses throughout the day. It was the sounds that haunted him as they moved through the camp, fear dogging his every step.

Eventually, he found Lydia helping a woman who had gone into labor following the attack. Though he was relieved that Lydia was safe, her presence wasn't enough to chase away the sounds...the hopelessness...the fear... They had embedded themselves in his mind, his heart, and his soul.

As darkness settled over the camp, he struggled to come to terms with what had happened and how he hadn't been able to do what he needed to in order to save more of the most defenseless ones in the camp.

And when he finally laid down to sleep, even exhaustion couldn't keep the nightmares at bay. The cries. The fear in the children's eyes.

Ryker woke with a jerk, his heart pounding as screams faintly echoed in his mind. He swung his feet over the edge of the bed and sat up, scrubbing his hands across his face.

Even knowing that nightmares would be likely after seeing the fear in Bryson's gaze, he still hadn't expected that. It had been awhile since he'd had one quite so vivid.

He tried to utilize the coping techniques Nick had taught him early on in their counseling sessions, but nothing helped him cope that night.

Well-meaning friends and family kept telling him to get on with his life, but they just didn't get it.

There had been just too many people who hadn't been able to get on with their lives.

They hadn't asked to be born in a war-torn part of the world.

They certainly hadn't asked to be forced into refugee camps where sufficient food and clean water were hard to come by. Not to mention medical care.

Those people had just been trying to survive as best they could, given the circumstances they'd found themselves in.

Too many of them hadn't been able to just *get on with their lives.*

Even the ones who had managed to survive had still been left in horrible living conditions. It felt wrong for Ryker to move forward with all the plans he'd had for his future as if the horror of the attack at the refugee camp hadn't fundamentally changed him.

He was back living in a safe place with plenty of food and clean water. It seemed that to strive for more was downright selfish. But more than that, he wasn't sure that he could actually carry out the job that he'd trained for so many years to do.

Though he'd done okay helping with Vivianne so far, he hadn't done more for her than the average person would have been able to do.

After seeing Sophia's little boy earlier and the fear in his eyes, something in Ryker had frozen. He knew without a shadow of a doubt that if he'd been required to treat Bryson while he'd been looking at Ryker that way, he wouldn't have been able to.

What would happen if he froze when a child's life was on the line?

He hadn't frozen that day in the refugee camp, but he was sure that was only because he hadn't had a chance to process everything. In the days following the attack, he'd struggled greatly to help the people, often needing the prodding of the other doctors there to stay focused.

The day he and Lydia had climbed on a plane to return to the US, he'd felt a mixture of relief and guilt. They had never really talked about what had happened on that day or any of the days that followed. Nick was the only one who'd managed to get him to open up even slightly about what he'd experienced and how he felt.

With a sigh, Ryker picked up his phone off the nightstand to see the time. 1:23. He'd been asleep for just over three hours, but he felt like he hadn't slept at all.

He pushed up off the bed and left the bedroom, knowing that he wouldn't be able to fall back to sleep right away. If at all.

The light over the stove in the kitchen was on, chasing away enough of the night that he could find his way to the fridge easily enough. He pulled out the jug of orange juice and poured himself a glass before putting the jug back. Carrying the juice, he went over to the glass doors leading to the small balcony of his third-floor apartment.

He slid the door open and stepped out onto the balcony, inhaling sharply at the chill in the air. It was nearly the end of April, which meant that while the days were fairly nice, the nights could still be chilly. Thankfully, he'd worn sleep pants and a long-sleeve T-shirt to bed, so it was only his extremities and face that felt the cold.

On any other night, he would have worried about the cold waking him up too much to go back to sleep, but a nightmare was always guaranteed to wake him up completely.

He slumped down in one of the lawn chairs he kept on the balcony and stared out over the neighborhood. It was a quiet part of New Hope. Not that any part of the town was particularly noisy. At least not when compared to a similar neighborhood in Seattle.

The houses opposite the apartment building were all dark at this time of night, with only the streetlamps casting any sort of light onto the street. It was an older neighborhood, which he really liked because it had lots of large trees on the boulevards and in the backyards of the homes.

It was a far cry from the refugee camp, and the quiet of the neighborhood went a long way to calming his mind. He took a deep breath, forcing his lungs to expand against his rib cage, then blew the air out before taking a sip of his orange juice.

For the next few minutes, he settled into a rhythm of sorts.

Inhale. Exhale. Drink.

Inhale. Exhale. Drink.

As he sat there, a feeling of calm finally settling over him, Ryker tried to figure out the best way to deal with picking Vivianne up. He had to do that for Michael, so somehow, he had to be able to deal with Bryson and the child's reaction to him.

He hoped that it was just seeing the little boy unexpectedly that had set his nightmares off so badly. If he could steel himself against the looks the little boy gave him, maybe everything would be okay.

One thing Ryker knew for sure was that if he'd walked into Sophia's to find Bryson having a medical event while looking at him the way he had, he would have frozen.

It was a horrible thought and was also the main reason why he didn't think he'd ever be able to practice medicine again. He didn't want to ever have the life of a child in his hands and then be unable to administer the medical care they desperately needed.

And if that meant he never *got on with his life*, then so be it.

Later that day, Ryker sat in his truck for a few minutes, mentally preparing himself to see Bryson once again. He was exhausted, both mentally and physically, since he'd only managed to get a couple more hours of sleep before having to get up for his day.

Thankfully, all the jobs that day had been physically demanding, but none had been dangerous. Michael was proof that sleepless nights and tree removals didn't go well together. Sleepless nights and garden preparation, on the other hand, usually worked out okay.

Knowing he couldn't put off the inevitable, Ryker climbed out of his truck and made his way up to the front door to ring the doorbell.

"Hi, Ryker," Sophia said with a small smile when she opened the door. "Vivianne is ready to go. She'll probably want to eat in a little while, but she hasn't been fussing, so I didn't give her a bottle."

"That's fine. Michael enjoys feeding her when I get her home, so that works out well."

Sophia handed him the diaper bag then set the car seat just inside the door. She hadn't invited him in, which was fine. He had a feeling that Sophia was trying to protect her son from whatever it was about Ryker that had scared him. It just so happened that not seeing Bryson worked for Ryker too, so he wasn't going to get upset with her for that.

What did upset him was knowing that he'd caused that fear in a child. When he'd made the decision to go into pediatrics, it had been because he enjoyed the idea of working with children. He had known that he would likely deal with children who were afraid of him in his role as a doctor, but Sophia's little boy seemed to be afraid of him simply because he was a man.

That didn't sit well with him, and it made him worry about why the boy felt that way. However, that history wasn't any of his business. Sophia seemed to be providing a safe environment for her son, and that was what mattered the most.

"I'll see you tomorrow," he said as he picked up the car seat and stepped back from the door.

"Yep. Enjoy the rest of your day."

"You too." Ryker smiled at her, then headed for his truck.

When he arrived at Michael's, it looked like the other man hadn't had a good night's sleep either, though his face lit up at the sight of the baby.

Ryker quickly freed her from the car seat and handed her over, then went to prepare a bottle. After giving it to Michael, he sank down onto the couch.

While Michael fed the baby, Ryker updated him on how the day had gone, doing his best to keep the other man involved in the business while he was removed from it due to his injury.

When Lani showed up, Ryker didn't linger, eager to get back to his own place. Though he was exhausted and wanted nothing more than to fall into bed, he wasn't sure how the night would go. The image of Bryson's fear-filled gaze wasn't quite as fresh in his mind, so he really hoped that his physical exhaustion would be sufficient to sink him deep enough into sleep that his dreams wouldn't torment him.

It was a bit of wishful thinking on his part, Ryker knew. But these days, if he didn't have that, he'd never be able to convince himself to sleep after what had happened the previous night.

CHAPTER THREE

"Momma."

Sophia looked up from where she sat on the lid of the toilet, scrolling through her phone. Bryson sat in a shallow amount of water in the tub surrounded by several toy boats, and he lifted one of them to show it to her.

Some might have said she'd gone overboard with the toys she'd bought him, but considering he'd had none for the first four years of his life, she wasn't going to keep them from him now. Shortly after their return to New Hope, Nana had given her three hundred dollars for each of them, stating it was for the birthday and Christmas gifts she hadn't been able to buy them for the past five years.

Though she'd protested at first, in the end, Sophia had accepted the money because she really did need things, especially for Bryson, and she hadn't had the funds to buy him anything. With money in hand, they'd gone to several thrift stores, and Bryson had picked out a bunch of toys, gravitating to the toy boats and cars as well as the books.

Thankfully, she'd been able to buy quite a few clothes for him and several things for herself as well at the thrift stores, so the money had stretched more than it would have had she gone to even the discount stores. She'd used some of it to buy groceries to set up the pantry at the house, then she'd put the rest in the bank. Once she'd had money coming in regularly from babysitting Vivianne, she'd established a budget and started to set aside a few dollars each week for future toy and clothing purchases.

"Are you almost done playing?" she asked him as she pulled a towel from the cupboard. "I still need to wash your hair."

He wrinkled his nose at that, but he nodded. Baths were a novelty for him since they'd only had access to showers where they'd lived before.

Together they put his toys into the bucket Sophia had brought into the bathroom to hold them. When that was done, she turned on the water and quickly washed his hair since it wasn't something he enjoyed very much, even though she now bought the shampoo that wouldn't irritate his eyes.

"All done, Momma?" he asked after she'd used the handheld showerhead to rinse the shampoo away.

"Almost, baby. Can you stand up?" She pulled the plug before quickly washing his body then rinsing away the soap bubbles. "All done."

"Yay!"

She helped him out of the tub to stand on the mat and dried him off, wrapping a towel around him since he had a tendency to get cold. Before leaving the bathroom, she grabbed another towel to dry his hair.

Because they'd previously lived their lives according to a rigid schedule, Sophia had initially thought that she'd abandon all schedules once they were free of that life. While she might have been okay with that, she'd quickly discovered that wasn't the case for Bryson. He needed to know what was coming throughout their day. So each night, he got a bath as part of his bedtime routine.

"Which pajamas do you want tonight?" Sophia asked as she herded him into the bedroom where his clothes were kept. Earlier, she'd laid out two different pairs on the bed in an effort to encourage him to make a choice for himself.

He stood wrapped in his towel, looking back and forth between the two pairs of footed pajamas. She didn't rush him, knowing that even though they'd been back in New Hope Falls for a few months now, being able to choose like this was still new to him.

"These ones," he said, patting the pair that had toy cars on them.

"Perfect." She smiled as she helped him into them, then put the other pair back in the drawer.

"Why don't you go pick out a book?" Sophia said as they left the room.

While he sat down to look through his stack of books, she made sure all the doors and windows were locked and the curtains were drawn.

"Do you want a snack while I read to you?" she asked as she returned to where he sat.

"Yes, please. Bananas and peanut butter?"

"Sure." Sophia knew from the doctor who had checked him over in Texas that he was underweight, so she fed him whenever he was willing to eat.

At the table in the kitchen, Bryson laid out the three books he'd been carrying. Since discovering books, he always requested more than one story, even if she told him to pick just one. And as with most things, she found it impossible to deny him.

Standing at the counter, Sophia sliced a banana in circles, then arranged the slices on a plate before adding a dab of peanut butter on top of each one.

"Is that man coming again tomorrow?" Bryson asked as she set the plate on the table in front of him.

She looked down into his serious, wide-eyed expression. "Yes, baby. He'll be back to pick up Vivianne every day."

He frowned at that, his brows drawing low over his eyes.

"Vivianne is safe with him," she said as she went to the fridge to pour a small glass of milk. "He wouldn't do anything to hurt her. Michael wouldn't let Ryker pick her up if he didn't trust him."

Sophia understood why Bryson was wary of the man. He'd been that way initially with Michael, too, though it seemed to be worse with Ryker. Likely that was because he had formed an attachment with the baby now that had brought out his protective instinct.

She'd been leery of referring to Michael as Vivianne's father at first because Bryson's experiences with his own father hadn't been good. She hadn't wanted to attach that relationship to Michael and Vivianne because then Bryson really wouldn't have let go of his wariness. Thankfully, Michael had explained his situation to her, so referring to him as Vivi's uncle wasn't a lie.

As she picked up the first book, Bryson shifted his attention to his banana and peanut butter, slowly eating one piece at a time and sipping at his milk as she read. By the time she finished the book, he was done with his snack.

"Let's brush your teeth, and then we can read the other stories."

They didn't even bother to go into his bedroom when they were done in the bathroom. He hadn't spent a night there yet, and she had no idea when he would.

Instead, she'd put a single bed she'd found for him in her room, sandwiching it between the double bed where she slept and the wall. It was slightly lower than her bed, so it didn't feel like he was sleeping with her, but she was close enough if he needed her. She hoped that that would make it easier for him transition to sleeping in his own room at some point.

She wasn't pressuring him to do that just yet though. It was too soon to take that step when they were both trying to adjust to the enormous changes that had already taken place in their lives.

After reading him the remaining two stories, she gave him the books to look at, knowing he'd fall asleep more quickly than if she forced him to try to sleep right away. She laid on the side of her bed closest to him and read a book of her own, waiting until he'd fallen asleep before getting back up.

Usually, once he was asleep, he stayed that way, barring any bad dreams. Thankfully those were coming less frequently the longer they were back in New Hope.

In the quiet, she cleaned up the kitchen, then straightened up the rest of the house. It wasn't something she needed to do every night since the two of them really didn't make that big of a mess, but she did it anyway since she didn't have anything else to do. Plus, old habits were hard to break.

As she worked, she puzzled over how to help Bryson with his reaction to Ryker. She wished she could afford professional counselling to help him work through that issue and the others he struggled with, but that was beyond her financial capability at the moment.

A solution eventually came to her mind, but it would require Ryker's cooperation, and she didn't know if he would be on board for that. For all she knew, he might not be interested in helping Bryson. Not every man would be.

Normally, she wouldn't have had the guts to ask him for his help, but this was for Bryson's sake. She'd do almost anything to help her son adjust to their new life.

It ended up taking her well over a week to work up the nerve to speak to Ryker about her plan. She'd hoped that Bryson would get better on his own, that his anxiety over Ryker taking Vivianne would lessen, especially after Lani brought her back each morning. But for some reason, that hadn't made any difference.

Despite all evidence to the contrary, he was still convinced that Ryker meant harm toward the little girl. Each night, he'd ask again about Vivianne and if Sophia was certain that she was safe. He just refused to believe that Ryker wouldn't hurt the baby, and he continued to view the man with an abnormally high level of distrust and fear each time he showed up.

When Sophia finally decided that she needed to carry out her plan, she suffered through her own bouts of anxiety over speaking to Ryker. He seemed like a perfectly nice man—just like she'd told Bryson.

But what would he say to her request? What if he thought she was nuts for what she wanted him to do? Maybe he'd tell Michael she was crazy and that he needed to find someone else to take care of Vivianne? Then what would she do to provide financially for herself and Bryson?

Apparently, just like her son, she had her own set of anxieties...

She spent the next few days praying about the situation, hoping God would help Bryson move beyond his fear of Ryker. Unfortunately, for whatever reason, it didn't appear to be God's will for Bryson to move on from his fear on his own. So then she began praying that God would prepare Ryker's heart for her request.

On the day she finally bit the bullet, Sophia met him on the porch, leaving Vivianne's car seat just inside the door. Ryker gave her a curious look, his brows drawing down over his light gray eyes.

"I was wondering if I could ask a favor of you," she said, bracing herself for his rejection even as she said the words.

"You can certainly ask," Ryker replied. "But I can't guarantee I'll be able to help you out."

Now that she was face to face with this man, she felt wobbly inside. Maybe she should have thought this through for a bit longer. Like, maybe if Bryson was still worried in a month's time, she could broach the idea with Ryker then.

But no...

Already Bryson spent his waking hours from the time Ryker picked Vivianne up until Lani dropped her off, worried about the baby. She needed to try and alleviate the anxiety he was feeling if she could. She would do anything for him, even if it meant dealing with this aloof man whose steely gaze made her feel like he could see right through her.

She wrapped her arms across her waist, trying to contain the nerves that fluttered wildly inside her. In that moment, she was as fearful of Ryker as Bryson had been. She had to remind herself that Michael wouldn't send someone to pick up his daughter who was capable of hurting her or Bryson.

But she also knew better than anyone how someone's looks and demeanor could be deceiving. However, she was placing her trust in Michael being a decent judge of character.

"I'm sure you noticed that Bryson has had a...not so great reaction to you."

"Yes, I did notice that," Ryker said with a nod.

"He's not super comfortable around men, and he's also gotten quite protective of Vivianne. Each time you take her away, he's worried that she won't come back."

Ryker's brows lifted slightly. "Really?"

"Yes. I've tried to reassure him that Michael trusts you and that you'd never do anything to hurt her."

"I wouldn't."

"I know that because I'm sure if there was any chance you would, Michael wouldn't have trusted you with her."

He nodded then said, "So what do you need from me?"

"Would you be willing to come in and hold Vivianne sometime, maybe talk to Bryson for a few minutes?"

Something flickered in his gaze, and for a moment, she thought that he'd reject her request outright. "Does he think I'll hurt him?"

She knew he noticed her brief hesitation because he frowned. Still, she shook her head. "He just doesn't know you, so that...worries him."

"Has he only been hurt by strangers?"

Sophia sucked in a breath. How was she supposed to respond to that? Clearly, she'd been naïve to think that Ryker would take her request at face value. That he wouldn't wonder about Bryson's previous experiences that had caused such fear to surface in the child.

"No. He hasn't been hurt by strangers. He just doesn't like people he doesn't know."

Ryker seemed to be on the verge of pushing the subject, but instead, he looked away from her to the large picture window in the living room. She followed his gaze and spotted Bryson standing there, his hands clasped beneath his chin as he stared at them with a worried expression on his face.

"Are you sure he'll respond positively to what you're suggesting?"

Sophia wasn't sure about any of this, but she had to try something. "I think he'll be okay if I'm there too."

Ryker looked back at her. "Let me think about it, okay?"

"Of course." Stepping back inside, she picked up the diaper bag and the car seat and brought them out to the porch. "Thank you for considering it."

"I'll let you know tomorrow."

Sophia watched as Ryker walked down the sidewalk to his truck. Well, that hadn't gone quite as she had hoped. But at the same time, he hadn't out and out refused her.

Back inside, she closed and locked the door, then drew Bryson to the rocker recliner in the corner. She sat down and helped him climb up into her lap.

As she rocked, she ran her fingers through his curls, doing her best to assure him that Vivianne was fine and that she'd be back the next day. If she thought he'd eventually get past this anxiety he had about Ryker, she would have just waited it out. But for some reason, he was as focused on it as he'd been the very first day Ryker had come by.

She had needed to do this. She just hoped Ryker could understand that, even though it didn't impact him one way or another.

~*~

Ryker sat down at his small dining room table and opened the flat box to reveal the pepperoni pizza he'd picked up on his way home. Now that Lani was bringing Michael food each evening, he was back to his own devices most nights. And after the day he'd had, he was more than happy about that.

Well, the whole day hadn't been bad, just the part where Sophia had asked for his help in putting her son at ease about his presence. It wasn't that he didn't want the little boy to be more settled about his role in Vivianne's life, but what would it cost him to do that?

Even now, several hours later, he could picture Bryson's expression as he'd stood at the window watching them. The thing was, it sat horribly wrong with him that there was any child who feared him in the way that Bryson seemed to.

So even though he'd asked for a little time to consider it, Ryker had known from the moment Sophia had posed the request that he would do it. He just needed a little time to prepare himself.

Though part of his willingness to help her stemmed from wanting to put Bryson at ease, he also wanted to know what had caused the boy to become like that in the first place. Sophia may have denied that Bryson had been hurt, but Ryker knew that abuse took many forms. Physical being just one of them.

As a pediatrician, he'd been taught how to recognize the signs. Plus, he'd heard plenty about them from his psychiatrist mom. It wasn't in his nature to let the little boy suffer if there was something he could do to help him out.

He wished that he could talk to his mom about the situation, but she'd want details that he just didn't have. And something told him that Sophia wasn't going to part with those secrets easily, so asking her about them would just be an exercise in futility. She trusted him to a certain extent now, but he doubted that it would be enough for her to confide in him.

As he thought of the mother and son pair, Ryker had to admit to a certain amount of curiosity. Whether that was because of the boy's intense reaction to him or the fact that they both carried a haunted look that wasn't helped by the fact that they looked like they were both underweight, he wasn't sure.

Ryker had a feeling that he was going to be as haunted by Sophia and Bryson as they were about whatever it was that had put those looks on their faces. Maybe it was time to go back to Nick. Certainly that would be the best course of action if he was about to find himself involved more deeply in their lives, and he couldn't see how that could be avoided if he was going to continue to pick Vivianne up each day for the foreseeable future.

Sighing, he lifted a piece of pizza out of the box. What had been a simple job for the past few years had gotten remarkably complicated in the past few weeks. He just hoped that he was up for the challenge.

The next afternoon, Ryker pulled over to the curb and parked. He sat for a moment, wondering if it was too late to change his mind. Realistically, it wasn't because he hadn't told Sophia that he'd talk with Bryson yet. However, in his mind, he'd already agreed. The problem was that he hadn't been able to talk himself out of it.

Not when he'd had a hard time falling asleep.

Not when he'd woken in the night with another nightmare.

Not when he'd crawled out of bed almost as tired as when he'd gone to bed the night before.

Throughout the day, he'd tried to keep from thinking about Sophia's request, but that had been impossible.

And now here he was, parked outside her house, hesitating yet again, even though he knew that he wasn't going to change his mind. So if he wasn't going to change his mind, he just needed to get himself together and deal with it.

Pushing open the door of his truck, he climbed out then shut it with a little more force than necessary. Well aware that Sophia was probably watching him, Ryker tried to keep his steps measured and steady, portraying confidence that he didn't really feel inside.

As he reached the bottom step, the door opened, and Sophia stepped out onto the porch. She wore a pair of jeans that hung loosely on her slender form, as did the large sweater she wore.

She crossed her arms as if warding off a chill that wasn't in the air on that sunny spring afternoon, though she was dressed as if it was the middle of winter. Her blonde hair was pulled up on the top of her head in a messy bun.

With a wary gaze remarkably like her son's, she watched him climb the steps to the porch. "Hello."

"Hi." Ryker blew out a quick breath and put them both out of their misery. "I'll do what you asked."

Relief filled Sophia's face, and her shoulders lowered. "Thank you so much."

"I hope this helps," he said. "It might not. It might make things worse."

"I know, but I really think he needs this."

"Do you want to do it now?" he asked.

"Yes. If you have the time."

"I do." He'd left work a little early, so he could do this without being too late getting to Michael's with Vivianne.

Opening the door behind her, she said, "Please come in."

Ryker followed her inside, then, being mindful of the mud and grass he'd trekked through that day, he toed off his work boots. Vivianne's car seat sat on the floor next to the couch, and beside it was Bryson. His fingers were resting on Vivianne's arm.

"Hey, baby," Sophia said. "Ryker is here to get Vivianne."

Bryson immediately frowned and shifted closer to the baby. Sophia walked over to the car seat and lifted Vivianne out, then glanced back at Ryker. "Do you want to sit for a few minutes?"

"Sure." Ryker went to the couch and settled down on it, feeling the puffy cushions suck him in a little.

Bryson got up from the floor and leaned against the far end of the couch, his gaze flitting between Ryker and Sophia.

"Would you like to hold Vivianne?" Sophia asked as she turned to him.

Ryker held out his arms, waiting for her to move close enough to give her to him. He'd held Vivianne several times by this point, but except for the very first time he'd helped Michael with her, none of those times seemed as important as this.

As he cradled her close to his chest, he ran his hand over her head, feeling the downy softness of her hair under his palm. He missed this part of his job.

"Do you like Vivianne?" Ryker asked, glancing at Bryson.

Once again, the boy's hands were clenched beneath his chin as he whispered, "Yes." Then he glanced at his mom and spoke more loudly, "Yes."

Had he been afraid that Ryker would get upset by his tentative response?

"Do you read her stories?"

The little boy's head bobbed hesitantly.

"I bet she enjoys that." Another bob of his head. "Does she tell you stories?"

Bryson's eyes widened, then his brows drew together. Once again, his gaze went to his mom, but this time, he seemed to be giving her a somewhat incredulous look as if to say, *is this man for real?* When he looked back at Ryker, the fear had eased a little bit.

"She can't talk," he whispered, as if letting Ryker in on a secret.

"Really?" Ryker looked down at Vivianne then back at Bryson. "So how do you know when she's hungry?"

"She cries," Bryson said, his words a bit louder.

"How about when her diaper needs changing?"

"She cries."

"And when she's tired?"

"She cries."

"Wow... Does she cry a lot?"

Bryson shrugged. "Sometimes. But usually not for very long."

"I bet your mom knows how to tell what Vivianne needs, huh?"

"Yep. Momma always knows how to help her stop crying."

"That's great," Ryker said. "I'll tell you a secret."

Bryson's eyes went large for a minute. "What secret?"

"Vivianne told me that there's this little boy at the place she goes to every day who she really likes."

A ghost of a smile crossed his thin face. "Really?"

Ryker nodded. "She thinks the stories that this little boy tells her are great, and she loves to listen to them."

"Momma!" Bryson exclaimed as he turned to Sophia. "Vivi likes my stories!"

Sophia reached out and carded her fingers through her son's curls. "I'm not surprised to hear that, baby. I like your stories too."

"Well, now that's not very fair," Ryker said. "Your momma and Vivi have both heard your stories, but I haven't."

"You want me to read you a story?" Bryson asked, his surprise clear in his voice.

"I would. Plus, I think Vivianne would love to hear another story."

"What story should I read?"

"Why don't you pick your favorite one?" Ryker suggested.

"Okay." With a slightly bigger smile, Bryson turned around and headed for the pile of books near the fireplace.

Ryker tried to commit the sight of that smile to memory, hoping it would push out the more fearful looks his brain had latched on to previously.

Time would only tell if his plan was successful.

CHAPTER FOUR

Sophia hadn't been sure what to expect when Ryker had agreed to what she'd asked. However, something like this hadn't even crossed her mind. The way the man interacted with Bryson made it seem like he didn't just tolerate children, he actually enjoyed being around them.

Did he have kids of his own? There was no way this man hadn't been around children on a regular basis. Not with the way he was relating to Bryson.

Not only had he managed to chase away most of the fear in Bryson, he had gotten him to warm up a little bit as well. And he'd done it in the most amazing way possible.

"What book is this?" Ryker asked when Bryson returned to the couch.

Sophia had known what book it would be even before he'd gone to his pile of books. It was the one he had her read to him each evening. The last one she'd read to him once he was in bed.

"*Love You Forever.*" Bryson showed Ryker the front of the book. "It's my favorite."

"Then I can't wait to hear it."

The thing was, Bryson couldn't read, though they were working on it since he desperately loved books. They hadn't had access to books at the compound, so he was behind where he should be with recognizing letters and even small words. She'd done her best to teach him colors from their environment when she had her time with him each week, but she hadn't had any paper or crayons to help him learn to read or write.

Sophia went to sit beside Bryson, just in case he needed help with a word. Bryson carefully turned to the first page and began to recite the words he knew by heart. Slowly they made their way through the book, and not once did he need her help.

"You're an amazing little reader, Bryson," Ryker said when they reached the last page.

Bryson looked up at Sophia then back at Ryker, his shoulders hunching forward. "I didn't really read it."

"What?" Ryker's perplexed gaze met Sophia's.

She looped her arm around Bryson's shoulders, disappointed that his fear was back. He had been punished frequently for lying...even though he had rarely actually told a lie. Sometimes, he'd given the answer he thought the person had wanted to hear, and then gotten into trouble for it. Other times, he told the truth, but some of the older children in the compound would make it seem as if he'd lied.

"He doesn't know how to read yet," Sophia said. "But we've read this story together so often that he has it memorized."

"That's amazing, Bryson. Most children your age couldn't remember all those words. You did a great job."

Bryson's shoulders relaxed slightly, but he'd had a bait and switch played on him too often for him to take Ryker's words at face value.

"It's great that you love books and that your mom reads to you," Ryker continued. "I'm sure you'll be reading on your own in no time."

Sophia thought the same, and she'd told Bryson that whenever he got frustrated that he couldn't read all the words in a book. That usually happened when she was tied up with something else and couldn't read to him when he wanted. Usually he was willing to watch kids' shows on television in the meantime, but she didn't want him glued to the TV.

"Do you have other books that you know the words for?"

Bryson nodded. "Short ones."

"Maybe next time I come, you can read me one of those, okay?"

Sophia had no idea why Ryker was going the extra mile with Bryson, but she was super grateful for it. Hopefully this would help Bryson get over his fear of Vivianne leaving with Ryker each afternoon.

"I'd better go," Ryker said, leaning forward to put Vivianne into the car seat. "Michael might be wondering where we are."

"Thank you for coming inside," Sophia said. "You didn't have to stay this long."

Ryker glanced up at her as he strapped Vivianne in. "It wasn't a problem. If I can help alleviate a child's fear, it would be wrong of me not to do it."

"Do you have kids of your own?" she asked, unable to contain her curiosity.

"Nope, but I do have a niece and nephew that I enjoy spending time with. Though they're a bit older that Bryson." Ryker got to his feet and lifted Vivianne's car seat, then took the diaper bag from Sophia.

If he was that way after just dealing with a niece and nephew, then he had a bit of a natural affinity with children. Too bad not all men had that.

She and Bryson followed him to the door, then after he said goodbye, they watched him walk to his truck. Bryson's hand tucked into hers, and she looked down at him, hoping she wouldn't see fear or worry on his face this time around.

"I think Vivi will be okay, Momma," he said.

With a rush of relief and not a small amount of gratitude, she smiled at him. This was definitely the answer to prayer she'd been hoping for. "Yes, baby. I think she will be."

"Can we have pancakes for supper?" he asked as she closed the door.

"Let me guess. You want peanut butter and bananas on them."

He grinned at her then, something he hadn't done much since Ryker had started picking Vivianne up.

"Just remember, if you have peanut butter and bananas for supper, you can't have them for a snack."

He seemed to consider that before saying, "still want pancakes."

"And you're going to help me, right?"

"Of course, Momma. You need my help."

That was something else he'd started doing since they'd come home to New Hope. For most of his life, he'd been told that cooking was women's work. It was just one of the many horribly wrong messages he'd been fed.

Thankfully, his devotion to her was as complete as hers to him. That meant that she'd been able to undo a lot of those erroneous messages, and she took great pleasure in doing so.

"I definitely need your help," she agreed as they made their way into the kitchen.

The recipe she used was the one Nana had taught her, so she was able to do it without looking it up in a book or online. In turn, Bryson was memorizing it, and she hoped that some day he would make the same pancakes with his children.

Her heart was filled with happiness, and with more hope than she'd had in a long time. If Bryson's life could just be filled with people who were as kind and patient as Ryker, maybe the trauma of the first years of his life could be healed.

Ryker lifted a hand to shield his eyes from the sun as he assessed the tree they were getting ready to remove. Normally, Michael took on the dangerous role of climbing to the top to trim down some of the branches. But since he was still out of commission, the decisions about the tree removal fell to Ryker.

He'd managed to eke out enough hours of sleep between the nightmares the last few nights that Ryker felt confident he'd be able to focus enough to safely tackle the job. With one of the crew's help, he put on all the safety equipment he needed, then together they began the slow work of removing branches and eventually, the rest of the tree.

By the time they were done, muscles Ryker had forgotten he had were screaming for relief. But it was a job well done, so he felt gratified. He'd honestly never thought he'd feel as much satisfaction doing landscape work as he did working in pediatrics, but there were times he did. It was a different sort of satisfaction, but it was still there regardless.

Once they got everything cleaned up and the equipment back to Michael's, it was time for him to go pick up Vivianne.

Though it was nice that Bryson no longer looked at him with fear, Ryker knew that he couldn't let himself get too close to the child. Even so, a couple of times over the past week, he'd stayed long enough to let Bryson read to him. He couldn't let it be more frequent than that, however, just because he needed to keep a distance of some sort between them.

On that particular day, he wasn't going to be able to stick around for a book. But so far Bryson hadn't gotten upset when he couldn't stay, so he hoped that was still the case that day.

"Hi, Ryker," Bryson said from the door as he approached the porch.

"Hey there, Bryson. How's it going?"

"Good! We're going to see Nana."

"Is that your grandmother?" Ryker asked as he followed the little boy into the house.

"She's my grandmother," Sophia said. "So his great-grandma. She lives in the care home."

"Sounds like Bryson likes to visit her."

"He does. We both do, actually."

"We made her some cookies," Bryson said. "Would you like one?"

"Uh...sure. Who am I to turn down a cookie?"

"Get both bags," Sophia said as he disappeared through an open doorway.

He reappeared a moment later with a couple of bags that looked to contain more than one cookie in each of them. "Here. These are for you, and this bag is for Michael."

"Why, thank you." Ryker took both bags from Bryson. "I'm sure Michael and I will enjoy them very much."

"They're Nana's favorite, and Momma lets me help her make them, even though only girls are supposed to cook."

Ryker had figured out that perhaps the influences Bryson had already had in his life weren't that great, so it didn't really surprise him to hear something like that from the child. Sophia, however, gazed at Bryson with a look of dismay.

"I know there are people who think that way, but I happen to think that anyone can cook, if they want to. I'm not a great cook, but I have to do it unless I want to eat pizza every night."

"Pizza every night?" Bryson's eyes grew wide. "That would be awesome."

"You'd think that," Ryker agreed. "But trust me when I say that after awhile, you want to eat something else."

Bryson nodded then. "I think I'd miss bananas and peanut butter. Especially on the pancakes Momma and I make."

"That sounds yummy. Do you help your mom a lot with cooking and baking?"

"Yep. Everything we eat, I help her make."

"That's good. I'm sure she appreciates that, and if you like to do it, don't let anyone tell you that only girls can cook, okay?"

"Okay."

"Well, I'd best get going, and it sounds like you have somewhere to be as well."

After he picked up the car seat and the diaper bag, Ryker said goodbye to the pair and left the house. Every time he was around the two of them, it was hard not to come away with more questions. Which meant he had to continually tell himself that their lives were none of his business.

When he got to Michael's, he handed him Vivianne and then the bag of cookies. "Those are from Bryson. He gave me a bag for each of us."

"I'll keep one for Lani, but I'm definitely having a snack now," Michael said.

"Do you want some coffee to go with them?" Ryker asked, already well familiar with Michael's coffee machine.

"That sounds great," Michael said as he cradled Vivianne in his arms.

He got Vivianne's bottle ready and gave it to Michael before turning his attention to the coffee. Once he had filled a couple of mugs, he set Michael's on the end table beside his chair.

"What do you know about Sophia and Bryson?" he found himself asking after taking a bite of the snickerdoodle and a sip of coffee.

Michael's brows drew together. "Why? Do you have some concerns?"

"Not where Vivianne is concerned. There are just some things I'm curious about."

"Like?"

Ryker considered if he should share his observations. After another bite and sip, he said, "Well, first off, Bryson's reaction to me—which seemed a bit over the top with fear. He worried every time I left with Vivianne, that he'd never see her again."

"Yeah. The first few times I saw him, he seemed a little reserved and wary of me too."

"So do you know anything about their past?"

"Not really," he said with a shake of his head. "Pastor Evans said that Sophia had just returned to New Hope Falls with her son after being away for several years. Her family still lives here and attends the same church as me."

"So you know her family?"

"I know *of* her family, but I don't know any of them personally. Pastor Evans said that Sophia was looking for a way to earn money while being able to stay home with her son."

"And you pay her enough for that?" Ryker asked, realizing as soon as the question was out of his mouth, that what Michael paid Sophia wasn't any of his business.

"I don't know what her expenses are, but I had asked a few people what a reasonable rate for childcare would be, and when Pastor Evans quoted me what she wanted, it fell in that range. So that's what I pay her."

What Ryker had seen of her home made him think that her rent was minimal. The place wasn't rundown, especially inside, but it had looked small and in need of some TLC, particularly on the exterior.

"So you don't know anything about what they may have gone through before coming here?"

"Afraid not," Michael said. "I've been a little preoccupied with stuff in my own life, so I haven't really indulged in much conversation with her." He paused. "Wow, that sounds really self-centered."

Ryker chuckled. "I think you can be forgiven right now. Having a baby dropped in your lap when you're a single man would be disconcerting for most of us."

Michael eyed him. "But you seemed to know what to do with Vivianne without missing a step."

"I have had some experience with kids," he said by way of explanation. "My older brother has two, so I've helped out a time or two with them."

All technically true, but he wasn't going to divulge more than that. He didn't want Michael to start looking at him differently when he realized that the man he'd trained to care for yards, do landscaping, and take down trees was actually a pediatrician by profession. Maybe some day he'd tell him, but it wasn't going to be that day.

"Well, since Vivianne is my only sibling's first child, I haven't had a chance to acquire those skills." Michael leaned his head back against his chair. "But I have a feeling that even if Taylor had had six, I wouldn't be as comfortable with babies as you are."

"Guess I'm just a natural," Ryker said, forcing a laugh. Not that that was a lie. He'd always enjoyed being around kids and taking care of them. "I also babysat as a teenager. One of the only boys in church that parents trusted with their kids."

"All I did when I was that age was mow grass and shovel snow. Look where I've ended up. Following that trajectory, you should have been a teacher or something."

Ryker shrugged. "Not all of us follow a trajectory that makes sense."

"True," Michael said. "Very true."

Though his thoughts about Sophia and Bryson lingered in the back of Ryker's mind, he allowed Michael to re-direct the conversation to the business. He understood that while he might have some concerns about the pair, Michael's concerns would be about the business since he wasn't able to be as hands on as he usually was.

"I might try and hit a couple of the work sites tomorrow," Michael said. "Since I'm able to drive, and I'm getting a bit steadier on my crutches, I think I'd like to get back out there. For at least an hour or two."

"As long as you think you're ready," Ryker said, eyeing the external fixator currently attached to Michael's fractured leg. "If you overdo it, you'll regret it."

Michael sighed. "Yeah. I know. But I'm going a little crazy just sitting here for hours every day. There's only so much daytime television I can handle. It's giving me a little too much time to think."

"How about I swing by and pick you up?" Ryker suggested. "That way you don't have to worry about driving too. The jobs are all local tomorrow, so I can drop you back home when you've had enough."

Michael sighed again. "I know I should take you up on that even though I don't really want to."

"You're a smart man," Ryker said, and despite the fact that Michael was essentially illiterate, Ryker truly believed that. "You'll make the right decision."

"Fine. Pick me up then."

Ryker chuckled. "It'll be great. I'll even bring you some coffee."

"And if I manage okay, will you let me go on my own next time?"

Ryker leaned back against the couch, stretching out his legs and crossing his ankles. "Maybe."

He almost said something about doctor's orders, but then bit his tongue. Although, Michael would probably just laugh, thinking it was a joke.

By the time Lani arrived, Ryker was ready to head to his apartment. His mom had sent him home with some food when he'd stopped by to see her and his dad on the weekend, so he was looking forward to a tasty meal for a change.

And he'd try to put Sophia and Bryson's situation out of his mind. After all, it wasn't really any of his business, even though one might argue that Sophia asking him for help with Bryson might have given him the right to ask some questions.

The problem was that in asking questions, he was opening himself up to knowledge that might be difficult for him to move beyond. It seemed that the two of them were safe now, so it wasn't as if there was imminent danger for either of them.

He could live without the knowledge of where they'd come from as long as they were safe now. And from what he could tell, they were.

~*~

Sophia stood at the picture window, gazing at the part of the front yard she could see from her vantage point. It was beginning to resemble a jungle, which was a shame because Nana had always taken such pride in her yard. Until she'd fallen and broken her hip, she'd taken care of it all herself. Mowing. Planting. Raking. Even trimming the hedges that lined the front of the yard along the sidewalk.

Since she'd taken up residence there, her dad had come by a couple of times to mow, but he'd been busy with overtime lately so hadn't been able to do it again.

The yard wasn't a huge piece of land, but so far, it was more than Sophia had managed to take care of. Part of the reason was that she just didn't have the experience, and another part was that she'd just never had the desire for it either. However, the biggest deterrent to getting the work done was Bryson.

He had never liked being outside. Where some kids enjoyed seeing bugs and other things out in nature, he never had. He'd been forced outside a lot, starting at around age three, but a horrific wasp sting had taken his dislike for the outdoors into the realm of a phobia. Now he tolerated walking from the house to the car and from the car to wherever it was they were going, but he never let Sophia dawdle.

Because of that, Bryson didn't want to come outside with her, which would be okay except he also didn't want her out of his sight. All of that meant that yard work was beyond her right then. She did feel bad though, because if Nana saw the state of the yard, she would have a heart attack.

She wondered if there was a teen in the neighborhood who would be willing to clean it up for a few bucks and some cookies...

Turning from the window, she said, "Bry? Do you want to sit on the porch so I can mow the grass?"

He looked up from the book he was paging through. With a frown, he shook his head.

"Then will you sit on the chair in front of the window while I go outside?"

Another shake of his head. Sophia stifled her sigh of frustration. She understood why he felt the way he did, but she needed him to learn to be a bit more independent. How she was going to achieve that, she didn't know.

"How about if I ask Madelyn to come over?" she asked, already knowing his reaction.

His eyes grew big as he shook his head more aggressively. "She's too...noisy."

That was definitely true. Whether she was in the midst of their big family or with just one person, she was loud. It was like she had no volume control.

She could ask her youngest brother to come over and mow, but getting the teen off his game console or phone was nearly impossible, if her parents were to be believed. He'd also probably want more money than she could afford to pay him. Madelyn would have wanted money too, if she'd come over to watch Bryson.

Frustrated, she decided to just let it go for the time being. She knew she was going to have to figure something out soon, though, or they'd be living in a jungle. Then insects would be the least of Bryson's worries...

"Let's go see Nana," she said instead.

Nana greeted them enthusiastically when they walked into her room a short time later, and happily relieved Bryson of the container of cookies he carried. Sophia sank into her chair with a sigh, watching as Bryson clambered up on his seat and pulled the coloring book and crayons closer.

"You doing okay, sweetheart?" Nana asked, a frown creasing her brow. "You look tired."

"I am," she admitted. "Bryson had a rough night last night, so we were both up a lot. He took a nap, but since I had Vivianne, I didn't feel like I should."

"I'll pray you sleep better tonight." Nana patted her hand. "Both of you."

"Thanks."

Nana turned her attention to Bryson when he wanted her to look at the picture he'd chosen to color. He began to talk to her about what he'd been doing, chatting even more than usual.

During their other visits, he would talk to Nana, but usually he focused on his coloring while she and Nana talked. This time, however, when Nana asked him a question, he answered it, then volunteered more information about what had been going on.

"Who is this Ryker that Bryson keeps talking about?" Nana asked.

"Hmm?"

Nana's brows lifted. "Ryker. Who is he?"

"Oh. He's the man who's been picking up Vivianne since Michael broke his leg."

"I thought Bryson was scared of him."

"He was," Sophia agreed, then went on to explain what had happened.

"Sounds like the boy has taken a bit of a shine to him now," Nana observed. "From fear to adoration? It would take a pretty special guy to help a little fella change like that."

Sophia happened to think the same, but she didn't say so, afraid that Nana would read something into it when she shouldn't. Instead, she just shrugged.

She wasn't sure she'd ever be able to trust her own judgment where men were concerned, which was why she would never look at Ryker as someone special except in relation to how he treated Bryson. However, she would always be grateful that Ryker had found a way to help Bryson with his fear.

She wondered if Bryson warming up to Ryker the way he had might spill over into how he related to his grandpa and uncles. She was also glad that he wasn't riddled with worry and anxiety about Vivianne leaving with Ryker each evening now, and she really hoped that maybe the experience would help Bryson deal with his other fears.

But regardless, what Ryker had done for Bryson was worth a whole lot to her. She'd never be able to thank him enough for that.

CHAPTER FIVE

A couple evenings later, Sophia tried to get Bryson to stay with Nana for just an hour so that she could tackle the ever-growing jungle at the house. Unfortunately, he wasn't willing to consider that, even though he probably trusted Nana more than any other person aside from Sophia.

She knew that his clinginess was a result of their experiences. Of him being taken away from her when he was barely a toddler. The memory of that crept in every time she considered trying to force him to be away from her even for a little while. He didn't know that it would only be for a short time. In his mind, it was possible his momma's absence could stretch on for much longer like it had in the compound.

So Sophia was forced to accept that the grass would continue to grow and the flower beds at the front of the house would fill with weeds.

She again considered asking her dad for help, but he already worked long hours. Plus, her relationship with her parents was still on rocky ground. Though they hadn't said *I told you so* when she'd come back to New Hope Falls, she knew it was what they thought.

Unfortunately, it was true. They *had* told her.

They'd only needed to meet Ezekiel once to see something that she hadn't been able to even after spending a lot of time talking with him. And because of that, she'd thought that she knew him better...that they were just trying to prevent her from being with someone who was treating her like she was important.

Given how she already felt about her place in their family, she really didn't think that they had her best interests at heart. After all, they'd let go of her easily enough as a child. How would they even *know* what was best for her?

Coming back to New Hope Falls had required her to do so with her tail between her legs, so to speak. If she'd had anywhere else to go, she probably would have gone there instead. But being broke with a young child relying on her had forced Sophia to return to the only place where she might have a support system...such as it was.

So for now, asking her dad to help with the yard would go to the bottom of her list of options. Her short—and getting shorter—list.

Maybe she should ask Ryker to encourage Bryson to sit at the window for a few minutes each day. Bryson might listen to the man in a way he didn't listen to her. She felt like she was too close to the situation, too emotionally invested in not upsetting Bryson to be able to move him through the intense separation anxiety he struggled with.

But she had a hard time with the idea of approaching Ryker for help again.

"Is Ryker coming today, Momma?" Bryson asked as he knelt on the chair in front of the window, arms hooked over the back of it as he stared out at the street.

"Yes, baby, he is." Sophia picked Vivianne up from the couch where she'd just changed her diaper. She placed her on a blanket on the floor then went to the kitchen to throw the diaper out and wash her hands before returning to the living room. "But it's not going to be for awhile. He doesn't come until after five o'clock, and it's only three o'clock now."

"Oh." He turned and slid down to sit on the chair, a look of disappointment on his face. "That's a long time, right?"

"A couple of hours," Sophia said. "But let's do something to help pass the time."

He brightened up at that. "Can we make him cookies?"

Sophia sighed. That wasn't quite what she had in mind, particularly since they'd made quite a few batches of cookies lately. And Bryson had insisted on giving Ryker some of them each time.

"How about we paint instead?"

"Okay." Bryson slid off the chair. "I'll paint a picture for Ryker."

Sophia closed her eyes and blew out a slightly frustrated breath, but she didn't argue with him. Nor did she suggest another activity because she was pretty sure Bryson would just somehow tie it back to Ryker. Instead, she picked Vivianne up and carried her into the kitchen where she had a small bassinette set up—one she'd scored in a thrift store.

After laying the baby down, she helped Bryson get set up with his paints at the small kitchen table, spreading the old plastic tablecloth she'd designated for painting over the table. Since they were in the kitchen anyway and Vivianne had drifted off to sleep courtesy of a full tummy and a clean diaper, Sophia decided to start on supper.

As she took out the ingredients for the stir-fry she was going to make, Bryson blabbed on and on about the picture he was painting for Ryker. Sophia had a feeling that the man was going to need Bryson to describe what he'd painted because while the boy loved painting, it was pretty rare that the pictures matched his descriptions.

By the time she finished chopping up the vegetables, Bryson had finished his masterpiece for Ryker. Since they still had time to kill, she suggested he paint a picture for Nana next.

When Vivianne began to fuss, Sophia picked the baby up and settled into a chair at the table to watch Bryson.

"Do you think Ryker will like my picture, Momma?" Bryson asked, peering up at her from beneath his curly bangs.

"I'm sure he'll love your picture," Sophia said. Strangely enough, she was quite confident of her response. Whether he really did or not, she didn't doubt that Ryker would tell Bryson that he did.

Bryson gave her a beaming smile as he turned his attention back to the paper in front of him.

"And I'm sure Nana will love this picture, too."

As she swayed back and forth with Vivianne, Sophia tried to figure out how to lessen Bryson's hero-worship of Ryker. She hadn't figured that he would deal with the situation of Bryson's fear so well that Bryson's opinion of Ryker would swing so completely in the other direction. She couldn't help but wish Ryker had been just a little less effective.

By the time Ryker arrived, Sophia had come to the conclusion that she needed to speak with him about maybe pulling back just a bit. She wasn't sure what his reaction might be, but hopefully, he'd understand.

"Ryker!" Bryson exclaimed when the man walked into the house.

"Hiya, buddy," Ryker said, holding his hand out for Bryson to smack.

Bryson hadn't even known about high fives until Ryker had taught him. Things like that made it hard to consider asking him to keep a distance from them.

In spite of that, Sophia was quite convinced that it was the right thing to do. Maybe if there were other men in her life who Bryson had connected with, the decision would be easier. Beyond Bryson's attachment to the man, the things Ryker did for Bryson was making Sophia feel certain...things. Things she needed to *not* be feeling when she'd resolved to steering clear of men.

She was doing this for both their sakes.

"Do you need some help with your yard?"

Sophia stared at Ryker for a minute, pulling her mind back from the decision she'd made. "What?"

"Your grass looks like it's getting a bit long," he said. "Do you need some help with it?"

Well, *phooey*. How was she supposed to ask him to keep his distance when he was offering his help with the one thing she needed help with right then?

"Yes. I could use some help," she admitted reluctantly, crossing her arms. "I've been trying to get around to tackling it, but it's hard since Bryson hates being outside and also hates having me out of his sight."

"Ah. I can see how that would make it difficult." She waited for him to ask why Bryson hated being outside and having her out of his sight, but he didn't. "I'll come back once Lani gets to Michael's to help with Vivianne. It should still be light enough for me to get some of the yard done before dark, though it will probably take a few evenings."

She could wait a few more days to speak to him about pulling back a bit. Though putting it off because he was helping her felt a bit like she was taking advantage of him.

"You don't have to do that."

"Do you have a lawn mower?" he asked, ignoring her statement.

She hesitated. It felt wrong to take him up on his offer, but it appeared that he wasn't going to give her much choice. "Yes. It's in the shed in the back."

"Why don't I go have a look at what's in the shed, so I know if I need to bring anything back with me." He headed out the front door, and she stood watching as he disappeared around the corner to the back.

Bryson came to her side and peered out the window. "Is he coming back?"

"Yes. He's coming back. He's just checking to see what he needs to mow the grass."

He looked up at her, his brows pulled tight over his eyes. "He's not afraid of bugs and bees?"

"I guess not."

It wasn't long before Ryker was back. "Looks like you've got everything I'll need, so I'll be back in a couple of hours to mow for a bit."

"Thank you," Sophia said. "I really appreciate it."

He left a few minutes later with Vivianne and the diaper bag. Sophia held the edge of the door as he walked to the truck, then sagged against it as Ryker drove away. She was grateful that Ryker was going to help her with the yard this time around, but she knew she couldn't let herself rely on him in the future.

The more she got to know Ryker, the more appealing he was to her. She had to remind herself that she didn't need a man...didn't *want* a man in her life. It didn't matter that he was amazing with Bryson. Plus, guys hadn't wanted to be with her before her life had become all messed up, so why would anyone want to be with her now?

Over the next few hours, she made supper and then they ate. After they'd cleaned up, she got Bryson ready to take his bath. Rather than play with his toys, however, he wanted her to get on with the job of washing his hair. She knew he wanted to be sure that he was out of the tub by the time Ryker returned.

Once he was in his pajamas, she took him back to the living room so that she could comb through his damp curls. He was surprisingly patient with her, not even getting upset when the comb caught on a knot. She'd toyed with the idea of cutting his hair short, but he'd been forced to live with a shorn head for most of his life, and she loved his curls.

"He's back, Momma," Bryson said, pointing to where Ryker's truck had parked at the curb.

"I see that."

He waved through the window, giving a squeak of excitement when Ryker lifted a hand in response. "Can I go say hi to him?"

Sophia stared down at Bryson. "What?"

"I want to say hi."

"You want to go outside and say hi to him?" Sophia asked. "What about the bugs?"

She wasn't sure why she wasn't just jumping at the chance for Bryson to go outside without the reason being a mad dash to the car. But why was Bryson willing to do these things for Ryker, but not for her?

"I...I won't stay out there long," Bryson said.

"Okay. But let's wait until he comes back around."

When Ryker pushed the lawn mower into the front yard, Bryson darted for the door, pushing it open so he could call out, "Hi, Ryker!"

Sophia followed him, putting her hand on the door to hold it open so Bryson didn't have to as he took just one step out of the house. Ryker greeted him but didn't come up onto the porch.

Bryson danced from one foot to the other while flapping his hands around. Sophia figured it was his "keep the bugs away" dance, since it wasn't something he usually did.

"I'm gonna watch you through the window," he told Ryker before retreating back into the house.

Ryker watched him go then looked at Sophia. "Guess he reached his outside tolerance?"

She nodded. "He got stung by a wasp awhile back, and he's been scared to spend any time outside ever since. I'm not sure how to help him get past that."

"That is a tough one," Ryker said. "When you're little, one bad experience can definitely spoil things for the future."

"Yeah." Too bad Bryson had had a whole slew of bad experiences in his short life.

"Well, I'd better get to it while there's still daylight," Ryker said, gesturing to the mower.

As she walked back inside, she heard the mower fire up. Bryson had reclaimed the chair he'd sat in earlier to watch for Ryker, staring out the window. While he was otherwise occupied, she got the laundry from the dryer and settled on the couch to fold it.

She found herself glancing out the window periodically to watch Ryker's progress. The evening was heading toward twilight, and she figured it wouldn't be safe for him to mow much longer.

When the mower switched off, Sophia got up and went to the door. She'd been contemplating how to pay Ryker for his work. Something told her that he'd decline money even if she could afford to offer it. But he might be interested in some food, and they had leftovers from supper.

"I think I'm done for tonight," Ryker said when she stepped out on the porch. "I'll do some more tomorrow."

"Have you had supper?" she asked.

"Uh...not yet. Why?"

"We had leftovers from supper if you'd like some."

"Sure. Just let me put this away."

She hadn't been sure if she should just offer him some to take home, but by the sounds of it, he was prepared to come inside and eat. Bryson would be thrilled at that.

"Come on in when you're ready." At his nod, Sophia headed back inside and went straight to the fridge, pulling out the containers that held the stir-fry and rice she'd made earlier.

She heard Bryson's enthusiastic greeting when the front door opened. "Are you staying here tonight, Ryker?"

Sophia was glad she wasn't in the living room when her son asked that embarrassing question. Hopefully Ryker didn't think that having overnight male guests was something that happened frequently...if at all.

"Nope, buddy. I'm going to sleep at my own apartment."

"Are you sure?" Bryson asked. "You can sleep in my room, since I sleep with Momma. I have my own bed though."

"Why don't you sleep in your room?" Ryker asked.

Sophia held her breath, waiting to see what Bryson would say. Anytime she'd tried to get him to sleep in his own room, he'd said he was too scared. Part of her hoped that Ryker wouldn't say anything that would hurt Bryson, even if that would solve Bryson's hero-worship of the man. Maybe.

"I'm...I'm too scared to sleep by myself."

"I understand. When I was your age, I would go to sleep in my own bed, but sometimes I'd have a bad dream. If that happened, I'd go to my mom and dad's room, and they'd let me stay with them."

Sophia felt relief that Ryker hadn't scolded Bryson for his need to sleep near her. Hearing footsteps headed toward the kitchen, she turned back to the counter where she'd been dishing up the food onto a plate. She'd just shoved it into the microwave when the two of them appeared.

"Momma, Ryker said he used to sleep with his mom too," Bryson said as he hurried over to where she stood.

"Sometimes," Ryker clarified. He didn't mention the fact that Bryson hadn't included his dad in that sentence. "I didn't always sleep with my mom and dad. Just when I was too scared to stay in my bed."

The microwave beeped, saving them from further conversation on that topic.

"I hope you like stir-fry and rice," Sophia said as she pulled the plate from the microwave.

"I can honestly say that there's not much I won't eat," Ryker said. "And I've been known to enjoy a stir-fry or two in my day."

"Well, hopefully your expectations aren't too high. Cooking for this guy means not a lot of spiciness, I'm afraid." She ruffled Bryson's now dry curls. "Why don't you have a seat?"

"Thanks." He pulled out one of the chairs and settled himself on it.

Bryson climbed up on the chair he usually used. "Do I get a treat, Momma?"

"Sure thing. Let me just get Ryker his food."

She set the plate in front of him then got a glass from the fridge. "Uh...are you okay with water? The other option is milk."

"I'm gonna have milk," Bryson said.

"Well, maybe I should join Bryson and have a glass of milk," Ryker said with a grin. "Never get enough calcium, right?"

Bryson's brow furrowed. "What's calcimum?"

Ryker chuckled. "Calcium is something that helps our teeth and bones stay strong."

"Oh. I drink lots of milk."

"Then your bones and teeth should be good."

Sophia poured them both glasses of milk, then set them on the table. While Ryker began to eat, Sophia quickly prepared Bryson's snack.

When she set it in front of Bryson, Ryker said, "Wow. Bananas and peanut butter. Classic combination."

"They're my favorite," Bryson informed him around a mouthful of banana.

"Not with your mouth full, baby."

Giving her an apologetic look, he swallowed. "Sorry, Momma." Then he turned his attention back to Ryker. "I like bananas and peanut butter on pancakes too."

"Yep. I like that as well."

While she put away the containers of food, Sophia listened as the pair continued to discuss food. She had to give Ryker credit for holding up his end of the conversation with a four-year-old. A lot of guys wouldn't even bother.

It was part of what made the idea of asking Ryker to back away so hard to accept. It appeared that Ryker was a decent guy, and if Bryson was in need of anything, it was good male role models.

He'd had plenty of negative ones, so she was eager to replace those with positive ones.

But how did she do that without him getting overly attached to someone like Ryker?

And honestly, without her becoming overly attached as well. She'd always fallen too quickly for guys, especially ones that weren't exactly good for her. Why that was, she didn't know. But being unable to escape the last bad decision she'd made, she wasn't in a rush to get into anything else.

Perhaps five years in hell had taught her to be a little more discerning in the men she allowed to get close. At least she hoped she'd learned that lesson, because she needed to be wiser about the people she let into her world now that she had Bryson to protect and take care of.

"Did you like your food?" Bryson asked.

Sophia swung around to see that both of them had empty plates in front of them.

"I most certainly did. It was very tasty."

"Momma's food always tastes good," Bryson said.

"That's because I usually only cook what you like," Sophia said with a laugh.

"Is he a picky eater?" Ryker asked.

"Not really, but he definitely eats more if it's something he likes. And right now..." She shrugged. "It's...it's important to get food into him."

Ryker's gaze held an assessing quality as it settled on Bryson, then he nodded. "He does seem to like healthy stuff, so eating more of that is always a good thing."

"Yep. Only not-so-healthy stuff he eats these days are cookies, and even those I try to work a healthy ingredient into if I can."

"Cookies are a food group all to themselves, I think," Ryker said with a grin.

"Nana and Bryson would agree with you," Sophia said as she sat down at the table. "I'm sorry we're out of cookies tonight. Somehow all the cookies go missing in the hours following me pulling them out of the oven."

Ryker chuckled. "Like they make their way into bags that get given away?"

"Nana gets the most," Bryson volunteered.

"I think she shares them with others in the care home."

"My mom always says sharing is caring," Ryker said. "Though my younger sister isn't about sharing when it's anything chocolate."

"Yeah. A few of my siblings feel the same way."

"How many do you have?" Ryker asked.

"There's seven of us," Sophia said, preparing herself for his reaction.

"Wow...that's...a lot. There are only three of us, and there are times when I feel like that's at least one too many," he said with a laugh.

"I have a sister who believes that there are about six too many of us."

"She would have preferred to be an only child?"

"Definitely. She's already vowed not to follow our mom and dad's example. She and our oldest sister argue a lot about their thoughts on having children. Chloe has four and is pregnant with her fifth, while Natalie has none and plans to keep it that way."

"Some people seem to be made to parent lots of children, but that doesn't mean that everyone should have lots of kids. Or any...if they don't want them."

"I agree. I get so tired of their arguing. It's not like Chloe can stuff her four children back inside."

Ryker chuckled. "Yeah. One way trip only."

"I figure if Chloe and her husband can provide for their family, size shouldn't matter."

"And is that the case?"

Sophia shrugged. "I think so. I mean, Henry has a job as a manager of a store. He's had it forever and from things Chloe has said, they have decent insurance. They have a small-ish house, but that doesn't seem to bother either of them or the kids. Honestly, I think they agreed early on that they wanted a large family, and that Chloe would be a stay-at-home mom. All their decisions seem to have been made with that in mind."

"That sounds responsible," Ryker said. "My older brother has two kids, and I think that will probably be it for them. My younger sister has none, and I'm not sure if she plans to have any."

Sophia wanted to ask about Ryker's plans for a family, especially given how good he seemed to be with kids, but that was too personal of a question. And hopefully he'd feel that way too, because the last thing she wanted was to answer any of those sorts of questions about herself.

"I should head home," Ryker said as he got to his feet. "Thank you for supper."

"Thank you for tackling my yard," she replied. "I was getting concerned that by the time I figured out how to handle it, we'd be living in a jungle."

"Living in a jungle wouldn't be all bad," Ryker said with a wink at Bryson. "Think how much fun you'd have swinging from branch to branch with the monkeys. Or being sprayed by the elephants at a watering hole."

Bryson's eyes got big at that. "Elephants? Monkeys?"

"Yep. Would you like to hang out with them?"

"I...don't...know." Bryson's brow furrowed once again. "I've never seen real elephants and monkeys. Just in my books and on TV."

"Maybe some day you can go to the zoo and see them in real life."

Sophia wasn't sure how they'd ever manage that. Such an idea seemed nearly impossible at that moment considering Bryson's refusal to spend any time outdoors.

"I'll be back tomorrow about the same time," Ryker said as they walked to the door.

"I'll have some supper for you again, if you don't mind relatively simple food."

"You don't have to do that."

"Consider it payment for your help with our jungle."

Ryker shrugged. "I don't need payment."

"Maybe you don't need it, but I need to offer something in exchange for you helping us out this way. It was becoming a stress for me."

"In that case, I'll happily relieve you of some food." Ryker pulled the door open and stepped out onto the porch. "See you tomorrow."

"Bye, Ryker!" Bryson called out as Ryker walked to his truck.

Ryker turned around and walked backward for a couple steps. "Bye, buddy."

"Time for bed, baby. Go to the bathroom, I'll be right there." Sophia locked the door and drew the curtains over the front picture window before heading for the bathroom.

Bryson stood on his stool, washing his hands. She quickly prepared his toothbrush and oversaw him using it since he still considered a single pass with the brush over his teeth sufficient.

When Sophia had him settled in his bed with the books he wanted her to read, he looked up at her. "Do you think Ryker likes me? Even if I don't like to go outside like him?"

Sophia hurt a bit at his words. She ran her fingers through his curls, feeling her heart pulse with love for him. "I think he likes you just fine."

Bryson's sigh of relief was audible, and Sophia was left wondering how she could ask Ryker to be more distant with Bryson when her little boy would likely take it as a rejection. Plus, she'd gone and asked the man to eat in her kitchen for the next few days...

That wasn't her smartest idea. Hopefully it wouldn't backfire completely on her.

CHAPTER SIX

Ryker walked up the sidewalk that led to Sophia's house. His plan was to just head on around to the shed in the back yard, but he spotted Bryson standing at the storm door, waving at him through the glass. He took a moment to wave back, but then he continued on.

It wasn't that he wanted to ignore the little boy, but he hoped that by staying outside, it might give Bryson the opportunity to think about venturing outdoors himself. He understood how his fear had developed, but it wasn't sustainable in a young child. At some point, he'd have to go to school—unless Sophia planned to home-school—and that would mean he'd need to be able to go outside.

And even if Sophia planned to homeschool, it would still make life difficult for them both if he was unwilling to spend any length of time outside. Case in point, her being unable to do yard work.

Ryker wondered again about approaching his mom for some advice, but he didn't have enough details about Sophia and Bryson's life before they came to New Hope Falls. She would ask him questions—because that's what she always did—and then wonder why he didn't have any answers.

In the meantime, he'd continue to hang out with the pair...at least until the yard work was done for the month. If he hadn't had anything else to do, he could have gotten it all done in one day. But instead of just one long day spent mowing, cleaning up the flower beds, and trimming the hedges, he was going to be there for at least three evenings doing the work.

He focused on mowing and weed-whacking the back yard since he'd managed to finish mowing the front yard the night before.

When the sun began to set, casting deep shadows across the yard, Ryker put all the equipment away. He'd been surprised by the quality of the tools he'd found when he'd checked them over the previous day.

The shed was organized, and everything in it was in good condition. Having things there made it a lot easier than him having to cart everything over from Michael's. Plus, then he'd have to answer questions from his boss about what he was doing, and he wasn't really in the mood to do that.

Frankly, he was rarely in the mood to answer questions from anyone these days. Except maybe Bryson. The boy's lack of experiences that most kids his age should have had made Ryker curious, of course, but it also made him want to help the little guy expand his horizons.

"You can come in this way, Ryker!" Bryson shouted from the back door.

"I'll be there in a minute," Ryker called back, then went about securing the shed for the night.

As he walked across the small deck to the back porch, the door swung open to reveal Bryson standing there in his pajamas. "Hi!"

"Hey, buddy." Ryker held out his hand for Bryson to smack it. "How was supper?"

"Yummy. Momma made sketti with balls."

"I do like spaghetti and meatballs," Ryker said as he tried not to laugh at Bryson's description. As he walked into the kitchen from the back door, he glanced over to where Sophia stood at the counter. "Are you eating bananas and peanut butter again?"

"Yep! It's my favorite, and Momma says it fills me up, so I sleep better."

"I think a tummy full of bananas and peanut butter would definitely make me sleep good." He paused then said, "Do you mind if I wash up in the bathroom?"

"Not at all," Sophia said. "Bry, can you show Ryker where it is?"

Bryson led the way out of the kitchen, then pointed to an open door in a short hallway. "It's right there."

"Thanks, buddy. I'll be back in a minute."

Once he was done in the bathroom, Ryker returned to the kitchen to find a plate of hot food sitting on the table. It smelled delicious, and he bet Sophia liked to make it for Bryson because there were all kinds of ways to hide vegetables in the meatballs and the sauce.

Bryson was already sitting at the table with a glass of milk in front of him. As Ryker sat down, Sophia set a small plate in front of Bryson. As he dug into the spaghetti and meatballs, Ryker quickly discovered that Bryson was quite right. The meal was definitely delicious.

It was a welcome meal after having worked all day then put in a bit more time on Sophia's yard. Plus, eating at Sophia's saved him from having to scrounge up something once he got home. Too often, he went the quick and easy route, which didn't necessarily add up to tasty or nutritious meals.

Sophia's phone rang as she was putting away the food. She picked it up from where it sat on the counter and stared at the display for a moment before answering it. "Can you hang on a second, Mellie?"

Lowering the phone to press in against her shoulder, she looked at Bryson. "Stay here with Ryker, okay? I'll be back in a couple of minutes."

He glanced at Bryson, catching a frown on his small face as he watched his mom disappear out of the kitchen. "Are you okay, buddy?"

"I don't want Momma to talk to her."

"To the person on the phone?"

Bryson nodded. "That's Mother Mellie."

The way he phrased that raised more than a few questions in Ryker's mind. Not the least of which was why Bryson didn't want Sophia to talk to her.

"And you don't like her?"

Bryson shook his head. "I didn't like any of the mothers. They wouldn't let me see Momma."

Ryker could hear the murmur of Sophia's voice in the distance, but it wasn't clear enough for him to understand what she was saying. The whole situation wasn't something that he could easily parse out with the limited information he had acquired about them. Nothing really fit what he knew of Sophia so far.

From what he'd seen, she was absolutely devoted to Bryson. If someone had kept her and Bryson apart before, it explained why she didn't try to separate herself from him now.

"What about your dad?" He asked the question even though he knew it really wasn't any of his business and probably a question he should be asking of Sophia, not Bryson.

Bryson's eyes widened, and he leaned closer to Ryker. "Father Zekiel wasn't nice. He told the mothers to take me away from Momma. He made me go outside even after I got bit." The little guy frowned. "He was a meanie. I *hated* him."

Ryker hadn't expected such an impassioned response from Bryson, but it was clear the boy felt very strongly about his dad. If the man even was his biological father. It was all very...weird.

Rather than press him further on a subject that was clearly upsetting him, Ryker decided to change the subject. "You better keep eating your bananas, or I might steal a couple when I get done with my spaghetti."

That seemed to work like a charm as Bryson tugged his plate closer and quickly ate one of the pieces of banana.

"Want to know what one of my favorite snacks was when I was your age?" Bryson nodded. "Apples and cheese."

The look Bryson gave him told Ryker precisely what the kid thought of that combination. "Eeww," he added for good measure. As if the horror on his face hadn't conveyed his thoughts sufficiently.

"Have you ever tried it?" Ryker asked.

"No. I don't like apples."

"Why not?"

"Too hard. Bananas are soft."

"Do you like cheese?"

Bryson shrugged. "Sometimes. I like cheese strings because I can pull them apart and eat them."

"That is a good thing."

"But no apples."

"How about if the apples are cooked?" Ryker asked, more to keep the conversation going than because he wanted to know how Bryson liked his apples. "Like in a pie?"

Bryson shook his head, sending his curls dancing. "No apples."

"How about oranges? They're not crunchy."

"I like oranges, but no seeds, and Momma has to peel them for me."

"Grapes?"

"Sometimes they're sour," he said with a shudder.

"Yeah. The green ones can be, but the red ones are usually sweet. Do you like raisins?" This got a nod from Bryson. "Did you know that raisins are made from grapes?"

His eyes went wide. "Really?"

"Yep."

"Momma keeps raisins in the cupboard. She puts them in cookies for Nana sometimes."

They continued to talk about different foods, Ryker chuckling at some of the reactions Bryson had. In some ways, they were so typical of kids his age, but every once in a while, he said something that made Ryker think that he'd only recently tasted some of those foods.

"Sorry about that," Sophia said as she walked back into the kitchen, tension etched on her face.

"Would you like a cookie or two for dessert, Ryker?"

"Uh...sure."

"Can I have one, Momma?" Bryson asked.

Ryker half expected Sophia to say no. But she just nodded, and when she carried a plate to the table, it had four cookies on it. She cleared away his and Bryson's empty plates and put them into the dishwasher.

"Mother Mellie isn't coming here, is she, Momma?"

Ryker saw tension lift Sophia's shoulders. She paused for a moment with her hands braced on the counter, head bent forward, before turning around.

Giving Bryson a smile that did nothing to alleviate the tension on her face, she said, "We'll talk about it later, baby."

"I don't want her to come, Momma. She's mean, and so are Charlie and Lisa."

Sophia sighed. "They just need a place to stay for a bit."

Ryker wasn't sure what to say about the situation. It concerned him that these people that Bryson didn't like very well would also be around Vivianne. He had to believe that Sophia wouldn't allow anyone to hurt either of the children. But still, it gave him pause.

"They won't be here for a few days yet."

Bryson scowled at the cookie in his hand, clearly unimpressed with the decision his mom had made.

"Well, I'd better get going," Ryker said as he finished off his cookies. "Gotta be up early tomorrow."

That was all true, but he could see Sophia's growing discomfort over having that conversation with Bryson in front of him.

"Thank you once again for your work on the yard," she said as she and Bryson followed him to the front door.

"I'll try to be back tomorrow, though I have to say, it might not work weather-wise. The forecast is for rain in the afternoon and evening." Which was one of the reasons why their day was starting earlier than usual. They needed to try and get as much work in as possible before it rained. Sometimes they could work in the rain, but mowing and taking down trees were two things they tried to avoid when the weather was like that. They had both those things scheduled for the next day.

"Bye, Ryker," Bryson said as he opened the door.

"See you tomorrow, buddy."

All the way home, he mulled over what he'd learned that evening. It felt a bit like peeling back the layers of an onion when it came to Sophia and Bryson's situation. Nothing was ever fully revealed, just another layer.

But concern was growing for the pair. He hoped that he'd be able to make a visit while the three people were there, if for no other reason than to check on Bryson and Sophia's welfare. It hadn't actually seemed that Sophia wanted them to visit either.

Should he just come right out and ask her about it?

He had no reason to think that either of them was in physical danger just yet. Even as a doctor, he would have needed more proof of abuse or reason to be concerned than a little boy expressing dislike for someone.

The *mother* reference was a bit...weird. But again, it wasn't anything he could bring to anyone out of concern.

Sighing, Ryker tried to force it from his thoughts for the time being. He couldn't let himself dwell on it too much, or he'd end up laying in bed awake for far too long when he needed to be able to get up early. And now there was a good chance that he'd have a nightmare too.

Still, shutting down his thoughts on everything was easier said than done. He knew that from past experience, so after he got home, he did a workout while listening to a true-crime podcast before taking a steaming hot shower.

Then he did something he'd kind of stopped doing in the past few years, and that was to say a prayer. He prayed for Sophia and Bryson, then just in case that prayer got God's attention, he tacked on a prayer that he'd be able to fall asleep quickly and have no nightmares.

~*~

Sophia waited until she was sure that Bryson was sleeping soundly before she slipped from her bed and went back to the living room. It had taken him longer than usual to fall asleep, which—given the events of the evening—wasn't at all surprising.

She just wished they hadn't had part of that conversation about Mellie and her kids in front of Ryker. God only knew what Bryson had said to Ryker while she'd been out of the room. Her mistake had been saying Mellie's name when she'd first answered the phone.

Settling in Nana's favorite rocker, she stared at the empty fireplace, her conversation with Mellie playing over and over in her head.

"I need someplace to go," Mellie said. "With someone who understands."

Sophia knew that not everyone had had a place to go back to like she had. Even if Nana hadn't stepped up and offered her house to them, she still would have had a place with her parents. In the days following the raid, she hadn't talked with Mellie about her plans. Hadn't talked to her much at all.

Which was why she really didn't understand why Mellie had called her. The woman had done some things that had made Sophia and Bryson's life extremely difficult. But Sophia hoped that her attitude had just been the result of the situation they were in and the things they were forced to do.

"If you come here, you can only stay for a week. Plus, if any of you tease or hurt Bryson in any way, you're out of here." She'd tried to inject her voice with as much firmness as possible. *"This is a safe place for him and me. Something we've both needed. I won't allow you to change that."*

"I promise. It'll be fine."

"I'm not alone here." She had felt the need to warn her. *"I have people who will be most unhappy if you bring any of your nastiness with you."*

"Sophia." Mellie's tone had been sweet—almost too sweet—and it had made Sophia have third thoughts. She'd already had second thoughts about even just talking to the woman. *"It wasn't my fault."*

"Wasn't it? I was in the same situation, and I didn't choose to turn on others. You had a choice, and you made the wrong one. The only reason I'm giving you a chance now is because I know that we were all under a lot of stress there. You will have other choices to make when you get here. Just be sure you make the right ones, or you'll be gone."

"You wouldn't just send us away, would you?"

"If you don't do as I've asked, yes, I would. It's now within my power to protect Bryson, and I'll do whatever I have to in order to accomplish that."

In the end, Mellie had promised that they would do as Sophia had asked. She'd warned her that she didn't have enough beds for all of them, and they'd have to share, but that hadn't seemed to be an issue for the woman.

Sophia sighed as she set the rocker in motion, leaning her head back against the chair. Until Mellie had come and gone without incident, she couldn't be sure that she'd made the right decision. She just hoped that being away from the compound and Ezekiel's dominating presence would allow her and Mellie to get along better.

They were both victims of the same scenario. Within the compound, Ezekiel and his minions had often pitted the women against each other in ways that left them viewing each other as competition...enemies. The unfortunate thing was that she had no way of knowing for sure which way things would work for them until Mellie was there.

After everything had gone down in the compound, most of the survivors had been too scared and confused to interact with each other in a real way. She'd stayed around to answer a million questions and get a bit of counseling, but then she'd left, eager to get Bryson away from Texas and the horror that had been their lives for the past five years.

Thankfully, there had been no trial because all the major players had been killed when the FBI had raided the compound...either by their own hand or, from what she'd understood, Ezekiel's before he'd gone down in a blaze of his own glory with a little help from the FBI.

She wanted to put it all behind her, so maybe this situation with Mellie wasn't the best decision. But she'd felt sorry for her, hating to hear that she and the kids had just been basically couch-surfing after leaving the care of the organization that had been helping them out after the raid on the compound. But would a week in Sophia's home really make any difference?

Another thought hit her then...Michael might not approve of her bringing people into her home while she was caring for his daughter. She couldn't lose the job she had taking care of Vivianne. It was the only reason she was able to stay at home with Bryson.

What had she done? Sacrificing the stability of her life all for a woman who had never been a friend?

Tension filled her body, bringing on a headache that made her want to cry.

Please, God, keep Bryson safe, and if this isn't a good idea, please help me see that before it's too late. I just...I just want to do the right thing.

Before canceling things with Mellie, she needed to talk to Michael. If he preferred that a stranger not be around his daughter, she would respect that. And then she'd let Mellie know that she couldn't come and stay with them.

The next morning, Sophia was surprised—and though she didn't want to admit it...happy—to see Ryker outside her door with Vivianne instead of Lani. Seeing him standing there, his hair tousled and with a smile on his face, made her heart skip a beat. She was conscious of the fact that she was dressed in her most comfortable leggings and a baggy T-shirt with her hair piled on top of her head. Definitely not how she wanted him to see her.

Ever since Michael's accident, Lani had been the one to drop Vivianne off each of the six days a week Sophia watched her.

"Hey. Didn't expect to see you this morning," Sophia said as she opened the door for him to bring Vivianne's car seat in.

"Ryker!" Bryson called out as he jumped off the couch and rushed to the door.

"Hiya, buddy." Ryker set the car seat on the carpet then held out his hand for Bryson to smack. Once the little greeting ritual was over, he straightened and looked back at her. "Uh... Michael and Lani have had a bit of a falling out."

"Oh no." Sophia frowned. "What happened?"

"It seems there was a lack of communication on something important that ended up causing some major issues. For today, I'm on drop off and pick up duty. Not sure what will happen next week."

"Is Michael back to work?"

"Not really. He comes to job sites, but more to supervise than to do any actual work. He's not back to full-speed yet."

"I'm sure that's frustrating for him," Sophia said.

"He's getting antsy, that's for sure. But his leg injury isn't anything to mess around with. Doing too much too soon could just mean it will take longer to heal."

Sophia nodded. "Well, I hope things get worked out between him and Lani. They both seemed really nice."

"They are," Ryker agreed. "I'm not sure if they can work through this or not. Only time will tell, I guess." He handed over the diaper bag. "I hope everything is in the bag. I think Michael and I got it all covered, but we were both in serious need of coffee, so who knows."

"It's fine. Michael originally brought over diapers and formula, so I have extra if I ever need them."

"Okay. That's good to know." He glanced at his watch then sighed. "I'd better get going. We have several jobs today, so I need to get on site before people start blowing up my phone to see where I am."

"Hope you have a good day," Sophia said.

"You guys too. I'll see you later."

As Ryker headed back to his truck, Bryson bolted over to the window to watch him leave. Sophia checked on Vivianne, not too surprised to see she was awake. She was awake more often now than when she'd first started watching her.

Scooping her up out of the car seat, Sophia went to sit in the rocker and cuddle her. Bryson came over and kissed the top of Vivianne's head. "Hey, Vivi."

Sophia loved to see how Bryson interacted with Vivianne. After everything he'd been through, she was so glad that his core of gentleness was still present. It was too bad that he'd never have siblings.

"Do you want to read her a story?" Sophia asked, knowing the answer before he even gave it.

"Yes!" He went over to his pile of books and picked one out.

When he came back to her, Sophia helped him up into her lap then angled Vivianne so that she could see the book. It was a chilly, gray day outside the house, but inside? She was filled with warmth as she held her little boy and the baby girl they'd come to love.

As Bryson "read" to Vivianne, Sophia considered what Ryker had revealed about Lani and Michael. She wasn't sure if they'd had a romantic relationship or just a friendship. But regardless, the news of a falling out between them was a sad turn of events.

She still needed to talk to Michael about how he would feel if Mellie came to stay with her for a while. Thinking of the conversation she needed to have made her a bit nervous because it was possible he would decide that he didn't want that to happen and take Vivianne to another babysitter.

Once Bryson finished his story, he slid off her lap and went to pick up the tablet that Nana had given them. Sophia allowed him to play a couple of children's games on it that she hoped would help him learn letters and numbers. He was a smart little kid, just a bit behind other children his age because of how he'd been raised.

She was doing everything she could to reverse the damage, but it was hard to not feel an enormous amount of guilt over what had happened.

CHAPTER SEVEN

Ryker had hoped he might be able to do more yard work at Sophia's, but as forecasted, rain started to fall as they were finishing up their last job in the middle of the afternoon. Resigned to the fact that it would have to wait for another day, he headed to Sophia's place to pick up Vivianne.

He was pretty beat, so his plan was to not linger too long at Sophia's. Both he and Michael had had fractured sleep since Vivianne had woken several times through the night. Though Michael had insisted that he would be okay caring for the baby on his own, Ryker hadn't been sure that would be the case, which was why he'd spent the previous night at Michael's place now that Lani wasn't watching Vivianne at night.

After he came to a stop in front of Sophia's house, he sat for a moment in the truck, not sure he wanted to get wet again. It had been a damp and chilly day, and he was looking forward to a hot shower.

Finally, he climbed out, tugging the hood of his waterproof windbreaker into place. Jogging up the sidewalk to the house, he was glad to reach the shelter of the porch.

"You look a little cold," Sophia said as she let him in.

"Cold and wet," he agreed, not moving further into the house since he didn't plan to stay.

The interior of Sophia's home was warm, and it smelled like they'd been baking again. It was probably greedy to hope that there was a Ziploc baggie with a few cookies in it waiting for him.

"Do you want cookies, Ryker?" Bryson asked.

Score! "I'd love cookies, buddy. Did you make them with your mom?"

"Yep. This time we made..." He looked at Sophia.

"Oatmeal cookies. Half with raisins for Nana, and half with chocolate chips for us."

"Do you want the raisin ones or the chocolate chip ones?"

"I have to say I'm a little partial to the chocolate chip ones," Ryker said.

"Can I go get them, Momma?"

"Yep. Go ahead."

Bryson darted away but reappeared not even a minute later with a bag in hand. "Is this the right one, Momma?" He lifted it up for her to inspect.

"It is, baby. Good job."

"Here you go, Ryker." Bryson held them out to him. "Hope you like them. They're yummy."

"I'm sure they are. You've done a good job with the other cookies you've given me."

"It's too bad babies can't eat cookies," Bryson said as he knelt next to the car seat. "You'd really like them, Vivi, but I'll eat some for you."

Ryker couldn't help but chuckle. "Is that how he manages to get extra cookies?"

"One of the many ways," Sophia said with a huff. "I have a hard time saying no to him."

"Well, I'd better take my cookies and go. I spent the night at Michael's last night to help him with Vivianne, so I'm running on empty. She's still not sleeping through the night."

"Yeah. I think she's a little young to expect that."

"Michael came to the job site for a bit today, but I told him to go home and get some rest since he'd probably be sleeping in short bursts again tonight. I'm going to drop Vivianne off, and then I'm going home to sleep as well. Sorry I can't do any yard work today. But with the rain, it's just not doable."

"That's quite alright," Sophia said. "I really appreciate what you've managed to do already. At least the grass isn't tall enough to hide a small child anymore."

Ryker chuckled. "That's true."

"I guess we'll see you on Monday then."

"Yep." Ryker tucked his cookies into the diaper bag and then picked it up along with the car seat, which was covered with a light blanket. "I'll be here."

After he said goodbye to Bryson, he headed back out into the rain, thankful that Sophia had covered the baby so she didn't get soaked.

He hadn't talked to Michael yet about what he'd heard from Sophia about her upcoming guests. Normally, he wouldn't have been concerned except for the fact that Bryson wasn't a fan of them and had called them mean. Though kids could be known for exaggerating, Bryson's obvious dislike of these people still concerned Ryker enough that he was contemplating mentioning it to Michael.

The only thing was...he felt kind of like that would be betraying Sophia's trust. Not that she'd asked him not to say anything. Still, he didn't want her to feel that he was tattling on her, which was why he really hoped that she took the initiative and talked to Michael about it herself.

"You get a chance to sleep?" Ryker asked Michael as he set Vivianne's car seat on the floor in front of the chair where the man sat.

"Yes. Thanks for sending me home. I had kind of forgotten how challenging it is to be up every two or three hours at night."

"Are you planning to talk to Lani?"

Michael sighed as he dragged his hand down his face. "I don't know. I suppose eventually I should, but what was her end game? Why was she working for us?"

"You know who could answer those questions?" Ryker asked as he dropped down on the couch.

The look Michael shot him told Ryker that he didn't appreciate the sarcasm in his tone. "Well, I'm not sure I want to know the answers, actually. Or if I could even trust what she tells me. After all, she kept her identity from me. Lying essentially."

After a few more minutes of conversation on the subject, Ryker knew he wasn't going to be able to talk Michael into calling Lani on that day, so he pushed up to his feet. "You okay for food and everything?"

"Yeah. I'm fine."

"And you feel confident getting around with her?"

"Yes. If you could put Vivi's car seat on the stroller, that would be great. That way, if I need to move around with her, I can put her in that and push it."

Ryker made quick work of attaching the car seat to the matching stroller, then lifted Vivianne out and handed her to Michael. She was starting to fuss a bit, so he said, "Want me to prep a bottle for her before I go?"

"If you wouldn't mind."

"Don't mind at all." He went to the kitchen and got it ready, then handed it off to Michael. "Give me a call if you find out that you need help."

"Thanks, man. I really couldn't do this without you."

"I think you'd figure out how to do it, but I'm glad to be able to help out."

After saying goodbye, he headed back to his truck, relieved to finally be heading home. He was looking forward to an evening of not having to do anything. Maybe he'd watch a movie or play a video game after his shower. And just because he could, he was going to order in some pizza.

It would probably be the most relaxed part of his weekend since he would be back at his folks' place for another family dinner on

Sunday evening. Hopefully Callie would be in a better mood because the past couple of times he'd seen her, it had been open warfare between them in only the way it could be between siblings.

After his shower, he threw on a load of laundry and straightened the apartment up a bit before placing an order for his favorite pizza. He was on the couch watching TV while he waited for it to arrive when his phone's text alert sounded.

Picking his phone up, he saw that the text was from his mom. Even before he opened it up, he knew what it was going to say.

Mom: *Hi darling. Hope you've had a good day! Are you still coming for dinner tomorrow?*

Ryker debated answering because he knew where the conversation was going. With a sigh, he tapped out his reply. *Yep. That's the plan.*

Mom: *We'd love to have you come to church with us in the morning.*

And there it was: His parents' concern over the fact that he hadn't darkened the door of the church since he'd returned from Syria. He knew it wasn't so much the fact that he wasn't attending church that bothered them as it was that he'd chosen to distance himself from all spiritual things.

Before heading to Syria, he and Lydia had been active in the large church his family had attended his whole life. They'd been involved in small groups and had attended pretty much every service their schedules allowed. They were committed to the church as much as they had been to their careers.

From what Callie had said on several occasions, that was still the case with Lydia. It made him feel a bit weak that somehow she'd managed to figure out how to accept that God had allowed that attack to happen, killing innocent people. So many of them children.

But he just hadn't been able to comprehend the events of that day and then move on with his life as it had been. Everything he thought he'd known about God was called into question that day. It had been just one more thing that had driven a wedge between him and Lydia.

Sorry, Mom. Not tomorrow.

He didn't have to imagine the disappointed look on her face. He'd seen it often enough over the years. But this wasn't something he was able to cave on. Maybe at some point in the future, church attendance might be possible, but not right yet.

Mom: *Just make sure you're there for dinner.*

I will be.

Mom: *xoxoxo*

xoxoxo

After sending his message, Ryker tossed his phone down beside him then leaned his head back, slouching into the couch cushions. Staring up at the ceiling, he tried to figure out how not to let the guilt consume him. He just wasn't sure that his parents—his mom, especially—would settle for him going to church just one Sunday. They'd expect him to continue to go every week.

And then it would be getting involved with a small group again.

Then going back to counseling.

Then getting back into medicine.

It seemed like a slippery slope that he wasn't all that keen to step on.

He was happy with life at the moment.

Okay, maybe *happy* was stretching it. He was definitely...okay with his life at the moment. He found satisfaction in his job, and helping Michael with Vivianne had revealed that he could tolerate casual interactions with children.

He was still of two minds about dealing with Bryson. During their interactions, he felt fulfilled and happy in a way that he hadn't thought he'd ever feel around children again. Making Bryson smile felt like a huge achievement. It was only at night when the nightmares came that he wondered if it was worth it to prolong their interactions.

Ryker knew, however, that if he told his mom that he was dealing with children again—who weren't his niece and nephew—she'd get all excited about how he might be healing from what had happened in Syria. And while he did feel that some healing was occurring, it still wasn't nearly enough to consider returning to a job in pediatrics.

There were still far too many nights when he woke in a cold sweat from nightmares of that day. Unfortunately, Bryson's smiles and earnest expressions weren't enough to completely overlay the other images in his brain, and in some cases, it was Bryson's face that stared back at him, a mask of fear and horror.

Something had fractured inside him that day, and Ryker wasn't sure if it would ever heal. In some ways, it felt wrong to want to heal from what had happened because so many others who had been there would never be able to. The ones that hadn't lost their lives had lost a loved one or suffered significant injuries or both.

Ryker covered his face with his hands, rubbing them vigorously as he tried not to let the tsunami of emotions drown him yet again. And despite his exhaustion, a sleepless night looked to be in the offing.

When his pizza arrived, Ryker tipped the delivery guy then went back to his couch. He was going to at least try and salvage the few plans he'd had for the evening: pizza and some entertainment.

As he lifted out a piece of pizza and set it on the plate, Ryker could picture Bryson's expression if he'd been there. He'd probably tuck his hands under his chin and gaze at the pizza, his eyes wide with anticipation. And then there would be Sophia...looking at her son indulgently. Because if there was one thing that Ryker had picked up on, it was that Sophia tried to give Bryson whatever she could to make him happy.

He didn't know the details of their past, but from the things Bryson had said, it was apparent it had been filled with fear and hurt. Those were emotions he could certainly identify with, even if he'd faced them in a different environment.

But regardless of their background, Sophia seemed to be doing what she could to provide a stable and safe life for Bryson. Ryker admired that about her.

He just hoped that the issues Bryson seemed to have would be dealt with or would resolve as he got older. The way the little boy had responded to Ryker once he had a chance to talk with him showed how resilient Bryson was. But some wounds to the psyche went deeper than others.

That was something he definitely understood from personal experience.

~*~

Sophia waited until Bryson was asleep before she sat down in the living room with her phone. She needed to talk with Michael. Should probably have talked to him before agreeing to let Mellie come.

Her nerves were fluttering badly as she turned her phone over and over in her hand. She could do this. Of all the difficult things she'd had to do in the past several months, this shouldn't even rank among the top ten. The problem was that her decision could possibly jeopardize her income and the stability of her life with Bryson.

Was this just another example of her making a bad decision? It kind of felt like it was, even though she'd thought that helping Mellie was the right thing to do.

But having made the decision to let Mellie come, she now had to talk to Michael about it.

"Hi, Michael," she said when he answered the call. "It's Sophia."

"Hey, Sophia. How're you doing?"

"I'm alright. How are you?" She didn't let on that she knew what had happened with Lani since he hadn't been the one to tell her.

"I'm hanging in there." He hesitated. "So what can I do for you?"

"I'm calling because I need to check with you about something." She searched for the best way to phrase everything. "I had a friend call me asking if she and her two kids could stay with me because they were in a bit of a bind. I said that I thought it would be okay, but I realized that I needed to check with you about that since I would still be watching Vivianne while they were here."

Michael was quiet for a moment. "When are they coming, and how long are they staying?"

"I think they plan to arrive on Monday night, and I told her that she could stay for a week. No longer."

"If you could still watch Vivianne on Monday, I could probably keep her with me for the rest of the week."

Though it wasn't the response she'd hoped for, at least it didn't sound like he was going to find another babysitter. Still, it would hurt her financially, having a week without pay. She had been trying to save up what she could, so it wasn't like she'd be unable to buy groceries for her and Bryson, but it would mean dipping into that money she'd been setting aside. Plus, now she'd have to try and make her groceries stretch to include three more people.

"Are you sure you're okay with that? I feel bad springing this on you on such short notice. I could still tell her it won't work."

"As it turns out, I think it will be fine. It'll allow me to spend some extra time with my little one."

"Okay. So I'll still watch her on Monday for you, and then I'll be available to watch her again on the following Monday."

"Just let me know for sure, one way or another, when you're available to watch her again."

"Thanks so much for being so accommodating about this," Sophia said, because truly, it was good that he was willing to give her the week off.

"No problem at all," Michael said. "Thank you for all you do for Vivianne. It gives me peace of mind to know that she's in the care of someone like you."

It was nice to know that Michael appreciated what she did for him and Vivianne, but she still didn't feel entirely at ease as they said goodbye. She kind of felt like she wouldn't feel that way until Mellie and her kids had come and gone.

She felt the weight of her decisions pressing down on her. There hadn't been a single day in her life when she'd enjoyed making decisions. Growing up the way she had, a lot of decisions had been made for her, and she'd gotten used to it. Once she'd graduated high school, she hadn't been prepared for all the decisions that would face her.

Should she go to college? And if she did, what should she take? Where should she work? Should she move out on her own?

It had been a struggle, and her parents hadn't been very helpful. Chloe and Natalie had managed to move into adulthood much more smoothly. By the time she graduated from high school, Chloe was already dating the man who would become her husband. And Natalie had boasted about an acceptance letter to the college of her choice.

Sophia, on the other hand, had floundered. Even as her twenty-first birthday approached, she was still working as a cashier at the local grocery store and living with her parents. Which would have been fine if she'd had some direction, but she hadn't.

Then Ezekiel Daniels had entered her life.

"You won't have to worry about a thing, darling. I'll take care of everything."

If she hadn't already been swept off her feet by the attention of the handsome man with sparkling blue eyes and wavy black hair that brushed the tops of his shoulders, his words would have guaranteed it.

Out of everyone in the bar that night, he'd zeroed in on her. Plenty of girls had tried to get his attention, but he'd stayed focused on her. And hadn't that just stroked her pride? For once in her life, she had been the sole focus of someone who chose to be close to her.

She soon came to understand that his ability to read people and then manipulate their weaknesses was his greatest skill. A skill he used for evil, only she hadn't realized that until far too late.

So why was it, after having been through everything with him, that she still wanted someone to help with her decisions? What did that say about her?

Sophia decided she wasn't all that interested in dissecting that right then...afraid of where she might end up. Tomorrow she'd be at her parents' house for dinner once again, and there would be plenty of people willing to dissect her there if she felt the need for it.

By the time she pulled up in front of her parents' house the next day, tension was holding her neck and shoulders taut, bringing on a headache. From the look of it, she was the last to arrive, which was both good and bad.

Glancing over her shoulder to where Bryson sat in the back seat, she said, "Ready?"

He looked at the house then back at her with a frown. "Do we have to go in there? It's so noisy."

He'd never really liked the noise that had come from a crowd of people, plus he still wasn't sure how he felt about her family. And she couldn't blame him for that.

After all, the people he'd been told for years were his family had treated them both horribly. She tried to reassure him that her *real* family was different. That they wouldn't hurt him.

So far, it hadn't worked.

"The sooner we go inside, the sooner we can leave," she told him.

With a resigned look, he nodded and undid his seatbelt. He waited for her to come around to his door and open it, then, hand-in-hand they ran up the sidewalk to the front door.

"About time you two got here," her dad boomed as they walked into the house.

He gave her a one-armed hug, but he didn't try to hug Bryson. That hadn't gone well in the past, so Sophia was glad that her dad no longer forced the issue.

"Sophia!" Her mom approached and gave her a hug. "Missed you at church this morning."

Well, that wasn't subtle at all, and it was the same thing she said every week. Though she'd tried to explain that it was too soon for her, and especially Bryson, to be sitting through a church service, they just didn't understand. Most Sundays, she watched the livestream of the service, but that didn't seem to be enough for her parents.

They seemed to assume that not going to church meant she'd lost her faith. The thing was, she kind of felt that if that were the case, it would have been justified. She'd spent the past five years being subjected to all kinds of hurtful things in the name of God. Yet, even though it had been a struggle at times, she'd tried to cling to her faith as best she could because she felt like she'd lost every-thing else in her life.

Going to church wouldn't have been an issue for her, but it def-initely was for Bryson. Because of that, she wasn't going to force him to go until it seemed like he was moving past the negative as-sociations he had about gatherings like church services.

How long it would take, she didn't know. All she did know was that they weren't at the point yet where she felt Bryson could sit through a service without freaking out.

"Come on, everyone," her dad called out. "Sophia and Bryson are here, so let's sit up."

The noise level rose as chairs screeched across the floor as everyone settled into their seats. There was a small table for the kids, but they'd stopped trying to have Bryson sit at it. Instead, it was just Chloe's oldest three kids who sat there.

Sophia sat with Bryson on one side and Natalie on the other. Madelyn was on the other side of Bryson. He probably would have done better with one of her brothers beside him since Devon and Chris weren't overly talkative and didn't try to hug him or engage him in conversation.

After her dad prayed for the meal, they all began to pass the food around the table, and Sophia focused on dishing up her and Bryson's plates. From the look of things, her mom had roasted a few chickens to go with the mashed potatoes, gravy, carrots, and rolls. It was one of three meals that she rotated for their Sunday dinners.

There was always plenty of food, and it always tasted good. Her mom was a great cook, and she'd tried—with varying degrees of success—to pass that skill on to each of her children.

After having another tense conversation with Chloe about her pregnancy, Natalie turned her attention to Sophia...much to her dismay. While Natalie didn't understand Chloe's need to have countless children, when it came to Sophia, she didn't understand why she didn't want to have a career that would give her financial freedom and fulfillment.

"You still babysitting?"

"Yes." Sophia had long since learned that where Natalie was concerned, the shorter the answers, the better.

That was probably part of the reason Natalie and Chloe clashed so much. Chloe liked to talk as much as Natalie did.

"How long are you planning to keep doing that?"

"As long as Michael needs someone to watch Vivianne."

"Don't you think you should try to get a job with some sort of benefits?" Natalie asked. "Seems a bit irresponsible to not do that when you have a child."

"Bryson has insurance through the state, plus I have other things to consider right now that are equally, or even more, important than having a job with benefits."

Natalie scoffed. "I can't imagine what would be more important than good health insurance."

"I'm sure you can't." Sophia resisted the urge to defend her decision...just in case it was yet another bad decision. She didn't think it was, but who knew. Only time would tell.

"At least Chloe is providing that much for her many children. You should be more interested in providing it for your one."

Well, it wasn't a big surprise that she ranked above Chloe on Natalie's list of bad decision makers.

"Hey, Soph," Madelyn said, pulling her attention from Natalie.

Happy to turn away from her older sister, Sophia shifted to look over Bryson's head to where Madelyn sat. "What's up?"

"Who's Ryker?"

CHAPTER EIGHT

Sophia stared at Madelyn. "What?"

"Is he your new boyfriend?" she asked. "Bryson seems quite enamored with the guy."

"He's not my boyfriend," Sophia said with what she hoped was enough conviction, but that didn't venture into the *she doth protest too much* territory. "He's the one who picks Vivianne up each afternoon, so Bryson has gotten to know him."

She was a bit surprised that Madelyn had managed to get that much out of Bryson. And while she was happy that Bryson was conversing with someone, did it have to be on the subject of Ryker?

"Well, from what Bryson's said, he seems like a god among men."

"Madelyn Rose," her mother said sharply. "We don't talk like that."

Madelyn rolled her eyes. "I'm talking about mythical Greek gods, Mom. You know...like Thor. Not *the* God."

"Still," her mother said. "I'd rather you didn't."

Madelyn just gave a shake of her head before she looked back at Sophia. "Is Ryker married? Does he have kids? What does he do?"

"Why does any of that matter?" Sophia asked.

"He's hanging around you and Bryson," she replied with a wink. "I think it only behooves us to make sure he's safe to be around you guys."

"*Behooves* us?" Chloe asked with a laugh. "Was that in your word of the day email?"

"No," Madelyn snapped with a huff, but then she grinned. "It was on my word of the day calendar."

"Idiots," Natalie muttered, showing once again that when they'd been handing out the sense of humor gene, she'd said *no thanks.*

Sophia didn't care what they joked about, as long as it kept the attention off of her. Of course, that was too much to hope for with her family.

"Are you going to answer Madelyn's questions?" Natalie asked.

"I haven't asked him if he's married or if he has kids. As for what he does, he works for Michael."

"So he mows lawns and plants flowers?" The judgment was clear in Natalie's tone.

"Nothing wrong with that," her dad said. "I'm pretty sure that you have people who do that for your home. You'd have to do it yourself if there weren't people who did it as their job."

It wasn't often one of her parents shut Natalie down, but she was glad her dad did it in this case. She was fairly certain the reason he'd done it this time was that he respected anyone who did an honest day's work. His career as a garbage collector had always embarrassed Natalie, but he'd worked hard to support their family, so he was likely to come to the defense of anyone else who worked hard, regardless of their line of work.

Whatever his reason, she was glad he'd done it because the last thing she needed was to have to defend Ryker herself. That would just make them think that there was more between them than there was.

As usual, Natalie's husband, Anthony, kept his head down and focused on the food on his plate. She didn't think Anthony necessarily disagreed with his wife on much, but he was smart enough to know that if he wanted at least one good home-cooked meal a week, it was best he kept his mouth shut.

Thankfully, the conversation moved off the subject of Ryker, but unfortunately, he didn't leave her thoughts. She had come to the conclusion that he wasn't married and didn't have kids, but she did wonder if he had a girlfriend. It was none of her business, of course, so she'd never ask. But she was curious.

What type of woman was he attracted to?

Probably not someone who struggled to make any sort of major decisions and who had no desire for a career. If she had her way, she'd be a stay-at-home mom to Bryson, but Natalie wasn't completely wrong. She did need to think about somehow getting a job that would offer good benefits for both of them.

But until Bryson was ready to spend a portion of his day apart from her, that wasn't going to happen.

After they'd had dessert, Chloe's older kids convinced Devon, one of Sophia's younger brothers, to go outside with them. Her dad had built a play structure and a treehouse when they were kids, and he'd kept them both in good repair over the years for the grandkids.

"Want to come with us, Bryson?" Devon asked as Owen and Aubrey tugged on his hands.

No surprise, Bryson gave a quick shake of his head. Sophia wished he could enjoy playing with his cousins without the fear of being stung by a wasp or bit by a bug, but she wasn't going to force him.

"What sort of boy doesn't want to play outside?" Natalie asked.

Sophia whipped around and glared at Natalie. "My sort of boy. He has his reasons that you know *nothing* about, so just leave him alone. Come after me all you want, but you leave Bryson alone."

"I think maybe we should leave," Anthony said as he approached his wife. "Thank you for a lovely meal, Marti. Good to see you again, Cliff."

Everyone fell quiet as Anthony and Natalie left, and with them gone, the tension dissipated, and it seemed to Sophia that she wasn't the only one who gave a sigh of relief.

"Anyone want a coffee refill?" her mom asked as she headed for the kitchen.

Sophia declined because she planned to be the next to leave, just as soon as it was polite to do so. Christopher was sprawled out on one end of the couch while Chloe and her husband were on the loveseat. Her dad and mom each had a recliner that everyone knew not to sit in. Madelyn had disappeared, most likely to her room.

Though she would have preferred to head right out the door, she settled on the couch next to Chris, with Bryson tucked up against her.

She listened to them talk, but she didn't participate. The conversation was interrupted by a shout from Owen as he burst into the house. Bryson jumped against her, but when the shout was followed by Aubrey's laughter, no one rushed to figure out if something was wrong.

Sophia could feel the tension in Bryson's body as his cousins came running into the room with Devon not far behind them with their four-year-old sister on his back. They all settled on the floor, with Owen focusing on his Nintendo Switch. Aubrey leaned over his shoulder, watching what he was doing.

That was something that Sophia really appreciated about Chloe's kids. They seemed to get along really well, and she'd rarely heard them fight with each other. They also were respectful of their parents and the other adults in the family. Natalie might like to lecture Chloe about it being irresponsible to have so many children, but Chloe and her husband were doing a great job raising them.

"I think we should probably go," Sophia said as she got to her feet. "Thanks for dinner, Mom. It was delicious."

She said goodbye to the others in the living room before heading for the front door with Bryson's hand in hers. When they stepped outside, they looked at each other and smiled. It was probably the only time Bryson actually enjoyed leaving the safety of the indoors.

Once home, she tackled getting Bryson's room ready for Mellie and her kids. There was only a double bed in there, but she'd found an air mattress in the basement that would probably do for Charlie. Hopefully it didn't have any holes in it.

After that was done, she and Bryson packaged up some cookies, then set off for the personal care home to spend some time with Nana. It was the best part of their Sunday. Kind of a palate cleanser, depending on how the time had gone at her parents'.

On that day, it was especially needed.

~*~

Ryker spent most of Monday wet and miserable. The rainy weather was the worst part of the job. He could handle the bugs, the scratches from branches, and mucking through the mud when necessary, but having rain drip on him constantly while he tried to work was the worst.

Wearing a raincoat was impractical, and though his waterproof windbreaker was a better option, it never kept one hundred percent of the rain off him. Moving around as he worked meant that rain slid down his neck or dripped off his hood onto his face. And there was no way to dry his face and neck because everything was wet.

Prior to getting a job that required him to work outside, Ryker had never really minded the rain. Now though, it was a pain. Especially when it also meant that some of their scheduled jobs wouldn't get done.

He hadn't been in a great mood that morning to start with, thanks to another family dinner the night before where his mental health and plans for the future came under the microscope yet again.

It seemed the more time passed, the more his mom and Callie seemed to feel he should be doing better. That he should be over what had happened to him in Syria. And while he could accept that Callie might think that way, he struggled with how his mom could since she was a professional in the mental health field.

So yeah, the dinner had left him tense, which had then led to a struggle to fall asleep, only to be woken by a nightmare. When his alarm had gone off, he'd still been exhausted. Dragging, he'd gone to work, only to be faced with a relentless drip, drip, drip of rain.

He didn't even get a chance to see Sophia and Bryson since Michael told him that he'd take care of dropping off Vivianne and picking her up at the end of the day. He'd mentioned that he'd be keeping Vivianne with him for the rest of the week since Sophia had let him know she had people coming to stay with her.

Ryker was relieved that Sophia had told Michael about the pending visit. He'd hoped to go by her place after work to do more on the yard, but the rain had derailed that plan. Thankfully, he'd gotten the grass mowed before the weekend, which had been the worst of the situation at her home. Still, he'd wanted to do some further work trimming up the bushes and cleaning out the flower beds.

While the rain didn't preclude him from doing those things, the fact that he'd already spent over eight hours in the rain did. He wanted a hot shower, dry clothes, and a warm meal. In that order. Too bad it wasn't going to be a meal in Sophia's kitchen with Bryson eating bananas and peanut butter.

Since there was rain in the forecast for Tuesday as well, it was unlikely he'd get back to Sophia's until at least Wednesday. But since she had company, it was probably just as well.

Still, as he dumped a can of chunky beef and potato soup into a bowl, Ryker found himself disappointed at the idea that he wouldn't get to see the pair for a couple more days. And it really wasn't just because of the meals Sophia fed him.

Ryker put the soup into the microwave, then popped a couple of pieces of bread into the toaster. Leaning a hip against the counter, his thoughts wandered as he waited for his food to be ready.

What was it about Sophia and, more surprisingly, Bryson, that made him want to spend more time with them? Sophia, he could kind of understand. Though she wasn't the sort of woman he'd ever dated, he could see that she was attractive and seemed nice. So spending time with her would only ever be a pleasant experience.

Bryson, on the other hand, still triggered nightmares for him. So even though the little boy didn't look at him with fear anymore, he should have been avoiding him, just to be safe.

But that wasn't what he was doing.

In fact, from that first time he'd actually spoken with Bryson, he'd continued to allow—and even pursue—further interactions with the boy. He could have still picked Vivianne up and been friendly to Bryson without going as far as he had in building a relationship with the child.

So what, exactly, was he doing?

Ryker hated introspection. Hated forcing himself to look at his motivations for things. Hated being forced to defend his actions— even to himself.

It was all kind of tied to his mother's career. For as long as he could remember, she always encouraged them to be honest about their emotions, actions, and motivations. When he'd been a kid, she'd had more roundabout ways of pulling that out of him, but as he'd gotten older, she'd become more direct about it.

Somewhere along the line, it felt like she'd managed to condition him to do it to himself without her help, except when it came to his current situation. She was no longer content to just let him deal with it on his own, especially after discovering that he had stopped seeing his therapist.

Deciding he needed a distraction of some sort while he ate, Ryker carried his food into the living room and searched for a movie to watch. His go-to movies of late were sci-fi, and since he'd already seen all the big name ones, he was down to having to pick which of the B-movie offerings on his streaming service he wanted to watch.

The next day promised to be as wet and exhausting as that day had been, so he didn't stay up super late once the movie was over. He did his workout, showered again, then fell into bed.

It ended up being Wednesday afternoon before he had a chance to get back to Sophia's. He'd texted her the night before to let her know he'd be there after he was done work. Since he didn't need to drop Vivianne off at Michael's and then wait with him for Lani to arrive, he was able to head over to Sophia's as soon as work was done.

The day had been overcast, with the sun poking out occasionally, but there had been no rain. For which Ryker was extremely grateful. And his sleep the night before hadn't been as fractured. All in all, he was feeling pretty good for the first time that week.

How much of that feeling he could attribute to the prospect of seeing Sophia and Bryson, he refused to consider.

As he drove to Sophia's, Ryker decided he wouldn't bother her while she had company. He'd just go to the shed and get the tools he needed to tackle the job of trimming down the bushes and, if he had enough time, do a little weeding.

After pulling to a stop at the curb in front of her house, Ryker climbed out of the truck. He headed up the sidewalk, then started across the grass toward the gate that led to the backyard.

As he neared the house, however, he heard terrified screams that stopped him in his tracks. *Bryson.* Though he'd never heard him like that before, deep down, he knew who it was.

But even as he identified what it was...who it was...his brain threw him back in time, freezing him in place. He bent over, covering his ears with his hands, trying...needing...to block out the screams from the past that had joined the ones in the present. A choir of screams, reaching into his mind...into his soul...pulling pain and agony from a place within him that he usually only visited in the midst of a nightmare.

No...no...

Ryker fought back against the whirlpool of emotion that was trying to pull him under. Someone needed help. *Bryson* needed help. Later...he could fall apart later. Right then, he needed to fight the pull and silence the screams of the past and focus on the present.

He jerked his hands from his ears and struggled to stand straight, fighting the weight pressing down on him that was made up of emotions from the past. Taking several deep breaths, he focused on the ground. The grass. The sidewalk.

A door managed to slam shut in his mind, trapping the screams of the past behind it. He knew that the door would fly open again in the dark hours of the night, but right then, it was setting him free to deal with the present.

Spinning on his heel, Ryker ran for the house on legs that were shaky but still held him up, taking the steps two at a time to the porch. The inside front door stood partway open, which explained how he could hear what was happening within the house.

Without pausing to consider that he didn't have the right to enter without Sophia's permission, he pulled open the outer door and stepped into cacophony. Immediately, his gaze sought out Sophia and Bryson.

He found Sophia first, standing in front of the couch with absolute fury on her face. Bryson was huddled against her, his face pressed against her hip as he continued to scream. Sophia's hand rested on his head, holding him close.

"I *told* you that if you or your kids hurt or teased Bryson, you were gone," Sophia yelled at the woman standing on the other side of the living room.

There were two children—a boy and a girl—with her. The girl seemed confused. However, the boy had an insolent look on his face, his chin jutting out as he stood there with his arms crossed. No one seemed to notice Ryker's arrival, which told him how intense this situation was for all involved.

"He didn't mean anything by it," the woman shot back. "It was just a bug, for goodness' sakes."

For a moment, disbelief crossed Sophia's face, but it was quickly chased away as anger returned. When Bryson's wails rose again, Ryker moved toward Sophia, hoping that Bryson would come to him so that Sophia could deal with the situation.

Crouching next to Bryson, Ryker reached out and took his hand. "Hey, buddy."

"Ryker?" His name was said in unison by mother and son. Bryson calmed enough to peer at him as he hiccupped, tightening his grip on Ryker's hand.

Ryker straightened and gazed down at Sophia. "Why don't you let me take him into the kitchen so you can deal with this."

She hesitated a moment before nodding, then she looked down at Bryson. "You go with Ryker, okay? I'll be right here."

Bryson stared up at Sophia with a tear-stained face that tugged *hard* at Ryker's heartstrings. Hard in a way that should have had him running in the opposite direction. But his desire to help a child in distress overrode his need to steer clear of anything that might trigger bad memories.

After a long moment, during which Bryson took several hiccupping breaths, he nodded and turned to Ryker. He stooped and lifted the small boy into his arms. Looking at Sophia again, he said, "I'll take care of him."

"I know."

Considering how protective she was of Bryson, those two words stirred something within him. Something he wasn't going to consider at that moment. There would be plenty of time for that later.

"Who on earth is that?" the other woman asked as he walked away.

"He is none of your business," Sophia said. "That is not what we're talking about right now."

"Good grief, Sophia. You and Bryson are such drama queens. Always have been. Always will be, apparently."

Ryker had to force himself to keep walking and not turn around to give the woman a piece of his mind. He had a feeling that this was a battle that Sophia had to fight for herself and Bryson, and he knew that she could do it.

Once in the kitchen, he set Bryson on the counter. When he spotted the bananas in a basket on the counter, he pulled one free then opened cupboards until he found the plates. Bryson pointed to where the peanut butter was without Ryker even having to ask.

"Want to tell me what happened, buddy?" Ryker said as he located a knife and began to slice the banana onto the plate.

"Charlie came in from outside with a bug. He said it was going to bite me, and I was going to swell up like a balloon until I popped."

As tears rolled down Bryson's cheeks, Ryker set the knife down and moved to pull the little guy into his arms again. "You're safe, buddy. It was super mean of Charlie to say that, but you're safe now. Your mom and I won't let anything like that happen to you."

He made a note to ask Sophia if Bryson had ever had an allergic reaction to a bug bite. It might help explain a little about Bryson's fear of bugs.

"I don't like him," Bryson said with a sniffle.

"I understand that." Ryker wasn't about to tell the little boy that he had to like people who were mean to him. Of course he would discourage any sort of retaliation, but Bryson seemed so gentle and tender that forcing him to be around someone like that would just make everything so much worse.

"He's a meanie, and I don't want him here."

Ryker wanted to reassure him that he wouldn't have to have him there, but Sophia had to stand firm in kicking the woman and her kids out. From what he'd seen of Sophia, Ryker knew that was going to be a hard thing for her to do. Only the fact that she'd warned the woman might give her the ability to stand her ground.

"Let me finish these bananas for you, then you can eat some while we talk. Okay?"

"Okay."

Bryson seemed to be reluctant to break their physical connection, so Ryker did his best to smear some peanut butter on each piece of banana while keeping his arms around him. Finally, they were all covered—although not nicely like when Sophia did them—but hopefully Bryson would eat them regardless.

Carrying Bryson in one arm and the plate in his other hand, Ryker went to the table. He set the plate down then sat down on one of the chairs, settling Bryson on his knee rather than putting him on a chair of his own.

Bryson stared at the bananas for a moment, and Ryker held his breath, waiting for the boy's rejection of his attempt at his favorite snack. Instead, Bryson glanced up at him then reached out to pick up one of the banana pieces and put it in his mouth.

As he continued to eat them, his body sagged against Ryker. He didn't force Bryson to talk. Instead, he listened to what was happening in the other room.

"Where am I supposed to go?"

"If you were worried about where you would go, you should have made sure that Charlie behaved. That was the only thing I asked of you. Make. Sure. He. Leaves. Bryson. Alone."

"They're brothers, Soph. Brothers tease each other."

Brothers? Ryker glanced down at Bryson.

"Nope. I'm not going to accept that. Any teasing between them only ever goes one way. Charlie teasing and hurting Bryson." There was a beat of silence before Sophia said, "You can stay here tonight, but you're leaving tomorrow, so tonight you'd better sort out where you're going. I'll drive you to the bus station in the morning."

"You are incredibly selfish, Sophia. You have a house and a family helping you. Not all of us have that."

"I understand that. It was why I agreed for you to come. But all I asked was *one* thing from you. *One* thing, Mellie. You knew that before you got here."

"You're being unrealistic to expect Charlie to not act like a boy."

"There is absolutely nothing in this world that says that little boys need to be outdoorsy, rambunctious, or mean. This home is my and Bryson's safe place after spending far too many years feeling scared. Now you brought someone here who I already knew made Bryson feel unsafe, but I gave you a chance. You allowed Charlie to turn our safe space into a scary one. That is *not* acceptable."

Sophia had struck him as being somewhat timid, so to hear her standing up for Bryson and herself made him feel good. He was glad to see that when she needed to, she could hold her own.

Ryker became aware of the fact that Bryson had stopped moving. He looked down to see that there were a couple more pieces of banana left, but Bryson had fallen asleep. That didn't surprise Ryker, as he suspected that the sleep had been brought on by the adrenalin crash after what had happened earlier.

Ryker pressed a kiss to his soft curls, then let out a breath. He'd spent so long trying to protect himself from this type of situation, and yet here he was, smack in the middle of it. But right then, holding this precious little boy, he couldn't find it in himself to regret his actions. Later on, he might, but knowing that Bryson felt safe enough to fall asleep with him kept Ryker from feeling any regret right then.

There was a lull in the conversation, then the woman herded her kids past the kitchen door in the direction of the bedrooms. Ryker stayed where he was, figuring Sophia would come looking for them now that the confrontation was over. She was probably as worn out by it as Bryson had been.

Some people would be energized by something like that—Callie, for example—but he was fairly certain that wasn't the case for Sophia.

A moment later, she appeared in the doorway, the strain of the situation showing on her face. Her brows drew together as she looked at Bryson.

"He fell asleep?"

"Yep. Conked out mid-snack. Hope you don't mind that I made these for him. I thought maybe he needed something to focus on that he enjoyed."

Sophia came in and sank down into a chair, seeming to deflate before his very eyes. "Thank you. Everything kind of...exploded." She sighed. "I thought I was doing the right thing, but clearly, I wasn't."

"Oh, I think you probably did the right thing. But for it to work out for all involved, the others need to do the right thing too."

Her eyes widened a bit at that statement. "Guess I never thought of it that way."

"Don't blame yourself when you try to do the right thing, and others do the wrong thing. That's on them. Not you."

Ryker wasn't sure why it was so important to bolster Sophia's flagging opinion of herself, but it was. Something *else* to think about later. He was going to have to start making a list pretty soon.

CHAPTER NINE

Sophia stared at Bryson as he slept on Ryker's lap, wishing that she could take a nap too. She'd never forget hearing Bryson scream while she had been in the bathroom. Her heart had literally stopped as she'd scrambled to get the door open with her hands still soapy and wet.

When tears pricked her eyes at the memory, she lifted a hand to rub her forehead, hoping to hide the rush of emotion from Ryker. She was glad he'd been there for Bryson, taking him so she could focus on dealing with Mellie, but she hadn't expected him to be there for her as well.

She could only imagine what he thought of everything. He may have brought Bryson into the kitchen, but that certainly hadn't meant he was out of earshot, especially since she and Mellie had both raised their voices. She just hoped he didn't start asking a lot of questions.

Aside from her family, only a handful of people in town knew about what had happened in her life. The only people she'd actually talked to about it had been her parents and Nana, and even then, it had been only the barest of details. Nana had attempted to get her to talk more about it, but Sophia hadn't been ready.

Maybe that was one of the reasons she'd agreed to let Mellie come...because without having to say a word, the woman would understand what she'd gone through. What they'd both gone through.

"You okay?" Ryker asked.

"Yeah." Sophia took a deep breath and blinked her tears away. "I kinda knew that that might happen, but I'd hoped that it wouldn't."

"Do you want to talk about it?"

"Not really." She hoped he didn't take offense to her response.

A corner of his mouth tipped up in a half-smile. "I get that. Plenty I'm not too keen to talk about in my own life."

Relief filled her. "It's all a bit of a mess now. I feel like I'll need to sleep with one eye open tonight."

Ryker's eyes widened. "Are you seriously worried about something happening?"

Well, until the words came out of her mouth, she hadn't been. "I think we'll be fine. Mellie's all bark and no bite."

"And Charlie?"

Yeah...Charlie. "He's only nine. I don't think he'll do anything."

"If you're really worried and don't have a lock on your bedroom door, take one of these chairs and hook it under the doorknob. A grown man might be able to get through it with some effort, but I doubt a nine-year-old could."

"I'll keep that in mind." She very much appreciated his suggestions for keeping her and Bryson safe. "Thank you."

As she took in the sight of her son slumped against Ryker, Sophia found herself wishing that Bryson had had a father who'd held him like that. But there had been no gentleness, let alone love, in Ezekiel's approach to any of his children.

She was glad that Bryson had men in his life now who treated him with care. Her dad loved him, even though he wasn't sure exactly how to relate to him. Chris and Devon had tried to interact with him like they did their other nieces and their nephew, and Sophia appreciated their efforts even if Bryson hadn't. At least she wasn't worried that they would ever hurt him intentionally.

Why Ryker had been the one who'd managed to break through Bryson's reserves, Sophia didn't know. Only that there was something about the way the man related to Bryson that made him feel safe.

Made her feel safe, too, if she was going to be honest, and she was too tired to lie, even to herself.

"How about I order a couple of pizzas?" Ryker suggested.

Sophia lifted her gaze from where she'd been watching Bryson sleep. "You don't have to do that."

That got another half-smile out of Ryker. "I know, but I remember Bryson being impressed that I had the option of eating pizza every night. I thought maybe having some tonight might help end the day on a high note. Or a higher note, anyway."

"He really would like that," Sophia agreed. Pizza wasn't something they had very often. At least not from a restaurant.

"So what type of pizza do you two like?" Ryker paused. "I'll make sure to order enough for everyone, but they'll have to make do with whatever we decide on."

"We're pretty basic when it comes to toppings."

"Well, as long as you don't want pineapple, we should be okay."

Sophia smiled. "No worries. Bryson doesn't care much for pineapple by itself, let alone on his pizza. We pretty much always get just plain cheese."

"I like pepperoni, so I think I'll get a large cheese and a large pepperoni. We can give half of each to your guests and keep half of each for ourselves."

Ryker pulled out his phone and made quick work of placing the order for delivery. When he was done, and silence fell between them, Sophia thought he might ask her again about what had gone on between her and Mellie. He didn't, though, and she was relieved. The events of the past five years didn't paint her in the most favorable light.

She shouldn't have been swept off her feet by a sweet-talking man simply because he'd paid attention to her. And people probably thought she was crazy for sticking with him, not realizing that there was just no way to escape. There had been no way past the walls of the compound. Walls that Ezekiel had insisted were there to protect them, but Sophia had known they were actually there to keep them imprisoned.

"Is Bryson allergic to bees?" Ryker asked, pulling her thoughts from the past she kept trying to move beyond. "You mentioned he was scared to go outside because he'd been bitten by a bee."

"They said it was actually a wasp—if that makes a difference. And he didn't have a reaction that affected his breathing, but his arm swelled up after he was bitten on his hand. It hurt him a lot too."

Ryker nodded. "Wasp stings can hurt a great deal, but it sounds like, while he had a reaction, it wasn't a bad one. But it does explain why he freaked out at Charlie."

Sophia frowned. "What did he tell you? I couldn't get it out of him and deal with Mellie at the same time. Just that it had something to do with a bug."

"Charlie brought a bug in from outside and told Bryson he was going to make it bite him, so he'd swell up like a balloon and pop."

She saw red as the meanness of the other boy was revealed more fully in Ryker's words. That went beyond teasing.

"Was Charlie there when Bryson got bit by the wasp?"

Sophia blinked back the angry tears that wanted to break free. "Yes. I wasn't, though."

"You can't be with your child twenty-four/seven, Sophia."

Couldn't she? These days she was certainly managing to achieve that, but Ezekiel never would have allowed it. "By the time I finally saw him, he'd been screaming for ages, and his arm was badly swollen."

"It sounds like a traumatic time for both of you."

Traumatic? Yeah, that described it perfectly. "He was so scared, not understanding what was happening to his arm. That's probably why he reacted like that to what Charlie said."

"That makes sense." Ryker looked down at Bryson as he began to stir. "Looks like his adrenalin-drop-induced nap might just about be over."

"Momma?"

Sophia smiled at Bryson as he blinked, lifting his hands to rub the backs of them against his eyes. "Hi, baby."

He looked up at Ryker then held out his arms toward her. Not like he was eager to get away from Ryker, but more that he needed to be close to her.

Before she could move to take him, Ryker stood up and deposited him onto her lap. She gave him a smile of thanks as she wrapped her arms around her boy. Burying her face in his curls, she inhaled the familiar scent of the baby shampoo she used on him.

He reached up and wrapped his arms around her neck. "Sorry, Momma."

"Sorry? What are you sorry for?"

"For screaming like that."

"It's okay, baby. I know you were scared."

She felt him take a deep breath and let it out. "Ryker made me some bananas."

"But your momma's are better, aren't they?" Ryker said with a laugh.

Bryson turned enough to peek at Ryker. "Her peanut butter is better."

"Do you want the rest of them?" Sophia asked. "You have three pieces left."

When Bryson nodded, Ryker slid the plate closer to them. She didn't bother to mention pizza coming because he probably wouldn't eat the bananas. It was her hope that he would eat the remaining bananas in addition to a piece or two of pizza—depending on how big the slices were.

Bryson finished the bananas, then asked for some milk. Keeping him balanced on one hip, she got a glass and poured milk into it. The doorbell rang as she finished pouring the milk, so Ryker went to answer it.

When he reappeared, he was followed by her dad. Sophia stared at him in surprise. It wasn't often that her dad came by.

"Hi, Dad."

"Nana reminded me that you probably needed some help with the yard," he said, his gaze settling for a moment on Bryson, whose face was still puffy from the tears he'd shed earlier. "I'm sorry I didn't think of it sooner, but it looks like you got it taken care of."

"Yes. Ryker has been helping me."

"Ryker?" He swung to face Ryker and stuck out his hand. "I'm Cliff Haldorson. Thanks for giving Sophia a hand with that."

"You're welcome. I'm happy to help."

"Did something happen?" her dad asked as he looked from Ryker to Bryson.

Sophia didn't want to hide anything from him, but she also didn't want to recount what had gone on with Bryson right there.

"Charlie was mean," Bryson volunteered. "He said the bug was going to bite me, and I'd swell up until I popped."

Sophia tightened her hold on him as he told the same story Ryker had told her earlier. It made her want to yell at Mellie again for allowing her son to hurt Bryson like that.

Her dad's expression darkened. "Well, that wasn't very nice. I hope he apologized."

He hadn't, and probably wouldn't, but Sophia decided to keep that to herself. The doorbell went again, and Ryker excused himself to get it.

"The man's answering your door now?" her dad asked as he watched him go.

"Only because he ordered pizza for all of us. That's why he answered it before. He thought you were the pizza delivery person."

"Okay. Well, if you don't need me to do the yard, I'll head home. I did try to call, but you didn't answer your phone."

Sophia glanced around the kitchen, then realized she'd left her phone in the bathroom. "I'm sorry about that. In the midst of everything, I didn't have it with me."

"Understandable. Hopefully the boy is okay."

"He'll be fine," she said as she bounced Bryson on her hip. "But it won't do much in aid of my efforts to get him outside, I don't think."

For once, there was real understanding on her dad's face about Bryson's fear of the outdoors. "We'll pray about that."

And she knew that by *we*, he meant him and her mom. Sophia hoped that God would answer their prayers in a way that He hadn't answered hers yet. "Thank you."

Her dad gave a single nod of his head, then turned his attention to Bryson. "You take care of your mom, okay?"

Bryson nodded, a small smile curving his lips. "I'll make her banana and peanut butter like she makes me."

Her dad gave a loud laugh. "That sounds perfect, little guy."

Ryker reappeared with two pizza boxes in his hands. Her dad eyed them for a moment. "I'm almost tempted to tell your mom I won't be home for dinner."

"You're welcome to stay."

"Thanks, hun, but I'd better get home to your mom." He came and gave her a hug, sandwiching Bryson between them for a moment. "See you on Sunday, or sooner if you need anything."

"Thanks, Dad."

When she moved to follow him to the door, he waved his hand. "You stay and eat your dinner."

She watched him go, trying to figure out if a shift of some sort had just occurred between them or if she had just imagined it.

"Everything okay?" Ryker asked as he flipped open the lids of the boxes.

"Yep." She looked down at Bryson. "Ready for pizza?"

"Yeah!" He punched the air with his small fist. "Lots of pizza!"

She doubted he'd get through more than one piece, if that. But as long as he was excited to eat, she would be glad for anything he consumed. Setting him down on his chair, she went to the cupboard and pulled down enough plates for all of them. After setting one in front of him, she put two more on the table for her and Ryker.

Feeling a bit guilty about relegating Mellie and her kids to the bedroom to eat, she said, "Do you think I should have them come in here to eat?"

"It's completely up to you," Ryker said. "I wouldn't hold it against you if you decided not to."

"Maybe I'll set their stuff up on the coffee table in the living room."

Ryker nodded as he moved pizza around between the boxes. Sophia took plates, napkins, and glasses into the living room and then returned for the pizza. After she set it on the coffee table, she went down the hallway to the bedroom and knocked on the door.

"What?" Mellie barked out.

"I have pizza for you and the kids in the living room whenever you want to eat."

She heard excited murmurs from the kids, but she didn't hang around to see if they came out or not. Her anger over what Charlie had done to Bryson still burned inside her. Not as hot or as bright as it had, and she knew in time it would fade away, but not just yet.

Back in the kitchen, she saw that Ryker had poured Bryson more milk and put a slice of cheese pizza on his plate. Bryson grinned as he picked up the slice then took a bite.

That big smile on his tiny face helped to dampen the anger a bit more. It might end up taking more time to get him to the point where he'd go outside to do more than just dash for the car, but it seemed that he was bouncing back okay after the altercation with

Charlie. She figured that part of that was due to Ryker stepping in and helping out with him.

Bryson talked with Ryker between bites, and Sophia was happy to let him. She was keeping an eye out for Mellie and the kids, figuring it was only a matter of time before the pair convinced their mother that they were starving.

She'd finished her first piece when she finally heard movement from the hallway. They went into the living room, but it wasn't long before Mellie appeared with glasses in her hand.

"Am I supposed to just stand outside and catch rain in these?" she snarked.

"Of course not," Sophia said. "I just didn't know what you might like to drink."

"I suppose a glass of wine is out of the question."

The edge to all of Mellie's words was starting to put Sophia on edge herself. "Sorry. I don't have any wine."

"Or maybe you just don't want to share it." Her gaze went to Ryker. "Is he your new boyfriend? I wouldn't mind sharing with you again."

Heat flashed into Sophia's face. "He's not my boyfriend, and sharing wasn't anything I ever did willingly."

"Not sure why you thought you'd be the special one to keep all of Ezekiel's attention to yourself."

She absolutely wasn't going to get into that in front of Ryker and Bryson. "Do you want milk for the kids?"

"Whatever." With a huff, Mellie plunked the glasses on the table, then turned her attention back to Ryker, popping out one of her hips. "If you're not interested in Sophia, I can hardly blame you. I'm available, however."

"Not interested," Ryker said, somehow managing to keep his words from being too sharp. "But thanks for the offer."

"Your loss," she said with a toss of her head.

"I think you might be losing sight of the true situation here," Ryker said, leaning back in his chair. "You need to be focusing on yourself and your children at the moment. A man isn't what you need."

"What I *need* is a friend who won't toss me out into the streets."

Sophia sighed as she poured milk into the glasses. "We were never friends, Mellie, and you know that. And you're tossing yourself out because you couldn't do the one thing I asked of you. The *one* thing."

"Do you know why we weren't friends?" Mellie asked. "Why no one was your friend?"

Sophia didn't really want to know, but she also knew that that wouldn't stop Mellie. The fact of the matter was, she had actually had a couple of women she would have considered friends. It was Mellie who hadn't been well-liked, but the woman definitely had her own version of events that she would never be dissuaded from.

"You seemed to feel that you and Bryson were special in a way the rest of us weren't."

The reality was that the only time she'd ever felt truly special in her life had been the time between when she'd met Ezekiel and when they'd ended up at the compound and she'd realized the truth of the situation. The moment that realization had dawned, she'd had to accept that she wasn't special at all...and likely never would be.

Though Nana and Papa had treated her like she was special, to her way of thinking back then, it was only because they felt sorry for her. And she'd also felt that a lot of their care for her had stemmed simply from her being their granddaughter, not because she'd been anyone special. Clearly she'd been blinded by the focus she'd had on needing someone to make the decision that she was special to them. Which was what had made her vulnerable to Ezekiel.

"Mom!" Charlie shouted from the living room. "I want another piece!"

Mellie picked up the glasses and left the kitchen with heavy steps. Even Bryson knew better than to stomp like that.

"She's mean like Charlie," Bryson whispered. "Only Lisa is nice."

"Yeah. She's nice," Sophia said, giving him a small smile. "Do you want another piece?"

Bryson shook his head. "Can I still have more banana and peanut butter before bed?"

"Of course, baby."

"I'll leave the pizza here for you," Ryker said. "Maybe you can have some for breakfast." He looked at Sophia and winked. "If your mom will let you."

"Oooh...can I, Momma?"

If he wanted pizza for breakfast, lunch, and supper the next day, she would always agree. "Sure. Why not?"

Ryker laughed and leaned closer to Bryson. "Your mom is a lot nicer than mine about pizza for breakfast."

"Your mom didn't let you eat pizza for breakfast?"

"Nope, and I never really understood that. After all, it's just bread, cheese, and tomato sauce. I think that's better than pancakes with syrup and whipped cream."

Bryson's eyes widened. "Better than pancakes?"

"Okay, maybe not better."

Even though Sophia could practically feel Mellie's displeasure radiating from the other room, she found herself smiling at the exchange between Ryker and Bryson. It helped her feel like maybe with time and patience, Bryson would get past the trauma he'd experienced during the first few years of his life.

Right then, it was all she wanted—her boy...happy and healthy.

~*~

Once they'd eaten pizza until they were full and then cleaned up, Ryker said, "There's still a bit of daylight, so I'm going to go do a little work in the yard. Will you be okay?"

"Yes. I'll be fine."

"Just yell for me if you need anything."

She nodded and gave him a smile. "Thanks for everything."

"You're very welcome." Ryker headed out the back door, feeling a bit wary of leaving Bryson and Sophia alone with Mellie and Charlie, but he'd have to do it at some point that evening.

His curiosity about everything to do with Sophia and Bryson was at an all-time high. But when she'd said she didn't want to talk about it, he'd backed off. Clearly, it wasn't a situation that had made Sophia happy, so he hated the idea of pushing her to relive it. He just hoped that when it came time for Mellie to go the next day that she departed without leaving mayhem in her wake.

When the sun began to set, Ryker put away the tools he'd been using to trim the bushes at the front, then loaded all the branches into the bed of his truck to get rid of out at Michael's. Before leaving, he knocked on the front door.

"Ryker!" Bryson exclaimed with a smile when he opened the door, making it seem like it had been days and not an hour or so since he'd last seen him. The boy had damp curls and wore some pajamas with boats all over them.

"I see you've had a bath," Ryker said as he stepped inside.

"Yep. Now I get a snack."

Sophia appeared from the kitchen, but there was no sign of her houseguests. When she joined him and Bryson near the door, Ryker took a moment to remind her about the chair under the doorknob.

"I'll do that," she said with a nod.

"And take anything valuable into your room with you," he said, keeping his voice low. "Purse. Car keys. Phone. Money." Her brows rose a bit at that. "I'm not trying to make you paranoid, but that woman seems like the type to take her anger out in unpleasant ways."

Sophia nodded. "Unfortunately, I think you're right."

"Would you...uh...text me tomorrow and let me know how it goes?" Ryker wasn't sure why he was asking for that, except he was quite worried about leaving the two of them with a crazy, angry woman.

She looked a bit surprised but went on to say, "I can do that."

"Good. Thank you." He looked down at Bryson. "Enjoy your snack, buddy." He held up his hand for Bryson to smack. "I'll see you tomorrow."

"You're coming back?" he asked.

"Yep. I've got a bit more to do in the yard, so as long as it's not raining, I'll be back after I'm done work."

Sophia rested her hands on Bryson's shoulders. "Thank you again for everything today."

Ryker flashed her a smile. "Anytime."

"Well, hopefully not under these particular circumstances."

"Yeah, can't argue there." After saying goodnight, Ryker headed out to his truck.

He wasn't in a big hurry to get home because even though he was alone in his truck, being alone in his apartment loomed like a dark shadow.

Though he'd been able to move past his initial moment of panic and had helped Bryson and Sophia, in the seclusion of his truck, Ryker felt a flush of shame over the fact that he hadn't been able to dash right into the house when he'd heard Bryson scream. That he'd had a moment of overwhelming weakness when the past had crashed into the present, rendering him utterly useless.

What would have happened if, instead of having an emotional reaction, Bryson's screams had been a result of someone physically hurting him or Sophia? What if his freezing up had made him too late to help?

Even thinking about that possibility sent chills up and down his back. It could have been so much worse, and he would have been responsible for failing to help yet another child.

Ryker jerked his truck to a stop at the side of the back road he'd been driving on. Taking shaky breaths, he leaned forward to rest his forehead on the steering wheel.

As long as his nightmares and issues from that time in Syria only affected him, he could ignore them and try to just take things day by day. But the incident with Bryson had shown him that at any time, those issues could keep him from being able to step up and help a child.

So unless he planned to avoid all children in the future—which he'd already tried to no avail since he now had Vivianne and Bryson in his life—he needed to stop living with his head in the sand. It would probably be easier to just quit his job and move to some remote place where there were no children.

But maybe it was time to do the hard work, regardless of how painful it might be. He owed it to Vivianne, Bryson, and any other children he might come in contact with in the future, to at least try to get himself to a place where he could help them if they needed it without freezing in the process.

CHAPTER TEN

"You look like you haven't slept in a week," Michael remarked as Ryker settled onto the couch across from him with a cup of coffee. His millionth of the day.

Truth be told, he *felt* like he hadn't slept in a week. The night had ended up being as bad as he'd anticipated. Despite all the things he did to try to tire himself out before bed, the nightmares had started almost immediately. By three-thirty, he'd given up on sleep, resigning himself to a day where he would have coffee as his primary source of energy.

"Just had a restless night," Ryker said, then took a sip of his coffee as he scratched Wolfie behind the ears.

Michael shifted Vivianne to his shoulder once she finished her bottle. "Something on your mind?"

He wished he could confide in Michael, especially after what had happened with Sophia and Bryson, but it wasn't his place to share any of that. And he certainly didn't want to share any of his past. Unfortunately, Sophia and Bryson's situation was now intrinsically connected with his issues from the past.

"Always stuff on my mind." Ryker gave him a grin that he hoped didn't look as tired as it felt. "But nothing to be worried about."

Michael studied him for a moment, then said, "Work was okay?"

"Yep. The guys managed to get all the jobs done since the weather was good."

"I'll be back on the job tomorrow. Sophia called a little bit ago to let me know that her guests had to leave early, so I can drop Vivianne back by."

Ryker was glad to hear that. Sophia had also called around lunchtime to tell him that she'd dropped Mellie and her kids off at the bus station. Apparently, she was going back to wherever she'd come from. He could hear the guilt in Sophia's voice as she talked about it, but he was glad she'd stuck to her guns.

From the start, he'd been able to see the gentleness in her, and he knew that she wanted to help others. But in this instance, he really felt she'd done the right thing. If it had been just her, he thought she probably would have just let Mellie stay, even though it was clear the woman didn't think much of Sophia.

But it *wasn't* just her. She had Bryson to consider as well. From what he'd seen, Bryson was her world, so she was trying her hardest to protect him. Ryker could definitely respect that.

"I'm sure Bryson will be happy to have Vivianne back. He loves her."

Michael laughed. "If they were older, I might be worried he'd make a move on her."

Ryker let his thoughts go to the future and how Bryson might still be protective of Vivianne. "If he keeps his sweet nature, Vivianne could certainly do worse for a boyfriend."

Michael glared at him. "Vivianne is not dating until she's in her thirties."

"Good luck with that," Ryker said with a laugh. "You'll have a fight on your hands, I'm pretty sure."

Michael settled Vivianne in the crook of his arm. "You're not going to ever argue with me, are you, Vivi?"

"I sure hope I'm around to see the two of you when she's in her teens. I want a front-row seat."

"You better still be around," Michael said. "I have a feeling you're going to be an important person in her life."

Ryker hoped that was true. He rarely thought more than a day or two into the future anymore, so thinking thirteen or fourteen years ahead was nearly impossible.

"Have you talked to Lani?" Ryker asked. It had been a couple of days since he'd last asked about her, so he figured it was time to nudge Michael into action.

Michael frowned. "No. I haven't."

"Don't you think you should talk to her? It's been almost a week."

"I don't know," Michael said with a sigh. "I'm still not sure what to think about everything."

"I think talking to her might help give you some clarity. Especially if you want to know why she was working for you."

Michael didn't respond, just kept his gaze on Vivianne. Ryker decided not to push it beyond that. He knew what it was like to be struggling with something and have someone continually harping on it. All he could do was hope that the two of them got things sorted out because he really felt like they were good for each other. Good in a way they hadn't acknowledged before things had gone awry.

"Which of the sites do you want to go to tomorrow?" Ryker asked.

Michael lifted his head, relief on his face. "I'll go to whichever site you think my leg will tolerate best."

Ryker considered what was on the schedule for the next day then discussed the pros and cons of each job with him. He tried as much as possible to keep Michael abreast of everything. Michael still took care of scheduling the jobs using voice notes to communicate them to him, but Ryker was often the one who went out to survey the sites to make sure they were prepared for each one.

Once they had the next day's jobs planned out, Ryker offered to run into town to pick up some supper for them. He would have liked to have gone to Sophia's, but he felt like Michael could use his company. He'd go to Sophia's the next day and do some more yard work and see how they were doing. Truth be told, he'd probably text her that night to see how the rest of their day had gone.

After he got back with burgers from *Norma's*, he took Vivianne and cuddled her so Michael could eat his burger with both hands.

"That is amazing," Michael said after he'd eaten about half his burger.

"What have you been living on?" Ryker asked.

"TV dinners and spaghetti." He gave a shrug. "It could be worse. I think TV dinners have come a long way. There's a lot more selection than there used to be."

Ryker knew he was right since he lived on the things himself. "My mom would kill me if she knew how many of them I eat."

"I wish I could cook better," Michael said. "But not being able to read very well has made following recipes quite challenging."

"Have you ever thought about taking adult literacy courses?" Ryker asked.

Michael took another bite of his burger and chewed before answering. "I have considered it. I never prioritized it, though, and now I have even more demands on my time. I don't think it's something I can take on."

"Well, if you do decide to tackle it, let me know. I'll help you in any way I can."

"I appreciate that, man, but you already help me more than you should have to."

"I don't mind taking on additional responsibility." And he didn't. The more he had to do, the less time he had to think. "I'm always up for a challenge."

Michael laughed. "You probably shouldn't tell me that."

Michael was unaware of just how much challenge Ryker had already gone through in his life. Between his career choice, which had resulted in long hours and lots of hard work, and what had happened in Syria, he'd had plenty of challenge.

Of course, he was backing down from the challenge of getting his issues sorted out.

After they finished eating their burgers, he gave Vivianne a bath while Michael had some coffee and a piece of cake from *Norma's*.

"I still can't get over how easily you handle her," Michael said as he watched him from the table. "I'm still scared I'm going to break her."

"I guess I'm just a natural," Ryker said with a laugh.

"For Vivianne's sake, I wish I was a natural."

"The nice thing is that she won't remember the details from this time in her life. All she'll know is that you stepped up when she needed you, and that's more important than anything else."

Ryker laid Vivianne on a towel on the counter next to the plastic tub, then dried her off, blowing a raspberry on her stomach and getting a squeal in response. Smiling, he quickly diapered her and put her in the sleeper he'd found in a drawer in the nursery. Once she was dressed, he handed her to Michael.

"Want me to prepare another bottle before I go?"

"I think I'll be okay. She'll be up for a while yet."

"Is she sleeping well at night?"

"Better than at the beginning, but definitely not a full eight hours."

"Yeah. That might not come for a bit yet."

"So people keep telling me."

"Just remember that there will come a time where she *will* sleep through the night, or if she doesn't, there will come a time when you don't have to get up when she does."

Michael frowned. "So she might still be waking up through the night when she's ten?"

"You never know," Ryker said.

"And here I thought you were my friend."

Ryker laughed. "Would you rather I lied to you?"

"Yes, actually, I think I would rather that."

Ryker rested his hand on Michael's shoulder as he went to the table to grab his jacket. "You'll survive. Just keep trying to sleep when she does."

"Should I be asking Sophia to call me when Vivi naps, so I know when it's time for me to nap too?"

With a grin, Ryker pulled his jacket on. "You could always nap in the truck. There are enough fathers on the crew that I think they'd understand."

"I think I'll stick to coffee to keep me awake."

"That's how I've gotten through many a day."

"Thanks again for all your help," Michael said.

"Anytime. I'll see you tomorrow." Ryker stepped out on the porch with Wolfie at his heels.

The dog scampered off into the trees as Ryker headed for his truck. He knew that Michael would let Wolfie back in when he was done his business, so he went ahead and slid behind the wheel of the truck then headed for home.

Despite his resolutions of the night before, he still hadn't called his therapist. He'd never been one to put things off, but in this particular case, he was taking the gold medal in procrastination.

Once he was home, he settled on the couch with his phone. He stared at it for a moment before he tapped out a message to Sophia.

Hope the rest of your day went well.

Ryker wasn't sure if she was in the middle of getting Bryson into bed or not, so he set his phone aside and went to change into his workout clothes. He hoped to get in a solid workout before bed to add to his lingering exhaustion from the night before.

On nights when he managed to sleep solidly, he wasn't sure if he still had nightmares but just didn't remember them. If that was the case, he was okay with that. If his psyche felt trapped by a nightmare, he didn't know about it if it didn't wake him. All he knew was that the ones that woke him were terrifyingly real.

When there was still no response from Sophia, Ryker climbed onto the elliptical he kept in his apartment and began to move. He'd been on it for about five minutes when his phone screen lit up at the same time his alert beeped.

He picked his phone up, grateful that he was adept enough on the elliptical that he could continue to work out while reading and responding to her message.

Sophia: *It did! Bryson was happy to have his house back, and I was happy to not have to keep track of where Charlie was all the time. We celebrated with the remainder of the pizza. What was left after I let him have a piece for breakfast.*

Ryker grinned and started to tap out a response when another message came through.

Sophia: *I blame you!*

He let out a bark of laughter, and his motions on the elliptical slowed to a stop as he focused on his phone. If he thought she really blamed him, he would have felt bad. But he knew that she was just happy to get food into Bryson.

I'm sorry?

Sophia: *Am I supposed to decide if you are or not?*

Yes?

Sophia: *Don't make me laugh! I might wake Bryson up...and then he'd want more pizza.*

Do you think I'm his favorite person now? I mean, aside from you.

Even as he pressed send, Ryker found a small part of him that would really have liked that. After steering clear of kids for so long, he wasn't sure why he wanted to be important to Bryson, but he did. There was no getting around that.

Sophia: *I think you became his second favorite person when you made him bananas and peanut butter.*

Ryker smiled as he stepped off the elliptical and sank into a nearby chair.

It was all I could think of that might make him feel a bit better while he waited for you. I think you still come out ahead of bananas and peanut butter.

Sophia: *Sometimes I wonder! If we run out of bananas, he has a meltdown.*

For some reason, the idea that Bryson might not have his favorite snack tightened something in Ryker's chest. They had bonded over bananas and peanut butter, and though he refused to consider too deeply why he was letting the closeness grow, he knew he couldn't let Bryson ever be without something that clearly brought him joy.

Well, consider me your banana backup. If you ever need some and can't get to the store, let me know and I'll grab some for you. Can't have him going without his bananas.

Sophia: *I've gotten better at making sure that I don't run out. If I'm down to two, I know I better make a stop at the store.*

Ryker felt kind of disappointed. With Michael doing Vivianne's drop off and pick up at Sophia's, he wasn't going to have many excuses to go by and see them. He should be glad about that...but he wasn't. At least the yard would be a good reason to return. But now that he'd gotten it under control, he'd only need to go by once a week.

I'll be by tomorrow to do a bit more work on your yard. Did you need me to stop for bananas??

Sophia: *lol I think we're okay for a few more days. He won't eat them if they've got any spots on them. If they happen to go bad too soon, we end up with banana bread.*

Though his mom liked to cook and bake, Lydia never had enjoyed it, and she'd made it clear that they'd either need to hire a chef or pay someone to prepare a week's worth of meals at a time for them to just heat up. Clearly Sophia was a bit more like his mom with her ability to cook and bake. Even if it was relatively simple fare, what he'd eaten with them had been tasty.

Ryker looked up from his phone, staring out the window as he took in the fact that he was comparing Sophia to his mom and his ex-fiancée. What on earth was going through his mind?

Getting close to Sophia and to Bryson should be the last thing he wanted to do. And yet...it was something that had become increasingly important to him.

So is it convenient for me to stop by after work tomorrow?

Sophia: *We're going to see Nana around 7. Would that work with your schedule?*

Yep. I won't be picking Vivianne up and taking her to Michael's anymore, I don't think. So I'll come right after I'm done work. Should be there around 5:30 or so.

Sophia: *Sounds good. See you then!*

Ryker was a bit disappointed that their conversation was over, but it was probably a good thing. *Yep. Have a good night.*

Without waiting for a response, he got back on the elliptical, and after finding a podcast to listen to, he set his phone on the display in front of him and got back to his workout. Sometimes he listened to music as he worked out, but he knew that on that night, music would still allow him to think too much. He chose to listen to a true-crime podcast that would hold his attention better, hopefully preventing him from continuing to think about Sophia and Bryson.

~*~

Sophia stood at the door with Bryson, watching as Michael pushed the stroller that held Vivianne's car seat to his truck. He was managing pretty well even with his leg immobilized. Though she'd carried the car seat down the stairs to where the stroller waited, it seemed that Michael had figured out how to cope with his temporary disability while caring for his daughter.

He'd looked tired, though. And sad. It seemed that perhaps what had happened with Lani weighed on the man. Sophia wished she knew the details, but she also knew that it was none of her business.

She was a bit sad about what had happened to them for personal reasons herself. She hadn't connected with any of her old friends since returning to New Hope Falls because she hadn't really felt like being judged by them for where she'd ended up. Lani would have been a nice friend to have. Someone who didn't know all about her past.

Once Michael had driven away, she closed the door and headed for the kitchen with Bryson on her heels.

"Is Ryker coming, Momma?"

"He should be here a bit later," she said as she put the meatloaf she'd made into the oven. "Do you want to wash the potatoes?"

Bryson nodded and pulled a chair over to the sink. Sophia filled a container with some warm water then put the potatoes on the counter beside the sink.

Sophia stood next to him, and when he finished with a potato, he handed it to her. She quickly peeled it, then cut it into cubes and dropped them into a pot of water. Though it would have been quicker to just do it all herself, she continued to teach Bryson about cooking and working in the kitchen.

Soon enough, the cut potatoes were rinsed and back in a pot to cook for the mashed potatoes she planned to have with the meatloaf. It wasn't Bryson's favorite meal, but as long as she gave him enough ketchup to eat with it, he didn't complain too much. He loved mashed potatoes, however, so that kind of balanced out his apathy toward the meatloaf.

She just hoped that Ryker liked meatloaf. If she'd had time to go shopping or had different ingredients on hand, she would have chosen something else. But ground beef was all she had in the freezer, so it was either meatloaf or meatballs. However, they'd just had meatballs, so meatloaf it was.

For the months since she'd been home, she hadn't cooked with anyone but Bryson in mind. So, considering someone else now was a bit disconcerting.

But most likely, it wasn't going to be something she had to think about too often. The yard was looking really lovely already, and if Ryker wasn't going to be picking Vivianne up, they wouldn't be seeing him very often.

She hadn't mentioned anything about that to Bryson, who was bound to be disappointed by the news. And she braced herself to have to answer a daily question of whether Ryker would be coming that day. Sophia had a feeling the answer to that question was going to be *no* more than it would be *yes.*

And though Sophia would deny it to anyone who asked, she knew that she'd miss seeing Ryker as much as Bryson would. But if she'd learned anything over the past several years, it was to not trust her heart or her emotions. They were both very bad judges of character and often led her to make bad decisions.

So she had a little crush on the man. That was understandable. He was handsome with his warm smile and sparkling blue eyes. Add in his kind nature, and it was pretty much inevitable she would find him attractive.

From the moment she'd discovered boys, she'd fallen in and out of crushes. Her emotions were easily swayed. Too easily swayed.

The longest she'd gone without harboring feelings for a man was the time she'd been in the compound. Anything she felt for Ezekiel had died the moment she'd discovered that even though she was pregnant with his child, he wasn't committed to her at all. No, she was just one of many that he felt was his due to have as leader of the cult.

She'd wanted to leave as soon as she'd realized what was going on, but he'd kept her prisoner, not even allowing her to go to the hospital to deliver Bryson. All babies were born in the compound, and if things went wrong, according to Ezekiel, it was God's will.

Those times had been absolutely horrible. Every emotion she'd ever had had been numbed during those terrible years, thawing only when she was able to hold Bryson close and whisper, *I'm your momma* and *I love you* over and over again.

But she was home, and they were both safe. And she would do her best to never be vulnerable again. To never be in a position where a man could manipulate her because of how she felt for him.

So while Ryker might be a nice man, she wasn't going to let anything she might feel for him show. Especially since she knew that she'd never be considered a catch by any man she'd actually want to be with.

"Momma!" Bryson called from the living room where he'd gone after he'd finished his job of washing the potatoes. "Ryker's here."

"Okay, baby." She didn't go into the living room to see for herself, even though her heart rate had picked up ever so slightly at Bryson's words.

Instead, she stayed in the kitchen, continuing to peel the carrots she still needed to prepare for their meal. She glanced over her shoulder as Bryson came running into the kitchen, going straight to the back door to unlock and open it. He stood in front of the screen door, his fingers pressed to the screen.

Sophia could see his desire to go outside and talk to Ryker, but it was definitely battling against the desire to stay inside where it was safe. She didn't say anything one way or another. This was a decision he had to make himself.

She was pretty sure that forcing him outside to just stand there in the yard would deepen the intensity of his panic. And so soon after Charlie's little "joke," it would only make things even worse.

Still, as she went to the sink to wash her hands, she couldn't help but look through the window to see Ryker in the shed, removing some tools. He wore a pair of faded jeans and a long-sleeve black T-shirt along with a ball cap.

"He brought flowers, Momma."

Sophia turned to look at Bryson. "What?"

"He put a box of flowers on the sidewalk at the front."

Sophia dried her hands on a dishtowel as she walked into the living room. Going to the large picture window, she looked out at the sidewalk. Sure enough, there sat a large flat of flowers in a variety of colors.

She lifted the hand clutching the dishtowel and rested it on the window. Flowers...

What was she supposed to do about that?

CHAPTER ELEVEN

Sophia was still standing at the window when Ryker walked around to the front from the back yard. Bryson came running to stand beside her. When Ryker glanced at the window and saw them, he smiled and lifted a hand in greeting.

"Hi, Ryker!" Bryson called.

Ryker's response was muffled, but Bryson reacted with a little dance beside her.

"He said hi, Momma."

"Yep, he did."

Together, they watched as Ryker knelt in front of the flower beds that lined the space right in front of the porch. The height of the porch blocked their view, and while Sophia figured that was a good thing, Bryson didn't.

"I can't see what he'd doing, Momma." He paused, pressing his hands flat against the window. "Can I...can I go outside for a minute?"

"You want to go outside?"

"Just for a minute." His voice wavered as he spoke. "If you stay with me."

"Of course, I'll stay with you." Sophia tried to keep from sounding as excited as she felt. "Let me just check the food, then we can go outside."

She hoped that delaying for a couple of minutes wouldn't give him enough time to change his mind. Maybe his anticipation would grow, and he'd be even more determined to go outside and stay out there for a few minutes.

After she stirred the potatoes and turned the burner under the carrots down, she went back to the living room. Bryson still stood where she'd left him.

"I'm ready," she said.

When he turned, she could see the apprehension on his little face. She wanted to kiss it away and tell him that everything would be okay. But she'd told him that plenty of times, and it had never made any difference.

Slowly he left the window and approached her. "You'll stay with me?"

"Of course, baby. I'll always stay with you." With a nod, he took the hand she held out, gripping it tightly. "When you want to come back inside, you just tell me."

She took a deep breath to calm her excitement and let Bryson lead the way to the door. He hesitated again, but then he pressed the handle of the storm door and pushed it open.

Ryker must have heard the door open because he got to his feet. His eyes widened as he spotted Bryson. He glanced at Sophia, and she could see that he was as amazed by this latest turn of events as she was.

"Hey there, Bry," he said. "Come to see what I'm working on?"

"Yep." Bryson pulled her cautiously toward the porch railing.

Clearly, he wasn't ready to venture beyond the porch, but just being outside with him was a victory.

"What are you doing?" Bryson asked as he peered over the railing.

Ryker knelt back down on the grass, reaching up to turn his cap around so the bill was in the back. "I'm pulling some weeds and preparing the soil to plant the flowers."

"You didn't need to plant flowers," Sophia said.

Ryker looked up at her. "I know. But we had some flowers left over from a job we did, so I thought I'd plant them here."

"They're pretty, Momma," Bryson said as he released her hand to grasp the railing.

Sophia noticed that he kept glancing around, and she had a feeling that he was on the lookout for any bugs or bees. She'd propped the screen door open, so he could dart back inside if he needed to. So far, so good, though.

"Yes. The flowers are very pretty," she agreed.

"And I think they'll look perfect in these beds," Ryker said. "They should get just the perfect amount of sun."

"Why do they need sun?" Bryson asked.

"Plants need water and sun to grow. Just like you need food."

"Do I need sun to grow?" Bryson asked.

Ryker glanced at her, then back at Bryson. "Sunlight helps our bodies produce a vitamin that everyone needs."

"So I'm not getting that...vi...vi..."

"Vitamin," Sophia provided.

"Vitamin," Bryson repeated.

"You can get it from food," Ryker said as he reached out to pull some weeds. "And if you take pills, you can get it there too."

"I take pills," Bryson said, then he looked up at her. "Right, Momma?"

"Yes." She rested her hand on his curls. "Every night before bed."

"So I don't have to go out in the sun?"

She and Ryker exchanged another look before Ryker returned his attention to the flower bed. Obviously, he was leaving the answer to that question up to her.

"You don't *have* to go in the sun, but it can be nice." The reality was that there were plenty of days when the sun didn't shine, so his going outside probably shouldn't be motivated by his desire to be in sunlight.

They watched Ryker in silence for a few minutes, then Sophia said, "I'm going to check on the food, Bry. I won't be gone long, but the door is open if you decide to come in. Will you be okay?"

Bryson peered at her, concern puckering his brow. "You'll come back?"

"Of course, baby. I just don't want the food to burn."

"I'll be here," Ryker said. "If you need anything."

"Okay."

Sophia took that as permission to go into the house. She hurried into the kitchen and went right to the stove to check the vegetables. After stirring them, she went back outside though she'd have to go in for a longer stretch in a few minutes to finish getting supper ready.

She stood in the doorway and watched Bryson as he peered over the railing at Ryker. No matter how much she told herself she shouldn't be feeling anything for Ryker, it was nearly impossible to keep from falling for a man this incredible. He'd done for Bryson what no one had been able to. That honestly, no other man in her life had seemed willing to do.

No one except for Nana had been willing to patiently connect with Bryson, accepting him as he was and yet allowing him to spread his wings when he cautiously made those attempts. No one else had taken the time to understand why he wasn't what people would consider a "normal" boy. He'd had experiences that had molded him in ways most boys his age hadn't been molded.

Sometimes it felt like her family just wanted her to forget the past five years and move on, as if it was that easy. If forgetting and moving on had been a simple thing, they would have done it already. But there was no way to forget everything that had transpired.

But even without knowing what had happened to them, Ryker seemed to have known that Bryson required gentle handling. That made him an exceptional man in her books.

"Look at the flowers, Momma." Bryson pointed over the rail.

Blinking away the moisture that had suddenly sprung into her eyes, Sophia moved to stand next to Bryson once again. She braced her hands on the railing and looked down into the flower bed. Sure enough. In the time she'd been gone, Ryker had put a couple of the flowers into the soil.

"They're beautiful," Sophia said.

"And they'll look even prettier as they grow," Ryker said as he continued to prepare the soil and then placed a plant into the ground.

"No bees, Momma," Bryson said, his voice firm. "And no bugs."

"That's great, baby." She knew it wouldn't always be that way. But if this encouraged him to come outside even for just a few minutes a day, they were making progress. "Will you be able to stay for supper, Ryker?"

He sat back on his heels and looked up at her. "Sure. If you have enough."

"We have plenty," she said, especially since Bryson wouldn't be eating all that much of the meatloaf.

"It'll probably take me another thirty minutes or so to finish the flower beds," he said as he gestured to the one on the other side of the sidewalk that led to the porch steps. It was a smaller flower bed on that side, but between the two beds, there would be an explosion of color at the front of the house.

She was going to have to take pictures to show Nana. The older woman would be so glad to see that her flower beds were being put to good use. Of course, that would also mean having to reveal that Ryker had had a hand in bringing her gardens to life again.

Sophia knew that Nana wanted her to find a good man, someone to be a father to Bryson, and it wouldn't surprise her if she started to think that Ryker was an option. He was the only man that Bryson had been even remotely interested in being around so far.

And now, with the flowers? Yeah, Nana would definitely think he might be worth keeping around. But Nana didn't realize that Sophia wasn't sure she could let Ryker close enough for a relationship—if that was even something he'd want. She still wasn't convinced there was any man on earth who wanted to take on the double whammy of a woman with issues and a child with issues.

"I have to go work on the food, Bry. Do you want to come back in?" Again, he hesitated. "You can stay out here, if you want. The door is open if you need to come in."

"I'll stay here."

"Good boy." She bent and pressed a kiss to his curls. "I love you."

"Love you too, Momma."

She glanced at Ryker to see him watching them with a smile. "I'll keep an eye on him."

"Thanks."

Back in the kitchen, she took a moment to compose herself, gripping the edge of the counter as she stared out the window above the sink.

She was happy that Bryson was making these steps forward, but she struggled with the fact that it was coming with Ryker's help. There was no guarantee that he'd be around to continue to help Bryson, and she certainly didn't feel comfortable asking him to keep coming around.

He'd already gone above and beyond her request to spend a couple of minutes putting Bryson's mind at ease about his intentions with Vivianne. From that moment on, Bryson had latched on to him, and Sophia had no idea how he was going to react to seeing Ryker less. But since it was inevitable, she would soon find out.

The sound of bubbling had her turning from the window toward the stove. She drained the potatoes then pulled out the stuff she needed to mash them. Once that was done, she drained the carrots, hoping that Ryker liked slightly mushy cooked carrots because, for whatever reason, Bryson liked that particular veggie to be either raw or cooked super soft. Nothing in between.

The timer on the oven went off, so she took the meatloaf out, then set the table. She wasn't sure if Ryker would finish in time to eat with them or if he'd eat later, but she went ahead and set a place for him.

Sophia was surprised that she managed to get everything ready with still no sign of Bryson. It felt weird to go this long without Bryson being within arm's reach. But she could hear the distant rumble of Ryker's deeper voice followed by Bryson's softer, higher one, so she knew he was okay.

When she went back to the door, she saw that Bryson had moved over to the other side of the porch. Sophia joined him there and looked over the railing. She was kind of amazed to see how quickly Ryker worked. But then again, he was a professional, so it made sense. But still, something that would have taken her hours had only taken him a matter of minutes.

"Supper is ready," she said as she rested her hand on Bryson's shoulder. "Why don't you go wash your hands, baby?"

"Are you eating supper with us, Ryker?" Bryson asked.

"Yep. I just need to clean this up." Ryker looked at her. "Do I have a few minutes?"

Sophia nodded. "It usually takes Bryson a little bit cleaned up."

Bryson skipped ahead of her into the kitchen, where he climbed up on a chair to wash his hands. All the while, he happily chatted about Ryker and the flowers.

"Okay if I wash up in the bathroom?" Ryker asked from the door of the kitchen.

"Definitely," Sophia said as she carried the mashed potatoes to the table.

By the time Ryker reappeared, Bryson had finished washing up and was seated at the table. She had the food on the table but was trying to figure out if it was enough. There was no salad or buns. It was plenty for her and Bryson, but Ryker might expect more.

"Smells delicious," he said, as if reading her mind. "So much better than the TV dinner I'd probably be eating at my place."

"Hope meatloaf is okay." She poured water into her glass, then said, "Would you like milk or water?"

"Water is fine," he said. "And meatloaf is more than okay."

"Can I get the ketchup, Momma?"

"Oh. Sure, baby."

Bryson slid off his chair and came back with the large bottle they kept in the fridge.

"That's almost as big as you, buddy," Ryker said with a laugh.

"I like ketchup on meatwoaf."

Sophia took the bottle from him and set it on the table. "Meatloaf, baby."

Once they were all seated, Sophia had a moment's hesitation, as she often did, where her instinct was to say a prayer. That had always been something her family had done, and it had definitely been part of every meal in the compound. Habits were hard to break, and it wasn't that she necessarily wanted to break the habit. She just wasn't sure how to approach things that had been part of their life in such a traumatic place.

Part of her kind of hoped that, if they had a long stretch of not doing things like praying before meals or going to church services, the memory of them would fade enough that he wouldn't assume she was making him do the same things that Ezekiel had forced them to do.

Was it the right decision? Her parents would likely say no, but they didn't know the scope of what she and Bryson had endured in the compound.

The one time she'd taken Bryson to the service shortly after they'd arrived back in New Hope, he'd refused to go to junior church with the other children, but then he'd begun to shake and cry softly as the service had gotten underway. It had been too much for her to handle, so she'd carried him out, and they hadn't gone back since.

Instead of making a decision on praying for the food that day, she slid the plate of meatloaf toward Ryker.

"Go ahead and serve yourself and Bryson," he said in response.

Sophia put a piece of meatloaf on Bryson's plate, then once again slid it in Ryker's direction before picking up the bowl of potatoes. "By the time I get Bryson's food ready, you'll have time to dish yourself up."

Ryker took the meatloaf, then said, "You can't always put yourself last, Sophia."

"I look at it as just being practical," she responded, keeping her gaze on Bryson's plate. "And when you're a single mom, putting your child first automatically means putting yourself last. It's just how it has to be right now."

There were times when some of the things Ryker said made her wonder about him. Like, for all that her dad loved her mom, she didn't think she'd ever heard him say something like that to her. They were a team, and he did as much as he could for the family when he wasn't working. Sometimes her mom served herself last. Sometimes her dad did. From what she could remember, it was usually just a matter of practicality.

Still, it made her wonder how Ryker might treat his wife...the mother of his children.

Which really wasn't something she should be thinking about.

As if realizing it wasn't a subject she was all that keen to be discussing, Ryker turned his attention to Bryson again. "Is meatloaf your favorite, Bryson?"

Sophia glanced up from where she was cutting his piece of meatloaf in time to see Bryson wrinkle his nose and shake his head. "Only with ketchup."

"When I was your age, I felt the same way. My grandma used to make meatloaf for us sometimes, and it had great big chunks of onion in it. I needed a lot of ketchup to help me eat that." He paused and looked down at his food. "It looks like you are much luckier in what your mom makes you."

"You don't like onions?" Bryson asked.

"I don't mind them now, but as a kid, I didn't much care for them."

"Do I like onions, Momma?"

Sophia squeezed some ketchup on his plate, then set the bottle back in front of him. "I don't really know if you do or not, baby. I don't serve them because *I* don't like them."

Bryson's eyes grew wide. "I thought you liked everything."

"Nana would be happy to tell you about all the things I don't like," Sophia said as she began to serve herself. "Some of which I'm still not fond of."

She noticed that Ryker waited until she had food on her plate before he began to eat his own meal. His manners seemed to be impeccable, better even than hers, and certainly better than her brothers.

"Do you like everything, Ryker?"

It was a little funny that so many of their discussions seemed to revolve around food. As Sophia listened to Ryker recount foods he hadn't liked as a child and those he still didn't like as an adult, she knew she shouldn't be enjoying these little tidbits of information about Ryker. However, once again, she wouldn't put a stop to the conversation since Bryson was actually interacting of his own accord with someone outside of her family.

She let the two of them talk, though Ryker would occasionally draw her into the conversation. It dawned on her then that she was far more used to listening to people talk than being the one doing the talking. The only person she ever conversed freely with was

Nana. With her, she never feared judgment like she did with her family. Especially Natalie.

Thankfully, most in her family didn't seem to expect her to talk, but it seemed that Ryker didn't have that same expectation of her. Where she felt invisible much of the time, Ryker made her feel seen. It was like he wouldn't allow her to fade too much into the background before pulling her back into the conversation.

It was a bit disconcerting, if she was being honest. The last time she'd felt so *seen* was when Ezekiel had turned his attention on her. And look how that had turned out.

She breathed a sigh of relief when the meal was over, then declined Ryker's help to clean up, figuring he'd done plenty already with his work in the yard.

"I guess I should head home," Ryker said after he took the bag of cookies from Bryson. "Thank you for yet another lovely dinner."

"Thank you for the flowers you planted. I know Nana will be thrilled to see that her flower beds haven't gone to the weeds this year."

"I was happy to help with that."

"Will you be back tomorrow?" Bryson asked.

"Sorry, buddy," Ryker said with a shake of his head. "I have work tomorrow, then I'm going to my brother's house for my nephew's birthday party."

"Oh." Bryson looked crestfallen, but Sophia didn't want Ryker to feel bad about not being able to come. "I've never had a birthday party."

Ryker glanced at Sophia with raised brows, apparently not sure if he should take that statement at face value or not.

"We'll have one when you turn five, baby," Sophia said. "I promise."

That brought a smile to Bryson's face. "Will you come to *my* birthday party too, Ryker?"

"That's still a couple of months away, Bry," Sophia said. "I'm not sure what exactly we'll be doing."

"When you have a plan, you can let me know," Ryker told him. "In the meantime, have a good visit with Nana."

With that, Ryker left the house and jogged down the stairs before heading to his truck. He probably couldn't wait to get away from the awkwardness of that last little conversational tidbit.

Part of her wondered if she should just tell Ryker everything and spare him from having to figure out why Bryson had never had a birthday party. But she hated the idea of having him look at her with pity and even the smallest amount of judgment for her bad decisions. He would be right to judge her—just like her family had—because she'd let herself be led right into the middle of a cult and had gotten pregnant without being married.

Well, that wasn't exactly right. She and Ezekiel had had a *spiritual* marriage.

She'd bought everything he'd sold to her during that time. Only coming to realize later that he'd wanted a *spiritual* but not *legal* marriage with her because he had other wives already. He may have railed against society and all its laws, but he didn't intend to get arrested for bigamy.

Looking back now, all she wanted to do was yell at herself for being so, so stupid and naïve. The only way she could live with herself and move forward was if she learned from her mistakes. As her father had always lectured them: those who didn't learn from their mistakes were doomed to repeat them.

She did not intend to be one of those who repeated her mistakes. Her goal from that point on was to devote her love and time to her son—the only good thing that had come from that time with Ezekiel.

Everything she did was to provide for him the life he deserved. The one he'd missed out on so far. And though she might not be able to afford the most expensive toys or the best places to live, she would love him with all her heart and do what she hadn't been able to do during their time in the compound to show him that he was important to her.

Ryker was playing a role in Bryson's life now, and because it brought Bryson joy, Sophia hadn't yet been able to bring herself to force Ryker away. But someday, Ryker would have his own children, and Bryson would fall below them in Ryker's priorities—which was as it should be. But if there was any way for Sophia to lessen Ryker's importance in Bryson's life before that occurred, it would make it easier for the child to accept.

She'd never imagined she'd be a single mother with only one child, but she accepted that that was her lot in life now. But what she hoped and prayed for was that there would be people in the years ahead who would fill the gaps in Bryson's life the way Ryker was filling a gap for him right then.

And as long as Bryson was happy, it would be enough.

CHAPTER TWELVE

"Thanks for coming," Silas said as he gave Ryker a hug, slapping him once on the back.

"You know I wouldn't have missed this for the world."

His nephew and niece had been the only children he'd been able to deal with in the dark months following his return from Syria. They'd been the solitary bright spots in his world, offering their love without any expectations for how he should be behaving.

"I just find it hard to believe that Jonah is turning eleven. You're going to have a teenager on your hands before you know it."

Silas groaned. "I already feel like I have teenagers on my hands. Emery already wants makeup and specific clothes that apparently all the cool kids wear. She's only *eight!*"

"You were the one who decided to have kids," Ryker said with a laugh. "I think you must have forgotten what we were like at that age, wanting all the big kid things."

Silas grimaced. "Well, come to the kitchen to have some pizza and a bunch of other junk food that Donna bought for the kids against my express wishes."

"You're turning into an old fuddy-duddy, Si. Let the kids have some fun."

Even as he said the words, his thoughts went to the night before at Sophia's and Bryson's announcement that he'd never had a birthday party. Ryker still wasn't sure what to make of that. It seemed that the more time he spent with the pair, the more questions he was left with. Would he ever get answers?

"Hi, Uncle Ryker!" Jonah called out from where he was seated at the table in the dining room with a few friends.

He knew that the party had started mid-afternoon with the boys coming to swim in the pool and to play video games.

"Happy birthday, Jonah," Ryker said as he went to where his nephew sat and bent over to give him a quick hug. "Have you had a good day?"

"It's been great." Jonah pushed up his glasses with a quick movement. "And we're going to watch a movie and play more video games when we're done here."

"Sounds like a stellar plan." Ryker held out his hand for a fist bump. "Did you save me some pizza?"

"I think Mom did. She's in the kitchen with Emery."

Ryker left the boys to their video game centered conversation and went in search of Donna, Emery, and some pizza. He found Silas with them, and he gave them each a quick hug before lifting a couple of pieces of pizza from the box.

"Did you have pizza, Silas?" he asked as he sat down at the island counter with Emery.

His niece giggled. "Daddy doesn't *like* pizza."

"I know," Ryker said with a shake of his head. "He's crazy."

"Hey now," Silas protested. "Don't go trying to plant ideas in my daughter's head."

"Oh, I don't think you have to worry," Ryker assured him. "She already thinks you're crazy for not liking pizza. Right, Em?"

She nodded vigorously enough to set her long curls dancing. "You're crazy, Daddy!"

"Oh, I'm crazy alright," Silas said as he stepped close enough to Donna to snag her around the waist and pull her close. "I'm crazy about your mommy!"

"Silas."

Ryker could tell that Donna had tried to inject some reproof in her tone, but the smile on her face when Silas kissed her cheek belied it.

Watching the affectionate interaction between his brother and sister-in-law caused an ache in Ryker. But as he thought about it, he realized it wasn't an ache for what he'd had with Lydia. While Lydia had been a lot of things, overly affectionate had not been one of them.

They were going to be a power couple in the medical world of Seattle, working hand-in-hand to care for the city's women and children. But would they have had enough time to care for each other?

He knew that Silas and Donna were both busy with their careers, as were his parents. Still, both couples made a concerted effort to keep the romance alive in their relationships. Back when they'd gotten engaged, Ryker had known that it would be an area that he and Lydia might have to work extra hard at, but he hadn't doubted that they could do it. If they had both wanted it.

Now he wasn't so sure that it had been an area where Lydia had planned to exert much effort. Even while they were dating, she hadn't always thought that it was necessary to meet up for a meal during the week, just the two of them. She'd seemed to be content to see him at church or small group, followed by meals with his family or hers or a group of their friends.

The cracks in their relationship had been very apparent in the weeks following the attack. She'd seemed to have little to no sympathy for the struggle he was having coping with what had happened in Syria. Even during the day of the attack and the ones immediately following it, if a patient died while she was treating them, she simply moved on to the next one, showing no emotion at all.

Ryker had assumed she'd just put her emotions aside so she could work—and he'd actually wished that he'd been able to be more that way himself. But once they'd returned to Seattle, she'd gone back to work...back to her life...like nothing had even happened. When he'd asked her about it, she'd said that it was a risk they'd taken when going to that part of the world.

And that was that.

Only Ryker hadn't been able to compartmentalize the way she had, and he'd like to think that none of his family would have acted the way she had either. Of course, they probably would have pursued therapy a bit more aggressively than he had.

"You didn't have to come here tonight, Ryker," Donna said as she stood in Silas's embrace. "Jonah's kind of caught up in his friends."

"I know." Ryker gave a shrug. "But I wanted to. As long as it's not an inconvenience for you guys."

"It's never an inconvenience," Silas said. "We love to have you come around. Especially if you're going to help us eat pizza."

"I'll always help you eat pizza." He bent close to Emery and jostled her arm. "As long as Em doesn't eat it all first."

Emery let loose a merriment of giggles, and Ryker realized he'd never heard that sort of laughter from Bryson. Or from Sophia, for that matter.

He needed to stop thinking about them. Stop wondering about what had happened in their lives that had left them both so...fragile. Because that was what he sensed when he was with them. A fragility...a vulnerability. Something that made him want to protect them.

What he did know was that he shouldn't even dare to consider something more serious with Sophia, and he really shouldn't be getting so close to Bryson either. When he woke up each night with nightmares that now featured him being unable to help Bryson because he was frozen in fear, Ryker resolved to put distance between himself and them.

But he just couldn't do it. In the light of day, he couldn't bring himself to walk away. At least not yet.

The reality was that they both appeared to be walking wounded. Though he didn't know *what* had wounded them, he recognized that *something* had, just like something had wounded him.

He would venture a guess that his mom would say that he shouldn't be getting involved on any level with them if he wasn't willing to seriously pursue therapy himself. And that they should probably be in therapy as well.

"So what's been keeping you busy these days?" Silas asked as he leaned against the counter opposite where Ryker and Emery sat, then took the cup of coffee his wife handed him.

"A little bit of mowing, garden preparation, tree removal. Same old, same old." He paused then said, "And I've been doing a bit of extra work for someone as well."

"Extra work?" Silas asked as he lifted his mug to take a sip.

"Single mom with a child who seems to have a bit of a phobia of being outside."

Silas's brows rose slightly. "Agoraphobic?"

Ryker shook his head. "If I had to choose one, I'd say maybe spheksophobia."

"Wasps?" Silas murmured.

"Possibly. He seems to have a fear of bugs, which, from what his mom has said, resulted from a wasp sting. Because of that, he has refused to go outside beyond going from the house to the car and from the car to other buildings."

"So he doesn't play outside, Uncle Ryker?" Emery asked.

As he glanced down at his niece, Ryker was reminded again that while the girl might only be eight, she was smart beyond her years. "No. He doesn't play outside."

"How does that factor into you doing their yard work?" Silas asked.

"He's only four and doesn't like his mom being very far away from him, so her going out to do work in the yard is next to impossible."

Silas had a thoughtful look on his face as he continued to sip his coffee. Ryker found that he wanted to spill everything that was going around in his head and his heart about Sophia and Bryson, but he wasn't sure if he should. His brother would only say what he already knew.

"Is the boy in therapy?" Donna asked as she joined them at the counter with her own cup of coffee.

"I don't think so. Single mom with no insurance, I'm pretty sure."

"I'm surprised you have anything to do with a child like that," Silas said, his blunt words not taking Ryker by surprise at all.

Ryker took a bite of his pizza, trying to decide if he should even bother responding to that. Of his two siblings, he was definitely closer to Silas, and while he might try and deny something like that with Callie, he knew that Silas wouldn't pester him for more information. Nor would he needle him into justifying his actions.

"I'm a bit surprised as well," Ryker said.

"How did you meet?" Donna asked.

In his mind, Donna and Silas were one, so what he could confide in Silas, he had no problem confiding with her there. Ryker knew that revealing all of this wouldn't mean they would begin to harass him about going back to therapy.

"She's the babysitter for Michael's daughter, Vivianne. The first time I went by to pick her up, Bryson—that's the little boy—was convinced I was going to run away with the baby and never bring her back. He's quite protective of her."

Donna's face softened as she smiled. "So he was worried about her?"

Ryker nodded. "This went on for a while, but I guess his anxiety over it was creating problems with him falling asleep, even though Vivianne was still coming back every day. Sophia, his mom, asked if I'd speak with him for a few minutes one day to try and put his mind at ease about me."

This time, it was Silas who smiled. "And the rest is history, huh?"

Ryker shrugged. He couldn't argue with Silas about how well he related to children. While his brother and father were both surgeons—though in vastly different areas of medicine—he'd wanted the more hands-on approach of being a pediatrician.

He'd been looking forward to starting in his practice. To building relationships with patients and their parents.

It dawned on him then that he was doing just that with Sophia and Bryson. Except it was turning into more. He couldn't imagine any situation where he would have done yard work for a patient and their mother whom he had met in his office.

"I'm happy that you were able to connect with Bryson," Donna said. "I'm sure that you helped put his mom's heart at ease. It's never easy when a little one is freaking out over something and, as a parent, you can't seem to do anything to help them."

Though he didn't have any kids of his own, Ryker knew that what Donna was saying was true. He'd experienced it during his residency. Though he hadn't been looking at it from a medical perspective when he'd agreed to do what Sophia asked since it wasn't a medical issue, he could see that it was the same. A worried parent was a worried parent, regardless of what the basis of that worry was.

"I know you're not ready to step back into a pediatrics practice," Silas began, "but I'm so glad that you're beginning to connect with children once again."

"I connected with children before this," Ryker said, trying to keep a defensive tone out of his voice. "What do you consider Jonah and Emery?"

"Relatives," Silas said. "They would never have been your patients because of that. Plus, I think you feel safe around them because being around them usually means I'm in the vicinity. If something happens to them and you freeze, I'll still be able to help them."

"And maybe you're able to connect with Bryson and Vivianne because you don't view them as your patients either," Donna added.

Ryker couldn't deny there was truth in that, but at the same time, he knew there had been moments when he'd looked at both Bryson and Vivianne through the eyes of a doctor.

"Mommy, can I go play on my iPad?" Emery asked, clearly bored with the conversation. She might have the ability to understand what she was hearing, but that didn't mean she was all that interested in it.

"Sure, darling," Donna said.

She slid off her stool then turned to look back at her parents. "You'll call me for cake, though, right?"

"No worries. We'll definitely call you."

After Emery had left the kitchen, Donna said, "So what's Bryson's mom like?"

Ryker saw the question for the trap it was, so he took another bite of his pizza. He also knew that if he didn't answer, they'd read even more into it. "She's devoted to Bryson. Very accommodating of his needs. I don't know her very well, though, since she seems very reserved."

"Shy?" Donna would definitely relate to her in that regard. Though she was a professor and had to deal with students and colleagues, Ryker knew that she found it difficult at times.

"Maybe a little." He thought back over their interactions and how things had gone down with Mellie. "I think she's been through quite a lot since Bryson was born. I don't know what, so don't bother asking me. It's just from comments she's said, plus she had guests earlier this week that said some really...awful things."

He usually wouldn't share things like that with people. Still, as he'd told them about Bryson and Sophia, he realized that he needed to talk to *someone* about what was bubbling around in his head. He couldn't talk to Michael about it since he knew Sophia,

and Ryker didn't feel it was right to reveal things about her to someone she interacted with. The chances of her ever meeting Silas and
Donna were slim to none.

"What sort of awful things?" Donna asked.

After a moment's hesitation, he shared what had happened to
Bryson, and even as he recounted his own interactions with Mellie,
Ryker realized how truly weird that all had been. Charlie's "joke"
on Bryson was understandable because there were kids who could
be mean like that. But Mellie's comments about being willing to
share him with Sophia because they'd shared before had just
been...so bizarre.

As Ryker talked, Silas walked over to the coffee machine and
refilled his mug. Ryker knew he wasn't ignoring him, which was
proven true when he came back to the counter.

"Do you think she might have been part of a cult?"

Ryker stared at his brother. "What?"

"The comment about them having shared a man in the past.
Plus the bit about their sons being brothers. We've seen situations
where an ex-wife and current wife develop a friendship of sorts for
the sake of the children," Silas said. "But the antagonism showed
by this other woman toward Sophia, plus some of her other comments make it seem like it was an ongoing situation. Like they were
pitted against each other while they were both involved with the
same man, you know?"

"It does make sense," Donna said. "If you have a cult leader
who fosters relationships with many different women in the group,
it can create a competitive environment. Women vying for the
leader's attention. Not every woman would react that way, but it
sure sounds like that woman did."

As Ryker considered everything he'd heard from Sophia and
Bryson, he realized a lot of things made sense when viewed in the
light of them possibly having been in a cult. The idea of it made
him feel a little sick.

"I'm not saying that's what happened to her," Silas said, clearly reading his thoughts. "Just that it's a possibility."

"That never really occurred to me," Ryker said. "What made you think that?"

"Don't you remember when Mom spoke at that conference last year about working with cult survivors?" Silas asked.

Ryker frowned as he thought back. He did remember it, but for some reason, it hadn't stuck with him the way it apparently had with Silas.

"Plus, there was a news report a couple of months back about an FBI raid on a cult down in Texas," Donna added. "So we've talked about it with your mom a few times."

Even though Ryker had all this new information, he realized it wouldn't make any difference because he couldn't exactly come right out and ask Sophia about it. If she wanted him to know, she had to be the one to tell him.

The worst thing would have been if he'd asked her about it, and it turned out that that wasn't what had happened with her. Still, it did make a lot of sense with regards to things she and Bryson had said. Like when Bryson had told him he'd never had a birthday party.

Now that the idea had been put in his head, however, Ryker knew that any time Sophia or Bryson said anything about their past, he'd be viewing it in light of this conversation. He wasn't sure if that was good or bad.

But if that really was the truth of their past, it just reinforced what he felt about the three of them all being wounded in ways that did not lend itself to anything beyond a casual friendship. He had a feeling that Sophia would agree with him, but Bryson? It wasn't hard to see that Bryson viewed him with a bit of a case of hero-worship.

Putting a bit of distance between them was almost imperative so that Bryson didn't come to rely on him too much. He'd already known that, but with this as a possibility now, he had to make the right decision.

~*~

"Is Ryker coming today, Momma?"

Sophia glanced over to where Bryson sat at the table, a cut-up pancake with peanut butter and bananas on the plate in front of him. It was the same question he'd asked every day so far that week.

"It's a workday, baby, so I don't think so." It wasn't a lie, but work hadn't been a reason that Ryker had stayed away before.

Bryson's shoulders slumped, and his head dipped as his feet swung slowly beneath his chair. His body language screamed despondency, and it broke her heart.

She'd made a huge mistake the day she'd asked Ryker to come in and talk to Bryson. It was never easy to see Bryson's fear and anxiety, but seeing his heartbreak was almost worse.

How was it that even when she thought she was making a good decision, it still ended up being the wrong one?

For probably the hundredth time in her life, Sophia wished she had a rewind button. She couldn't make bad decisions like picking the wrong color paint for a room or choosing to go on a diet right before Christmas. No, her bad decisions had to have devastating effects on her life and now on Bryson's.

As she turned her attention back to the bottle she was preparing for Vivianne, a realization dawned on her. All her bad decisions centered around people she chose to allow into her life.

From there on out, she needed to be warier of who she interacted with. It might lead to a solitary life for her, but if it meant she didn't have to deal with heartache for herself or Bryson, maybe it would be worth it.

Bryson's upset over Ryker not coming back showed itself in his refusal to spend any more time outside. All week, she'd asked him to come out and see the flowers with her, but he wouldn't. Going between the car and the house had once again become the extent of his time outside.

"Do you want to get pizza for supper? We can take it to Nana's and eat with her."

Bryson shrugged, which was just more proof of how much he was struggling with Ryker not stopping by. It made her angry at the man, but she knew she really had no right to feel that way.

He'd stepped in to help them out, but they weren't his responsibility. It wasn't like they'd been dating or that they'd even been good friends. After he'd finished the work on the yard, there was no reason for him to return. This had been inevitable.

There was nothing she could do but continue to love on her son and keep to their schedule, which included caring for Vivianne each day. It was oh-so-tempting to ask Michael about Ryker, but she hadn't so far, and she didn't plan to.

Later that afternoon, once Michael had picked Vivianne up, Sophia phoned in a pizza order for pick-up then got Bryson ready to go. She didn't really have the money to spare for pizza, but it was her hope that the treat would buoy his spirits a bit, and she knew that Nana would enjoy it as well.

It was drizzling a bit as they left the house, and Sophia couldn't keep from glancing at the flower beds. She'd taken pictures of the flowers earlier in the week and showed them to Nana. As she'd thought, the woman had been thrilled to see them.

Bryson climbed into the back of the car and buckled himself into his car seat. Sophia checked to make sure that he was secure, then they headed off to pick up the pizza.

After she pulled into a spot in front of the pizza place, she tried to judge if the rain was heavy enough that they should wait a few minutes before going in to pick up the pizza. As she looked around, she noticed Ryker's truck was parked a few spots down.

She glanced back at Bryson, glad to see that his attention was on one of the books they kept in the car. The large glass windows at the front of the pizza place allowed her to see that Ryker was inside talking to someone. She had a weird feeling in the pit of her stomach at seeing him again, and she knew that she needed to get out of there before Bryson spotted him.

After checking that Bryson was still focused on his books, Sophia looked at the restaurant one more time. Ryker was on his way to the door, so she knew it was now or never. Grateful that there wasn't much traffic on the street, Sophia backed out of the spot and began to drive toward Main Street. She would circle the block, and hopefully, Ryker would be gone by the time she got back.

"What about the pizza, Momma?" Bryson asked.

"We'll come back for it in a couple of minutes, baby. Why don't you tell me about your book while we drive?"

After she'd taken her time circling the block, Sophia approached the pizza restaurant again, slowing when she saw the rear of Ryker's truck as it pulled away. Normally, she wouldn't have tried to avoid a meeting with him, but she didn't think it would be beneficial for Bryson to see him. Especially not if they weren't going to see him again for a while.

No. This was the better way to handle things...she hoped. She might have made a mistake asking Ryker to come more deeply into their lives, but she didn't think she'd made one by keeping distance between them right then.

CHAPTER THIRTEEN

Ryker glanced out the pizza restaurant window as he waited for them to bring his order to the counter at the front. When he saw a car that looked like Sophia's, he headed to the door. As he pushed it open, the car began to back out of the spot, but not before he was able to get a clear look at Sophia behind the wheel and Bryson in the back.

Getting a glimpse of them like that, after resolving to stay away, had been a bit like getting a bite of chocolate cake after deciding to go on a diet. All he wanted was to see more of them. To talk to them.

Why had she driven away? There weren't any other shops or restaurants in the vicinity of the pizza place. She'd parked but then left without coming inside.

"Ryker Bennett?"

He turned away from the door, then walked back to the counter. "Do you have an order for Sophia Haldorson?"

The teenage boy behind the counter frowned then turned to look at some slips pinned to a board. "Yeah. I've got one for her."

"I'd like to pay for her order in addition to mine."

The teen looked puzzled. "Her order won't be ready for a few more minutes."

"I don't want to pick up her order. I just want to pay for it."

"Oh. I don't know if you can do that."

"What's the problem, Trev?" When a man in his twenties approached the counter, Ryker hoped he might understand the concept a bit better.

"He wants to pay for an order, but he doesn't want to pick it up."

The man looked at Ryker with raised brows. "I'm afraid I might need you to translate that."

"He's not wrong," Ryker said with a laugh. "I want to pay for my own order and pick it up. However, I also want to pay for a friend's order. She's a single mom, so I thought I'd pay for it so when she comes in to get it, it doesn't cost her anything."

"Ah. Gotcha. We can definitely do that for you."

"Excellent." Ryker was relieved when the man sent the teen into the back and took care of things for him.

Even though he'd stayed away from the pair that week, he'd planned to see if he could stop by the next day to mow again. But now having seen them briefly, he wanted to go by their place right then. But he had promised Michael he'd bring pizza back to the house for supper so he couldn't. He'd text Sophia later to see if the next day would work for her.

At least he felt good about having covered the cost of their meal. He knew that money was likely tight for them, so helping them out even just a little bit in that way felt good.

Back at Michael's, he carried the pizza boxes into the house, holding the door so Wolfie could follow him in.

"You're gonna wish you could eat pizza, Wolfie," Ryker said as he set the boxes on the table. "And you too, Vivianne."

"I'm hungry enough to fight either of them for mine," Michael said from where he sat, feeding Vivianne her bottle.

Ryker was a bit surprised at how well Michael was managing Vivianne on his own. But while he was doing good in that regard, Ryker could see that whatever had happened with Lani weighed heavily on the man. He wished he knew what to say to help him.

He'd been toying with the idea of going by to see Lani. Was she doing any better than Michael? Ryker didn't think he'd been mistaken in thinking that something more than just friendship had blossomed between the pair. He thought perhaps they'd each realized their own feelings for the other but were still oblivious to the other's feelings for them.

Sometimes looking at a situation from the outside provided clarity that being too close to it obscured.

"Is Vivianne's sleep schedule getting better?" he asked as he handed Michael a plate with a couple of pieces of his pizza of choice on it.

"Thanks." He took the plate and set it down on the end table beside him. "No two nights seem to be the same, so I can't really tell if it's getting better or worse. I think I've just reached a point where I've accepted I'm going to be without sleep for the next eighteen years."

Ryker chuckled. "My brother has two, and they're both sleeping through the night now. One is eight, and the other just turned eleven. I think you'll be fine in a few years."

Michael stared down at Vivianne. "Sometimes I wonder if I'm going to be able to be a good father to her. A single dad to a daughter? What do I know about girls?"

"At this age, boys and girls aren't really that different...body parts aside."

"Yeah, but how am I supposed to do ponytails and braids and...makeup?"

Ryker smiled at that. "You can learn those things. YouTube is helpful. Plus, you might not always be on your own."

"I was going to say that that was how I planned to live my life," Michael said with a humorless laugh. "But I had also planned to never have kids, and I've got this little one now."

Ryker found his thoughts drifting to Sophia and Bryson, and even Vivianne. It had been his plan to avoid being around children—especially young ones—and yet, in an effort to help his friend, he'd ended up with two of them in his life.

He was sure his parents would suggest that perhaps God was trying to say something to him, but he kind of doubted that. Why would God care where he worked or who he spent his time with...or without? Would God really care if he didn't practice medicine? Would He care if Ryker chose to not surround himself with children like he had originally planned?

If God hadn't cared enough to protect the children in the refugee camp, Ryker had a hard time believing that He cared much about the decisions Ryker had made in his life in recent years. Not that he'd say anything of the sort to his family. Silas might listen and try to reason a bit with him. Callie, however, would just flat out tell him he was stupid.

He'd never let on to Michael that he had once been an active Christian, attending church regularly and doing all he could to encourage others in their faith. But since the attack, he'd felt dead inside. It was the only way he'd been able to function.

Although his family would surely say he *wasn't* functioning as long as he was wasting his time mowing grass and chopping down trees. And not going to therapy.

"You okay, dude?"

Ryker looked up from his pizza. "What?"

"You seem distracted. What's going on?"

What *was* going on? Ryker didn't quite know how to handle the distractions he was dealing with. His dead emotions had been slowly coming back to life—starting the moment he'd held Vivianne in his arms.

The love he'd felt for his family had always been there, but it had felt muted while everything else had felt dead. But now, those dead emotions were starting to press up through the rubble of his life like fresh green shoots.

A part of him wanted to treat those green shoots like he did weeds that found their way up through the cracks in sidewalks or wood chips in a garden. Yank them out and throw them away.

"Just...stuff." Ryker wanted to confide in Michael, needing to unload everything without having to deal with all the input that would come from doing that with his family. But he wouldn't. It would require too much explanation and would likely change the nature of their friendship and work relationship.

"Women stuff?" Michael asked.

Ryker chuckled. "Nope. At least not in the way you're referencing."

"I feel bad that you've had to deal with all *my* stuff, but I'm not offering to do the same for you."

"You don't have to worry about that. I'm more than happy to help you out."

"I'd be happy to help you out too," Michael said. "Might help to distract me from my stuff."

"Most of my stuff is just related to my family. I'm sure you understand after what you've gone through with Taylor. My sister is being testy, and my mom is trying to run my life."

"Has your sister kept a pregnancy secret and dropped a baby in your lap yet?"

That made Ryker laugh again. "You definitely win the "best" sister award, I do have to say, but Callie can be a royal pain. She's been that way since birth, as best as I can remember."

"How old were you when she was born?"

"Three. Until then, my older brother and I lived in sibling bliss, having no clue about the terror that was going to be unleashed in our lives when Mom and Dad decided to have a third child. I think Silas was especially taken off-guard since he'd had such a wonderful experience welcoming me into his life."

Michael's brows lifted at that. "I have a feeling he might have a *slightly* different feeling about that."

"Maybe," Ryker agreed with a laugh. "But I still think Silas would say I'm his favorite sibling."

"I've been wondering what would have happened if there had been more than just the two of us. If there had been another sibling my sister could have chosen to give Vivianne to."

"Do you think she would have chosen them over you?"

Michael shrugged. "If they could read and deal with their life without her help, probably."

"I will say this now, and I'll say it every day from here on out: Vivianne is *lucky* to have you as her dad. There is more to parenting than being able to read. Don't sell yourself short because you struggle in one area. I would say this...Vivianne is better off with a parent who loves her and can't read than one who can read but views her as a burden."

A ghost of a smile crossed Michael's face as he looked down at the baby he held. "I do love her. I never thought I'd ever be able to trust myself with a child, but I can't imagine ever treating her the way my dad treated us. Never."

"That's because you're a good man, Michael." Ryker understood the man's uneasiness when dealing with Vivianne, so he'd do what he could to help shore up the man's confidence.

"Oh, by the way," Michael said, looking up at him. "Bryson asked me if you were going to come pick up Vivianne soon."

"And to think that at the start, he didn't want me to pick Vivianne up."

"He has definitely changed his tune." Michael paused. "He told me all about how you planted flowers in front of their house. And mowed the grass. And cut the bushes. And got them pizza."

"Wow. He's really gotten chatty."

"Took me by surprise since he hasn't said that many words to me...ever. But he's certainly become your biggest fan." Michael gave him a considering look. "Is there something going on between you and Sophia?"

"Nope. I'm not in a good place for any sort of relationship, and I get the feeling that Sophia isn't either."

"And yet you think I'm in a good place for a relationship with Lani?" Michael asked with an incredulous tone.

"Well, the difference there is that I think the two of you were moving towards something more than just friendship when Taylor dropped her Vivianne-shaped bomb into your life. I think it was more than just being a nice person that drove Lani to help you out."

"Why don't you think you're in a good place for a relationship?" Apparently he was going to ignore Ryker's comment on Lani.

Ryker considered just brushing the question off, but then he decided to give the man a little explanation. "I was engaged a few years ago, but my ex broke it off. Since then, I've not been interested in getting into a relationship again."

"Did that happen before you started working for me?"

"Around that time," Ryker said.

"So you just don't plan to ever get involved in a relationship again?"

Ryker shrugged. It wasn't that he didn't want to get married and have kids one day. That desire hadn't completely evaporated, but getting to the point of that happening from where he currently was seemed impossible, requiring so much emotional hard work.

"I mean, I guess I'm one to talk," Michael commented. "Since I never planned to get involved with anyone either."

The thing was, if he were in a better place, Ryker could see himself getting involved with Sophia. Well, if that was what she wanted. She really hadn't given any indication that she might be interested in that.

She was the opposite of Lydia in pretty much every way. But in his mind, that wasn't necessarily a bad thing.

In hindsight, after everything they'd gone through, he could see that while he and Lydia may have been on the same page career-wise, they definitely would have had struggles emotionally in their relationship at some point. And honestly, he wasn't sure that they would have stayed on the same career trajectory after a while either.

"Anyway, I told Bryson that maybe you'd drop by at some point."

"I had planned to go by and help Sophia out with her yard once a week or so."

"I feel bad that I didn't realize that she needed the help. That was rather short-sighted of me."

"You had other things demanding your attention," Ryker said. "So don't worry about it."

"So you're going to help Sophia out again soon?"

"That was my plan," Ryker said. "Honestly, I sensed that Bryson was getting a little...attached to me, so I wasn't sure that it was a good idea to spend as much time there as I had been."

"I guess that explains why he looked so disappointed when I told him I wasn't sure when you'd be by next." Michael frowned. "Like bordering on heartbroken. Maybe you keeping some distance came a bit too late?"

Ryker sighed. Was it possible that Sophia had also realized that Bryson was getting too close to him? Was that why she hadn't come into the restaurant?

Since that was what he'd been trying to accomplish, why did the idea that she also wanted distance between them make him feel bad? With all his experience, he should have known better. He should have realized that in drawing Bryson out of his shell, he was drawing the boy to himself.

He owed Sophia an apology. Both for allowing such a closeness to develop between them and then for backing away.

Maybe the reason Callie told him he was stupid sometimes was because he really could be. Of course, he hadn't ever been in this sort of situation before. Any kids he'd come in contact with prior to his trip to Syria had been patients during his residency or the children of family or friends.

"I think I may have messed up," Ryker murmured, as if saying it any louder would carry the words straight to Callie's ears so she could use them against him.

Rather than comment on what he said, Michael shifted Vivianne to his shoulder, rubbing her back when she began to fuss.

"I thought I was doing the right thing, but I think I went about it the wrong way."

He had approached Bryson using his previous experience with scared young patients in order to put him at ease, but it was clear from the start that Sophia and Bryson hadn't viewed him as a doctor. And why should they have? They didn't know his background.

"Well, there's no reason you can't try and make things right," Michael said.

"Except I think I should still keep my distance." Ryker set his empty plate on the couch beside him. "I should just never have gotten as close to them as I did."

"Do you think that Bryson would read something into you being around? Like is he going to ask if you're his mom's boyfriend?"

Ryker really didn't think that would happen. At least, not yet. If Bryson and Sophia really had come out of a cult, the boy might not even know what a boyfriend was. But that would change at some point. Especially once he started going to school.

"I think maybe I just need to tell him I'll be back once a week to do yard work. That way, he knows I'll be back, but I won't be there are much as I have been." Ryker grimaced. "It's probably what I should have done in the first place."

"Live and learn, my friend," Michael said with a smile. "I'll probably be doing plenty of that in the years to come, so I'm glad to have you trailblazing."

Ryker got up and went to the table. "Want some more pizza?"

"Sure."

After Ryker gave him a couple more slices, he got them both a couple of cans of pop from the fridge. "Want me to lay her down?"

"That would be great," Michael said as he lowered Vivianne from his shoulder.

Ryker scooped her up then settled her into the bassinet that sat beside Michael's chair. She wasn't asleep, so he turned on the mobile that hung above her.

Thankfully, they didn't return to the subject of Sophia and Bryson. Instead, they discussed some work issues ahead of the meeting they were having with all the employees the next day. The meetings were only held once a month, but they gave the employees a chance to air their concerns and hear any concerns that he and Michael might have.

Once they were done talking about the meeting, Ryker decided he should head for home. He put Michael's pizza into the fridge then, after saying goodnight, took his own box out to his truck.

As he drove to his apartment, he debated what he should say to Sophia. It had been almost a week since he'd been there, so maybe he should just see if it was okay for him to drop by the next day, then talk to her about his plan moving forward.

He'd just pulled into his parking spot at the apartment building when his phone chirped. Thinking it was probably his mom, Ryker climbed out of the truck and grabbed his pizza box, leaving the text to check until he was climbing the stairs to his third-floor apartment.

Sophia: *Thank you for paying for our pizza. You didn't need to do that.*

Ryker came to a stop mid-way up the flight of stairs as he read her message. Given what he and Michael had discussed earlier, he'd needed to do that and so much more.

You're welcome. I hope Bryson liked it.

Sophia: *He did and so did Nana. We went to the care home to have dinner with her.*

Ryker smiled as he imagined Bryson and his great-grandmother sharing a pizza. Slowly he began to walk up the stairs again, using his thumb to tap out a reply.

I'm sure you all enjoyed that.

Sophia: *Yes. We did.*

When he reached his apartment, Ryker let himself in then sent her another message.

I was wondering if I could come by tomorrow afternoon.

He pressed send, then waited. Since he was staring at the screen, he noticed when the three bubbles appeared. But almost immediately, they disappeared and didn't show up again.

Frowning, Ryker put his pizza into the fridge then went to sit on his couch while he waited for Sophia's response. He wondered if she was trying to come up with a way to ask him to stay away. If that was the case, perhaps he needed to give her a way out.

If it's not convenient, that's fine.

After more waiting, he glanced at the time and realized that it might be right around Bryson's bedtime. He hoped that was what was causing her delayed response, but he really had no idea what might be going through her mind. Clearly, he was out of practice when dealing with women. Or maybe it was just dealing with some-one like Sophia.

With Lydia, the woman never held back. She always said what was on her mind with seemingly no regard for how her words might make another person feel. Strangely enough, however, she seemed to be able to temper that when dealing with her patients. Still being straightforward with them, but doing it in such a way that the preg-nant women were receptive to whatever she said to them.

She and Callie were very similar in their direct, blunt interac-tions with people, which was probably why they got along so well. They'd been friends for years, and it had been through Callie that Ryker had initially met Lydia. It hadn't surprised him that the two of them had remained close friends after the breakup. They were essentially two peas in a pod.

However, when it came to Sophia, Ryker had never gotten the feeling that she was one who spoke her mind. Still, he hoped that Sophia would feel comfortable enough to do what was right for her and Bryson, regardless of how it might make him feel. Especially if they *had* come from a cult, it was important that she feel able to voice her opinion now.

Rather than continue to just wait, Ryker went to change into his workout clothes. There happened to be a hockey game on, so he watched it as he used the elliptical. He wasn't a huge hockey fan, but he enjoyed sports in general, so he tended to watch if a game was on.

He'd finished up and was on his way to the shower when his phone's text alert dinged.

Sophia: *I think perhaps it would be best if you didn't come by anymore.*

Ryker felt a little sick at her words, but he couldn't argue with her. *I understand. I'd still like to help you with the yard. You could just let me know when you and Bryson won't be home.*

Sophia: *You don't need to do that.*

Ryker ran his hand through his hair, then gripped the back of his neck. He completely understood where she was coming from, but the prospect of not seeing the two of them again made him sad. Sadder than it should have.

I know, but I'd like to.

Sophia: *It's just that I'm worried that Bryson has gotten too attached to you.*

You don't need to explain your reasons to me. If this is what you feel is best for you and Bryson, I will respect that.

Sophia: *But you've done so much for us already. I feel like I owed you an explanation.*

To be honest, I was kind of worried about his becoming too attached to me as well. I should have explained that I'd be back once a week rather than just disappearing the way I did. I'm sorry that my decision upset Bryson. I made a mistake.

Sophia: *I never envisioned where things would go when I asked you to speak with him that day. He responded better to you than he has to any man, including those in my own family.*

Ryker knew he shouldn't be pleased by that, particularly because Sophia was concerned about how things had developed because of that.

Sophia: *I know he'll be upset that he can't see you, and maybe that's not good either. I don't know what to do.*

That last sentence of hers reached out and tugged at his heart. He knew she was trying to do the best she could for her son, and he wanted to support her in that, not make things more difficult.

He stood there for a minute, mulling things over in his mind, knowing he needed to respond to her.

How about we let him know that I'll come by once a week to work on the yard? That way, he can still see me, but it won't be as much as it was.

Sophia: *I hate to ask you to do that. You've already done so much for us.*

Ryker reflected back over the time he'd spent with Sophia and Bryson. It was true that he'd done a lot for them, but what she didn't realize was that both of them had done a lot for him too. But how could he explain that without going into all the details of his past?

You're not asking me for anything. I'm offering. I enjoy spending time with both of you, so don't think it's a hardship for me to come to your place. It really, really isn't.

CHAPTER FOURTEEN

Sophia stared down at the words on the screen of her phone. Was it possible that someone else's message had somehow come through on her phone?

She had a hard time believing that Ryker actually *enjoyed* spending time with her and Bryson. Her own family didn't even seem to enjoy doing that, especially with Bryson. It was like it was just too much work for them to try and understand his issues.

But then there was Ryker...not just willing to understand and work with Bryson's issues, but actually enjoying spending time with them...him. *Him.* Sophia had to remember that this was about Bryson. Not her.

It was so very tempting to take Ryker up on his offer. Maybe one day a week would be better than nothing. And it would get Bryson used to Ryker only being around periodically.

As for her, it would probably be better if she didn't see Ryker at all. Since she was already experiencing feelings for him, it wouldn't help if she continued to spend time with him.

But this couldn't be about her. She just had to be strong enough to not let any of her emotions get the better of her.

If you're sure that would work for you, I think Bryson would be thrilled.

Ryker: *It would work fine for me. How about I come by Saturday afternoon?*

That would work.

Ryker: *See you then. Probably around 4:30 or 5.*

We'll be here.

Once the conversation was finished, Sophia lowered her phone into her lap and wrapped her hands around it. She pulled her legs up to rest on the arm of the rocker recliner she had settled in after Bryson had fallen asleep.

She hadn't turned on any lights in the room though twilight was descending on the town. The days were getting longer, but sometimes it was hard to tell since gray clouds hung low over the town.

It was at this time of day that she wished she had something to do to keep her mind busy. Being alone with her thoughts wasn't necessarily a good thing. She needed to find more to do in the evenings once Bryson had gone to sleep.

She'd filled pages of her journal. She'd spent time reading her Bible and devotional books, trying to find her spiritual focus again after it had been warped over the past five years. She'd also read a lot of fiction, but she needed to find more to do.

Nana had told her that she could decorate the house however she wanted, but she wasn't sure how to do that. From things Nana said, it seemed that she viewed the house as Sophia's now, but Sophia was reluctant to view it that way herself. She was sure that if— or when—that officially happened, the rest of the family would say she wasn't entitled to it.

And maybe they weren't wrong. She didn't know if she really was entitled to it.

But whose fault was it that she and Nana were close?

Nana had said on more than one occasion she felt like Sophia had been more like a child than a grandchild to her. They definitely shared a relationship that none of the others in the family understood.

Her parents didn't comment on it—at least not within her hearing—and she thought it was because they accepted their role in the closeness that had developed between Sophia and Nana. But Chloe and Natalie—especially Natalie—had gone on and on about it when Nana had told Sophia to move into the house after they'd come back from Texas.

Initially, they'd tried to live with her parents, but there had been just no room, and the noisiness had set both her and Bryson on edge. Nana's offer of the house had been a godsend, that was for sure. Especially since Nana wouldn't accept any rent for it.

She wished that she could find a way to make additional money during the evening hours, but she had no idea where to start. Since her main goal in life had always been to become a wife and a mother, she'd never really explored ways to make money beyond the job she'd had as a cashier.

A few nights earlier, she'd searched out *how to make money at home* on the internet, but nothing she found through the search had looked doable.

She dropped her head back against the chair then turned her head to look out the picture window that faced the front yard and the street. The streetlights had come on, casting pools of light on the ground.

As she watched, someone walked by with a dog on a leash. Maybe Bryson would like a dog. Even as the thought entered her head, she shook it right out again. She couldn't take on something that would require her to stretch her already thin budget.

And there was no guarantee that Bryson would even like a dog. They'd had dogs in the compound, but they certainly hadn't been pets. No, the dogs that prowled the compound at night and had been chained up near the entrance during the day had been guard dogs. Used as much to keep people in as they had been to keep people out.

She reached out to turn on the light and picked up her journal from the end table next to the chair. Opening it to the previous entry, she read it over then sighed. There was not much to add to it as it was already a recap of what was going on in her head.

It was a bit like she was chasing her tail, going around and around without reaching any solutions. Every time she wrote in her journal lately, it was always the same thing. Writing it all out again would just be a waste of paper and ink.

How she wished that she was more decisive like Natalie. Her sister would never be so wishy-washy. She went after the things she wanted aggressively, never letting anything stand in her way. And then there was Sophia...barely able to make a decision, let alone figure out how to move forward with her life.

Knowing she wouldn't be solving any of her problems that night, Sophia closed the journal and set it aside before picking up her phone. Without anything else to do, she opened the app to continue reading the book she'd started a couple of nights earlier.

For an hour or so that night, fictional characters would be the ones keeping her company. She could lose herself in their world and forget about her own problems for a little while.

"Is he almost here, Momma?" Bryson asked as he ran into the kitchen.

Sophia glanced at him, then turned her attention back to the potatoes she was cutting. "I don't know, baby, but I think he'll be here soon. Just be patient."

She realized that she'd made a mistake telling Bryson that Ryker was coming that day. It had just been hard to see the sadness on his little face when she knew that hearing that Ryker was coming would brighten his day.

All she hoped was that nothing came up to keep Ryker away. At least it wouldn't be anything weather-related since it had been a mainly sunny day. He hadn't texted to say he *wasn't* coming, so Sophia was fairly certain he would show up. She didn't think he'd leave Bryson hanging in that way.

"Why don't you keep watching out the window?" she said as she put the cubed potatoes into a pot of water and set it on the stove.

"Okay." He skipped out of the kitchen.

While she waited for him to yell that Ryker was there, Sophia stirred the ground beef in the pan on the stove. She wasn't sure if Ryker planned to stay for dinner or not, but she'd have enough food if he did. Shepherd's pie was a pretty basic dish, but she'd discovered that Bryson liked it, so she made it at least once a week.

That night she planned to pair it with some biscuits. Bryson liked the biscuits, too, because she would let him eat leftover ones with his beloved bananas and peanut butter.

She liked the dish because she could add vegetables to it, and Bryson would eat them. So she added peas, carrots, and corn into the ground beef and gravy mixture.

"Momma! Momma! Momma!"

Even without him saying the words, Sophia knew that the man of the hour had arrived. She pressed a hand to her stomach as butterflies came to life. For all the lectures she'd given herself about not getting excited about Ryker's visit, apparently, her emotions hadn't gotten the memo.

"Can I open the door, Momma?"

"Go ahead," she called back, knowing that he wouldn't ask to open it if it wasn't really Ryker.

She took her time stirring the meat mixture, her hand gripping the handle of the wooden spoon at the sound of Ryker's voice as he greeted Bryson.

"How're you doing, buddy?"

"I'm good!"

Sophia heard the smack of skin on skin and knew that the two had performed their greeting ritual. Picking up the dish towel that was on the counter, she rubbed her hands on it and walked to the door of the kitchen, knowing that the longer she waited, the weirder it would look.

"Where's your momma, bud?" Ryker asked as she walked in from the kitchen.

"Right here," she said. "Sorry. I was just stirring some stuff on the stove."

"It smells delicious." He gave her a broad smile, the skin crinkling at the corners of his blue eyes. "How've you been?"

"Good." She twisted the dishtowel in her hands. She'd forgotten how his smile and warm gaze made her feel. Or maybe she'd pushed it out of her mind in an attempt at self-preservation. "How about you?"

"Busy, but good. Lots of people wanting help with their gardens and landscaping."

"And then you have to come over here and do *more* work."

Ryker shook his head. "There's no *have to* about it. I'm here because I want to be."

"Surely you have somewhere you'd rather be."

"Not really. No birthday parties tonight, and when my family gets together, it's usually on Sundays."

"Same with mine. Big Sunday dinner after church."

"Loud," Bryson said as he reached up to grab her hand, forcing her to release the dish towel. "They're too loud."

"They certainly are that," Sophia agreed.

"My sister is loud," Ryker said. "The loudest of everyone."

"Does she be quiet if you ask?" Bryson asked.

"Nope. She doesn't listen to me."

"They don't listen to Momma either." Bryson leaned his head against her hand.

"Well, as long as you always listen to her," Ryker said. "That's most important."

"I do listen to her."

"Good boy." Ryker flashed him a smile. "Are you going to come help me outside today?"

Bryson's hand tightened on hers as he looked up at her. "I...I..."

"It's okay if you don't want to," Ryker said. "I'm going to mow the grass, so it would be loud anyway."

"I'll watch you from the window."

"Sounds good."

"You're welcome to join us for supper afterward, if you have the time." Sophia knew she shouldn't be prolonging their contact with him, but she felt like she owed him *something* for the work he was doing for her.

"It smells so good, I think I will."

"Just come back inside when you're done," she told him.

"Will do." He smiled down at Bryson. "See you in a bit."

Once he had gone back out the door, Bryson took up a position at the window. Sophia returned to the kitchen, going straight to the stove to stir the food. But she couldn't help but glance out the window to watch Ryker pull the lawnmower out of the shed.

It was great to see Bryson smiling so broadly, but would he keep smiling when he had to wait another week before seeing Ryker again?

With a sigh, she turned her attention to the food, draining the potatoes so that she could mash them. After they were done, she transferred the meat into the round dish she planned to bake it in then topped it with the potatoes. Once it was in the oven, she turned her attention to the biscuits she'd made using the recipe Nana had taught her all those years ago.

The meal was ready before Ryker had finished, but letting the food sit for a bit wasn't a big deal. Not that she really had any choice since Bryson had no interest in eating until Ryker came in.

"Let me just wash up, buddy," Ryker said when he finally came through the front door.

Bryson came into the kitchen and climbed up on his chair to wait. Since the shepherd's pie would still be hot for Bryson, Sophia lifted some out of the dish onto his plate to cool.

"Can I have a biscuit, Momma?" he asked as he gripped the edge of the table.

"Yep." She put one on his plate then poured him his milk.

Though she wouldn't admit it to anyone, it pleased her that Ryker felt at home enough to settle into the chair he'd used before without waiting for her to tell him where to sit. This time, because she'd already dished up Bryson's food, he insisted she take her food before he did.

"This is delicious," he said a short time later. "You like it too, huh, buddy?"

Bryson nodded. "I like potatoes."

"So do I."

Sophia once again ate in silence, listening as Ryker and Bryson talked about all kinds of things. On this night, Ryker also talked about Michael's dog.

"His dog is a wolf?" Bryson asked.

"No. His dog is a dog, but his name is Wolfie."

"Does he bite?"

"No. He's very friendly." Ryker leaned closer to him. "Do you know who his favorite person is?"

Bryson shook his head.

"Vivianne. He loves Vivianne." Ryker grinned. "When Michael puts her down on a blanket on the floor, Wolfie will sniff her head, then he lays down beside her. Here." He pulled out his phone and swiped at the screen then angled it toward Bryson.

Bryson's eyes went wide as he took in whatever was on the phone. "Momma, look."

Ryker held out the phone so that she could see the picture. Sure enough, there was a dog lying with his head close to Vivianne's. It really was quite a picture.

"Do you have a dog?" Bryson asked.

"No. I live in an apartment, and I'm gone a lot of the day, so it wouldn't be fair to the dog."

"Does Wolf...Wolfie stay by himself?"

"Sometimes, but there are times Michael brings him in his truck."

"Does he have to use a seatbelt?"

"Nope." Ryker grinned. "He likes to poke his head out the window when Michael drives."

"Momma wouldn't let me do that."

"That's because your momma's smart."

Bryson smiled. "She's the smartest. I love her."

Ryker looked at her then, and Sophia felt her heart speed up just a bit. There was affection in his gaze, and even though it was for Bryson, it did something to her too.

After she'd left the compound, she never imagined that there would be a man who would ever care for her son. His own father hadn't exhibited any affection for him.

If only she could have found a man like Ryker before she met Ezekiel. Of course, a man like Ryker wouldn't have looked twice at her. At least not one who didn't have an ulterior motive in seeking out someone like her.

Her stomach soured at the thought, and she shifted her attention back to her food. She'd accepted that the real danger of Ryker's presence in her life was to her heart. But it was a risk she'd have to take in order for Bryson to not just be happy but to grow and thrive from having a positive male role model in his life. One he actually wanted to be around.

And maybe once he was more settled in his life, he'd be more accepting of other men like her dad and brothers.

After they were finished eating, Bryson helped her dish up the brownies they'd made earlier, then she added a small scoop of ice cream to each plate.

"I love brownies and ice cream," Ryker said.

"Me too," Bryson agreed as he picked up his spoon. "Momma said everyone likes brownies and ice cream."

"I'd have to say that I agree. Brownies and ice cream are the best."

Bryson lifted a piece of brownie and stared at it. "I helped make the brownies."

"Good job." Ryker took another bite. "Very yummy."

The one thing Sophia really appreciated about Ryker and how he related to Bryson was how he gave such positive feedback and reinforcement. Bryson didn't talk about cooking as being women's work anymore, and she knew part of that was because Ryker had told him that men cooked too.

After they were done with the dessert, Bryson convinced Ryker to let him read a story to him. Sophia took advantage of Bryson's attention being elsewhere to clean up the dishes from the meal. There were enough leftovers that they'd be able to have it for supper again the next night.

When she was done, she went into the living room to find them sitting on the couch. This time, Ryker was reading to Bryson. He used different voices and sounds as he read, which Sophia knew was no easy feat, and yet he did it with ease.

This man... He seemed perfect, which made her wonder what was wrong with him. He really couldn't be that perfect, could he?

But if he really was that perfect, why didn't he have a girlfriend or a wife already?

She didn't have a boyfriend or a husband, but perfection was so beyond her that it wasn't even on the horizon. So far, she couldn't see any faults in him, but part of her hoped she saw some soon. Maybe it would help slow the growth of her feelings for him.

"I need to get going," Ryker said after he finished the book and handed it back to Bryson.

Bryson clutched the book to his chest. "Will you come back?"

"I'll be back in a week."

"A week?"

"Seven days. Maybe your momma can make a countdown so you can see how many days it is until I'll be here again."

Sophia nodded when they both looked at her. Bryson looked relieved, and Sophia hoped that this week would be better for him without worrying if Ryker would be coming back. Plus, it might help him learn how to count.

CHAPTER FIFTEEN

The next few weeks fell into a pattern of sorts. Ryker would show up on either Friday or Saturday to work on the yard, then he'd stay for supper.

Bryson was sad when Ryker left each time, but he dutifully made a countdown chart and then colored in the circles each day. It seemed to help him to have that to focus on. At least he wasn't as despondent as he'd been the first time around.

They filled some of their time with visits to Nana, and each Sunday, they went to her parents' place. Sophia wished that there was a place for Bryson to meet other children, but so far, she hadn't found a place that wouldn't cost money.

The one good thing that had happened over the past couple of weeks was that Lani had returned from Hawaii, and she and Michael had apparently worked things out and were now officially a couple. As a result, the not-so-good thing was that there were days now when Michael didn't need a babysitter for Vivianne.

Not a lot of days, but once a week or so, he'd let her know that he wouldn't be bringing Vivianne by. Usually it was on a Saturday, so she tried to use that day for grocery shopping and other errands even though she would rather have been earning money by babysitting the little girl.

Still, she'd been super careful with her money, and that, along with some good sales at the grocery store, meant she'd been able to set aside a bit. Whenever Nana asked how she was doing for money, she told her she was fine because the last thing Sophia wanted was for Nana to give her money when she already was giving her so much with the house being rent-free.

That week, Michael had told her that he wouldn't be bringing Vivianne on Friday or Saturday. Normally she would have been more upset, but Bryson had been cranky for the past few days. He wasn't one to be cranky for no reason, so she was worried that he was getting sick.

"My ear hurts, Momma," he said as she got him ready for bed on Wednesday night.

He hadn't had an ear infection before, so she wasn't sure what to do. It was already too late to go to the small clinic in town. After googling what to do for a possible ear infection, she decided to give him some medicine for the pain in hopes he'd be able to sleep.

As she lay there with him, waiting for him to fall asleep, she texted Michael to let him know that she was going to have to take Bryson to the clinic in the morning. Thankfully, Michael said it would be okay. That he and Lani would take care of Vivianne.

It was one more day without pay, and she wasn't sure how much it might cost at the clinic. She had the state insurance for Bryson since her income was so low, but she didn't know if there was any sort of fee that she had to pay out of pocket since she hadn't used the healthcare system yet.

Worry kept her awake most of the night, and Bryson woke a few times as well, crying because of the pain in his ear. He didn't even want to eat breakfast once they were up for the day, not even when she tried to tempt him with bananas and peanut butter.

She wanted to cry along with him, seeing him so miserable and in pain. She managed to get them both dressed and into the car, then drove to the clinic in town. Hopefully, they'd see her even though she didn't have an appointment. If they turned her away, she didn't know what she'd do.

Thankfully, they weren't sent away. Instead, after Sophia had filled out several forms, the nurse showed her to a room and said the doctor would be in soon.

"Will he hurt me, Momma?" Bryson asked as he curled up in her lap.

Sophia ran her fingers gently through his curls. "No, baby. He will want to look at your ears, though, but it shouldn't hurt."

She hoped that she wasn't lying about it not hurting. The last thing she wanted was to layer fear on top of the pain he was dealing with. It was bad enough that she was worried and scared. She didn't know how to deal with this. In the compound, if he'd ever been hurt or needed some medical help, someone else provided it for him—though never an official medical person.

As she sat there, holding Bryson close, Sophia realized that God had answered at least one of her prayers while they'd been in the compound. Each morning and each night, she'd prayed that God would keep Bryson safe and healthy. She'd known that if he had gotten really sick, there would be no doctor or hospital to care for him.

She had seen what had happened to others who had gotten sick or hurt there. Sometimes they were able to get better with the care they got from others in the compound. Sometimes...they didn't.

Bryson had always been on the small side, more fragile than a lot of the other kids his age. But thankfully, he'd still been relatively healthy.

So while she was upset that he was sick now, Sophia was very grateful that it had taken this long and was after they had left the compound that he had gotten sick enough to require the attention of a doctor.

When the doctor finally showed up, *he* was a *she* with a warm, friendly smile.

"So how are we doing today, Bryson?" the woman asked as she settled on the chair at the desk, then rolled herself a little closer to them.

Bryson lifted his hand and gestured to his ear. "Hurts."

"How long has it been hurting?" The doctor's gaze flicked to Sophia for a moment before focusing back on Bryson.

He shrugged, pressing further into her, so Sophia answered for him. "He mentioned it for the first time yesterday though he's been a bit out of sorts for a couple of days."

"Can I look into your ear, Bryson?" the doctor asked. "It will help me see why your ear is hurting."

Bryson's body tensed, and he tilted his head to look up at Sophia.

"It will be okay, baby."

"How about I look in your mom's ear first?" the doctor suggested. After Bryson nodded, the woman looked at Sophia. "Will that be okay, Mom?"

"Sure," Sophia said with a nod.

The doctor got to her feet, washed her hands, then pulled a black instrument from a holder on the wall. She fitted a tip to the pointed end, then sat back down and rolled her chair closer to Sophia, going to the side opposite where Bryson was sitting.

Sophia had to admire the woman's patience and skill as she explained to Bryson what she was doing as she checked Sophia's ear. By the time she switched out the disposable tip and approached Bryson, he was more relaxed.

The doctor checked his good ear first to let him feel what it was like before going to the ear that hurt him. He tensed up and whimpered a bit as she moved his ear around, but he didn't cry.

"You're such a good boy," Sophia whispered to him. "Momma's so proud of you. I love you, baby."

He gave a little sniff and clung to her more tightly. "Love you too, Momma."

The doctor put everything away, then rolled back to her desk. "On the info you gave, you didn't list a pediatrician for Bryson."

"No. I just moved back to the area a few months ago and haven't gotten him a pediatrician yet." Which she realized now was a mistake—yet another bad decision on her part.

The doctor made a note on the chart. "Unfortunately, we don't have a pediatrician here in New Hope, but I can give you some names for doctors in other clinics that aren't too far away." She paused again, her attention on the papers in front of her. "Is he up to date on his vaccines?"

Sophia hesitated, aware of where her answer might lead. "No. He hasn't had any vaccinations."

The doctor looked up at her then, her brows pulled together. "Is there a medical reason why he hasn't had them?"

There was no obvious judgment in the doctor's voice, but Sophia still felt defensive even though it really wasn't her fault. "No. We were just in a...situation where I wasn't able to get Bryson to a doctor for checkups and shots."

The doctor's brows rose at that, and she glanced briefly at Bryson. "Are you still in that...situation?"

Sophia shook her head. "That was in Texas. We're here now because I have family here."

"Good. Well, it's even more imperative than ever that you find a pediatrician."

All she could do was nod. It wasn't that she didn't want Bryson to have a pediatrician. It was just one more thing she had to make a decision on. Since he hadn't needed a doctor so far, finding one had been something she hadn't pursued aggressively. Especially because the doctors in Texas had said he was healthy, if a little underweight. But she would need to move finding him a doctor up to the top of her to-do list.

"In the meantime, there is a definite infection in the one ear, and the other is a bit inflamed as well. You'll need to keep an eye on them over the next couple of days. Often, these clear up on their own, and if possible, we prefer to let that happen. If it doesn't, we'll look at giving him some antibiotics."

"So what do I do to help him?" Sophia asked. "He's in pain."

As she listened to the doctor give her instructions on how to make him as comfortable as possible, Sophia felt overwhelmed. Not by what she had to do...she would do anything she could for Bryson...but that she was responsible for making sure he wasn't in pain.

What if she did everything, and it still wasn't enough to keep him from hurting?

Though he was almost too big for her, Sophia carried him out of the clinic to the car. Once she had him buckled in his seat, she slid behind the wheel and then just sat there for a moment, saying a prayer that God would heal Bryson and give her wisdom in dealing with him.

"Do you want some chicken nuggets and fries, baby?" she asked, looking back at Bryson.

He sat with a hand over his ear, but he still nodded. She thought he might as that was very much a favorite of his. So even though she really couldn't afford it, Sophia drove to the closest fast-food restaurant that served the nuggets and fries he liked.

Because there wasn't one in New Hope Falls, it was almost an hour before they got back home. She'd let Bryson eat in his seat as she drove back, hoping that once they were home, he might be able to take a nap. That they'd *both* be able to take a nap.

He didn't eat as much as he normally would have, but anything was better than nothing since he hadn't had breakfast. Once he had taken some more pain medicine, they laid down on her bed with several books.

Halfway through the second book, she glanced down to see Bryson had fallen asleep. Relief coiled through her. He'd eaten. He'd taken some pain medicine. And he'd fallen asleep. For now, she'd done all she could do for him.

Her own tiredness soon had her sliding down to rest her head on the pillow beside Bryson. As she closed her eyes, she began to pray again, asking God to heal Bryson quickly and to free him from pain.

Please, God, help my baby feel better soon.

~*~

"Hey there," Ryker said on Friday morning as he crossed to where Michael had parked his truck.

"Hey." Michael gave him a quick smile but didn't move from where he leaned against the door of his truck.

"What's up?" He glanced into the back seat of the truck and spotted Vivianne's car seat. "You have Vivianne today?"

"Yeah. Lani was going to watch her at the shop today, but she ended up with a potential wedding client wanting to meet with her at short notice."

"Sophia couldn't take her?"

Michael shook his head. "She called me on Wednesday night to say that she thought Bryson had an ear infection and needed to take him to the doctor yesterday morning."

"Did she let you know what the doctor said?"

"Yeah. They confirmed it was an ear infection. She said that he was in pain and kind of cranky, so I didn't want her to have to deal with Vivianne on top of that."

Ryker frowned at the idea of Bryson being in pain. He knew all about ear infections in children and the likely treatment the doctor would have recommended. Hopefully, Sophia had medicine to help with his pain.

Maybe he'd give her a call later to check on Bryson. And Sophia too, for that matter. From the times they'd spent together, he knew that she worried about Bryson a lot, and with him being sick like this, she was probably even more worried.

Yeah. He'd definitely contact her later.

In the meantime, he and Michael discussed what was happening on the job, sticking close to the truck since Vivianne was napping.

Once Michael had left to visit another site, Ryker returned to the crew working at the landscaping site. Unfortunately, he found it very difficult to stay focused for the remainder of the afternoon.

He debated just going over to Sophia's place. But in the end, he waited until he got home, then settled on his couch and sent her a text.

Michael said that Bryson wasn't feeling well?

It took a few minutes, but eventually, a text lit up his screen.

Sophia: *He has an ear infection.*

How is he doing?

Ryker leaned forward, resting his elbows on his thighs, his eyes on his phone screen.

Sophia: *He says it hurts, but the medicine the doctor said to use seems to help. At least for awhile. It wears off though and that's when he says it hurts.*

Ryker had a bunch of questions he wanted to ask her, but he had to trust that the doctor she'd seen had done their job and explained to her things to watch Bryson for.

Has he been able to sleep?

Sophia: *As long as I give him medicine before bed, he sleeps for a few hours. Definitely not as well as he usually does though.*

Ryker rubbed the back of his neck, then slumped back into the couch. *Do you need anything? I could pick stuff up for you before I come tomorrow if you do. Some bananas maybe?*

Sophia: *Maybe a couple. He hasn't been eating much, so the ones we had have gone bad and I haven't been to get to the store yet.*

Ryker frowned at her words. The little guy needed to be eating and drinking, but Ryker understood it could be painful to chew or to suck on a straw. He'd get the bananas, but maybe he could find some other things that Bryson might like that would still get some calories into him.

I can do that. If you think of anything else, just text me. I'll probably be by around 2.

Thankfully, they only had one job on the schedule for the next day, and provided it wasn't raining, they would be done with it in the early afternoon. He probably would have called an early day of it regardless, now that he was worried about Bryson.

His worry stayed with him as he got himself something to eat, then worked out. And then it followed him into his dreams, tormenting him with images of Bryson being deathly ill and Ryker unable to help him.

When he jerked awake, soaked in sweat and shaking with the scope of his helplessness, Ryker fought the urge to text Sophia to make sure that Bryson was still okay. He stumbled out of bed and into the bathroom to splash water on his face.

Right then, feeling so weak and powerless, Ryker resolved to call Nick and make an appointment to see him again. It wasn't the first time he'd said that over the past few weeks, but this time...this time he really meant it.

He left his bedroom and, without turning on any lights, made his way to the kitchen to get a drink of cold water, then went out on his balcony to breathe in the fresh air. Gripping the cool metal of the railing, he inhaled deeply, held his breath, then exhaled.

The night held New Hope firmly in its grip. There were no lights on in any of the houses across from his apartment building. The streetlamps cast yellow puddles of light on the ground beneath them. He heard a car in the distance, but there was no traffic on his street.

He felt like it was just him and the night in a battle of wills over who held the greater darkness.

Ryker tipped his head back to stare up at the cloudy night sky. The moon was there, but its light only shone through in the barest of streaks where the clouds were thin enough. He knew how brightly the moon could shine, and he'd seen stars glowing in the night sky like diamonds scattered across black velvet.

The light of the moon and stars was still there even when he couldn't see it, and he had to believe the same thing about moments like these when it all felt very, very dark. There was still light in his life, even in the darkness. Even when the clouds covered that light completely.

Shivers raced over his skin the longer he stood out in the cool night air. The sweat from the nightmare had dried on his skin, making him feel the chill right to his bones.

With a shove, he pushed back from the railing and turned to go back inside. He didn't know if he'd be able to go back to sleep, but since it was just after midnight, he needed to at least try.

As he lay under the blanket on his bed a few minutes later, trying to get warm, Ryker found himself praying. Something he rarely did anymore.

Once upon a time, he'd lived by the verse in First Thessalonians that talked about praying without ceasing. Throughout the day, he'd send up little prayers. If he was seeing patients as part of his residency, before stepping into the room, he'd pray for wisdom for himself and calm for the patient and their parents. Afterward, he'd pray for them regarding whatever concern they'd had.

Praying had felt like breathing to him. Something he'd done unconsciously but also with confidence in knowing that God was listening to him.

Until that day when he'd felt as if God had completely tuned him out.

What made him think that God was listening to him now? He could only hope that for Sophia and Bryson's sake, He was.

When another nightmare woke him just before five, Ryker abandoned his bed and began to prepare for the day. The sooner he got it underway, the sooner he could get to Sophia's to check on her and Bryson.

"Something wrong, man?" one of the guys asked when Ryker snapped at them yet again over something miniscule.

"Sorry." Ryker pulled off his cap and ran his hand through his hair before replacing it. "I've got some stuff on my mind. I need to be somewhere this afternoon, so I just want to make sure everything gets done."

"No worries." The guy clapped him on the shoulder. "We'll get it done."

True to his word, the job was done by one-thirty. After apologizing to them for his impatience earlier, Ryker made sure the site was good to go then headed for the grocery store in town. Thankfully, they had everything he wanted to take to Sophia's.

When he got to her place, he grabbed the grocery bags and got out of the truck. He hurried to the house, taking the steps two at a time before ringing the doorbell.

He'd thought she'd answer it fairly quickly, but when she didn't, he began to get worried. He was just about to try the doorknob to see if it was unlocked when it swung open to reveal Sophia in obvious distress. As he stepped into the house, he was hit with the scent of sickness.

"What's happened?" he asked as he took in the tears spilling down Sophia's face.

"He's worse." She stopped to take a gulping sob. "His fever won't go down, and he's been throwing up."

Fear wrapped its hand around Ryker's heart and squeezed. He felt panic flutter at the edges of his mind, but he fought hard to keep it at bay. He couldn't let it take over because someone needed him. *Bryson* needed him.

He could do this.

Taking a deep but shaky breath, he said, "Where is he?"

"In the bedroom."

With no regard for the frozen items in the bags he carried, Ryker dropped them on the floor and followed Sophia down the hallway to a bedroom, trying to ignore everything but his need to help Bryson. His gaze landed on the boy where he laid on the larger of the two beds in the room.

Sophia crawled up on the bed beside him, then looked at Ryker. "I don't know what to do."

Ryker did know what to do. He just needed to move past the panic building in him, competing for space with the fear. He *had* to do this. There was a scared mom and a sick little boy—both of whom had come to mean an awful lot to him—and he couldn't let them down.

The thing was, it wasn't just fear over being faced with a sick child that had wrapped itself around him. It was fear for what he suspected Bryson was sick with.

"Hi, buddy," Ryker said as he went to the edge of the bed.

Taking in Bryson's fragile appearance, his heart pounded hard as he glimpsed the rash on the one arm he could see. He used the thermometer he found on the nightstand, registering the temperature when it appeared in the digital display.

"When did you last give him something for the fever?" he asked, glancing up and seeing the fear he felt inside reflected on Sophia's face. He hoped he was doing a better job at hiding his fear than she was.

She answered that question and every other one he put to her without asking why he was asking them.

Unfortunately, none of her answers made him feel any better about what he suspected. It didn't make any sense, though, because what he suspected Bryson had wasn't all that common anymore. Regardless, his suspicions meant that he needed to get the little boy to the hospital.

"Sophia, I think we need to take Bryson to the ER."

Her eyes went wide, and more tears spilled out. "The ER?"

He decided not to scare her with the worst-case scenario that was playing through his mind. "Between his fever and vomiting, I think the ER is the best place for him. They'll have medicine to help with both those things, plus he's probably dehydrated because he can't keep anything down."

"Okay. Okay." She took a deep breath as she slid off the bed. "I'll take him."

Ryker touched her arm as she looked frantically around the room as if trying to figure out what she needed to do first. "I'll take you both."

"You will?" The relief on her face was immediate and immense. "You'll go with us?"

"Yes. Now let's get him ready to go."

While Sophia gathered up her things, Ryker put the items he'd gotten at the store into the fridge and the freezer.

Returning to the bedroom, he picked Bryson up in his arms, hating how frail he felt and how out of it he seemed.

Sophia picked up a bowl and towel along with her purse, then led the way out of the house, pausing for only a moment to lock the door.

"We'd better take your car," Ryker said. "I don't have a car seat."

She opened the door of the car so that he could put Bryson into his seat. When he held out his hand for the car keys, she handed them over.

"Go ahead and sit in the back with him in case he's sick again," Ryker said as he opened the other rear door.

Without saying a word, Sophia did as he suggested. It was only as he pulled away from the house that she spoke. "Is he going to be okay?"

Ryker knew better than to promise anything, but he found that he *had* to offer her some reassurance. "The hospital is where he needs to be. They'll take good care of him there."

He wished he could promise her everything was going to be fine with Bryson, but if what he suspected was true, there were no guarantees. And even if it was fine in the end, the road to get to that point was going to be bumpy.

CHAPTER SIXTEEN

Sophia tried to stop crying, but it was hard, especially now that they were on their way to the ER. This was beyond scary for her because it meant that Bryson was way sicker than she'd thought.

When he'd woken up crying that morning, it had been clear pretty quickly that he'd taken a turn for the worse through the night. Friday had been hard, seeing him so lethargic and not wanting to eat anything, still complaining about the pain. She'd done her best to keep getting fluids into him, and he'd been drinking in small amounts.

However, when he'd started vomiting around noon, she'd begun to get really worried since that meant even the little bit of liquid she managed to get into him was coming back up. And then the fever...when that had spiked, she'd started to panic.

She was sure it didn't say much about her as a mother that it had taken Ryker to get her moving in the right direction. But there had been something calming about his presence, even with all the questions he'd asked her.

As he deftly drove her car out of New Hope to the hospital in a nearby town, Sophia was glad that she could focus on Bryson. Although seeing him so lethargic and pale, except for the weird red rash that had popped up, was so scary for her. She could only hope that once they got to the hospital, the staff would be able to help him quickly.

When they got to the ER, Ryker parked the car in front of the doors then jogged around to lift Bryson from the seat once Sophia had unbuckled him. Sophia followed them into the hospital, glancing back at the car, uncertain if it should be left there. But she had bigger concerns than a towed car at that point.

When they reach the ER desk, Ryker began to recite a bunch of information to the nurse there. The woman stared at him for a moment before she began to make notes on a pad in front of her.

Sophia didn't understand everything Ryker said, but whatever it was, it was enough to have a nurse come to guide Ryker to a room.

"You'll need to fill out some forms," the woman at the desk said to Sophia.

Sophia reached out to grab Ryker's arm, fearful of being separated from him and Bryson.

"Bring the forms to her in the room," Ryker said in a tone that had the nurse nodding. "I'll make sure she gets them filled out for you."

Before Sophia had much chance to wrap her head around how Ryker seemed to operate so easily in the hospital setting, they were in a small room with a bed, which was where Ryker placed Bryson. A nurse appeared right away and began to attempt to put an IV in Bryson.

When he started to whimper without even fully waking up, Sophia wrapped her arms around him to keep him still while the nurse kept trying. The heat of his forehead against her neck was horrifying and made her want to cry again. She didn't think she'd ever felt him that hot before.

Ryker placed a hand on her shoulder, and she appreciated the comfort from that gesture even as she tried to offer comfort to Bryson.

When the nurse finally got the IV placed in his hand, she positioned a protective plastic covering over top of it then opened the IV line. After that, she took his temperature and checked some other things that were unfamiliar to Sophia.

Sophia felt a bit of relief as she watched the nurse. Like Ryker had said, they could help him here. They would make sure that he was okay.

He *had* to be okay. She just couldn't imagine any other outcome. Ducking her head, Sophia blinked hard to keep her tears at bay. She had to be strong for Bryson.

She heard someone else come into the room and looked up to see a nurse there with a clipboard.

"You need to fill this out for us," the nurse said.

Sophia nodded and reluctantly laid Bryson back down on the bed, then took the clipboard from the nurse. There was a pen trapped under the metal clasp at the top of the board. She moved a chair close to the bed so that she was within sight of Bryson, if he woke up. *When* he woke up... It had to be *when* not *if.*

"I need to go move the car," Ryker said. "I'll be right back."

She looked up at him and nodded. "You don't have to stay if you need to get back to New Hope."

"I do need to stay," he said. "I *want* to stay. I'll be back."

Though she'd felt obliged to say he could leave, she was incredibly relieved when he didn't take her up on her offer. His presence gave her strength, and she knew that if Bryson opened his eyes and saw Ryker there, it would make him smile. Hopefully...

After running her fingers through Bryson's hair and telling him how much she loved him, she turned her attention to the forms she needed to fill out. She was grateful that they hadn't made her leave the room to give them the information they needed, and she tried to fill it all out as quickly as possible.

She had to dig out her wallet to get some of the information for them, and some of the questions on the form were the same as what had been on the form she'd completed for the clinic. Would the staff here also zero in on the lack of pediatrician and Bryson's unvaccinated status? Probably. Still, she filled out all the information to the best of her ability.

Before Ryker got back, a doctor arrived. A man, this time, wearing scrubs. Sophia watched him warily as he approached the bed and greeted her, introducing himself with a warm smile. Before turning his attention to Bryson, he skimmed over the chart where the nurse had entered her observations earlier.

"Does Bryson have a pediatrician?" he asked.

This was asked without him even looking at the form she had just filled out. "No. Not yet. We just moved back here a couple of months ago."

The doctor nodded, then asked, "Has he had all his vaccinations?"

That was the one question she had hoped he wouldn't ask, but she had to be honest. "No. He hasn't had any."

Because she was watching the doctor, she saw his features tighten for a moment. "And the reason for that?"

Again, there was no judgment in his voice, but Sophia knew he wasn't happy with her response. "Bryson and I were in a situation where medical decisions were made for us." The doctor's brows rose slightly at that. "I had no say in his medical care. If I had, I would have made informed decisions when it came to his vaccinations."

"Are you now able to make those decisions for both of you?" the doctor asked, his voice soft.

"Yes. He's all mine now, and we're back here with my family."

"Good. I'm glad to hear that."

He asked her some more questions about what had happened with Bryson over the past week, then he turned to the nurse who was in the room with them and gave her some instructions. As the nurse got to work carrying out the doctor's orders, he swung back to Sophia and began to explain what he thought was going on with Bryson.

He hadn't gotten far with that when Ryker walked back into the room. The doctor glanced over at him then did a double-take, a smile spreading over his face.

"Well, Ryker Bennett, as I live and breathe." He held out his hand, which Ryker took, a look of discomfort clearly visible on his face. "How're you doing?"

"I'm good. You?"

"I'm doing well. Very well." The doctor looked at Sophia then back to Ryker. "Is this your girlfriend?"

Ryker shook his head without hesitation. "Sophia and Bryson are friends of mine."

"Oh well." The doctor cleared his throat. "I was just talking with Sophia about what I believe is going on with Bryson." He looked down at the chart he held. "It says you suggested a diagnosis when you brought him into the ER."

"Yes. Based on what I saw and what Sophia told me, I thought it was a possibility."

"I would have to say that I agree with you," the doctor said with a nod. "But as you know, we'll have to do a test to confirm our suspicion."

"What's wrong with him?" Sophia couldn't keep from asking, fear spiraling through her.

Both men turned to face her, and Ryker moved to her side, crouching down beside her chair. "We think that it's likely that Bryson has bacterial meningitis."

"Is that...is that serious?"

"It can be, yes," Ryker said, taking her hand in his. Ryker's words should have made her fear worse, but there was something calming about his presence. "But if it's caught early enough and treated promptly, patients can make a full recovery."

"Did we catch it in time?" Sophia asked, clutching hard at Ryker's hand. "Did I not see things soon enough?"

"You did fine," Ryker said, smoothing his other hand over hers. "The test they need to do is a lumbar puncture."

Even though Sophia didn't know what that meant exactly, it sounded worse than just a simple blood test. "What will they do to him?"

As she listened to Ryker explain the procedure, a heavy sense of dread settled over her. She pressed her free hand to her stomach as nausea rose up inside her.

"Will it hurt him, Ryker?" she whispered, feeling a bit dizzy at the thought.

"They'll give him an injection to numb the area before they do the procedure." Ryker seemed to be well-informed about it, so his assurance that it wouldn't hurt Bryson settled her a bit.

"Can I stay with him?" she asked, unwilling to let Bryson out of her sight unless it was absolutely necessary.

Ryker glanced to where the doctor stood watching them, then looked back at her. "Yes. You can be with him while they do it." He paused then said, "Do you have any questions about this?"

The only questions that circled around in her mind were one that she couldn't bring herself to voice yet. *Did I do something that caused this? Did I make another bad decision somewhere that has resulted in this?*

As Ryker got to his feet, the doctor said, "Where are you practicing these days, Ryker?"

"I'm not."

Ryker was a *doctor?* Sophia stared at the man as pieces of the puzzle began to fall into place.

"Uh...sorry about that. I just assumed..." The doctor's brow furrowed. "I heard about what happened in Syria. Glad you and Lydia were okay."

"Yeah. Me, too."

"So what are you doing if you're not practicing?"

"Working for a friend," Ryker said without going into more detail.

"You still have the touch, man," the doctor said, his gaze going to Bryson and then to her before landing back on Ryker. "You always were the best of us when it came to that."

"This is an exception," Ryker said with an edge to his voice that Sophia had never heard before.

The doctor didn't seem put off by it, however. "Well, if you do set up a practice, let me know. I'd love to be able to refer patients to you."

"I'll keep that in mind."

"Doctor Barkman," a nurse said as she came into the room. "They have some questions about the test you've ordered for Bryson."

The doctor clapped Ryker on the shoulder. "Take care and keep in touch."

Ryker nodded and stood watching as the doctor and the nurse left the room, then he turned his attention to Bryson. "Did they explain what all this is?" he asked as he gestured to the equipment now surrounding Bryson.

"Sort of," Sophia said, though she wouldn't remember most of what they said.

Ryker nodded. "Okay. The most important thing you need to know about at the moment is this." He moved to the IV stand. "This is dispensing fluid to keep Bryson hydrated as well as an antibiotic to begin the fight against the bacteria that's making him sick. Once they get the results back from the lumbar puncture, they'll probably change to an antibiotic that is more specific to the bacteria."

"Thank you for explaining all this to me," she said, then paused, biting her lip for a moment. "Did him not being vaccinated cause this?"

"He's not vaccinated?" Ryker asked, his brows drawing together.

"No." Admitting that to him was harder than it had been to the doctors. "Could it have caused this?"

Ryker seemed to be considering his words. "Though some vaccines can help to prevent certain types of meningitis, it still isn't a one hundred percent guarantee. There's no way to know for sure how Bryson came down with it. I think it was just an unfortunate series of events, and likely not something you could have prevented."

Though she knew that Ryker was trying to reassure her, it didn't stop her from still feeling responsible. Sophia bent her head, pressing the heels of her hands into her eyes.

She tried to keep the tears at bay, but her fear for Bryson and now feeling like his sickness was her fault was almost too much. Her bad decision making had already impacted him so greatly, and it was too much to bear that now his life was at risk because of what she'd done or not done.

"Hey." Ryker's voice was soft as his hand settled gently on her back.

She wanted to lean into his strength, but she couldn't. It was her fault that they were there, and she owed it to Bryson to be strong for him.

"Hey," Ryker said again. "I know there are no guarantees in life, but Bryson is in good hands here. He'll receive the best care possible."

Sophia lowered her hands to her lap, clenching them into fists. Looking at Bryson through watery eyes, she nodded, not confident that her voice would work.

"Why isn't he waking up?" she asked after swallowing a couple of times.

"That's mainly because of the dehydration and the fever. But it's not necessarily a bad thing. His body is fighting against the bacteria. Once the IV starts to deal with his dehydration and his fever begins to drop, he'll be more alert, but it might take a couple of days."

Sophia hoped that Ryker was right. She just couldn't let herself consider any other option.

Ryker moved a chair over next to hers, then sat down in it. They sat in silence for a few minutes, and Sophia leaned forward to take Bryson's non-IV hand. In direct contrast to the heat she'd felt on his forehead, his hands were cold.

She began to gently rub his fingers, trying to get them warm again, unnerved by how cold and lifeless they felt. "Why is his hand so cold?"

"That's not uncommon when a fever is present. Particularly in a child," Ryker explained. "The body does some weirdly effective stuff in its quest to fight off sickness."

Sophia continued to hold Bryson's hand between hers though she looked at Ryker. "You're a doctor?"

Ryker sighed before he nodded. "I'm a pediatrician, to be exact."

She stared at him for a moment. "I'm so glad." He lifted his brows at her response. "If you didn't have that expertise, you wouldn't have known what was wrong with Bryson."

He seemed to consider her words before responding. "I think you would have gotten him to the ER on your own."

Sophia hoped that was true. "Maybe. But probably not as soon as you did."

"It doesn't matter now. Bryson's here, and that's all that matters."

"Why aren't you working as a pediatrician anymore?" Sophia asked.

Ryker looked at her for a moment, then his gaze moved to Bryson. For a moment, Sophia wasn't sure he was going to answer her question, let alone respond in any way.

"When all this is over, maybe we can exchange stories," he said without looking at her.

"What?"

"I suspect you have a story about your and Bryson's life before you came back to New Hope." Sophia tensed at his words. "I have a story about why I'm not a practising pediatrician. When Bryson is better and back home, I'll tell you my story if you tell me yours." He glanced at her. "You don't have to agree right now."

Sophia was glad he said that because right then, she didn't want to share her story with him. She didn't want to see judgment on his face when she revealed all the bad decisions she'd made and how those decisions had negatively impacted Bryson.

"Right now, let's just focus on Bryson, and I'll do my best to explain things to you if you have questions."

"Thank you," Sophia said.

Ryker gave her a small smile, softening the tension on his face. "I am more than happy to help you with Bryson. He's...special."

That was something Sophia could absolutely agree with. But in that moment, she was also thinking that Ryker was pretty special himself. Thinking those kinds of thoughts might lead to heartache later, but right then, Sophia found she didn't care.

She was beyond grateful for Ryker's actions, and the fact that he'd been willing to risk revealing a fact about himself that he'd kept private in order to help Bryson, showed that he was a good man. Someone she was happy to know and happy to have in Bryson's life in whatever manner he wanted to be.

~*~

Ryker waited for regret to fill him. He'd known there was a chance that coming into the ER with Bryson the way he had would expose his background to Sophia. Of course, the risk had sky-rocketed when the doctor attending Bryson in the ER had been a former classmate and casual friend from Seattle.

Being outside of Seattle, he hadn't considered that he might come across someone he knew. But as luck would have it, his old friend had somehow ended up in the hospital closest to New Hope Falls that had an ER.

But the regret didn't come. Even though he wouldn't have thought he wanted to involve himself in a medical situation, especially with a child, he was glad he'd been able to in this case. Helping Bryson and Sophia brought on absolutely no regret. The only thing he would have changed would have been Bryson needing medical help, to begin with.

He wished that the little boy had never gotten sick at all. But since that wasn't something he could change, Ryker was happy to be able to use his medical knowledge to help them in any way he could.

Thankfully, the feeling of panic had lessened considerably, but the feeling of helplessness still weighed heavily on him. There was nothing he could do to help Bryson beyond what he'd done already. From this point on, someone else would be responsible for Bryson's care.

Ryker actually itched to be the one in charge of this particular case. He knew that Fred Barkman was an excellent doctor, but like he'd told Sophia, Bryson was special. He was important to Ryker. Just like the woman sitting beside him was.

The doctor came back into the room, giving Ryker a nod before focusing on Sophia. "After consulting with some of my colleagues, I've made the decision that it would be best for Bryson to be transferred to PNW Children's Hospital in Seattle."

"What?"

Ryker could hear the panic in Sophia's voice. He leaned forward and reached out to cover her hands where they held Bryson's.

Fred gave him a look before turning his attention back to Sophia. "He is stabilized for now, but he's likely going to need to be in intensive and possibly isolated care for the first phase of his treatment and recovery."

"What about the test?" Sophia asked.

"We'll do it here and send results to the hospital in Seattle as soon as we have them."

Sophia looked at him. "Ryker?"

"The children's hospital is the best place for kids like Bryson who need medical care."

"It doesn't mean he's worse," Fred said. "It's just that they are better equipped to deal with sick children like Bryson."

Ryker knew that this was the right decision from a medical standpoint. However, it was going to put him right back into a hospital he'd once worked in. Even if he hadn't known Fred Backman at this hospital, he *would* know people at PNWC.

Fred went into detail about how the transfer would take place. Ryker didn't say anything, waiting until the other doctor was finished to see if Sophia had any other questions.

"Can I go with him?" Sophia asked.

Ryker already knew that he'd be driving her car to the hospital regardless. He wasn't going to be leaving her or Bryson's side unless he had to.

Over the next several hours, the test was done, then Bryson was transferred to the children's hospital and settled into the PICU there. Those hours definitely had their ups and downs. Bryson had roused as they prepped him for the test, crying and scared.

So as Sophia had comforted him, Ryker had done what he could to comfort Sophia. By the time Bryson was in a room in the PICU, Ryker could see the exhaustion on Sophia's face. Her shoulders slumped as she sat down beside Bryson's bed.

He knew without asking that she planned to stay there with Bryson, probably for the duration of his hospital stay, if she could manage it.

As he observed Sophia, he started to worry about her as much as he was worrying about Bryson. She had a frailness to her that matched the fragility in her son.

He stayed in the room with Sophia and Bryson, stepping out only long enough to get them both food and something to drink. Not that Sophia had eaten much of what he'd gotten. Though to her credit, she had tried.

It was odd, being on this side of things...having knowledge of what they were telling Sophia but no real right to voice an opinion unless she asked him to. And she did ask him about pretty much everything, apparently choosing to trust in his medical knowledge.

By nine o'clock that night, Ryker knew he had a decision to make. Sophia was definitely staying at the hospital with Bryson, needing to be there for him in case he woke up. However, Ryker knew he needed to get some sleep, and that wasn't going to happen in a chair in a PICU room.

Plus, he couldn't risk having a nightmare while in the same room as Sophia and Bryson.

"Sophia," he said, drawing her attention from where Bryson lay sleeping once again.

He knew Bryson's lack of wakefulness weighed on her even though he'd explained that it wasn't necessarily a bad thing. But he understood. Though Bryson had never been a super active child, he also was never this still.

"I'm going to head back to New Hope."

Alarm flared in her eyes, but she didn't voice it. Instead, she just wrapped her arms across her body and said, "Okay. Thank you for staying with me today. I really appreciate it."

"I'm going to be back first thing tomorrow morning. Do you want me to bring anything from your house?"

She looked down at herself and frowned. It was clear she would have liked a change of clothes, but he doubted that she wanted to ask him to pick those out for her.

"How about I ask Lani if she'd be willing to pack up a few things for you?" he suggested, feeling fairly certain that the woman would help him out.

"If she would do that, I'd really appreciate it."

"I'll give her a call, and if you think of anything else that you'd like for Bryson, let me know."

She glanced at where he lay. "I think there are a few things he might like."

"Okay. I'll text you when Lani and I are at the house, then you can tell us what you'd like."

"Thank you," she said. "Thank you so much."

Ryker knew he needed to leave, but he approached her chair and dropped down onto his haunches. Taking her hands in his, he said, "Bryson is in the very best place for him right now. Try not to worry too much and get some sleep tonight. You need rest so that you're able to deal with everything."

She nodded, and from the tiredness apparent on her face, Ryker hoped that meant she'd be able to sleep despite the interruptions that would likely come as the nurses checked on Bryson throughout the night.

"I'm going to go, but text or call if you need to talk to me, okay? Don't worry about what time it is. Just call."

He could see the emotion on her face, and he wanted to be able to comfort her more, but that really wasn't his place. So rather than prolong his departure, especially since he wanted to make a couple phone calls on his way home, he gave her hands another squeeze then said goodbye.

Walking away from Bryson's room was the hardest thing Ryker had done in a very long time. It felt wrong, even though he knew it was what he needed to do right then.

CHAPTER SEVENTEEN

As soon as he got into Sophia's car, Ryker phoned Michael, putting the phone on speakerphone so that he could talk while he drove.

"Sorry to call you so late," Ryker said when Michael answered. "Hope I didn't wake you or the princess."

"Nope. You're fine," Michael assured him. "What's up?"

Ryker explained what had happened with Bryson as he drove out of the hospital parking lot.

"That's terrible that he's so sick," Michael said. "Is what he has contagious? Should I be taking Vivianne to her doctor? I don't suppose you'd know. Sorry."

"Actually, they said they wouldn't know if he was contagious or not until they got the test results. But because this developed after an ear infection, they think that's what caused it. In the meantime, it probably wouldn't hurt to contact her pediatrician, just to be safe."

"Okay. I'll do that."

"In the meantime, you'll need alternate childcare. Bryson will probably be in the hospital for a little while."

"Really?" Michael sounded shocked. "Is he like...really, really sick?"

"Yes. This is pretty serious, but the doctors are hopeful that he'll make a full recovery since they caught it in time."

"I'm so sorry to hear this has happened to him, and to Sophia as well. I know she dotes on that boy."

"Yes. Sophia is taking it quite hard. And that's the second part of my call. She's not likely to leave Bryson's side any time soon. I was hoping that Lani might be willing to meet me at Sophia's house tonight or tomorrow morning to pick out some things for me to take to her."

"I can call and ask her, if you'd like," Michael said. "Or would you rather talk with her yourself?"

"If you could call her, that would be great since I'm on the road at the moment."

"Sure. I can do that. I'll give you a call back."

Ryker let out a sigh as Michael ended the call. Though it had been a long day already, he kind of hoped that Lani might meet him that night. If she could, that would mean he could leave early the next morning to get back to the hospital.

Thankfully, when Michael called him back, he said that Lani would meet him at Sophia's in an hour.

"Thank you so much," Ryker said. "I appreciate her help with this."

"Please keep us informed about what's going on with Bryson. We'll be praying for him and Sophia."

"I'm sure she'll appreciate that."

"Take care, my friend," Michael said.

After he hung up, Ryker instructed his phone to call Sophia. When she answered after the first ring, he let her know that he'd be meeting with Lani in an hour.

"Do you think you'll still be awake then?" he asked. "So you can tell her what you'd like her to pack for you?"

"Yes. I'll still be awake."

From the sound of things, Sophia didn't seem to think she'd be able to sleep at all that night. He hoped that wasn't the case, but he understood why she might feel that way. Maybe he'd be able to encourage her to rest when he got back there the next day. He liked to believe that she trusted him enough to sleep, knowing he'd wake her if Bryson needed her.

"Okay. I'll have her call you when she gets to your place."

"Thank you for doing that, Ryker," she said.

"You're welcome. I'll talk to you in a bit."

He made it to Sophia's place with a few minutes to spare and used the key Sophia had shown him that was on the same keyring as the car to unlock the front door. As he walked into the house, he was assaulted again by the smell of sickness in the air.

While he waited for Lani to show up, Ryker stripped off the bedding and gathered it up with the towels that were on the bed then went in search of the washing machine. He knew he'd have to stay around a bit longer so that he could put the load into the dryer, but it had to be done. There was no way he'd let Sophia and Bryson return home to a house that smelled of sickness and that would remind them—most especially Sophia—of that awful day.

He'd just started the load in the washer when the doorbell rang. Opening the door, he found Lani on the porch.

"Thank you so much for coming," Ryker said as he stepped back to let her in. "Sophia needs some clothes, and I don't think either of us was comfortable with the idea of me going through her drawers to get them for her."

Lani smiled at him. "You're such a good guy, Ryker."

"I try," Ryker said. "I told Sophia that you'd call her so she could tell you what she wants."

"Oh, sure thing." Lani pulled out her phone. "Where's the bedroom?"

Ryker led her down the hall to Sophia and Bryson's room. "Sorry about the smell. Bryson was throwing up before we took him to the ER."

"Poor baby," Lani said with a sad frown as she looked around the room. "That can't have been easy for either of them."

"No. It was...difficult to see," Ryker confessed. "They were both in a bad state."

"It's hard to see people we care about in a situation like that." She held up her hand. "And don't even bother denying that you care about Bryson and Sophia. I'll know it for the lie that it is."

Ryker chuckled. "Okay. I won't say anything."

"Excellent. Now I'm going to phone Sophia."

He gave a nod and then left her to it, going into the bathroom to see if he needed to clean up in there. Armed with a spray bottle of bleach cleaner and paper towels, Ryker made his way through the house, spraying down any surface that Bryson might have come in contact with when he was throwing up. And even a few surfaces that probably hadn't.

"Well, it certainly smells clean in here now," Lani said when she came out of Sophia's bedroom a bit later. "I left the bag with Sophia's stuff on the bed. She also asked for some of Bryson's books. She said you might have an idea on those."

Ryker nodded. "Yeah, I do."

"I think that's it then." She slid her phone into her pocket. "Keep us up to date, okay?"

"I certainly will."

"And let Sophia know not to worry about Vivianne. Also, you don't have to tell her this, but Michael and I spoke about it, and he'll still pay her for the time she's off to take care of Bryson. We know she is reliant on the money Michael pays her to make ends meet."

"That's super generous of you guys," Ryker said. "I won't say anything to her about it, though, because I'm sure she'll protest. You can share that info with her when things have settled down a bit with Bryson." He walked her to the door. "Thanks again for coming out this late."

"It wasn't a problem, especially given the circumstances. Are you going back to the hospital tonight?"

Ryker shook his head. "I'll head back first thing in the morning."

"We'll be praying for her and Bryson," Lani said as she stepped onto the porch. "And we'll share with our group from church, so they can pray for them as well."

"Thank you. I'm sure that will be much appreciated."

It was only as Lani was walking to her car that Ryker wondered if Sophia had let any of her family know what was going on with Bryson. She hadn't mentioned anything about it to him, nor had he heard her make a phone call. Maybe she'd made contact with someone after he'd left.

While he waited for the laundry to finish in the washer, he went through Bryson's books, picking out the ones he knew the boy liked, the ones Bryson had read to him repeatedly. He took them into the bedroom and added them to the floral duffle bag that Lani had left on the bed.

He set the bag by the front door, then pulled fresh sheets from the hall closet and put them on the beds. Without knowing when he might get back to the house, he wanted to make sure it was ready for Sophia and Bryson when they were able to come home. Finally, the washer finished so he could transfer the load to the dryer.

By the time he got to his own place half an hour later, Ryker was exhausted. But he wasn't foolish enough to think he was going to drop into bed for a solid eight hours of sleep.

No, he'd come face to face with his worst nightmare that day: a sick child...a *very* sick child...and being able to do nothing himself to help Bryson except drive him to the ER.

He had frozen up, though, when he'd realized how sick Bryson really was. Sure, he'd managed to move past it and do what was required to help Bryson, but freezing up was unacceptable. He'd done a rotation in the ER. He knew that seconds could mean the difference between life and death.

Memories of the night he and Silas had witnessed an accident take place right in front of them flooded his mind. Silas had already been working in the ER, and as soon as he'd seen the accident happen, he'd pulled over and gotten out of the car, telling Ryker to call 911, before he took off running to where the cars had come to rest. There had been absolutely no hesitation in Silas' actions.

Ryker had done what Silas had asked then had joined him at the accident to see if he could help too. He wanted—needed—to get back to the confidence he'd had in his abilities that he'd had before what had happened in Syria. He wanted to get back to believing that he could help in any situation he was presented with.

The fact that he'd gotten past his initial fear and panic with Bryson was a step in the right direction. Well, he was sure that's what his therapist would say anyway.

The problem was that his brain was going to treat it as just another excuse to bring up other memories from when he'd experienced that feeling of panic followed by helplessness. And he had no doubt that no matter his exhaustion that night, the nightmares were going to come.

Right then, however, Ryker was experiencing something new. The desire to just get the night behind him. To crawl into bed, knowing full well the nightmares would come, and just not caring. He wanted to get what hours of sleep the nightmares would allow and then get back to the hospital to be with Sophia and Bryson.

To that end, he skipped his workout and went to take a quick shower, then fell into bed. As he lay there, staring up at the ceiling, he found himself sending up a prayer for Bryson and Sophia. During his residency, he'd seen plenty of parents dealing with sick children, and his heart had always gone out to them.

This was the first time though, that the child who was sick also held a piece of his heart. He'd tried to reassure Sophia that everything would be okay, but he knew better than most, that things could take a turn for the worse.

Don't let me have lied to her. Please, God, let Bryson be okay.

It took him awhile to fall asleep, and as he'd expected, the nightmares came, dragging him down into the depths of despair before releasing him to consciousness.

Sitting on the edge of his bed, Ryker took several deep breaths and tried to get his heart rate to settle back down. Though his sleep had been fractured, he'd managed to get five hours of sleep in total, so he was going to call it a win for the night.

He took another shower, then got dressed before making himself some coffee, knowing he'd need several cups to make it through the day ahead. It was still too early to head to the hospital, even with an hour or so drive, but he decided to leave anyway.

Once he made it to Seattle, he found a drive-thru fast-food restaurant and picked up an assortment of breakfast items in hopes that one of them would appeal to Sophia. He'd eat whatever she didn't.

He'd stuck in a banana and a container of peanut butter just in case Bryson felt like eating. Though he hoped he did, Ryker also knew that Bryson was a very sick little boy, and it might be awhile before he wanted to eat his favorite snack.

Ryker only stuck the peanut butter and banana in because if, by some miracle, Bryson *did* feel like eating, that particular combination was sure to make him happy. And if there was something Ryker really wanted to see that morning, it was a smile on the little boy's face.

Thankfully, visiting hours had started by the time he finally got to the hospital. He made sure he had his visitor badge on—the one they'd done up for him the previous day after he and Sophia had arrived at the hospital—then made his way into the building, juggling the duffle bag, the bag of food, and the tray of drinks.

When he got up to the unit where Bryson's room was located, several nurses greeted him by name. Well, by the name *they* knew him as.

"Hey there, Doctor Bennett," one of the middle-aged nurses said with a warm smile. "Haven't seen you around in ages. How's it going?"

"It's going fine, Dianna," he replied as he stopped walking, knowing it was only polite to engage in a bit of conversation with her. "How are you doing?"

The woman had been the PICU supervisor even back when he'd been working in the hospital, and he had always enjoyed working with her. She was professional but also warm and friendly. Parents and patients always responded well to her comforting nature.

"Are you working here again?" she asked, her gaze going to the badge he wore.

"Nope. I'm here as a friend of a patient, not as a doctor."

"Ah. Well, lucky friend," she said with a smile. "You've always been a favorite doctor among the kids. Who're you here with?"

"Bryson Haldorson," he said. "He just came in last night with a possible meningitis diagnosis."

A look of concern crossed her face, but Ryker knew better than to ask her for any details. He'd get them soon enough when he had a chance to talk to Sophia.

"He still in the same room?"

"Yes." Her brow furrowed as she hesitated before saying, "If you could get the boy's mother to rest at some point today, it would be a good thing. She looks like a stiff breeze could blow her over."

Ryker nodded. "I suspected she wouldn't get much rest last night. I'll see what I can do."

"Is she your...girlfriend?" He knew why the question was asked hesitantly. If he'd still been working as a doctor there, it would have been out of line. But since he wasn't there in a professional capacity, it was more acceptable.

"No. Not a girlfriend. Just a close friend."

"Okay. Well, if you could help her out, that would be a good thing for her and for Bryson."

"Definitely," he agreed. "I did bring her breakfast, so I'll get in there and see how they're doing."

"So nice to see you again, Ryker," Dianna said. "Don't be a stranger."

If only he could be, he thought as he headed to the door of Bryson's room. From the moment he stepped through the door, he could see why Dianna had been concerned.

Though Sophia smiled when he walked in, she looked pale and exhausted. He returned her smile, then looked at the bed where Bryson lay, his eyes closed, presumably sleeping.

"How's he doing?" he asked as he set the bag with her things down on a chair near the window. He put the bag of food on the small table next to the chair. His fingers itched to check the chart, but he didn't.

"They said he's producing good amounts of urine now, so they're not concerned about dehydration."

"Has he been awake?" he asked as he moved to stand next to the bed, categorizing the boy's appearance.

He was still frail-looking, but at least the sunken look and the dark circles under his eyes weren't quite as stark as they'd been when Ryker had seen him at the house the day before.

"Yes. He woke up twice through the night, and he did throw up a couple of times, but his fever isn't as high as it was."

Ryker ran his gaze over the monitors, glad to see that the numbers indicated the boy was stable. He looked back at Sophia. "Has the doctor been by yet?"

She shook her head. "Just the nurses."

"The doctor—or maybe several doctors—will be by sometime this morning to check Bryson over and to talk to you." He moved back to where he'd set the bag of food. "But first, let's have something to eat."

As he pulled the food out of the bag, Sophia got up and came to the table. She peered down at the food. "You've brought a lot."

"I wasn't sure what you might like."

"What do you like?" Sophia asked as she glanced up at him, her light eyes framed by a sweep of dark lashes.

"I like it all, so you pick what you want to eat."

With tentative movements, she picked up one of the hash browns, and then her fingers rested for a moment on the pancakes.

"We can save the pancakes for Bryson," Ryker said, though he wasn't sure the boy would be up to eating just yet.

She looked up at him, her eyes bright with tears. "Thank you."

After that, she picked up a wrapped breakfast sandwich.

"I wasn't sure what you'd like to drink, so I got both apple and orange juice as well as a smoothie. I didn't know if you'd like coffee."

"Did you want the smoothie?" she asked.

"Nope. I have a travel mug of coffee." He worked the smoothie cup free from the tray and held it out to her. "Does Bryson like apple or orange juice?"

"He'll drink both, though he seems to like orange juice a bit better," she said as she sat down on a chair next to the small table.

"We'll leave them for him along with the pancakes." He went and got his travel mug from the duffle bag, pulling out the bananas and peanut butter. As he set them on the table, he said, "I brought these for him too."

Sophia's gaze moved to the items, and he could see that tears were once again threatening to fall. "Thank you, Ryker. You've done so much for us. For him. How can we ever repay you?"

Setting the items he'd chosen for his breakfast along with his travel mug on the table, Ryker settled in the chair opposite Sophia. "I don't expect you to repay me, Sophia. I...care about the two of you, and because of that, I *want* to help you."

Without looking at him, she broke off a small piece of the hash brown and put it in her mouth. Ryker was glad to see her eating, and he hoped that the doctor wouldn't show up until after she was done. Then once the rounds were done, he planned to get her to rest.

In between bites, he began to tell her a bit about when he'd worked there at the hospital. It seemed to be a good distraction for her, and for some reason, the idea that she might like to learn more about him was appealing. Especially since his curiosity about *her* was growing by leaps and bounds.

He knew he should be more wary, but he was being drawn further and further into their lives by things beyond his control. Sure, he could have just dropped them off at the ER the day before and left them there, but if he'd have done that, he wouldn't have been able to live with himself.

"Have you let your family know about Bryson?" he asked when they'd finished eating.

Sophia's shoulders slumped as she sighed. "No. Not yet."

"Why not?"

She met his gaze for a moment before looking back down at her hands. "I don't want to worry them."

"But they're your family. Part of their job is to worry about you." He certainly gave his family plenty to worry about, and he'd been worried about each of his family members at different times in his life.

"I've already given them a lifetime of worry," she murmured. "I don't want to add to it."

"What about Bryson's father?" Ryker knew he probably shouldn't be pushing, but...well, he was curious. And he'd moved to the point where he'd answer any question she put to him. Which was more than he'd do for anyone else.

Her features tightened as her gaze shifted to Bryson. "He's dead."

"Should I offer my condolences on that?" Ryker asked.

She looked at him and frowned. "No. It's for the best."

He'd suspected that that was the case, but having it put so bluntly left him speechless for a moment. Thankfully, he was saved from formulating a response by the arrival of the doctor with three residents in tow.

Ryker groaned inwardly at the sight of Doctor Ellis, a man he knew quite well from his own time as a resident at the hospital. His reaction was selfish, though, because he knew from experience that the man was the best doctor at the hospital. The older man's steely gray gaze swept the room, freezing when it landed on Ryker. His bushy brows jerked up as he stepped closer to where they sat.

"Doctor Bennett," he said as he held out his hand. "This is most unexpected."

"Good to see you again," Ryker said as he got to his feet and shook the doctor's hand. "I'm here as a friend of the family. This is Sophia Haldorson, Bryson's mother."

With a nod, he turned to introduce himself to Sophia, giving her his full attention. Ryker sat back down in his chair while Sophia walked to the bed, where she took Bryson's hand. He listened as the doctor interacted with Sophia and the residents.

At one point, Bryson stirred and began to cry. Ryker got to his feet and moved to stand beside Sophia as she bent over to console him.

"You're okay, baby. Momma's here."

Doctor Ellis waited patiently—the man's patience was endless— as Sophia comforted Bryson.

"Look who's here," Sophia said, then moved back a bit so that Bryson could see Ryker.

"Ryker." A teeny-tiny smile lifted the corners of his mouth.

"Hi, buddy."

"Do you like Ryker?" Doctor Ellis asked as he moved closer to Bryson.

Bryson shifted his gaze warily then gave a small nod that made him wince a bit. All his movements were sluggish and lethargic still. "He's nice."

"I happen to agree with you," the older doctor said with a smile and a wink at Ryker.

Ryker couldn't deny that seeing that smile from Bryson had loosened a knot of tension in his stomach he hadn't even really been aware of. He lingered near the bed with Sophia as the doctor finished up his time with Bryson. Doctor Ellis was very calming, even though he wasn't able to tell Sophia what she wanted to hear: that Bryson would be just fine.

So much could go wrong with bacterial meningitis. It would be a few days before they'd know for sure that Bryson was out of the woods, and Ryker prayed that he'd be one of the fortunate ones. Because he was a fragile boy to start with, Ryker knew that the medical staff would err on the side of caution when it came to his care.

One thing he knew for sure, he'd be talking to Sophia about getting Bryson a pediatrician. If Silas was correct about their past, he knew it wasn't her fault that Bryson was had never received proper medical care, but that was something that needed to be rectified.

After the doctor had led his little posse out of the room, Ryker turned his attention back to Bryson.

"Are you hungry?" Sophia asked as she perched on the edge of his bed. "Ryker brought some bananas and peanut butter."

"Really?" Bryson looked at him with half-closed eyes, not even trying to sit up. Ryker was sure he was going to fall back asleep in a matter of minutes.

"Really," Ryker assured him. "The bananas and peanut butter were lonely for you, so I brought them along."

He knew that he had to be careful with the peanut butter since they didn't know if anyone else on the unit had an allergy, which was why he'd brought a plate and knife from home along with a pack of wipes. It was just that if Bryson was resistant to eating, he hoped that the bananas and peanut butter would entice him to eat.

"Do you want me to cut some up for you?" Ryker asked. "There's also pancakes."

Bryson just stared at him as if trying to completely understand his words. Though he'd been hoping that he might be able to entice the boy to eat, it was pretty clear it was too soon. Bryson's gaze shifted to Sophia, and he blinked slowly before saying, "Tired, Momma."

Ryker heard Sophia take a quick breath, then she leaned over to press her forehead to the side of Bryson's head.

"Go to sleep, baby," she murmured. "I'll be here when you wake up."

Ryker felt like his heart was being squeezed with emotion. He had to look away from the pair because the pain inside him was overwhelming. There was nothing he could do to spare either of them from what lay ahead, though he wished with all his heart that he could.

The helpless feeling was back again, and Ryker found that he wanted to rage against it. He didn't want to feel helpless anymore. He didn't want to feel like there was nothing he could do to help them.

But the truth of the matter was that there wasn't anything he could do to help Bryson. At most, he could be a support for him and Sophia. But there was nothing he could do to make sure that Bryson recovered fully.

It made him want to gather them both into his arms and hold them tight. But that wasn't something he could do. So he stood there with his hands fisted at his side, watching Sophia be the strength her son needed.

CHAPTER EIGHTEEN

Sophia woke with a start, jerking upright in the armchair she'd apparently fallen asleep in, grateful that the room had comfortable furniture for the families of sick children. The room almost seemed like a hotel room—until you saw the hospital bed.

Glancing around, she noticed a nurse was in the room speaking with Ryker. She blew out a breath and rubbed her face. She was so tired. More exhausted than she'd ever been before. But considering she hadn't slept more than a couple of hours in a row since Bryson had been admitted, that wasn't too surprising.

Getting to her feet, she moved to stand next to Bryson's bed, happy to see that he was awake. In the three days since he'd been admitted, he'd shown some signs of improvement, but it had been slow going. She'd thought that once the fever had gone down, everything would be better, but then it had gone up again.

The only area they hadn't had a set back in was the dehydration he'd been experiencing on admission. She'd been glad that even though he wasn't drinking as much as he should have been or when he'd thrown up again, she didn't have to worry about him getting dehydrated because of the IV fluids he was receiving.

"Everything okay?" she asked, directing her question to Ryker.

It seemed that the staff now understood that she would turn to Ryker first with her questions if he was around. It wasn't that she didn't trust the nurses and doctors. She just trusted Ryker *more*.

"They're going to be coming to draw blood soon."

"I can still stay with him, right?" He'd had a couple of blood draws so far, and neither of them had been great. She wasn't sure which of them had been more upset by them.

He nodded. "It's best that you do."

"And you'll be here too?"

236 · KIMBERLY RAE JORDAN

"Of course."

Sophia had a moment of apprehension, worried that she was expecting too much of Ryker. He'd gone over and above what anyone should have had to for someone that they weren't even related to.

"If you need—" A look from Ryker stopped her words. She bit her lip to keep from saying anything further.

The fact was, however, that he'd spent a lot of time at the hospital with them. She had no idea what Michael was doing since for the past two days Ryker had been at the hospital each day by three o'clock. Clearly, he wasn't putting in the full day of work he usually did.

She'd finally let her family know what was going on, and while her parents had come up to the hospital earlier that day, they hadn't stayed very long. Nana had been extremely worried and had voiced more than once that she wished she could come to see them. Unfortunately, having to use a wheelchair for mobility made it nearly impossible for her to visit.

When the nurse left the room, Sophia tried to shake off her tiredness as she moved closer to Bryson. He was dozing again after having been awake for a little while. She wasn't used to him sleeping so much, but Ryker assured her that extra sleep was a good thing at this point. But no matter how many times he told her that—and it had been several—she just couldn't seem to grasp the truth of what he said.

The person coming to do Bryson's blood draw arrived just as Ryker's phone rang. He moved closer to the window to answer it while Sophia prepared to keep Bryson from getting too upset. She wasn't sure why they were drawing his blood again, but they'd said something about checking some levels.

She wanted to worry, but Ryker said it was just routine. So, hopefully, he was right.

"It's okay, baby," Sophia murmured as she wrapped her arms around Bryson when he began to get agitated when he spotted the lab technician.

The technician was a soft-spoken woman who, from what Sophia could see, was trying her best not to traumatize Bryson further. Unfortunately, Bryson had already endured so much over the past few days that he wasn't calm about anything anymore.

When his whimpers turned to cries, Sophia heard Ryker say, "Mom, I've got to call you back." She felt Ryker at her side, his arms wrapping around her and his hand cupping the back of Bryson's head. "Hey, buddy. It's going to be okay."

Bryson looked up at them both, his eyes wet with tears. Sophia's heart broke, and she couldn't help but slump against Ryker.

"It hurts," Bryson whispered in a shaky voice.

"I know, buddy," Ryker said. "But Gina is good at her job. If you hold still, it won't hurt as much. You can do that. I know you can."

Bryson blinked a couple of times before he nodded and lowered his head to rest against Sophia again. Ryker plucked the stuffed animal he'd brought for Bryson from his pillow and settled it against Bryson's chest.

He wrapped a thin arm around it, and as Gina began to do what she needed to with his other arm, Sophia sang softly to Bryson. It was a song that Nana had sung to her as a little girl.

Be not dismayed whate'er betide,
God will take care of you;
Beneath his wings of love abide,
God will take care of you.

She felt his body relax against her, save for a slight tensing when the technician inserted the needle into his arm. It was all she could do not to tense in sympathy with him.

When it was all done and the technician was gone, Ryker let go of them and moved to the other side of the bed. "You did so well, buddy. I'm proud of you."

He held out his fist close to where Bryson's hand was. It meant Bryson didn't have to lift his too far to give Ryker a tiny fist bump.

As Sophia watched Ryker interact with Bryson, the crush she'd had on the man had blossomed into something so much more. He should have been too good to be true, and maybe he was. Still, she refused to believe that he hid any sort of ugliness beneath his handsome exterior the way that Ezekiel had. Which, given how badly her track record was in judging men, probably made her a fool.

But as long as he was there for Bryson, she'd accept that character assessment of herself. A fool in love...because there was no denying that her emotions were fully engaged in this man. But he would never know. No one would. Her mistakes in the past hadn't been in her feelings but in revealing them. In letting them dictate her choices. *That* would be the mistake she wouldn't repeat.

He might be a good man, but he'd never be *her* man.

Ryker was a *doctor*, even if he wasn't practicing currently, which meant that he was far above her. A doctor needed someone who could match his intellect, and that certainly wasn't her.

Sophia had never dreamed of being the wife of a man like Ryker. She'd only hoped that she could find a man who would love her. A man who would care for his family the way her father had.

And she could see that while Ryker might be working a simple job, he was not a simple man. He was someone with incredible knowledge and, from what she'd heard while they'd been in the hospital, was also very well-respected.

She had no idea what the staff thought of his presence in the room with her and Bryson, but it probably wasn't that they were a couple. Though she didn't want to, she knew that she needed to encourage Ryker to get back to his life. The life she was sure he'd put on hold in order to be there with them.

From what she had gathered, though Bryson wasn't completely out of the woods, he was at least headed in the right direction. She didn't need Ryker to be there every day, helping her understand what the doctors and nurses were saying.

She knew that other families who had children in the hospital didn't have someone with medical experience like Ryker running interference for them. They asked their questions of the nurses and doctors if they didn't understand. That was what she needed to do.

Be the adult her age said she was and deal with this situation on her own.

"I need to go make a phone call," Ryker said, drawing her thoughts from...well, him. "I'll be back in a few minutes."

She watched him go, accepting that the thing she'd resolved to never want in her life again was becoming something her heart longed for. But accepting it didn't mean she was going to do anything about it. Her brain was holding strong so far. Not only was it reminding her of what had gone wrong in the past, but it was also telling her that Ryker was someone she didn't have a chance with. She needed to put some distance between them before she completely broke her own heart.

As she sank down into the chair beside Bryson's bed, taking his small hand in hers, she wished more than anything that they were home. She missed their little house. She missed Bryson running into the kitchen as she cooked, chattering on about one thing or another. She missed seeing him move around with energy and life.

But she knew that beyond all that, she needed to just be thankful that God had heard the prayers she'd cried, asking Him to spare Bryson's life. Everything else from this point on was gravy—the icing on the cake. The doctors had said Bryson might have some lasting effects from this battle, but as long as she still had *him*, she'd deal with everything else.

And when Ryker came back, she'd do her best to encourage him to go back to his daily routine and stop spending so many hours at the hospital. A place she wasn't altogether sure he really wanted to be, despite his profession. Because if he still wanted to be involved in medicine, wouldn't he still be practicing?

They needed to get back to the schedule they'd fallen into before Bryson had gotten sick. He should only visit once a week like a friend, not be there every day like he was more than a friend. It would be the best for her and for him.

~*~

Ryker headed to the family room, hoping that it was empty so that he could call his mom back without having to leave the hospital. When he found it, it wasn't empty, but there were only a couple of people there who didn't even look up from their phones as he walked into the room.

Choosing a seat on the opposite side of the room, Ryker sank down on it and leaned forward, bracing his elbows on his thighs. As he stared down at his phone, he tried to formulate responses in advance to the questions his mom was sure to have.

Given how well known his family was in the medical world in Seattle, he'd been naïve to think that word wouldn't get back to at least one of them that he was spending time in his old stomping grounds. And depending on who word got back to, it would quickly spread to the rest of the family.

Since it was his mom calling, he could assume that it hadn't been Silas who had heard. His older brother would have called him directly to find out what was going on.

No, this had Callie's grubby hands all over it. She had friends everywhere, so likely someone had called her to gossip about him. And she wouldn't have called him to demand answers since she knew he would just clam up. Nope, she would have put a bug in their mom's ear, knowing Ryker wouldn't be able to resist her questioning.

With a sigh, he fished his Bluetooth earpiece out of his pocket and put it in place. Once it was connected, he placed the call to his mom.

"Ryker James Bennett," she said when she answered the phone. "Why are you hanging up on me?"

"I didn't hang up on you, Mom." Ryker ran a hand through his hair. "I told you I'd call you back, and here I am, calling you back."

"Why did you have to go?" she demanded. "Did I hear a child crying?"

Ryker wondered if he should just go ahead and blurt it all out or let her drag it out with a game of twenty questions.

"Yes. You heard a child crying."

There was a pause, then a sigh before she said, "And whose child was crying?"

And...a game of twenty questions it was going to be. "A friend's son."

"Ryker." Her voice held a warning.

"Fine. Tell me what you know, and I'll fill in the gaps."

"What makes you think I know anything?"

"Because you rarely call me in the afternoon."

"Rarely, but not never."

"What did Callie tell you?"

His mom sighed. "She said that someone had seen you at PNWC. In the PICU."

"Guess she has a spy here."

"A spy?" his mom scoffed. "They're called friends, Ryker. Might be smart of you to get a few for yourself."

"I have friends, Mom."

"Like the people whose son was crying."

Ryker leaned back in the chair, crossing his arms. "Yeah. Just like them."

"So what's wrong with the child?"

"He's been diagnosed with bacterial meningitis."

From the intake of breath he heard in his ear, he knew she understood the seriousness of it. "Is he okay now?"

"He's doing better but still has a little way to go."

"Why are you at the hospital so much?" she asked.

"He was just transferred here Saturday night. I've been trying to help her understand what's happening."

"Her?"

Ugh. That slip of the tongue was going to make his life even more difficult where his family was concerned. "The boy's mother."

"And where's the boy's father?"

"Dead."

"Oh."

The long pause that followed told Ryker his mom wasn't quite sure how to respond to that. She may have been caught off-balance, but it wouldn't last long.

242 · KIMBERLY RAE JORDAN

"Does she need someone to help spell her off?"

Huh. Well, that was a bit unexpected. "She probably does, but she won't take anyone up on that offer."

"Why not?" she asked. "She won't be able to help her son if she burns out. We all know that no one gets adequate rest in the hospital."

"She and Bryson are inseparable. I have a feeling he'll have a meltdown if he wakes up and she's not there. I've been trying to get her to sleep once I'm here since Bryson knows me and will at least accept my presence enough to let his mom rest as long as he can see her."

"You seem...close to these two."

And there it was. Not an unexpected conclusion, but one he would have preferred she not come to quite so quickly.

"I met them through Michael when I was helping him out by picking Vivianne up. Sophia is Vivianne's babysitter."

"How did you go from seeing them for a couple of minutes a day to spending hours with them in the hospital?" She hesitated. "Not that I'm not happy that you seem to be willing to be around children again and are back at the hospital."

"Mom, don't read too much into this. Don't jump to the conclusion that I'm going back into practice just because I'm helping out a friend."

"Ah, Ryker." She gave a soft laugh. "That's not the conclusion I'm jumping to at the moment."

"Well, don't jump to that one either," he said. "Whatever it is."

She sighed. "How have your nights been since helping out this boy?"

He could lie to her, but he doubted she'd accept his denial as truth regardless. "I've had a few nightmares, but I'm surviving."

"Is he appearing in your nightmares now?"

Ryker leaned forward again, rubbing his forehead. "Yeah. A few of them. When I saw him Saturday, he was in bad shape. I knew we had to get him to the ER, or he was going to be in trouble."

"Did you freeze up?"

"Yes, but not as badly as I'd always imagined myself freezing up."

"I'm glad to hear that. Now get yourself back to Nick and see if you can get those nightmares under control. You don't need your PTSD to have yet another source of inspiration, if you will."

"I've been thinking about it," Ryker confessed.

"Less thinking and more doing in this case, sweetheart."

"Yes, Mom."

"And if your friend needs a place to go for a few hours, our home is always open."

"I'll let her know, but don't hold your breath."

"In the meantime, we'll be praying for her and her son," she said. "And you too, of course."

"Thanks, Mom."

"I'll let you get back to them, sweetheart. Keep us appraised of the situation."

"I will if you won't give Callie details about what's going on. This situation doesn't need her barging into it."

"I won't."

He was sure she still had a lot of questions, but she'd obviously picked up on his reluctance to talk more. Not that he thought this was the last they'd discuss the situation, but she was a good enough therapist to know when to push and when to pull back.

"Love you, Mom."

"Love you too, sweetheart. Talk later."

That was both a promise and a threat, but it gave him a sense of security as well. Whatever else he might be feeling about having revealed so much to his mom, he knew that she would keep his secrets, and she'd also pray for him.

With a long exhale, he leaned back and tipped his head against the wall, staring at the ceiling. He was tired.

His fragmented sleep, early mornings, and late nights along with his physical job, were all combining to leave him drained. If he could just get eight solid hours of sleep at night, he could handle everything else, but the chance of that happening was slim to none.

And he knew that his exhaustion wasn't even close to what Sophia was experiencing. Her sleep was likely as fragmented as his, with the nurses coming in to check on Bryson every couple of hours through the night. Even though he tried to get her to rest once he arrived each afternoon, she never slept for longer than an hour or so.

To that end, he needed to get back to the room to see if he could convince her to sleep for a bit.

Pushing up to his feet, he headed back to Bryson's room. When he walked in the door, he was relieved to see that the boy had settled down and that Sophia wasn't crying. Things like the blood draw episode could be as hard on the parent as they were on the patient. Maybe harder since the parent understood exactly what was going on.

Bryson was sleeping once again, but Sophia wasn't.

"Go lay down for a bit," he said. "I'll wake you if he needs you."

It was the same thing he said every day, and it was a testament to how tired she was when all she did was nod, then walk to the single bed and lay down. Ryker went to the windows and lowered the blinds before switching off the overhead lights, hoping that the darkened room might help Sophia sleep longer.

The hospital was a relatively new building—only about a decade old—and they'd gone all out to make the rooms in both the PICU and on the regular units family-friendly. That meant they had a bed for a parent to use when they stayed overnight with their children, as well as a loveseat and a table with chairs—a home away from home...sort of.

He took the seat she'd vacated, settling back into it, glad for its comfortable cushions. Hopefully, the nurses wouldn't be in to check on Bryson for a little while, so they'd be able to get some uninterrupted sleep.

Surprisingly enough, he was able to catch a little sleep himself before waking to the sound of the door opening and conversation from the hall. He frowned as he sat forward, wanting to tell whoever had made the noise to be quiet.

His brows rose when he spotted the man standing just inside the door. Was Callie responsible for this as well? Or had one of the staff given him up to the chief of staff of the hospital?

With a glance at both Bryson and Sophia, Ryker quickly moved toward the door, motioning with his hand for the man to go back out into the hallway. He pulled the door nearly closed before turning to face the man.

"Uncle Landon," he said, keeping his voice low. "What are you doing here?"

"I heard a rumor you were in the building, so I thought I'd check and see if it was true."

Ryker gave a shake of his head. "Not even going to ask who gave me up."

His uncle's brows drew close. "Were you here undercover?"

"No," he said with a huff of laughter. "Just didn't realize that my presence here was going to create such a stir."

"Really?"

Ryker sighed. "Okay. So you've seen me now with your own eyes."

His uncle glanced at the door Ryker stood in front of. "Who's the patient to you?"

Was it any surprise that his mom's brother was also willing to take on a game of twenty questions?

"A friend's son."

He seemed to be about to ask another question, but instead, he just nodded. "Let me know if there's anything I can do."

"I will."

"I'll let you get back to it then."

"Tell Callie to keep her nose out of my business."

The older man chuckled. "Will do."

Ryker waited until he disappeared around the corner, then went back into the room, happy to see that Bryson and Sophia hadn't stirred. He sat back down, his gaze automatically going to the numbers on each of the machines that monitored Bryson.

He didn't fall back asleep though. The stretch of sleep he'd managed to get had been enough to take the edge off his exhaustion for the time being. He was just grateful he hadn't had a nightmare that had woken them all up.

As soon as Sophia was awake again, he'd head out to get them some supper. Bryson had his meals delivered. Not that he was eating much yet, even when it was something he had once enjoyed. Unfortunately, Sophia wasn't eating a lot either. Neither of them had body fat to spare, so Ryker did his best to bring food that he hoped might appeal to one or both of them.

He heard movement from the bed and glanced over to see Sophia sit up, sliding her legs off the bed. She braced her hands on the edge of the mattress, her head bent forward.

After a moment, she lifted her hands to brush back the strands of hair that had escaped the messy bun on the top of her head. Looking up, she met his gaze, and for a moment, they just stared at each other.

Then her gaze slipped to Bryson. "He's still sleeping?"

"Yep, and his vitals are all stable." It was what he told her each time she woke up, knowing that that was what she needed to hear from him.

She stayed on the bed, staring at Bryson for a few minutes before she said, "I think you don't need to keep coming back every day now."

"What?" He'd heard her perfectly fine but couldn't quite understand why she'd tell him that.

"I know Michael relies on you a lot, and it's probably hard for him to have you here, especially when he has to worry about care for Vivianne too."

Ryker couldn't deny that it had been a bit of a juggle for Michael and Lani, but they understood his situation. "I don't think it's good for you to be here on your own."

"I'll see if someone from my family can come to stay with us."

That didn't offer him much reassurance. After all, her family hadn't seemed all that eager to help her out so far. It seemed that the one person who wanted to be there was her grandmother, but unfortunately, she wasn't physically able to come on her own.

"I really don't mind being here," Ryker said, which was the truth.

"But it's a lot for you to drive back and forth every day, especially after working."

"I'm not comfortable leaving you on your own here."

"I'll be fine. If I have questions, I can always phone you, right?"

"Well, of course, but..."

Though she still had a fragile air to her, Ryker could see that she was trying to show him that she was strong. He didn't want to abandon her, but he couldn't deny that having even just one day of solid work would be helpful. Not just for him, but for Michael and Lani as well.

"Please," she said. "I feel like we've taken up so much of your time. Now that Bryson is improving, there's no need for you to be here every single day."

He knew that she was already worried about owing him for what he'd done for them. With a sigh, he said, "Just one day. I'll be back on Friday."

"Saturday."

Ryker lifted his brows at her response. "Are you actually trying to get rid of me?"

"No," she said with a shake of her head. "I'm trying to give you a break."

He wanted to insist that he was fine to come back, but he also didn't want to run roughshod over what she wanted. Even if he didn't necessarily agree with it. "I'll call you each evening to check on the two of you, and you have to promise to call me if something comes up that you need to talk to me about."

"I promise."

Ryker really didn't want to leave her, especially when he wasn't sure she'd take care of herself if he wasn't there. How would she get food? She still wasn't willing to leave Bryson for more than a few minutes at a time.

Still, he did owe Michael for being so accepting of his truncated workdays so far that week. At the determined look on Sophia's face, Ryker found himself agreeing to her request. He'd stay in New Hope for a couple of days and hope that he wasn't making a mistake.

CHAPTER NINETEEN

Sophia felt decidedly shaky the next day. After Ryker had left the night before, she'd cried. It was so stupid because she was the one who had insisted that he go. But it wasn't until he'd left, knowing that he wouldn't be back for a couple of days, that it had struck her how alone she would be.

After she'd stopped crying, she'd called her parents to let them know how Bryson was doing. Unfortunately, when she'd asked if either of them could make it up the next day, they'd said they wouldn't be able to since her dad was working overtime and her mom had already committed to watching Chloe's kids.

She hadn't been too surprised. For as long as she could remember, her dad had picked up extra hours at his job whenever he could. After all, providing for a large family on a single income wasn't exactly easy. Also, Chloe often dropped her kids off with their mom, especially now that she was pregnant again.

So Sophia wasn't disappointed, especially as they did say they'd try and get up later in the week. She'd learned long ago to not have high hopes of what her parents were able to do for her and now for Bryson. Low expectations meant less disappointment.

Still, it did leave her feeling very alone. But that feeling was an old friend. She'd felt alone in her family's crowded home, and she'd felt alone in a compound full of people. The only times she hadn't felt alone had been when she'd had Bryson to focus on, or during the times they spent with Nana and Ryker.

The fact of the matter was, it had been her own choices that had led to her being alone. She could have rekindled former friendships upon returning to New Hope, but she'd chosen not to. Now she was reaping the consequences of that decision—perhaps yet another bad one.

In the meantime, she'd try not to wear out those who *were* still in her life with requests for help.

Once she'd calmed herself to the point where she would hopefully not cry again, she called Nana.

"How is Bryson, darling?" Nana asked as soon as she answered the phone.

"He's doing a bit better each day, it seems."

"I've been talking to the nurses here, and I think perhaps you didn't tell me how sick he really was."

Sophia looked at the bed where Bryson was sleeping yet *again.* "I didn't want to worry you too much."

"It's my job to worry," Nana insisted. "You need to tell me everything."

"But there's nothing you can do."

"You're wrong, Sophia Marie," she said, an edge of reproof in her voice. "I can pray."

"Are you telling me you haven't been praying?" Sophia asked. "Aren't you the one who always said that God knows the details we might not?"

"Don't throw my words back at me, young lady," Nana said.

Sophia found herself smiling for just a moment. "I really just didn't want you to worry."

"I know, and I love you for that. I wish I could be there to see you both. I miss you."

"How about we do a video chat tomorrow when Bryson's awake?" she suggested, hoping that Bryson would be a bit perkier, because if he wasn't, Nana was going to be even more worried.

"I'd like that very much."

Before they ended the call, Nana prayed for them. It wasn't the first time Nana had prayed with her, and Sophia knew it wouldn't

HEALING HEARTS · 251

be the last. The thought of Nana's prayer support gave her a sense of comfort, and she felt a little less alone when she hung up.

She sat at the table, staring out the window at the neighborhood around the hospital. Though she'd grown up not far from Seattle, she'd rarely traveled to the city. It was just after her twenty-first birthday that she'd come there with some of her friends. Since they were all officially legal, they'd decided to head to a bar in Seattle to celebrate.

It was there that she'd met Ezekiel for the first time. She still wasn't sure why he'd been there, or what he'd seen in her that had made him approach her.

Though Sophia wanted to say that their meeting had been the worst thing that had ever happened to her, she really couldn't. Ezekiel had given her Bryson, and for that reason alone, she couldn't regret everything that had happened because of their meeting. What she wanted more than anything was for her and Bryson to be able to forget everything from that time with Ezekiel. Too bad that wasn't possible.

As she sat there, her stomach cramped, reminding Sophia that she hadn't eaten anything for supper. But she hated the idea of leaving Bryson for more than just a few minutes to go to the bathroom, let alone going to find food. She'd even waited until Ryker had come to use the showers that were made available for parents who were staying at the hospital with their children.

It wasn't going to be easy without Ryker around for the next couple of days, but she was quite sure that she wasn't the first single parent to have a child in the PICU. She needed to just buck up and do what she needed to for Bryson. And if that meant she missed a couple of meals or had to go for longer than a day without a shower, she'd survive.

Leaning over, she dragged the duffle bag out from under the table. She found her journal and pulled it out. She'd hesitated to ask Lani to put it in the bag, but she needed it. In years to come, she wanted to have memories of this time. Not because she was a sucker for emotional pain, but because she hoped that she could look back and see how far she and Bryson had come. And how God had been with them through yet another horrible time in their lives.

During her growing up years, she'd begun to keep a journal, pouring onto its pages all the things she hadn't felt like she could tell anyone else—even Nana. Of course, now, looking back, she realized that she could have told Nana about her crushes and her hopes and dreams, and the woman never would have dismissed any of it.

There had been times when she was in Texas that she had wished she could have written down her feelings. But by then, Sophia had known that should those written words fall into the wrong hands, it would have been rough going for her. So she had kept everything bottled up inside, only once again taking up journaling when the therapist she'd met with a few times before leaving Texas, had suggested it might help her.

But this particular journal was more than just a place for her to record her feelings. She also used it to keep track of her income and expenses. It was her least favorite thing to do, but also one of the most important since she didn't want to get behind on her bills.

Opening her journal, she decided to focus on her feelings. She slid the pen from the spiral binding and turned to the next blank page. Sometimes she had to mull over what she wanted to write, but not that night.

His eyes are closed, but is he just sleeping? Is he still here with me? Or is he lost to the disease that's waging war on his body? His stillness worries me.

Ryker's not here to reassure me, and I miss that. I miss him. And I know that Bryson does, too, even though he's not alert enough most of the time to voice that.

But I need to do this on my own—just the two of us like it's been from the very start. Even when we weren't together, it was the two of us against the world. Bryson deserves more than I can give him, but no one deserves to be drawn into the mess our lives are.

I'll be so glad to get past this. I want to count down the days until we're home again, but no one can tell me when that will be. Even Ryker hasn't given me a definite date, and I'm pretty sure that he would if he could.

I just need to remember that in spite of everything going on right now, I'm doing okay. We're doing okay. Things could be a whole lot worse than they are. So much worse.

As her thoughts began to circle around Ryker, she stopped writing and stared out at the lights that had begun to come on in the buildings around the hospital. She'd already written plenty about her thoughts and feelings for the man, so it seemed like there was nothing more to say...except her heart seemed to overflow with emotions.

Before she could begin to write anything more, the door opened behind her. She glanced over to see one of the nurses walk in. Sophia closed her journal as the nurse approached her.

"Are you doing okay, darlin'?" The middle-aged African American nurse gave her a look of concern.

"I'm alright," Sophia assured her.

The woman had become one of her favorites among Bryson's nurses. Maybe it was because she reminded Sophia of Nana with her warm and affectionate nature.

"I know this isn't much, but you need to keep your strength up," she said as she set a couple of items on the table.

Sophia glanced at them, surprised to see a sandwich sealed in a plastic packaging and a container of milk. Looking up at the nurse, she said, "Thank you."

"You need to eat. Bryson needs his mama strong."

"I know," Sophia said with a bob of her head. "I just don't have much of an appetite these days."

"I understand that, but you already look like you're fading away." The nurse held up her hands, then grinned as she lowered them to pat her ample midriff. "I know. I know. I shouldn't be commenting on a person's body. But seriously, take care of yourself."

"I'll try." Sophia's hunger grew when faced with food, overcoming even the anxiety that had been robbing her of her appetite. "Thank you so much for this."

"You're welcome." She rested her hand on Sophia's shoulder for a moment. "Now eat up."

Sophia picked up the sandwich, then paused to thank God for the food and to ask Him to continue to heal Bryson. Then before saying amen, she thanked Him for the people who had been supporting her through all of this. *Ryker. Nana. The medical staff. Michael and Lani. Her family.*

"Everything okay?" Sophia asked as she peeled back the plastic on the sandwich, watching the nurse make notations as she checked the monitors.

"Everything looks stable," she said.

"When will he start staying awake for longer stretches?" Sophia knew she shouldn't bother to ask because the answer would likely be the same one Ryker had given her.

"Right now, his body needs to conserve its energy for fighting the infection. He is just sleeping, though. You don't have to worry."

That was what Ryker had told her, too, so she just nodded.

"I know you think we won't tell you if things aren't going right, but we'll keep you informed. If there's a concern, we'll let you know."

Again, Sophia nodded, lifting the sandwich to take a bite. The nurse gave her a smile, then left the room.

She was halfway through the sandwich, sipping at the milk as she ate, when her phone vibrated. As she looked at it, she registered two things. The caller was Ryker, and it was a video call.

Though she was a bit uncertain about a video call, she still answered it and waited for Ryker's image to fill the screen.

"Hey there," he said as soon as the call connected. "How're you doing?"

"I'm fine." Not exactly a lie now that she had eaten something. "How are you?"

"I'm good." He seemed to settle back in his seat, and Sophia found herself curious about his home. "Has Bryson had a good day?"

"As far as I know. Did you want to see the monitors?"

"Sure."

Sophia got up and tapped her phone screen to flip the camera, then moved to stand by the machines that monitored him. Holding the phone as still as possible, she kept an eye on Ryker's face as she showed him each display. His nods were encouraging because out of all the people with medical knowledge who were caring for Bryson, she trusted him the most.

"Everything looks good," he said after she showed him the last one.

She let the camera pan over Bryson. "He's sleeping again."

"That's good. Hopefully, you'll be able to sleep as well."

Moving away from the bed, she flipped the camera view even though she didn't feel like she looked her best. That feeling wasn't helped any when Ryker's brows drew together as he stared at the camera.

"Are you sure you're okay?" he asked. "Did you eat today?"

She sat back down at the table with a sigh. Lifting up the sandwich, she showed it to him. "Still have half to eat and some milk."

"Is that all you've eaten today?" When she didn't answer, Ryker frowned. "You *need* to eat, Sophia. You can't expect me to stay away if you're not going to take care of yourself."

"It's not your responsibility to take care of me," she said softly, her gaze dropping to her half-eaten sandwich.

"Be that as it may, if nothing else, you need to eat. What good will you be to Bryson if you collapse?"

She knew he was right. But she was scared to leave Bryson, even if he was sleeping, in case he woke up and freaked out because she wasn't there.

"He's sleeping a lot right now, so I think you'll have enough time to scoot down to the cafeteria to pick up something to eat," he said. "And if you think you can only make one trip down, pick up extra to eat later in the day. There's a fridge in the family room where you can leave stuff if you label it."

And there was the second part of her issue: The cost of buying food every day. It wasn't in her budget. Not if she hoped to be able to pay her bills that month. With no money coming in, things were going to be super tight for awhile. She would need to be able to buy food for Bryson once they got home. Good food that he would eat and would give him the nutrition he needed to help him recover completely.

"Okay. I'll do that tomorrow."

"Please do," Ryker said. "I'm more worried about you right now than I am Bryson."

"I'll be fine." Desperate for a change of subject, she said, "How are Michael, Lani, and Vivianne doing?"

"They're doing good. Vivianne will be a pro at floral arrangements any day now."

Sophia smiled at that. "I hope it's not been too much trouble for Lani to have her at the shop."

"Both Michael and Lani have told me to let you know that everything is just fine, but that Vivianne can't wait to see you and Bryson again."

"Wow. Vivianne has certainly excelled in the few days I've been away."

Ryker smiled. "I know she misses both of you."

"We miss her too." Sophia was sure that Bryson would have agreed with that if he'd been awake and alert.

Ryker hesitated for a moment before saying, "Things will go back to normal. Maybe not all at once, but you both will move past this."

She knew that there was a possibility that Bryson would struggle with some things afterward, but they would cross that bridge when they got to it. And if that was a bridge she never had to cross, she'd be so very grateful.

"Do you want me to come tomorrow?" Ryker asked.

Though she very much *wanted* him to come, she didn't need him to. "No. We'll be fine, and I promise to eat."

"Glad to hear it. I'll call you again tomorrow night, okay?"

She nodded. "Thank you for calling tonight."

"You're welcome." He paused, staring intently at the phone. "Take care of yourself."

Sophia wanted to say more—to share more of what was in her heart—but instead, she just said, "I will. You too."

"Goodnight."

She stared at the dark screen on her phone for a moment before setting it aside. With an aching heart and a bit of a headache, she picked up her sandwich and finished it, acknowledging that all of Ryker's admonitions about her eating enough were valid.

Once she was done with the sandwich and milk, she put the garbage in the trash can then went into the small, attached bathroom to get ready for bed. It didn't take long to change into a pair of sleep pants and a T-shirt and brush her teeth. She quickly washed her face with the soap provided by the hospital, then used the towel there to dry off.

When she settled onto the bed a few minutes later, she opened her Bible app to the verse of the day. She let out a huff of laughter as she read it.

Rejoice always, pray without ceasing, in everything give thanks for this is the will of God in Christ Jesus concerning you.

Definitely a reminder that she needed right then. But it was a struggle to find things to rejoice in considering their surroundings. And giving thanks in everything? Yeah, that was even harder.

But she forced herself to think about their situation and find three things to be thankful for.

I am thankful that Bryson is doing better.

I am thankful for the medical staff who take care of him every day.

I am thankful for the care and concern of Nana and Ryker.

She paused, then added on *I am thankful for my family.*

After resolving to make a thankful list each night, she squeezed her eyes shut and began to pray. After she'd prayed for Bryson and for God's provision for her bills, she prayed for Ryker and whatever it was that had led him away from practising medicine.

It was so evident that he had a natural gift for dealing with children. She'd seen that even before Bryson had gotten sick.

She knew that if God did lead him back to medicine, there was a pretty good chance that she and Bryson wouldn't see him much at all. But other children deserved the opportunity to be the recipient of his caring nature, especially when they were dealing with particularly stressful diagnoses.

The thought of not having Ryker in their lives deepened the ever-present ache in her heart, and in the dimly lit hospital room, she once again ended her day in tears. Crying made her feel weak. But she knew that with everything else going on, she needed to let the emotions out when she was alone. If she didn't, she was sure to have a meltdown in front of everyone at some point.

Bryson needed her to be strong, so strong she would try her very best to be.

But not right then.

~*~

"You heading to the hospital?" Michael asked as Ryker unloaded the leftover bags of mulch that they'd used on a small job that afternoon.

"No." He hefted a bag up onto his shoulder and headed into the large building where Michael stored the equipment and products they used for their jobs. When he came back to the truck, he said, "Sophia told me to stay away until tomorrow."

Michael's brows rose. "Really? She doesn't seem to be the sort to tell you what to do."

Ryker shrugged. "I think she felt guilty about all the time I was spending driving back and forth from here to Seattle. Also that being with her and Bryson was taking me away from work."

"We were doing okay without you for the last couple of hours of each day."

"I know." Ryker pulled another bag of mulch toward him, then rested his hand on the smooth plastic. "I'm just respecting what she wants."

"But you don't want to," Michael stated with a contemplative look on his face.

"Oh, I do want to respect what she wants." Ryker lifted the bag up onto his shoulder. "I just wish that what she wanted wasn't for me to stay away for a few days."

"I must say I'm enjoying this," Michael called after him as Ryker walked to the building.

Ryker rolled his eyes even though Michael couldn't see it. He knew what the guy was getting at, but he didn't want to have that conversation with him.

When he returned to the truck to get the last bag, Michael was still there, leaning against the lowered tailgate.

"Vivianne with Lani?" Ryker asked, hoping his friend would leave the previous subject alone.

"Yep. I'm going to the shop to meet up with her for supper. I think we're going to *Norma's*. Do you want to join us?"

"Nah. I'm just going to head for home." His agitation was growing, and he needed to be in his own space so as not to have to explain what was going through his head. There was no way to explain it without having to share everything.

"Oh, come into the house before you go," Michael said as he turned and headed for the mobile home he lived in, Wolfie at his heels.

Ryker stared at his friend until he disappeared into the house. Resigned to whatever Michael wanted to talk to him about, he finished unloading the last few things from the truck, then made his way to the front door.

He'd become familiar with the house over the past few months. It was almost like a second home to him now, so he just opened the door and walked inside.

Michael was standing at the counter with a small diaper bag in front of him. "Lani asked me to pack another outfit and bottle since we hadn't planned to stay out for dinner when I got her stuff together this morning."

"Date night?" Ryker asked.

"I guess you could call it that. We haven't really gone out without Vivianne, so maybe it's just a family dinner."

Ryker smiled at that. "I'm glad you two finally worked everything out."

Michael's usually serious face was suddenly transformed when he smiled. "Me too."

Figuring that his friend might take the conversation back to Sophia, Ryker said, "What did you want to talk to me about?"

Michael turned and picked up an envelope from the counter. "Can you give this to Sophia?"

Frowning, Ryker took it from him. "What is it?"

"On Sunday, I mentioned what was happening with Sophia and Bryson to our Bible study group," he said. "Jillian—one of the women in the group—said that when her grandmother was in the hospital, the extra cost of buying food each day while she spent time with her there, added up quickly. She suggested that maybe we should collect some money to help Sophia out with that."

Ryker stared down at the envelope he held. This was something he would have been a part of back before he'd decided to separate himself from the church. The body of Christ coming together to help others.

"I've also put in the money that I would have paid her for this week to take care of Vivianne."

He looked up to find Michael watching him. Ryker had to swallow hard before he could respond. "I'm sure she'll appreciate that."

A small smile lifted the corners of Michael's mouth. "*I'm* sure she'll be resistant to accepting it."

Ryker gave a gruff laugh. "Yeah. You're probably right. But what's she gonna do? Since this is from you and not me, she won't be able to give it back."

"She'll probably still try." Michael's expression sobered. "But just let her know that we care about her and are praying for her and Bryson."

"I'll tell her that."

"Also, I think Lani would like to visit her. Is that possible? Or is Bryson coming home soon?"

Ryker shook his head. "I think he'll be in the hospital for a while yet. He's improving a little bit every day, but he's still in the PICU. Hopefully, he'll be moved to a regular unit early next week. Lani could probably visit then."

"I'll let her know."

He ran his fingers along the edges of the envelope. "I think she'd enjoy a visit from Lani. I'm pretty sure they haven't had many visitors."

Michael frowned. "I thought she had a large family."

"She does," Ryker said with a shrug. "But they haven't been able to get to the hospital to see her very much."

He had hoped that her family would be by to visit, and that had been part of the reason he'd agreed to Sophia's request that he not come for a couple of days. Unfortunately, it didn't appear that anyone else had been to see her and Bryson aside from her parents, which made him angry.

What kind of family didn't circle around one who was sick?

His mom would have been up at the hospital in a heartbeat if Sophia had been her daughter. Frankly, even now, he had a feeling that his mom would gladly go up to the hospital to see Sophia if he asked her to.

"That will make Lani even more determined to visit if it's okay."

"Thanks, Michael," Ryker said. "This means a lot."

"I'm glad that I've been given the opportunity to pay it forward." He leaned against the counter, taking the weight off his broken leg. "I know it's hard to accept help, but I'm so glad that you and others reached out and persisted when I needed it."

Ryker nodded, remembering conversations they'd had when Michael had struggled to accept the help Ryker, Lani, and others had offered him. No doubt Sophia would feel the same way. But for Bryson's sake, Ryker figured that she would accept the help.

"Well, I'd better go, or Lani is going to think I stood her up," Michael said as he zipped up the bag on the counter.

"I'll see you tomorrow," Ryker said as they walked out of the house.

Michael opened the door of his truck. "You don't have to work tomorrow."

"I know, but I think I need to."

His friend and boss gave him a curious look, but he didn't say anything, just nodded.

After Michael had driven away, Ryker sat in his truck for a moment, contemplating what the next couple of days held. He couldn't wait to get back to the hospital to see Sophia and Bryson.

CHAPTER TWENTY

Ryker shifted in his seat, but it wasn't because the chair was uncomfortable. Heaven forbid a therapist would have an uncomfortable chair.

"I'm glad you made the decision to come back," Nick said from where he was seated in a matching plush armchair.

"This doesn't mean I'm going back to work as a doctor," Ryker warned him.

"I'm not here to convince you to do something you don't want to. We wouldn't make much progress if I tried that."

Ryker wasn't sure that Nick wouldn't try to convince him to do things he didn't want to, but he knew that it would take small efforts...baby steps...in order to move him forward in his life.

"Why *are* you back in counseling?" Nick asked.

The question was one Ryker had expected, but he hadn't been able to come up with an answer. Or at least not an answer that he was really willing to consider just yet.

"I've been confronted by the very thing I've dreaded ever since returning from Syria."

"A sick or hurt child?"

Ryker wasn't surprised that Nick guessed correctly. Before he'd bailed on therapy, they'd spent plenty of time talking about his reaction to the children in Syria and the helplessness he'd felt at the time.

"Yeah." Ryker rubbed his hands on his thighs as he stared at the carpet. "It started with my boss unexpectedly ending up with a newborn baby. His sister gave birth without Michael knowing she was even pregnant, and then she left the child with him." He looked up at Nick. "I couldn't just not help him when I had the experience to make life a bit easier for him."

Nick nodded. "Of course you couldn't. You didn't lose your love and desire to care for children after what happened in Syria. It might have made life easier if you had."

Wasn't that the truth? "Then the woman he hired to babysit Vivianne had a little boy. At first, he was scared of me when I would drop by to pick up the baby. His mom asked me to spend a few minutes with him, thinking that it might put his mind at ease."

"You said yes."

"Yeah," Ryker said. "Yeah, I did. Once the little guy got past his fear, he sort of attached himself to me."

Nick smiled at that, the skin at the corners of his eyes crinkling. "Children have always been drawn to you."

"Well, one day there was an incident when I heard Bryson screaming, and I froze. Not for long, but long enough that if the scream had been because he was hurt, my hesitancy could have made a big difference."

"But he was okay?" Nick asked.

"That time," Ryker said with a nod. "But then last Saturday, I dropped by the house to help Sophia with the yard, and Bryson was sick. Seriously ill. We got him to the ER, then they transferred him to PNWC."

"I bet that was difficult for you," Nick observed.

Frowning, Ryker considered his words. "Actually, it wasn't as difficult as I'd always imagined it would be to be back in that atmosphere."

"So you've been with him at the hospital?"

"Yeah. Well, I was. I spent a couple of days going back and forth between New Hope for my job and the hospital. Sophia told me to take a break, so I haven't been there since Wednesday. I'm going back after this time with you, though."

"So why are you here?" Nick asked again.

Ryker sighed. "I'm not entirely sure. I'm still having the nightmares. I'm still not comfortable with the idea of a child's care resting in my hands. But Bryson and Sophia..."

"Where's Bryson's dad?"

"Dead." Ryker considered sharing his suspicions about Sophia's past. Then, knowing that Nick wouldn't tell anyone, he decided to go ahead with it as her story factored into a lot of his conflicted feelings.

When he was done, Nick looked at him for a moment then said, "Do you have feelings for Sophia?"

Ryker let out a long exhale. "Yeah, I think I do. I didn't expect that at all, but the more time I've spent with her and Bryson, the more I've begun to feel love for both of them."

"It's not just Bryson, is it?" Nick asked.

He didn't even have to think twice before shaking his head. "No. It's true that I began to spend more time with them because of Bryson, but in doing so, I began to get to know Sophia better. It's just...unexpected."

"Why is that?"

"I don't know. Maybe it's just that she's so different from Lydia. I always thought I wanted a woman as devoted to a career as I was, but that's not Sophia. Her devotion is to her son, and I find myself admiring her for that. She looks fragile, but I've seen that she has strength within her, and yeah... I'm drawn to that too."

"How do you think she feels?"

"If I'm right about her past, my guess is she's not interested in a relationship."

"So what does that mean for you?"

Ryker shrugged. "I'm not in a hurry. I know I still have work to do on myself, and maybe that's why I'm here again."

"Maybe?" Nick asked with an arched brow.

"Yeah. Maybe there's no maybe about it. I want to be the best version of myself for her and Bryson, and I know that that starts with coming to terms with what happened in Syria."

Nick nodded. "I wasn't surprised when you stopped coming. You'd been struggling with the idea of getting past the events of that day when so many were still suffering. Parents who had lost children. Children who had lost parents. You'll never forget what happened to you on that day, Ryker. You know that. But allowing yourself to continue to suffer won't change anything for any of those who suffered unimaginable loss."

He knew that Nick was right. He'd known that even back then, but it still hadn't felt right to put that time behind him and move forward. And yet, there were moments when all he wanted was to forget what had happened. The conflicting feelings made his head spin at times.

"You were spared, Ryker. Not all of your medical team were. But you choosing to suffer won't bring them back. It won't change what happened that day." The man leaned forward, his brow furrowed. "You know what this is. We've talked about it at length. The guilt you feel over surviving that day, for struggling with the feelings of helplessness, for the lives you weren't able to save, it's time to let that go."

Ryker closed his eyes and sank further into the chair. Since that day, guilt had definitely been his constant companion. Survivor's guilt. He knew all about it. He'd read up on it. He'd talked with Nick about it. He'd done everything but overcome it.

"Are you ready to work on that?" Nick asked, his voice low.

Ryker opened his eyes, not surprised to find them damp. Swallowing the emotion down, he whispered. "Yes."

It was a single word—just three letters—but it was the hardest thing to say. The guilt didn't immediately leave him, but he felt as if a weight had fallen away. It was as if he'd been drowning in a sea of guilt, held down by a weight around his ankles. The weight was

268 · KIMBERLY RAE JORDAN

gone, but he was still in that sea. It would take work to get to shore, but for the first time since that horrific day, he found himself wanting to do the work.

Nick reached across the distance between them and grasped his arm, a compassionate look on his face. "You won't be doing this alone."

"Thank you," Ryker said as he laid his hand on top of Nick's. Some might have said it wasn't a good idea for him to come to someone so closely tied to his family for therapy, but Nick had felt safe, and Ryker knew that he'd made the right decision to come back to him.

When he left the office a short time later, after thanking Nick for making time on his Saturday to see him and making another appointment for later in the week, Ryker headed to his folks' place. His mom had made him promise to come by and pick up some food to take to the hospital.

"Hi, sweetheart," she said when he walked into the house. She wrapped him in a tight hug, the scent of her perfume a familiar comfort. "I know you don't want to hang around too long, so come right on into the kitchen."

Appreciating her understanding, Ryker followed her into the spacious kitchen. He hadn't told her yet about returning to Nick for therapy, and he knew Nick wouldn't reveal it. But he didn't say anything right then either because she'd want to talk to him about it, and he didn't want to hang around that long.

"It smells great, Mom," he said as he settled on a stool at the island.

"I hope she likes it." His mom picked up an insulated bag from the counter and slid a couple of containers into it. "This is for supper tonight. It should stay warm as long as you leave it in the bag."

"They do have a family room that has a microwave," Ryker said.

"Well, that works too." She picked up another bag and began to put more things into that one. "Here are the items you asked me to make, plus these are cinnamon buns and cookies. They're your favorites, but don't eat them all yourself."

Ryker chuckled. "I won't, Mom. I learned to share a long time ago. Well, I would make an exception for Callie."

"Leave your sister alone," she said with an exasperated look.

"If only she'd leave *me* alone."

"You know that she cares about you and only wants the best for you."

"Which, according to her, apparently means returning to my career and getting back together with Lydia."

His mom stopped what she was doing, resting her hands on the counter as she regarded him for a moment. "And that wouldn't be something you wanted?"

"Mom, if I wanted those things, I would have taken steps to get them. I'm on a different path right now," Ryker said, then paused. "I'm not sure where it's going, and I'm not ruling out returning to medicine, but it's not going to happen right now."

"And getting back together with Lydia?"

"That's not going to happen," he said with more conviction. "Not now. Not ever."

He wasn't sure what he'd expected as a reaction from his mom, but it wasn't, "Good. You two weren't right for each other."

Ryker stared at his mom in surprise. "I thought you liked her."

"Oh, I like her just fine, sweetheart," she said. "But I never really felt she was right for you."

"You didn't say anything."

"The thing is, I didn't think she was exactly *wrong* for you either."

"Now I'm confused."

She gave him a smile. "What I mean is that I didn't doubt that the two of you would make it work. You loved each other and were committed to your relationship. I just thought that maybe a different sort of man might have made her happier in the long run. And a different sort of woman might have made you happier down the road too."

"What sort of woman?"

"One who wasn't quite so focused on becoming the top obstetrician in the state."

"Hmmm."

"Lydia is very goal-oriented and not just for herself. I had a feeling that she would eventually have wanted you to take a career path that you might not want. Like taking over Landon's job at PNWC."

Ryker shuddered at the very thought, but he could see now that his mom was probably right. Lydia's career plans had never been to just be an obstetrician. She'd hoped to end up in a higher position within the obstetrics community.

He hadn't wanted—didn't want—that for himself. Dealing with patients directly had always made him happiest, so an office job like his uncle had as the chief medical officer at PNWC was the absolute last place he would have wanted to end up. However, he could definitely see that Lydia would have wanted that for him.

He'd been attracted to Lydia partly because of the passion she had for her career. But if that passion had been directed to his career and where she thought he should go, it would have undoubtedly been the cause of some heated arguments.

"Well, it's a moot point," he said. "I'm not interested in getting back together with her, and I really can't believe that she would want me back either. Regardless of what Callie has said."

This time his mom's smile was loaded with affection as she looked at him. "You're quite a catch, sweetheart. Any woman would be lucky to have you."

"You have to say that," he said with a laugh. "You're my mom."

"Though your lack of drive to reach the top might not have been what Lydia wanted, you have many other things that I'm quite sure

drew her to you. Which may be why she's still willing to consider
something with you."

Ryker shrugged. "It's not going to happen."

This time it was his mom who hummed in response before saying, "You seem very certain of that. Has your heart moved in
another direction?"

He didn't even bother to answer her. The fact that she was packing up a bag of food for Sophia and Bryson told him that she
already had her suspicions.

Reaching out, she patted his hand. "We're praying for you."

"Thanks, Mom." He glanced at the arched doorway that led out
of the kitchen. "Where's Dad?"

"He and Jonah went to the museum," she said as she zipped up
the bags she'd finished packing. "There was some sort of science
display on somewhere."

That didn't surprise Ryker. His nephew enjoyed science, and
while he hadn't expressed any interest in the medical sciences,
Ryker expected that he'd have a career in the sciences somewhere.

"There you go." She patted the bags with a smile. "Sure you
don't want some company?"

"I'm sure," he said with a little bit of regret.

Something told him that Sophia would probably be a little overwhelmed by his mom. But at the same time, she and Bryson could
probably both use a little bit of spoiling, which his mom was really
good at.

"You'll be back later?" she asked as they walked to the front
door.

"Yep." He'd decided to spend the night in Seattle since it would
save him a trip back to New Hope. Now that word was out that he
was spending time at the hospital, he might as well take advantage
of closer sleeping arrangements. "But probably not until around
nine or so."

"Whenever you get here is fine. You know all the codes if Dad and I are in bed already." She gave him a tight hug. "Love you."

As he walked to his truck, Ryker found himself more grateful than ever for the support of his family. Even Callie...in her own way.

Now that he was on his way to the hospital, he was impatient to get there. Traffic moved far too slow. It took too long to find a parking spot. And too many people stopped him to chat as he made his way to Bryson's room. Okay, so it was only two people. But after having been gone almost three days without seeing Sophia and Bryson, he didn't like having to wait even longer.

As he approached the door, he slowed his steps a bit and took a deep breath. He was well aware that the feelings he had for Sophia might not be reciprocated, so he didn't want to overwhelm her by running into the room and sweeping her into his arms.

The very idea made him grin, and he wondered if Sophia would enjoy romantic gestures like that. He hadn't had much of a chance to be romantic with Lydia. The few times he'd attempted romance, she'd let him know she preferred a more practical approach to their interactions.

It had been a bit of an adjustment since the example he'd always had from his dad had been one of romantic gestures. Bouquets of flowers even if there was no special occasion. Cards with no reason other than to say he loved his wife. Her favorite chocolates if she was feeling a bit down. Dinners out, just the two of them, to a restaurant they both enjoyed.

And while his mom didn't do those sorts of romantic gestures in return, she had her own ways of showing her husband that he was important to her. Every morning she had a cup of coffee waiting for him, doctored just how he liked it. Each Saturday, she made them breakfast, then the two of them ate together in the sitting room attached to their bedroom. And just like his dad brought his mom her favorite chocolates, she would make his favorite cookies, often sending them to work with him in a cookie jar for him to enjoy throughout the week.

All of their actions had been a good reminder for them as kids that their parents were more than just Mom and Dad. They were a couple. Husband and wife. And they believed their relationship with each other was important.

Now that he was open to having another relationship, Ryker couldn't help but wonder if things might be different with someone like Sophia.

Already he found himself eager to do things for Sophia and for Bryson too. Which was why he'd found it difficult to respect her request that he not come back for a couple of days. He was sure that she'd done it mainly for his sake, but also because she didn't want to feel obligated to him.

Of course she didn't know that he didn't expect any sort of re-payment for what he'd done for them. However, he could tell her that until he was blue in the face, but he had a feeling that only time would show that to her.

Suddenly eager to see them, he walked quietly into the room, not wanting to wake either of them if they were sleeping. It was silent, and his gaze went to the bed where he saw Bryson asleep. Even though he knew that Bryson sleeping a lot wasn't necessarily a bad thing as his body healed from the infection that had invaded it, Ryker couldn't deny that he would have liked to have seen him awake.

His gaze moved around the room in search of Sophia, knowing that the likelihood of her not being there was slim. He found her seated at the table, her head resting on her folded arms, facing the window.

Mindful that she might be sleeping, Ryker kept his steps light as he walked toward her. He moved around to the other side of the table, which allowed him to see that her eyes were open, staring out the window. She became aware of his presence at the same time as he made his observation, because immediately, she straightened up.

She blinked a couple of times, then said, "Ryker?"

"In the flesh." He smiled, then pulled out the chair opposite her, setting the bags he carried on the floor. "How are you doing?"

Her brow furrowed, and for a moment, Ryker thought she was going to cry. He could see that the dark smudges under her eyes seemed worse, and overall, she just looked...frail. Ryker regretted agreeing to her request that he not come for a few days.

"Are you okay?" he asked when she didn't reply to his other question.

She took a deep breath, then nodded. "It's just...hard. I want to take him home."

"I get that," Ryker said. "Being in the hospital is difficult, especially when you're essentially doing it on your own."

Her gaze dropped as she lifted her hands and rubbed her face.

"Has anyone come to visit?"

She sighed as she nodded. "My mom and dad came by this morning."

"That's great," Ryker said, happy to hear that someone had been to visit her.

"Yeah. It was nice to see them," she agreed. "But they didn't stay too long."

"How's Bryson doing today?"

She glanced at the bed. "He's been awake more, but they came to draw blood for yet another test, and that upset him. I think crying like that wore him out."

"And you too, probably," he said.

It said a lot that she nodded. "I know why they have to do it, but it's still really hard to see him so upset and in pain."

"Most kids have trouble with blood draws, and it's never easy on the parents."

She didn't respond to him right away, and he was starting to get concerned. Finally, her gaze focused back on him. "How have you been?"

"Busy, but good. I went to see my mom before I came here, and she gave me some food for you."

Her eyes widened at that. "You told your mom about us?"

"Well, actually, someone saw me here, and they told my sister, who in turn blabbed to my mom."

"I'm sorry if your being here with us caused you any issues with your family."

"It didn't cause any issues," he assured her. At least not the way she was likely thinking. "Mom sent food because she knows how hard it can be when you have a loved one in the hospital."

"Is she a doctor too?"

"She's a psychiatrist." Ryker settled back in his chair. "My dad is a plastic surgeon."

Her brows lifted. "Are you all in the medical field?"

"Basically. My older brother is a trauma surgeon, and my sister is a cancer researcher."

"You're all pretty smart, huh?"

"I guess," Ryker said with a shrug. "It seemed that we were destined to end up in careers associated with medicine somehow."

"But you're not practicing now?"

For a moment, Ryker contemplated how to answer that before finally saying, "How about you eat something while I tell you a story."

"Are you bribing me?" she asked, a small smile tugging up the corners of her mouth.

"Maybe? Although my mom's food is delicious, so I know you'll enjoy it."

"What did she make?"

Ryker bent over and picked up the insulated bag. He unzipped it and pulled out the two containers his mom had placed in there earlier. "To be honest, I'm not one hundred percent sure, but it smelled like lasagna when I walked into the house."

He set the containers on the table, glad to feel they were still warm, then pulled the top off one of them. "Yep. I was right."

After sliding one container across the table to Sophia, he looked through the other bag his mom had given him. Along with the cookies and cinnamon buns, he found garlic bread and some disposable forks.

"Have you been able to get food?" he asked as he gave her some of the bread and a fork.

She didn't reply right away, so he wasn't surprised by what she said when she did.

"I tried to go when my folks were here, but Bryson woke up while I was gone, and it took forever to calm him down when I got back."

"Well, I've brought some stuff that you can keep in the room in case you aren't able to get yourself some food. Oh, I forgot." He bent over to pick up the bag he'd packed in New Hope and pulled out the envelope that Michael had given him. "This is for you."

She frowned as she took it from him. "What is it?"

"Michael asked me to give it to you."

After a quick glance at him, she turned her attention to the envelope. She carefully slid her finger under the flap and worked it open before pulling the card out. Ryker thought about warning her to be careful when opening it but then decided to just let the bills fall where they may. It wasn't like they were out in public.

It was clear she hadn't been expecting anything in the card because she opened it right away and the money inside fell into her lap. She froze for a moment before looking up at him. "What is this?"

"People in Michael and Lani's Bible study group contributed to the card, thinking you might be incurring some unexpected expenses while Bryson is in the hospital."

"But this..." Sophia's voice faded away as she gathered up the bills. "This is too much. I can't accept this."

"Sure you can," Ryker said, though he understood why the concept was difficult for her. "These people want to help you and Bryson. Jillian, one of the women in the group, shared how when her grandmother was in the hospital, she'd had to spend money on food each day. The group has been praying for you and Bryson, and I guess they wanted to do something a bit more tangible too."

By that point, she'd gathered up the money and set it on the table, not even bothering to count it. It seemed that to her, even if it was a stack of ones, it was still too much. He would have added some to it himself, but since the envelope had been sealed, that hadn't been possible.

"If it helps to ease any of the stress you're under, it's a good thing," Ryker said. "You need to be able to just concentrate on Bryson."

She nodded, still staring at the money, then looked up at him. "I really do appreciate it. Please don't think I'm ungrateful. It's just so...much."

"No one forced them to give you the money. They did it because they wanted to, so accept it knowing that." He gave her a smile. "Now, you eat, and I'll tell you why I'm not practicing medicine anymore."

"You don't have to tell me if you don't want to," she said as she set the card and money aside, then picked up her fork. "You said you were going to tell me when Bryson was home from the hospital, and that hasn't happened yet."

It wasn't a story that he was excited to tell, but Ryker wanted to take her mind off the card and its contents. Plus, he found that he wanted Sophia to know, and if his willingness to open up helped her divulge parts of her own story to him, then that would just be an added bonus.

CHAPTER TWENTY-ONE

Sophia felt so choked with emotion, she wasn't sure she'd be able to eat any of the delicious smelling food that Ryker had set in front of her. She honestly had as much trouble believing that his mom had made her food as she did that Michael and his friends had given her a card with money.

If she had opened it in private, she probably would have broken down in tears. But since Ryker was there, she hadn't wanted to take the chance that once she started crying, she wouldn't be able to stop. She'd been teetering on the brink of tears ever since her parents had left, and Bryson's meltdown over the blood draw hadn't helped.

And since the day had already been on a downward trajectory, she'd managed to convince herself that Ryker wouldn't show. At the end of their call the night before, he'd said he would see her, but he hadn't told her exactly when he'd show up. It was super, super concerning to her that she was becoming so dependent on him.

But she'd think about that more when he wasn't around. Right then, she had some food to eat—if she could get her emotions to settle down—and a story to listen to.

Ryker worked the lid off his container then picked up his fork. She saw him hesitate a moment before closing his eyes, and she wondered if he was praying. They hadn't touched much on spiritual things in any conversations they'd had.

"So I need to go back a few years," he began after he'd finished a bite of his food. "I had made the decision to spend a month on a medical mission after I finished my residency and before moving on to the next stage of my life, which was supposed to be joining a pediatric practice. My fiancée and I went with a group of nurses and doctors, each who had different specialties, to work in a refugee camp in Syria."

He'd had a fiancée?

The bite Sophia had just swallowed settled heavily in her stomach. She didn't say anything, though, because it wasn't her place to react to that. Earlier in their acquaintance, she'd wondered about his relationship status, but given the time he'd spent with them, she'd come to the conclusion that he wasn't married or in a relationship.

She hoped that she wasn't wrong because the idea that she had feelings for a man who was already in a relationship made her feel positively ill. It would also be an indication that she'd completely misjudged the man because she'd assumed he wouldn't spend that kind of time with her and Bryson if he had a girlfriend or wife. And he'd certainly never mentioned having a significant other in any of their conversations.

Sophia hoped that whatever he shared with her would clear it all up because she couldn't handle the uncertainty. And it would change so much if he was involved with someone.

"We spent the first three weeks at the camp doing our best to treat the people there under conditions that were less than ideal." He paused, staring down at his food. "You know, we never truly understand how even the worst of conditions in this country are still far better than what many people in the rest of the world have to live in."

Sophia didn't know how to reply to that, so she just continued to eat small bites of food, for once hoping that Bryson would take his time waking up. For some reason, she *needed* to hear Ryker's story. Maybe it was because she hoped it would give her the courage to share her own.

"Already, I'd felt a bit haunted by what I'd seen there, but I still enjoyed being able to help the children in the camp. Despite the difference in situations, they were just like the kids here. Some were outgoing. Some were mischievous. Some shy." Ryker looked up as a smile crossed his face. "I'd taken a ton of candy to give out, and no matter their personality, they would grin with so much happiness when I gave them some."

Sophia returned his smile, unable to keep his momentary joy from pulling that response from her. "Candy and happy kids seem to go hand in hand."

"So true," Ryker agreed.

She thought he'd dive right back into his story, but he focused on his food for a few minutes, so she did the same. There was still no movement from Bryson, but she glanced over at him anyway, just to be sure he hadn't woken without them noticing.

"During our last week there, we were determined to do as much as we could. In order to do that, a few of us had gathered to discuss treatments for some patients who were overlapping in our specialties."

He fell quiet again, his fork coming to rest on the side of the plate as his gaze shifted to the window, though Sophia wasn't sure that he was actually seeing what lay beyond the glass. She had the overwhelming urge to hold his hand or even wrap her arms around him like she did to Bryson when he was upset.

"In the blink of an eye, everything changed," he murmured. "There had always been a bit of a chaos in the camp, but the bombs took it to a whole new level."

Bombs? Her heart began to pound at what might still be to come in the story. Obviously, he hadn't been killed, but she doubted that was true of everyone who had been there.

"We stepped out of the half-collapsed tent where we'd been meeting into unbelievable destruction. Devastation." He blew out a breath. "And death. So much death."

Sophia clutched her fork but didn't bother to eat anything, knowing her stomach would revolt. Ryker's expression was sober, but it held an edge of despair that she'd never seen on him before.

"I tried my best to help those who were so badly injured. But the shock of seeing those who were beyond my help...the children I'd given candy to...made it difficult for me to function. We worked long into the night, searching for survivors and treating them. All the while worried that more bombs were coming."

Sophia wasn't sure that she would have been able to keep going under those conditions, and she admired him for pushing on.

"By the time the sun came up the next morning, we were faced with the real devastation. Among those killed were a doctor and two nurses who'd gone over with Lydia and me. It took a few days to get everything sorted out, but in the end, over half the inhabitants of the camp had been killed. Whole families were wiped out. There were children left without parents and parents without children. I'd never seen anything so awful in my life."

The horror he felt was easy to read on his face, and Sophia realized that despite the time that had passed, the attack was still very real and vivid for him.

"By the time I got back to Seattle, I was a wreck. I could hardly sleep because of the nightmares. But even when I was awake, I still couldn't block out the memories. I thought that as time passed, I'd move beyond it. But I couldn't. I came here for a shift, just to see if I could handle the patients, but I couldn't. I just...couldn't."

Now there was sadness on his face, and Sophia wished she had the words to say to erase that from him.

"The experience in the camp left me feeling helpless and hopeless. I had tried so hard to help the children there, but for far too many, it wasn't enough. I just couldn't get past the feeling that I'd fail more children if I continued to practice." He looked at her then, one corner of his mouth lifting slightly. "And before you ask, yes, I went to therapy. My mom was insistent on that."

Given what he'd said about his mom, that made sense, but Sophia knew from experience that therapy could be hard. Regardless of it being the right thing, sometimes it felt like it was so much work for so little in immediate return.

"It soon became apparent to me that regardless of being in therapy, I couldn't face treating children—or anyone else, for that matter—anymore. That's when I began to look for something else to do. Something that, should I freeze up or fail somehow, wouldn't result in someone's death. Around that time, I saw Michael's ad for people to work at his landscaping business."

He took a bit of his food then, so Sophia did the same, figuring the worst of the story was behind them. After a couple of bites, he continued.

"I soon realized that the job could be a godsend for me. I could move away from Seattle. Away from people who knew who I was and what had happened. I wanted a place to heal—if healing was even possible. I'd hoped for a life where I wouldn't have much—if any—interactions with children."

Sophia thought of Vivianne and Bryson, realizing that he'd been sort of forced into close contact with both of them. Was that why he'd begun to limit the time he'd spent with them?

"So I applied for the job, and even though I'd put down no previous experience of any sort, Michael agreed to interview me and then gave me a position working with him. It ended up being a good thing because shortly after I started working for him, my fiancée called it quits on our engagement. She's an obstetrician, and she'd had great plans for the two of us. Plans that hadn't included me being weak and unable to deal with the tragedy we'd both experienced."

Sophia couldn't keep from asking, "She didn't have the same reaction as you did to what happened?"

Ryker shook his head. "Lydia has always been a strong woman, and while she has the ability to soften her interactions with the patients she sees, she's also able to keep her emotions in check the rest of the time. For her, it seemed like what happened in Syria was simply an event she had to handle to the best of her ability. But once we left there, it was in the past. It was as if it had been a shift in the ER. A trauma to focus on, then forget. I just couldn't view it that way."

Sophia couldn't help but think of the women from the compound and how varied their responses to the cult experience had been. When Ezekiel died, some had been devastated and had mourned him in ways that others, like her, hadn't. There had been a couple of women who had immediately left the area, returning to their families to presumably move on with their lives without looking back.

Mellie was one who had mourned Ezekiel, but she'd also seemed to move on quite quickly from the whole experience. Sophia's reaction to what had gone on stemmed more from how things had impacted Bryson. She might have been able to move on sooner if she hadn't seen Bryson's struggle to function in the world beyond the compound.

"Anyway, I wasn't heartbroken over the end of our engagement. I think my heart was already too broken from what had happened in Syria."

Sophia was glad to hear that his fiancée hadn't been one of the people who had died in that camp because he'd already suffered so much as a result of that event.

"And though I haven't been going to therapy for the past year or so, my nightmares aren't quite as frequent as they were at the start."

As she mulled over everything he'd told her, Sophia realized that dealing with Bryson in this way might have pushed him to a place he wasn't comfortable being. She didn't want him to be there if it hurt him in any way.

"Are you having more nightmares recently?" she asked. "Because of being around Bryson, and what's happened with him?"

When his gaze met hers, Sophia could read the answer in it and in his hesitation to answer her. She hoped that he'd be honest with her. For reasons she couldn't pinpoint, she needed him to be honest and not lie in order to spare her feelings.

His gaze dropped to his food as he picked up his fork, but he didn't scoop up any of the lasagna. Instead, he sighed and looked up at her again.

"Yes. Seeing his fear the very first time I met him did a number on me, I'll admit. I had a nightmare that night, seeing his fearful gaze mixed in among the ones from the camp. I'll confess that it shook me up."

Sophia's shoulders slumped, and she felt a bit sick to her stomach. "And then I asked you to spend more time with him."

"It was okay, Sophia," he said, an urgent yet gentle tone to his voice. "I could have said no. I could have stayed away."

"You tried to stay away," she reminded him.

He nodded. "But that wasn't just because of the nightmares. I mean, I hate the nightmares, but honestly, I'm kind of used to them. I have methods that I use to try to prevent them, but if they don't work, I do have things I do to help me deal with the aftermath that usually...sometimes work."

Frowning, she said, "So you really did just stay away because of him getting too attached to you?"

"Yes," he said. "And maybe I was getting too attached to him as well." His gaze met hers, and this time there was something besides devastation in his eyes. There was an emotion she was almost afraid to name. "To both of you, actually."

At one time in her life, his words would have delighted her. But right then? All she felt was fear. Fear that she would once again be led by her feelings and not make good decisions. But beyond that, there was a fear that whatever he thought of her, it would all change once he heard what she'd done. What she'd been a part of.

"I'm sorry if what's happened with Bryson brought you back to this place when you didn't want to be here," she said, choosing not to address the subtle indication that he might be feeling things for her and Bryson, especially since it was clearly something he was trying to avoid.

"I think I needed to be brought back here." Ryker shifted in his seat, resting his arms on the table, pushing the container of food away from him. "It was time, and though it was difficult at first, it helped me see that I could face a medical emergency with a child and not freeze up completely."

"Do you think you'll practice medicine again?"

"Yes." The answer came without hesitation, but it appeared to take Ryker by surprise. A smile curved his lips. "Yes. I will practice medicine again. Not right away, of course. But where I once thought it was impossible, I now think I can do what I need to in order to reach that goal."

It wasn't lost on Sophia that Bryson had helped to give Ryker back the one thing that would eventually take him out of their lives. Everything else aside, there was no way she could ever imagine being involved with a doctor. Even *if*—and that was a big if—they were both open to a relationship, his ex-fiancée was a *doctor*. His whole family was involved in the medical field.

And what was she? A single mom whose sole aspiration had been to be a stay-at-home mom. She was only able to keep a roof over her son's head because of her grandmother's help. And that didn't even take into account all the issues she had from the years she'd spent under the thumb of an egotistical maniac. An egotistical maniac she'd thought she loved.

"I've made the decision to go back to therapy," he said. "In fact, I had my first session earlier today."

Sophia sat back, what little appetite she'd had was gone now. "Is your mom your therapist?"

Ryker gave a huff of laughter. "I'm sure she'd like to be, but no. I see another therapist in her practice. He's a good fit for me, but I've been...resistant. Going back this time, I'm doing it because I want to do the work now. Last time, I felt like I was going more because it was expected of me."

Sophia knew how that was. It was why she'd gone to the sessions initially offered by the group who had stepped in to help the survivors of the cult. Would she want to go back now if she was able to? For sure, she'd want Bryson to go. It was more important that he get the help he needed in order to be able to live a full life.

With Ryker dealing with so many of his own issues—issues brought on by his desire to help those less fortunate—she couldn't see any way for him to be interested in someone who also had a lot of issues. And her issues weren't the result of anything so selfless. Nope, her issues were the result of a desire to feel special to someone.

Thankfully, Sophia was saved from having to make further conversation by sounds coming from the bed. She got to her feet and made her way over to check on Bryson.

"Hi, baby." She leaned over the side of the bed as he blinked up at her. Though she really hated how lethargic he still was, she refused to focus too much on that. Feeling Ryker come to her side, she said, "Look who's here."

Bryson's gaze flicked to Ryker, and a small smile curved his lips as his eyes lit up. "Ryker."

"Hey there, buddy," Ryker said as he held out his fist close to where Bryson's hand rested on his blanket.

Sophia held her breath, hoping he'd respond how he usually did to Ryker. Relief flooded through her when he lifted his hand, making a small fist and bumping it against Ryker's.

She lifted the cup of apple juice with a straw while Ryker went around the other side of the bed to help Bryson sit up. Once he was sitting more upright, Sophia held the cup and straw close to his mouth.

"Have a drink, baby," she said.

Though there was no fear of him getting dehydrated because of the IV, he needed to start drinking more on his own because there was no way they'd let him go home if he wasn't eating and drinking enough.

"You need to drink a bit, buddy," Ryker encouraged.

After a glance at Ryker, Bryson opened his mouth and allowed Sophia to move the straw into position. She watched with happiness as he took a couple of sucks on the straw. The battle to get him to drink threw her back in time to just after he'd been born when she'd struggled to nurse him. She'd known that there wouldn't be money for formula, so it had been imperative that she get him to nurse.

Thankfully, there had been another woman there who had enough experience that she was able to help Sophia successfully nurse Bryson. If Ryker was going to be the person who helped Bryson make forward moves when it came to eating and drinking, it would be just one more thing she'd be thankful to him for.

"Want to try drinking something else?" Ryker asked. "I brought something from my mom you might like."

He went back to the table then reappeared with an insulated cup in his hand. Popping up the straw, he said, "Do you want a taste?"

Bryson frowned at it, then glanced at his mom. "No."

"How about we let Momma have a taste and see what she thinks?"

This time Bryson nodded, so Sophia hoped that her trust in Ryker that he wouldn't feed her anything too awful wasn't misplaced. He held the cup out to her with a smile. She reached for it, expecting that he'd let go. But as she wrapped her fingers around the smooth surface, he kept hold of it, so her fingers brushed against his.

His smile grew as she leaned forward across Bryson and took a sip. At the explosion of the taste of banana and peanut butter in her mouth, she took another small sip before straightening with a smile of her own.

"I think you'll love this, baby," Sophia said as she turned to face him. She leaned closer to him. "It tastes just like bananas and peanut butter."

He didn't look convinced, but just as she'd decided to trust Ryker, he apparently decided to trust her.

Ryker held the cup for him, just like he'd held it for her, and Sophia waited with bated breath. Not surprisingly, Bryson's first sip was tentative. When his eyes widened, and he went back for another sip, Sophia wasn't sure if she was going to laugh or cry.

Something told her that Ryker had asked his mom to pack as many calories into the peanut butter banana smoothie as possible. She stood there, watching in amazement as Bryson kept taking tiny sips of the smoothie.

"You don't have to drink it all right away," Ryker said. "It will stay cold in the cup, plus I have another one you can have later on."

"I love it," Bryson whispered with another small smile, his hands going up to grip over Ryker's as he pulled the cup forward for another sip.

"Thank you, Ryker," Sophia said, blinking back tears that she knew he'd understand.

"You're very welcome. I thought this might be a good way to get some nutrition into him."

"And thank your mom too," she added.

It was hard not to compare his mother's help for her and Bryson to her own mom's. Sophia knew it wasn't fair to do that since

Ryker's mom had medical experience, and Ryker could advise her on what he wanted her to make for Bryson. Also, her family didn't have much experience with people being in the hospital. From what her parents had said, aside from Chloe's regular admissions to have her babies, no one except Nana had ever been in the hospital.

From what Nana had said about her own hospital stay after breaking her hip, Sophia's dad had visited her every day and her mom every couple of days. However, they hadn't hung around long. Sophia figured that was just who they were, and given that they weren't that close to Bryson, it made some sort of sense. Maybe.

Or maybe she was just trying to make excuses for them. Trying to justify why they'd never been that invested in her life, and now by default, Bryson's.

"You okay?" Ryker asked.

Sophia looked up, not even having realized she'd dropped her gaze from him and Bryson to where her hand rested on Bryson's leg. She gave him a smile that would hopefully reassure him since she didn't feel like discussing her family right then. If ever.

"Yes. I'm just happy that he's enjoying something."

Ryker gave her a look that told her that he wasn't completely buying that response, but he didn't say anything about it. "I found a recipe online, then gave it to Mom to make with a couple of tweaks."

"I might need to get a copy of that recipe because I have a feeling that even once we're home, he's still going to be wanting these in addition to his regular bananas and peanut butter."

"I'm more than happy to give it to you." Ryker set the smoothie cup on the wheeled table that sat across the end of Bryson's bed. "Let me know when you want more, buddy, okay?"

"Okay."

Bryson's reply was still weaker than normal, but Sophia knew she couldn't focus on that. In comparison to where he'd been a week ago, his current state was a considerable improvement. That was what she needed to focus on. Small steps forward were still steps in the right direction, even if they weren't great strides.

When the nurse came in a few minutes later, she greeted Ryker with a friendly smile before turning her attention to Bryson and the monitors.

As she listened to Ryker interact with the nurse and Bryson, Sophia couldn't help but think once again that any patient of his would be so very fortunate. His caring and loving nature shone through even in his conversations with the staff. It was probably why so many still remembered him even though it had been a while since he'd last been there.

Sophia understood that completely because she was quite sure that in years to come, both she and Bryson would remember Ryker and how caring he'd been to them.

CHAPTER TWENTY-TWO

Ryker settled back in his chair at the table, watching as the nurse spoke with Sophia and Bryson. Though he'd interacted with the staff, he knew it wasn't his place to participate in any medical discussions. It seemed that she'd been doing just fine without his help over the past few days, so he wasn't going to barge in now.

If she asked him for his advice on something or needed clarification about anything she was told, he'd definitely help her out. But otherwise, he needed to remember that he was there strictly as a friend...even if he might want to be more.

The nurse wanted Bryson to move around more, and though he was sure Sophia thought he was still too weak, Ryker knew it was necessary. The long road to recovery needed to be pushed forward with small steps. Physical movement being one of them. Eating and drinking being another.

Seeing Bryson enjoy the smoothie had been very gratifying since Sophia had been so worried about his intake. If that was something he'd consume willingly, Ryker wasn't going to tell him that there was more than just bananas and peanut butter in it. Things like whole milk and some peanut butter flavored protein powder had been added to bulk up the nutritional content.

He wasn't sure yet if Sophia was going to ask him to stay away again—it was fifty-fifty on that—but even if she did, he'd make sure that Bryson had the smoothies. It was an unexpected blessing that the little guy had been so obsessed with something that could be healthy for him.

"See you later, Doctor Bennett," the nurse called over to him as she made her way to the door.

"Sure thing," he replied as he got to his feet.

"Lots of people asked where you were during the days you weren't here," Sophia said as he joined her at the bed again.

"What did you tell them?" Ryker asked.

"That you had other things that required your attention."

"That was true enough," he said. "Do you want to grab a few minutes for yourself? Take a shower or go for a walk? I'm happy to entertain him for a bit."

She glanced at Bryson. "I'm not sure he'll let me go if he's awake."

"What do you say, buddy?" Ryker said as he turned to the little boy who lay back against his pillow watching them. "Want to read some books with me while your mom goes out for a few minutes?"

He could tell that Bryson wasn't totally on board with the idea, so he didn't push too hard, but he did push a little. "You can have more of your smoothie, and I'll read your favorite stories to you."

"Ryker will stay with you the whole time," Sophia said. "And I'll be back before too long."

"And she'll take her phone just in case we need her to come back sooner. She's not leaving the hospital, just your room for a few minutes."

It was like they were tag-teaming Bryson in an attempt to get him to agree. This was more than just getting Sophia a bit of a break. He knew from things Sophia had previously said that the boy was reluctant to let her out of his sight, especially when they weren't in their own home. Ryker was hoping that Bryson liked him enough to accept him as a substitute for his momma. Albeit a poor one.

The furrow of Bryson's brow had Ryker braced for a refusal.

"Okay."

He lifted his brows as he exchanged a look with Sophia. "Perfect! Now tell me, which stories are we going to read? I think I picked up your favorites when I was at your house."

Picking up the books stacked on the table beside his bed, Ryker spread them on the bed in front of Bryson. He heard Sophia moving around behind him, and he lifted his gaze in time to give her an encouraging smile as she pulled open the door.

"So, which one are we going to start with?" Ryker asked, returning his attention to Bryson.

He was pleased to see Bryson choose one that he knew that the little boy had memorized. It gave him hope that he might be willing to read with him. There were always neurological concerns—among others—that followed a diagnosis of bacterial meningitis, so if the little guy could remember his stories, it would be very encouraging.

After stacking up the books he'd hadn't chosen, Ryker angled himself to hold the book so that Bryson could see it. He read the first page slowly, waiting to see if Bryson would chime in. Hoping that he would.

It took two pages before Bryson began to recite the phrase that was repeated at the bottom of each page. Fighting the urge to fist pump the air, Ryker continued to read. He took it slow so that even with his whispered words, Bryson could keep up with him.

When they finished that book, Bryson chose another one and asked for his smoothie. Ryker could hardly contain his joy as he began to read through the next one. In between sips from the cup that seemed almost too big for his small hands, Bryson would either recite a few words with him or make a comment on the pictures.

It seemed like he hadn't even noticed his mom was gone, but Ryker definitely wasn't going to draw his attention to her absence. Though he was happy that Bryson seemed content with him while his mom was out of his sight, Ryker wasn't convinced that that would extend to a nurse he didn't know as well. Still, it was a step in the right direction.

They'd slowly read through four books by the time Sophia re-appeared, her hair damp from the shower she'd apparently taken during her time away. Part of him had thought she might just hang around outside the door in case Bryson started to cry for her, so he was glad to see she'd gone further than that, to a place that was guaranteed to take her out of earshot of her son.

"We read books, Momma," he said with a smile, his eyes wide. "Four of them!"

"That's great, baby." Sophia set her things down on a chair then approached the bed, bringing with her a subtle scent of flowers. "Did you help Ryker with the words?"

Bryson nodded. "And I drank more smoothie."

Ryker wasn't sure if the boy had been talking this much in the days he'd been gone, but from the look of joy on Sophia's face, he was going to guess that perhaps he hadn't. Not that he thought he was some miracle worker or anything, but Ryker had a feeling that Sophia tended to baby Bryson a bit. Afraid to push him too far.

Ryker, on the other hand, tried to present Bryson with things that he'd done before in hopes of having him rise to the occasion. Though the boy had definitely recited the stories with more gusto and accuracy in the past, the fact that he'd done what he had was encouraging.

"Thank you for staying with him," Sophia said as she sank down on the other chair next to the bed. "I'm happy he's staying awake for longer periods now, but it does make it challenging for me to get away for even a few minutes. I worry that he'll wake up and..."

Ryker nodded. "Understandable. But we did fine, didn't we buddy?" He held his fist out to Bryson, smiling when Bryson's smaller fist bumped against his.

"I'm going to step out for a few minutes," he said as he got to his feet. "Do you want me to heat up the rest of your lasagna?"

"Sure. That would be great."

With a nod, Ryker went back to the table and picked up the containers with their food, then left the room. Before heading to the family room to heat up the food, he went to the nurses' station.

"Hello, Doctor Bennett," the nurse who had come into Bryson's room earlier greeted him. "Is everything okay?"

"Yep. I'm not sure how the neurological assessments are going on Bryson," Ryker said. "But I thought I'd report what I've seen given that I knew him before he got sick."

"Okay." She grabbed a notepad and set it on the elevated counter in front of him. "You can write it out, and I'll leave a note for the doctor to review it on rounds tomorrow."

"Thanks." Ryker set the containers down and took the pen she held out.

Writing quickly, he made a note of Bryson's abilities before the illness, then added information about what he'd observed during his interactions with him that night. If the doctor had been anyone but his old mentor, he might have been a bit more concerned about stepping on toes. However, one of the reasons he'd so admired and appreciated the older doctor was his ability to put his patients' wellbeing above his pride.

When he was done, he handed both the pen and notepad back to the nurse. "Thanks so much."

"You're welcome."

With that done, he headed for the family lounge, where he knew there was a microwave. There were a couple of people in the room who looked up as he walked in. Their expressions showed the stress that came with having a child in the PICU, which was likely their situation given that this room was used most often by the family members of children in that unit.

He gave them a sympathetic smile and a nod as he made his way to the microwave. It didn't take long to get the food warmed up, then he carefully carried the containers back to Bryson's room.

When he walked in, he noticed that Sophia was still at Bryson's bedside, her hand slowly carding through his curls. It appeared that the boy had fallen asleep once again.

After he set the containers on the table, Sophia joined him there, sitting down on the chair she'd occupied earlier.

"Thank you," she said as she looked down at the food. "I feel like I have a bit more of an appetite now."

"That's good. I was starting to wonder if I needed to bring you a smoothie too." He smiled at her in an effort to take the sting out of his words. "You need to be taking care of yourself."

"That smoothie was a genius idea," she said after she took a bite of her lasagna, possibly to mollify him.

"It was, wasn't it?" He chuckled, so he didn't come across too vain, but he *was* really proud of that flash of inspiration.

After they'd talked a bit more about how Bryson had been while she'd gone for her shower, Sophia fell silent, focusing on the small bites of food she was taking. Ryker wanted her to keep talking, but he didn't push.

"I worry so much about him," she finally said, setting her fork down and leaning back in her chair. She wrapped her arms around herself and kept her chin tucked close to her chest, her gaze lowered.

"I think that's a parent's job," Ryker said, hoping to reassure her that she wasn't doing anything wrong in that regard.

She nodded. "I just want to protect him from anything that might hurt him." He saw her let out a quick exhale. "I haven't always been able to do that, and it feels like I've failed him yet again."

Ryker ran several responses through his head, trying to figure out which one would reassure her and maybe also encourage her to share, if she needed an outlet.

However, before he could say anything, she spoke again.

"I'm sure you're curious about our past," she murmured. "I know I would be."

"You're right. I am," he confessed, knowing that to deny it would be to utter a lie they both would recognize. "But you are not under any obligation to share anything with me. That's not to say that I wouldn't listen if you want to tell me about it."

"I think I would." She glanced up and met his gaze. "The main reason I hate telling people about it is because my past doesn't paint me in a very good light. I come across as naïve, gullible, and desperate."

"I'm not going to think less of you, Sophia," Ryker assured her. "I've seen how much you care for Bryson, and I see the person you are now."

Though she sat forward, she kept her hands in her lap, and her gaze lowered. "Growing up, all I wanted was to get married and have kids. Not as many as my mom had, but still more than just one or two. The guys my age didn't really interest me much because I wanted someone who could support my dream, and that wasn't too likely to be a nineteen or twenty-year-old." She sighed. "Anyway, I was here in Seattle celebrating my twenty-first birthday at a bar with a few of my friends. My parents and Nana wouldn't have approved, but I didn't tell them where we were going."

Ryker wasn't surprised to hear that. His parents probably wouldn't have approved if he'd done that either. They'd viewed bars as places where someone could get into far more trouble than was good, especially as a twenty-one-year-old.

"While we were there, this guy approached me. At first, I was sure that he was setting me up. I mean, there were much more attractive women in the bar who were clearly more adept at flirting and holding a guy's attention. But he stayed focused on me, and at the end of the evening, we exchanged phone numbers." She let out a sigh. "I thought I wouldn't hear from him again, but he texted me the next day to see if I was available to go out for dinner. Of course, I said yes.

"Over the next few days, he picked me up each day after my shift and took me out for dinner. We didn't go to expensive restaurants, which was fine, but he was inventive. We went on picnics and to food fairs. It was fun, and he was engaging, always encouraging me to talk about myself rather than just talking about himself. I thought he was perfect."

Even though Ryker knew the guy wasn't in the picture anymore, he couldn't stop the pang of jealousy that shot through him. If there was one thing Sophia now knew about him, it was that he wasn't perfect. If she was on the lookout for perfection in a man, he was definitely out of the running.

"When he had to go away for a week, I felt absolutely bereft, even though he texted and called me every day while he was gone. Though logic would say that it was too soon, I knew that I loved him. In my mind, we were in the midst of a whirlwind romance. That meant that when he proposed to me just a month after us meeting, I said yes without hesitation. The only thing was that I knew my parents wouldn't agree. That *they* would say it was too soon."

She lifted a hand and rubbed it across her mouth. "When I told Ezekiel that, he said that maybe we didn't need a big church wedding. That we could have something for just the two of us."

"Like eloping?" Ryker asked when she didn't continue right away.

She shook her head, keeping her gaze lowered. "Not really. He said we didn't need a preacher or anyone to make our wedding legal. If we stood before God, just the two of us, that would be enough. He knew my faith in God was a big part of my life, and it seemed that he felt the same way about God. Though I'd never imagined that I wouldn't have a hand in planning my own wedding, he said to leave everything to him. All I had to do was get myself a wedding dress and let him take care of the rest. So I did."

The alarm bells started to clang a bit for Ryker then. He could recognize the manipulations in their relationship already.

"So on the day we'd chosen, he arrived to pick me up wearing a suit and with a bouquet of flowers. He took me to a spot overlooking the ocean, and as the sun set, we pledged our love to each other. It was all super romantic in my mind. I couldn't believe that this handsome man had planned something so wonderful for just the two of us. I didn't feel like it was missing anything even though there was no pastor there to perform the ceremony or guests to witness our vows."

Ryker could see how the romance of it might appeal to someone young and yearning for a romantic connection with another person. But at his age, with everything he'd seen and experienced in his life, he saw something more sinister at work. And, of course, he was listening to everything she told him with the knowledge of how she and Bryson were now, and the things he already suspected.

"My parents were livid when we told them we were married, though we didn't mention that it wasn't exactly legal. I knew they wouldn't understand, even though in my mind, we were very much married." She hesitated then, biting on her lip and keeping her gaze lowered. "He hadn't pushed for anything physical between us before the wedding, saying we needed to wait until we were married. I thought it was him being respectful of me, of my upbringing and my faith."

If what he suspected was true, the roughest part of her story was still to come.

"He'd told me to pack all my things, anything that was important to me, before we told my parents that we were married, just in case they wouldn't let me take my stuff. He said we'd move into our new place together when we got back from our honeymoon. His family lived in Texas, and he wanted me to meet them, so that was

300 · KIMBERLY RAE JORDAN

where we were going to go for a couple of weeks before we returned to start our new life in Seattle."

Ryker had to make a conscious effort to relax his hands when
the handle of the plastic fork he held bit into his palm. He had
always hated when people preyed on the vulnerable. And though
he wouldn't say it to her, Sophia's naivety *had* made her vulnerable.

Still, no one should have taken advantage of that. People should
be allowed to be who they were without fear that others would prey
on them because of it.

He had to admit that her gentle air was attractive to him, but he
didn't want to take advantage of her. He wanted her to continue to
have that because it was part of the person he found himself falling
in love with.

"The first sign of trouble came when we arrived at a walled compound where he said his family lived. Only it wasn't his family that
lived there...at least not ones who were all related to him. There
were men and women there who called him Brother Ezekiel. Children there who called him Father, and other women who called
him Husband. It was...horrible."

"Did you ask him to bring you back to New Hope?" Ryker
asked as his mind filled with all the possibilities of how things had
been for her.

"Not at first because he kept me with him in a cabin separate
from everyone. By the time I fully understood everything, it was
too late to leave. Once I was pregnant and trapped, he introduced
me to the rest of the *family*." She emphasized the word as well as
putting air quotes around it. "They quickly showed me that I wasn't
anyone special, and that became my life for the next five years."

"What happened with your family here?" Ryker asked. "Did
they try and find you?"

"Ezekiel let me use a phone to call and tell my family that we'd
decided to stay in Texas. I was pregnant already, and I just didn't
know what else to do. I already felt like my parents were mad at

me for marrying him. I kind of figured that they would say that I'd made my bed."

Ryker's brows lifted. "Really?"

"Looking back," Sophia said with a sigh, "I'm pretty sure that they would have come to get me if I'd managed to let them know what was happening. Ezekiel convinced me otherwise, however, telling me that my parents didn't want what was best for me."

"So it was a cult?"

She stared down at her food for so long without answering that Ryker wasn't sure she was going to. "Yes. Although Ezekiel called us a family. Eventually, I found out that the cult had been started by his father, some eccentric rich Texan who'd made his fortune in oil years and years ago. When he'd died, Ezekiel assumed control. I don't know where or even who his mother was. There were older women in the compound who were all called mother, so maybe one of them was his actual mother. I never asked. I didn't really want to know anything."

"What was the premise of the cult?" he asked.

After giving him a considering look, she said, "I don't know, really. I mean, there was definitely a spiritual element to it. I recognized enough of Christianity in what was preached and what actions were expected from us to know they'd drawn some from that. I got the feeling that they kind of looked around at a bunch of different religions and picked the most conservative or fundamentalist aspects of them, usually carrying them out in a way that only benefitted the men."

"So they cherry-picked what they wanted to incorporate?"

Sophia nodded. "Like women were supposed to only wear dresses, not cut their hair, and also wear head coverings. I know many women do those things as an act of submission to God. But in the compound, it wasn't encouraged for that reason. They were acts of subservience to Ezekiel and the men there.

"Then there were the spiritual marriages. Several women married to the same man. Those were usually the teenage daughters of the members who had been around when his father had been the leader. There was a lot more rules, but I remember those because they impacted me the most."

"How about the kids? How were they treated?"

"Out of everything there, the situation with the children was the worst." Sophia glanced over at the bed where Bryson was sleeping. "Every birth was at the compound, regardless of the risks to the mom or the baby. If things went wrong, they didn't seek medical help. The compound had its own cemetery for when the worst happened."

The hand she lifted to her forehead trembled slightly, making Ryker want to pull her close and offer her comfort.

"And if a mother couldn't nurse her baby, she had to hope that another nursing mom would help her out because there was no formula available. We did have animals that provided milk, but Ezekiel said it was the mom's job to provide what the baby needed. That he didn't want to take from others already in the compound to provide for a baby."

Ryker was speechless. Okay, no, he wasn't really, but he also wasn't going to blurt out what he was thinking. He was well aware that there were ruthless people like Ezekiel had shown himself to be, but it hurt his heart to think that Sophia and Bryson had been exposed to that.

"As long as your baby was nursing, they let you keep them with you, but once they were weaned, they became family property. We were moms to all of them, though they made sure that the children we interacted with the most were not our own. Once a week, if we'd been good, we had time with our own kids." She hesitated, swallowing audibly. "When I had my time with Bryson, I spent most of it just holding him and whispering *I'm your momma and I love you* to him over and over."

That explained so much to Ryker. Bryson's attachment to his mom and Sophia's protectiveness of her son. "How did you get away?"

"Over the time I was there, Ezekiel had the men go out to work and bring money in. Apparently, they were also procuring weapons for the compound. I guess they must have attracted the attention of the authorities because eventually, the compound was raided. As soon as I realized what was going on, I found Bryson and hid. Ezekiel and all of his top men were killed in the standoff."

"And you came back here afterward?"

"Not right away. I wasn't sure what sort of reception we'd have here. After all, I hadn't been in contact with any of my family in years. For the first month, we were cared for by an organization that helps people in situations like we'd been in. They offered us counseling and assistance to re-enter the real world. A lot had changed in five years, you know? We hadn't had access to television or the internet to know what was going on."

"How come it took that long for the authorities to intervene?"

"I don't know. Maybe if more families of the people in the compound had tried to get us back, though honestly, I'm not sure that many were able to be tracked. Ezekiel made sure that most of the women were never seen outside the compound."

"I guess what matters is that you're both free now."

"Yeah, but unfortunately, we're not free of the consequences of the decision I made to trust Ezekiel. We probably never will be."

Ryker heard the desolation in her voice and tried to find the words to assure her that life could...would...get better. But could he really guarantee that? As they sat in a hospital room where her son was recovering from a potentially deadly disease, Ryker wasn't sure that he could.

CHAPTER TWENTY-THREE

Sophia fought the urge to just lay her head down and sleep. Every time she'd shared her story, it exhausted her. First with the counselor after the raid, then with her parents and Nana, and now with Ryker. And she hadn't even shared all of it. There were parts she didn't want to think about, let alone talk about.

Even telling the little bit she had to Ryker didn't get any easier. Or maybe it was just because she knew that once Ryker was aware of her past, his impression of her would shift.

She'd needed him to know, though. People who were less involved in her life than Ryker currently was, knew her story. It was only fair that he did as well. And maybe knowing that he knew the worst about her would help to curb her growing feelings for him.

"I assume that Mellie was also in the cult," Ryker said.

Sophia winced at the reminder of the woman and what she'd said to Ryker. "Yeah. She was there already when I got there. Not everyone was there against their will."

Ryker's brows rose. "Really?"

"Most of the men were there by choice, and for the most part, they could come and go as they pleased. Some of the women were also there because they wanted to be. Some, like Mellie, actually *wanted* to continue to be with Ezekiel even after realizing the truth of the situation."

"Was that why she was so hateful toward you?"

"I don't know why she was like that, to be honest. I never tried to vie for Ezekiel's attention. In fact, I went out of my way to stay off his radar."

"You could actually do that?"

"Yes. As long as Ezekiel didn't think I was getting close to any other men, he would leave me alone. And if I did what I was supposed to, I could see Bryson for a little bit each week." Though she'd often wished she'd been seen more within her own family growing up, she'd been ever so grateful to blend into the background at the compound.

Ryker's brow furrowed as his gaze shifted to the window. Sophia wondered how long it would be before he excused himself for the day and then just didn't show up ever again. She'd dumped an awful lot on him when he already had so much trauma in his own life.

"I'm surprised that you and Mellie have so few children. So many of those types of cults operate on prolific procreation."

"Ezekiel seemed to be of two minds when it came to children. Yes, he wanted to pass on his genes, but he also didn't want the compound to be overrun with kids. More mouths to feed and all that. What he wanted most when it came to offspring were sons. If you gave him a son the first time around, he was happy with that. If you gave him a daughter, he'd want to keep trying for a son.

"And after you gave him a son, he might pass you off to one of his favored soldiers—as he liked to call them—if he was feeling generous. It was his way of making sure there was some fresh blood in the next generation. Mellie, however, had two children who she claimed were both Ezekiel's, though most of us assumed her daughter was actually someone else's."

"So it was good that you had a son first?"

"Yes." Sophia recalled her relief when the woman attending Bryson's birth had said he was a boy. By then, she'd become aware of what that meant. Why Ezekiel hadn't passed her on to another man, she didn't know, but it was yet another thing she'd been grateful for in the midst of so much pain and suffering.

After she'd returned to New Hope, Nana had told her how she'd prayed constantly for God's hand of protection to be on Sophia. As she'd thought back over times at the compound when there had been potential trauma or unpleasant situations for her, Sophia had wondered if some of them had been diverted from her because of Nana's prayers.

There was really no other explanation for why she'd been spared the worst of what had been possible in the compound.

"Thank you for sharing your story with me," Ryker said after she'd lapsed into silence, her thoughts mired in the past.

"Thank you for sharing *your* story with *me*."

Ryker's brow furrowed. "I know I talked about us exchanging stories, but I hope you didn't feel obliged to tell me about your past simply because I'd shared about mine."

"It wasn't that," Sophia said. "It's just that you're so involved in our lives, it felt...right to tell you about what happened."

"I'm glad you told me." Ryker leaned forward, his gaze intent. "I want you to always feel like you can trust me, Sophia."

As she looked into his light blue eyes, Sophia knew that she would take him at his word. After all she'd experienced at the hands of a man who knew how to use his words to entice, one would think she'd know better. But she desperately wanted to trust Ryker, especially after he'd been so good to her and Bryson.

"I know that you have no reason to trust me," he said, seeming to read her thoughts. "And I understand that. All I want you to know at this point is that you are important to me. You and Bryson both. I care about you, and if you let me, I'd like to be a part of your life in whatever form you're willing to have me."

Sophia's heart skipped a few beats at his words, making it difficult to take a breath. Was it even possible that a man like Ryker could want her and Bryson in the way she'd always longed for a man to want her in his life?

"I'd never..." Sophia swallowed, hoping she wasn't misinterpreting his words. "I'd never turn you away. You're important to Bryson and me as well."

A smile spread across Ryker's face, lighting up his eyes. Sophia wasn't sure how to take his expression because it seemed like her response had truly made him happy. Maybe even more than just happy. Was that even possible? That even with all her issues, the idea of having her in his life made him happy?

"I can see that you don't really understand how I'm feeling," Ryker said, his smile turning gentle. "And that's fine. I'll happily take the time to show you until you do understand."

After enduring so much darkness over the past several years, was it possible that things were turning around? But more importantly, could she trust herself to make a good decision where Ryker was concerned?

It wasn't that she needed time to heal from a previous relationship—her feelings for Ezekiel had died years ago—but she carried a lot of baggage. Most of it tied to how much she'd failed Bryson over the years. Normally she'd be wary of allowing a man to get too close to him, but Ryker had blown past those concerns already with Bryson's help.

She wasn't even entirely sure they were speaking about the same thing. Maybe Ryker was just talking about friendship while her mind—and heart—had jumped right to happily-ever-after. She needed to pump the brakes on her emotions for the time being. Give Ryker time to reveal what he truly wanted from her.

And if she ended up with another broken heart...well, that seemed to be a theme in her life, and she'd survived it before. She'd survive it again. But it would be the absolute last time she listened to her heart. Absolute *last* time.

Ryker's phone vibrated on the table, and he glanced at it before frowning. "I need to take this. I'll be back."

After he left the room, Sophia stared down at her reheated lasagna, not sure that it would survive yet another reheating, no matter how good it was. She took another small bite, surprised that even with it not being hot anymore, it actually didn't taste bad.

Though her stomach was still not settled after recounting what had happened with Ezekiel, she knew she needed to eat a bit more. She really wasn't trying to starve herself, especially when she still hadn't put on the weight she needed to after leaving Texas. Both she and Bryson had still needed to gain weight before this latest setback. It was something she would have to focus on even more once they were back home again.

In the quiet of the room, she continued to take small bites of lasagna interspersed with nibbles of the garlic bread that was really quite delicious. It still amazed her that Ryker's mom had gone to the trouble of providing food for her and the smoothie for Bryson.

She didn't know the woman's motivations, but she'd like to think that she was just a really nice person. That wasn't beyond the scope of imagination, given that Ryker seemed to also be a really nice person.

When Ryker came back into the room, the frown was still in place as he sat down across from her. "That was my sister, doing her best to annoy me. I swear, if my folks had had her first, there would be no me or Silas."

Sophia let out a soft laugh. "Don't bet on it. I have a very difficult sister, and from everything I've heard, she's been that way since birth, and my parents still went on to have five more kids after her."

"Do you get along with her?"

"As long as I don't disagree with her, sure. We get along great."

"Sounds like Callie. The woman thinks she knows what's right for the whole world. You'd think she had enough going on in her own life to not be meddling in mine, but no. She has plenty of thoughts on all my life choices."

"Just yours?"

"Not much she can comment on with Silas. His chosen career is going well. He has two great kids, and he has a lovely wife who · puts up with Callie. But she knows better than to go after Silas's family. She's welcome to take pot-shots at him and me, but the people we care about and have chosen to have in our lives, are off-limits."

Sophia wondered if that would apply to her and Bryson. She had to admit that the thought of coming under the scrutiny of a woman like that made her cringe. There were so many things about her life that Callie could pick apart and find fault with. No matter how she felt about her brother, it was possible she'd look at Sophia and Bryson and decide that they weren't good enough for Ryker.

Maybe it would be better if Ryker *was* only in this for the friendship.

"Let's just say that I don't think she'll be calling me back today, and thankfully, we don't have a family dinner tomorrow night. I have another week before I have to face her down."

The conversation veered away from the difficult things they'd shared that day, and Ryker told her about what had happened that week at his job. She found his joy in the work he did with Michael interesting, given he was trained to do something so very different. But from everything he said, he really enjoyed working with Michael doing landscaping and yard work.

"How is Vivianne?" Sophia asked.

"She seems to be doing fine."

Sophia found that she missed the little girl. Though she'd never been like Chloe, wanting a family the size of baseball team, she'd always sort of hoped that she'd have at least two or three.

"And is Michael's leg doing okay?"

"Yep. He's in a walking cast now, and that should be coming off in a bit. He'll have to do some physio, though, because he's lost muscle in that leg."

"I'm sure he'll be thrilled to be back to normal." Sophia knew that *she'd* be thrilled when she and Bryson were back to normal. When that would be, she had no idea.

Since neither of them had eaten all the lasagna, Ryker left to get them something for a late dinner. She'd thought he would just go to the cafeteria in the hospital and grab a couple of sandwiches, but when he returned, he had a takeaway bag from a restaurant.

"Hope you like Chinese," he said as he set the food on the table. "I suppose I should have asked before I left."

"Chinese is fine," she told him.

Bryson was awake again, but he wasn't interested in eating anything. He did accept the other cup of smoothie that Ryker had brought, however. She really hoped that this was the start of his appetite returning. The day he asked for actual bananas with peanut butter, she'd know that he was officially on the mend.

Ryker let her dish up her food first, then filled his plate. They took their plates over by Bryson's bed so that they could interact with him too.

"When can we go home?" Bryson asked.

Sophia's eyes widened. It was the first time that he'd asked about that. Emotion swamped her, making her eyes sting with tears at this latest evidence of his improvement.

"There are a few things that need to happen first," Ryker told him.

As he laid out what those things were, Sophia was grateful that he could explain them in a way that Bryson would understand. She wasn't sure she would have been able to do that, but she supposed that Ryker's ease with Bryson came from his experience as a pediatrician.

After they finished eating, Ryker read with him again while Sophia curled up on the small armchair by the window, grateful that he wanted to spend time with Bryson like that. And now there was the prospect that Ryker actually wanted to be there for both of them.

Sophia let her gaze linger on the two of them, and she prayed that she wasn't reading the situation wrong. Bryson needed someone like Ryker in his life, and she couldn't deny that she did as well. That he had taken her revelations in stride gave her hope. She knew she wasn't a great catch, but if Ryker would let her, she'd love him as fiercely as she loved Bryson. And if he'd love her even a quarter as much, she'd be happy.

Bryson was beginning to nod off when the nurse popped in. She was friendly and listened with interest when Ryker explained what was in the insulated cup that sat on the table across the bed.

"Well, it's definitely good to hear that he's drinking now," she said. "Even if it is a peanut product."

Ryker held up his hands. "I promise, I'm making sure that there is no transfer to anywhere outside this room."

"I should reprimand you." But then the nurse sighed. "The ridiculous thing is, we've had peanut products in the vending machines and the cafeteria, and you're not the first to bring in peanut-based food. But at least you know enough to take precautions. At this point, I'm just happy he's taking something by mouth. He hasn't been particularly interested in eating or drinking more than a couple of mouthfuls at a time."

"I'm hoping that this will help jumpstart his appetite," Ryker said. "We've got to start somewhere."

"We certainly do," the nurse agreed. "Not that we want to see him go, but you know he needs to be well enough to leave the PICU for a step-down unit before they'll consider letting him go home."

Sophia watched as the nurse looked over the monitors and tried to get Bryson to talk to her. But Bryson being Bryson, he only gave her wary looks and single word answers spoken in a whisper.

"I'll be back later to check on him," the nurse said to her. "Get some sleep."

"I'll try," Sophia said, though that would be a first. What she wouldn't give for a night with the two of them in their own beds at the house.

Once Bryson had fallen asleep, Ryker began to gather up the bags he'd brought with him. "I'll bring more smoothies for him tomorrow. Here are some cinnamon buns and cookies for you to snack on if you get hungry."

"Thanks." She had a pit in her stomach at the thought of him leaving, but she knew he needed to go. He'd spent a lot of time with them, and she knew it was selfish to want more. But still, she did.

Ryker set the bags on a chair and came to where she stood. He grasped her upper arms, his grip gentle. Giving her an affectionate smile, he said, "You've got this, sweetheart. You're stronger than you know, and Bryson is *so* lucky to have you as his mom."

For the second time that evening, she blinked back tears. "I haven't often felt that way."

It was a relief to be able to say stuff like that, knowing he'd now understand where she was coming from.

"I know, but the reality is, he is blessed to have a mom who is looking out for his best interests now that she's able to. Things might look a little rough at the moment, but you're here with him, showering him with love, and he feels that."

Lifting her hands, she gripped his forearms, trying to draw on the strength she felt there. "He's lucky to have you in his life too. We both are."

At those words, Ryker drew her close, wrapping his arms around her as she tucked her head under his chin. In his embrace, she felt protected and cared for. She'd never imagined that she'd want to be that close to a man again. In fact, she'd accepted that the life she'd once dreamed of wouldn't be hers.

However, Ryker was changing that, offering her hope that she wanted to reach out and grab with both hands. But even though she'd accepted that she might get her heart broken again, she really didn't want that, which made her afraid to hope too much. Too many times, her hopes had been dashed, and she had a feeling that this time would hurt the most because Ryker was a genuinely good man who Bryson also adored.

The feeling of loss would be immense if he decided that he really didn't want to take on all their issues. Maybe she needed to protect her heart for just a little while longer. Just to be sure he wasn't going to change his mind.

Stepping back, Ryker cupped her face in his hands, gazing down at her with an emotion she wasn't sure she trusted just yet.

"Try to sleep tonight. I know it's hard, but you're still close to him. You'll hear if he needs you, and the nurses will be checking on him throughout the night."

She wished she could assure him that she'd sleep, but all she could do was say she'd try. She doubted she'd sleep a solid night until they were back in their own home, and Bryson was over the deadly disease that had brought him to the hospital.

"I'll be back tomorrow," he said. Then, after the briefest of hesitations, he leaned forward and pressed a light kiss to her forehead.

She gave him a smile that felt weak, but she tried. "We'll be here."

After Ryker had left the room, she sank down on the bed she used and covered her face with her hands. With Bryson already asleep, she felt utterly alone. Even though she'd shared about her past, and Ryker seemed willing to help her with Bryson, the weight of it all fell heavily on her right then.

She wanted to be strong, not just for Bryson's sake but also because she didn't want to appear weak to Ryker. Though honestly, that ship had probably sailed already.

She let out a shaky breath even as tears pricked at her eyes yet again.

Fear not, for I am with you;
Be not dismayed, for I am your God.
I will strengthen you,
Yes, I will help you,
I will uphold you with My righteous right hand.

The verse echoed through her mind, offering her comfort and hope, if only she accepted it.

Every part of it seemed so relevant to her current situation.

She was afraid of what the future held for Bryson—*fear not.*

She was alone—*I am with you.*

She felt weak—*I will strengthen you.*

She was often confused and worried—*I will help you.*

And when she felt like she couldn't go on—*I will uphold you.*

Closing her eyes, she thanked God for the reminder that He was there for her in every way she could ever need. She also thanked Him for sending Ryker to them. He was a blessing that she didn't feel worthy of but was so very grateful for.

Visiting hours had just started when Ryker appeared the next morning, once again bearing bags of food. After he set the bags down on the table, he turned to where Sophia stood next to Bryson's bed.

"Good morning," he said with a smile as he approached them, an insulated cup in his hand.

Sophia gripped the edge of the bed as she smiled back at him, feeling a little bit shy for some reason. "Hi."

Through her restless sleep of the previous night, she'd spent a lot of time replaying the conversation she'd had with Ryker, wondering if she'd read things into what he'd said. It was hard not to second guess everything because she didn't trust herself to see things for how they really were. Because of that, she'd also spent time praying for wisdom and God's will with regards to Ryker's role in their lives.

Seeing him again in the cold light of day, the worries she'd had over whether or not he'd really been talking about a possible relationship between them came roaring back to life. She needed to watch his actions, not just listen to his words. Right then, his actions showed care for her and Bryson.

"Hi, Ryker," Bryson said, his voice soft.

"Hey, buddy." Ryker held his hand out for a fist bump.

Sophia had to admit that she appreciated how Ryker wasn't treating Bryson any differently just because he'd been sick. She probably should have done that a little more with him, but she couldn't keep from babying him. He *was* her baby, after all.

Bryson seemed to want to try and respond to Ryker the way he had before getting so sick. He took the cup from Ryker with a bigger smile than she'd seen from him in over a week.

If it had been for anyone other than Ryker, she might have felt jealous that she hadn't been able to evoke such a reaction from him. But at this point, she was just so relieved to see sparks of his old personality that it didn't matter that it was someone other than her who had brought them to life.

"How're you doing?" Ryker asked as he turned to her, concern in his gaze. His hand rested briefly on her back. "How did you sleep?"

She shrugged. "About the same. I just don't know how to sleep more soundly here."

Obviously reading her exhaustion, he slipped his arm around her. Sophia couldn't help but slump against him, letting him take her weight for a moment. He didn't stagger or seem to have any trouble holding her, and it made Sophia want to cry, but she didn't because she'd cried far too much over the past week.

"Well, if you want to lay down for a bit, I'm here."

It was something she'd done before, so she'd probably take him up on that offer again.

"Is that good, buddy?" Ryker asked as he watched Bryson sip at the cup.

Sophia didn't know why God had brought Ryker into her life. She certainly didn't feel that she deserved him. But there was no denying that she and Bryson needed him. Ezekiel had never

316 · KIMBERLY RAE JORDAN

offered his strength to either of them. If anything, he'd used his strength against them.

Ryker wasn't like that at all. He had only ever used his strength and abilities to help them. How long would it take for him to realize that he was getting short-changed? Especially when it came to her?

As she stood there with Ryker's arm around her, Sophia wondered if it was wrong to lean on him, to accept the things he offered, when she felt certain that, in time, he would realize that she and Bryson wouldn't be a good fit for his life. Maybe not wrong, but certainly selfish.

But every time she'd tried to get him to go back to his life, he'd resisted. And even when he had agreed to take a couple days away, he'd come back. Maybe he really did want to be there with them.

CHAPTER TWENTY-FOUR

When it came time for Ryker to leave later that night, it was the hardest thing he'd had to do in a long time.

"I'll be back tomorrow," he said as he'd gathered up the bags he'd brought with more food from his mom.

"You don't have to," Sophia said from where she stood next to Bryson's bed. Her arms were wrapped across her waist, and even though she'd slept a little that afternoon, she still looked exhausted and fragile.

"I know I don't have to." He moved closer to her and lifted his hand to cup her cheek. "I want to be here for you. With you."

Her eyes fluttered shut for a moment before she looked up at him. "Thank you for being here today."

"I'm glad I was here for the good news," he said with a smile as he lowered his hand. "I know you're probably a bit worried about leaving the monitoring of the PICU, but they wouldn't be moving Bryson to a regular unit if he wasn't ready. Him eating and moving around more is a good sign."

"I know."

"Just think of it as one step closer to him going home, which is what we all want for him."

"Yes. I really do want that."

"Do you need anything from your house that I can get for you?"

She shook her head. "I think I'm okay."

He didn't know how she was for clothes, but he figured she wasn't comfortable asking him to pick up more for her. Hopefully, now that Bryson was on the mend, it wouldn't be too much longer until he could go home. Then they could move forward, and Ryker

318 · KIMBERLY RAE JORDAN

hoped that he and Sophia would be able to start to build something between them.

He could see that she wasn't entirely sure what he wanted from her, and he knew that a lot of that came from her inability to trust herself after getting caught up in a cult the way she had. That was okay. They had time.

Though he was ready to acknowledge and embrace his feelings for Sophia, he still had some work to do emotionally in order to deal with his reactions to what had happened in Syria.

He knew that some might question his sense in starting a relationship while also going back to therapy. Callie would probably tell him that if he was trying to get better for someone else, it wouldn't work.

What Callie wouldn't understand was that yes, he wanted to get better for someone else. But it wasn't just for Sophia or even Bryson. He wanted to get better for any children he might come in contact with in the future...whether that was in a medical practice or just in life in general.

Being around Bryson and Vivianne had reminded him just how much he loved children. The two of them had managed to break through the defenses he'd put up, making him more vulnerable to his nightmares, but also reminding him of the joy he felt when he was around children.

But more than that, everyone in his life deserved the best version of him. For years, the best version he could manage was the one that allowed him to function, even if it was just barely. Now, though, he felt like with God's help he was strong enough to reach for an even better version of himself. To strive to become the man God wanted him to be.

He wasn't going to leave Sophia alone while he did it, though. Doing that didn't feel like it would help him be a better version of himself.

"Text me when you're in the new room with Bryson, okay?" he said, glancing to where the boy slept. "And I'll be back here as soon as I'm done work."

This time, she didn't tell him he didn't need to come back. She just smiled wearily and said, "Okay."

He slid an arm around her and let his cheek rest on her head for a moment. "If you need me for anything, call. And if you think of anything that you need from your house, text me what it is. I still have your keys."

She leaned against him for a moment, and Ryker found that he enjoyed the feel of her body against his. He knew she could be strong when she had to be, but he appreciated that she seemed willing to lean on him when she needed to as well.

"Try and get some sleep," he said, then pressed a kiss to her hair, waiting for her to straighten up before moving his arm from around her. "See you tomorrow."

She nodded, and for a moment, he thought she might cry, but instead, she took a deep breath. "Drive safe."

"I will." He gave her one last smile, then left the room.

As he walked out to his truck, he was already counting the hours until he was back again and with a surprise that he hoped would brighten her day.

"You're a sweet boy," the older woman said as she reached over and patted his arm. "A real blessing to my Sophia and Bryson. I feel like I know you already because Bryson has talked about you so much."

Ryker glanced at the woman in the passenger seat of Sophia's car. When he'd first approached her on Friday evening about taking her to see Sophia and Bryson, he hadn't been sure what she'd say.

"I'm glad you felt up to coming with me." He'd thought that the hour-long drive might be too exhausting for her, but she'd insisted that she would be fine.

"I'm not really an invalid," she told him. "It's just that after breaking my hip twice and not having it heal correctly, it was better for me to stay in the care home since my house isn't exactly wheelchair friendly. But it all worked out because now Sophia and Bryson can make my house their own."

"That was very generous of you to let them stay in your house."

"They needed it," she said, and out of the corner of his eye, he could see her watching him. "Has she talked much to you about her life?"

"Well, I know that she's from a large family," Ryker said, though he suspected that wasn't what she was asking.

"That is definitely true." Then, instead of telling him about Sophia's life in the cult, she began to tell him about when Sophia was a baby and how it was that she ended up closer to her grandmother than her own immediate family.

As her grandmother told him about her past with Sophia, Ryker came to understand a whole lot more about the woman he loved. He didn't feel like the older woman was revealing anything she shouldn't because this story was certainly hers as much as it was Sophia's.

All he could think about was how it had been for Sophia, with her quiet, gentle personality, to be part of a large, and from what she'd said, boisterous family. It would have been very easy for her to fade into the background.

He knew from his experience that the loudest and most forceful people got the lion's share of attention. It was easy for them to demand that people listen to them because their personalities supported that aggressive approach.

Callie was a good example of that in their family. Silas, on the other hand, was more reserved and quieter, rarely getting into debates with anyone.

As the middle child, maybe it wasn't too surprising that Ryker fell in the middle personality-wise as well. While he didn't seek out attention the way Callie did, he could hold his own if he needed to. Especially with her.

"I don't think Sophia trusts her own judgment these days," Nana said, interrupting his thoughts. "Particularly with the people she allows into her and Bryson's lives. Which is probably why she basically has no friends at the moment."

Hearing sadness in the older woman's voice, Ryker glanced over at her. "Didn't she have friends from when she lived in New Hope before?"

"Yes, she did, but it seems these days that a lot of the young people end up leaving town for college or better job opportunities. I think that's what happened with some of her friends. I think the bigger part of it, however, is that she's ashamed of what happened." She paused. "Has she talked to you about that?"

"She's told me about Ezekiel and the cult," he said.

"Good. That tells me that she trusts you—as much as she trusts anyone these days—and that makes me happy."

"Did you wonder where she was those five years she was gone?" Ryker asked.

"I knew where she was," Nana said. "I hired a private investigator to find her when it seemed that she'd dropped off the face of the earth. It didn't take too long for him to figure out where she was, but it was impossible to gain access to her. From what the private investigator was able to determine, she never left the compound. He spoke to others who were also trying to find their children at the compound, and they reported the same thing.

"The only people who left appeared to be very loyal to the cult and would divulge nothing when approached by family members.

All I could do was pray that something would happen to free her from the situation."

"And then the compound was raided."

"Yes. When I heard that on the news, I saw it as a definite answer to prayer. It took a bit to get her back here. I think she was scared to come home, but this is where she needed to be in order to heal." Nana fell silent for a moment, then cleared her throat. "I needed her here so I could see that she was okay. Bryson was a lovely surprise. A blessing in the midst of turmoil."

"He's a great little boy," Ryker said.

"I'm so glad you see that. Far too many people—and yes, I'm counting my own family in there—only see him as a little boy with a bunch of issues. There's no denying he has those, but to expect him not to, would be unreasonable given the situation they've been in. I just wish people would be more patient and understanding of him. Well, and of Sophia too."

"I have issues of my own," Ryker found himself confessing. There was just something about the older woman that made him feel safe and comfortable, much like he had with Sophia.

"Well, dear," she said with a pat on his arm. "We all have issues to varying degrees."

"Isn't that the truth."

Ryker shared his own story with her as they finished the drive to the hospital, and just like her granddaughter, Nana was sympathetic and understanding. When he helped her from the car once they'd reached the parking lot, she gave him a tight hug before settling into the wheelchair.

He found himself even more eager than usual to reach Bryson's room, but first, he had to get Nana's visitor badge sorted out. Thankfully, when he'd arrived with Sophia back when Bryson had first been transferred, she'd listed him as a guardian, so he was able to get the ID for Nana without any issues.

Once that was all sorted, they made their way up to the unit where Bryson had been moved. Thankfully, no one stopped him to chat as he pushed Nana's wheelchair, and soon they were at the door to Bryson's new room. It stood open, so he hoped that meant they weren't sleeping.

Slowly he pushed the wheelchair into the room, glancing around for Sophia and Bryson. He smiled when he spotted the two of them curled up together on the small loveseat that sat against one wall, a book open on their laps.

Sophia glanced up, her eyes widening as her gaze landed on Nana. Moving carefully, she shifted Bryson slightly. When she was free of him, she got up and moved quickly toward them, dropping to her knees to press her face against Nana's leg.

Hearing her sobs, Ryker went to where Bryson sat, his brow furrowed in obvious concern. He lifted the boy onto his lap, being careful of the IV he still had in his arm.

"Momma's crying?" he asked as he glanced worriedly between them.

"Yes, she's crying," Ryker said, not wanting to lie to the boy. "But it's because she's happy to see Nana."

Bryson stared at the women for a long moment before he said, "I'm happy to see Nana too."

Ryker figured that the little guy was wondering if he should be crying too. He rubbed his hand on his back as he said, "Not everyone will cry every time they're happy. I think your momma really missed Nana."

Bryson leaned back against Ryker, tension leaving his body. "Did she miss us?"

"Yes, buddy. She's definitely missed you too."

Nana was bent over Sophia, her hands smoothing over her hair. Ryker felt a surge of emotion as he watched the two women together. He hadn't been one hundred percent sure about bringing Nana to the hospital. Still, now that they were together, he was glad that he'd made the decision to go to the personal care home and speak to her about visiting Bryson and Sophia.

"Do you want to keep reading your story?" Ryker asked.

Bryson's head rubbed against Ryker's chest as he nodded, then he patted the book he still held. "This one."

As they began to read the story together, Ryker saw out of the corner of his eye that Sophia had gotten to her feet and had wheeled Nana over to the table by the window. Knowing they probably had plenty to talk about, he chose to focus his attention on Bryson.

After they finished the book, Ryker helped Bryson stand then walk over to where his mom and great-grandma sat, guiding the IV stand so it didn't get caught on anything. From the emotion on Nana's face, he could see that it was difficult for her to see him unsteady on his feet. But given where he'd been even just two days earlier, seeing him walk like that was a wonderful thing.

"Look at you go," Nana said, giving Bryson a wide smile as she held open her arms.

He basically fell against the woman as he reached her, then Sophia lifted him up so he could sit on Nana's lap. It took a bit of arranging to get him situated on the side of her uninjured hip, then he and Nana began to talk.

Sophia walked over to where Ryker stood, looking up at him with an emotion-filled gaze. "Thank you."

He smiled down at her as he lifted his hand to brush it across her cheek. "You're welcome."

She stepped closer to him then, and Ryker wrapped her in his arms. Her arms went around him, and he felt her grip handfuls of his shirt as her forehead rested against his shoulder.

"You don't know how much I needed her," Sophia murmured. "She's been my strength for so long, and seeing her... Well, maybe I didn't know how much I needed her until that moment."

"I'm glad you have her in your life," Ryker said softly. "I enjoyed getting to know her on our drive. She seems like a very special person."

Sophia lifted her head and tipped her chin up so their gazes met. She smiled as she said, "She is the very best person. I'm so glad that God blessed me with her. I couldn't have asked for a better grandmother."

"How have things been here today?" he asked, letting his arms drop as she turned to look at Nana and Bryson.

"The move went off without too much hassle," she said. "He was disappointed that he didn't get to leave his IV behind."

Ryker chuckled. "I'm sure. I've yet to meet a person—adult or child—who enjoys having an IV in, so he's in good company."

"It's an experience that I've never had," she said.

Ryker was going to say something about her obviously not having an epidural with Bryson but stopped the words in time. Of course, she hadn't had an epidural since she hadn't had a hospital birth.

"How about I go get some supper for everyone?" he suggested when Bryson slid off Nana's lap.

Sophia lifted Bryson onto the chair next to Nana then they began to discuss food options. In the end, they decided on a nearby deli that served soup and sandwiches. It was a spot he'd frequented over the years, and he knew that the food was good.

Leaving the three of them chatting, Ryker smiled as he walked down the hallway to the elevator. It made him happy that he'd been able to do something that had made Sophia so happy.

When he got back with the food, the four of them huddled around the small table. Bryson ate half of the child-size grilled cheese sandwich that Ryker had bought for him. That made Ryker, Sophia, and the nurse very happy. He'd brought another smoothie, but he didn't offer it until after Bryson had eaten part of the sandwich.

He could see the concern on Nana's face, but he knew that she was comparing Bryson to how he'd been before he got sick. If she'd seen him a week earlier, she'd understand how much of a win this truly was.

For a couple of hours that evening, Ryker was able to see flashes of how Bryson had been before ending up in the hospital. It gave him hope that the little boy would be recovered enough to go home soon.

Sophia got emotional when it was time for them to leave. Ryker wished that he could bring her grandmother every day to visit, but he knew that the travel time alone would be exhausting for the older woman. Maybe he'd try and bring her back again on the weekend if it looked like Bryson would be staying in the hospital for another week or so.

Once again, Sophia encouraged him to not come back the next day. But unlike the last time, she didn't suggest that he stay away for several days. When he said that maybe he would come back the day after, she'd been quick to agree to that.

Still, once he'd dropped Nana back at the care home, Ryker wasn't sure that he'd be able to stay away for that long. If he thought Sophia would take care of herself, it would be a bit easier to space out his visits. So even though he'd agreed to her suggestion, he reserved the right to do what he wanted the next day.

~*~

Sophia still wasn't sleeping well, but the exhaustion had begun to lift. It seemed that maybe a lot of that exhaustion had been mental because, with the move to the new unit and Bryson's improvement, the tiredness that had felt so overwhelming didn't feel like it was going to drown her anymore.

And Ryker...she couldn't believe that he'd gone to the trouble of picking Nana up and bringing her to the hospital. Being able to spend that time with her had been amazing, and she was glad that Nana had had the chance to get to know Ryker a little bit.

When she'd hugged Sophia right before leaving, Nana had told her that he seemed like a really decent guy. She'd always valued Nana's opinion, so knowing that Nana shared her opinion of Ryker made her feel even better about how things were progressing.

And even though she knew she wouldn't be seeing him that day, the happiness she felt stayed with her.

Bryson was smiling more, and she was starting to see more of the boy he'd been before getting sick. Even though it had been just twenty-four hours since moving from PICU to the regular unit, she could see such a difference in him. It stood to reason that the doctors wouldn't have felt that he was ready to move unless they could see that Bryson was on the right path.

It seemed like maybe everything had turned a corner, and Sophia felt like she could take a deep breath without feeling like she had a vice constricting her chest.

Since the nurses were encouraging Bryson to walk more—and he was actually becoming more stable on his feet—she had him walk with her to the family lounge where she heated up some supper. Ryker had brought extra soup and sandwiches the night before so that she'd have food for lunch and supper without having to leave the unit.

They would still bring Bryson supper, but she kind of liked to have some options for him in case he wouldn't eat what was on the hospital menu. The aide brought Bryson's supper, and thankfully, he seemed willing to eat it. He'd begun talking more, and as they ate, he chatted about what he would do when he got home.

Every day that passed where he seemed more and more like his old self, the worries she'd had ever since hearing that he could have neurological issues began to fade. He had enough issues as it was. Adding more would have felt really unfair.

After they were done eating, she helped Bryson into the bath-room to get cleaned up. They'd just come out, and Sophia was helping Bryson into the bed when a couple of women walked into the room.

She waited for them to identify themselves, like the medical people usually did when they first arrived. However, it seemed ra-ther late in the day for anyone new to be coming around. As far as she was aware, Bryson wasn't scheduled for any tests or evaluations that evening.

Neither of them wore any sort of medical uniform like she was used to seeing on unknown people who came into Bryson's room. The shorter of the two women was dressed more casually in a pair of jeans and a plain light blue T-shirt. She had short, medium blonde hair and light blue eyes and was what people would proba-bly consider to be cute.

The other woman was more statuesque and wore a dark blue pantsuit with a pink blouse. She had long dark hair and dark brown eyes and held herself with an almost regal bearing.

They were both regarding her with looks of curiosity and some-thing else that Sophia couldn't identify. When they didn't say anything right away, Sophia said, "Can I help you?"

The shorter one smiled at her then. "We heard that Ryker's been here in the hospital and stopped by to see him."

"He's not here at the moment," Sophia said.

"Will he be back soon?"

Sophia wasn't sure about giving them any information about Ryker without knowing who they were. It just felt very weird.

"What did you say your name was?" she asked, ignoring the woman's question.

"Oh. I'm sorry," the woman said. "My name is Callie."

Dread settled into Sophia's stomach, leaving her feeling slightly panicked. From the things Ryker had said about his sister, it didn't seem like she was exactly a nice person.

"You're Ryker's sister."

Callie's brows rose at Sophia's statement. "He's mentioned me?"

"Yes." Sophia didn't bother to mention that it hadn't necessarily been in a good light. All she wanted right then was for this woman and her friend to leave.

"Did he happen to mention Lydia?" Callie asked, gesturing to the woman beside her. "His fiancée?"

Sophia wanted to tell them that he'd mentioned Lydia, his *ex*-fiancée. But face-to-face with these two formidable women, any nerve she might have had, vanished. She was saved from answering, however, by the arrival of yet another unexpected person.

"What on earth are you two doing here?" Ryker demanded from the doorway behind them, anger tightening his features as he glared at the women.

CHAPTER TWENTY-FIVE

Ryker was later getting to the hospital than he'd wanted to be, but their afternoon job had run longer than planned. With Michael tied up with Vivianne, he'd had to stay on the site until the job was finished. But he'd made up his mind to go to the hospital, so even though it meant it would be later when he got there, he still went.

He'd gone through a drive-thru on the way, but he hadn't picked up anything for Sophia and Bryson, figuring they'd eat what he'd left for them the previous night. By the time he reached the hospital, he'd finished his food, so he went straight up to Bryson's room.

The plan had been to surprise Sophia, but he was the one who got a surprise. Or maybe it had been more along the lines of a nasty shock.

At the sight of not just Callie but Lydia too squaring off with Sophia, anger surged inside him. When he demanded to know what they were doing there, Callie immediately went on the defensive.

"Why shouldn't we be here?"

"Out," Ryker said with a jerk of his head toward the door. "We'll talk in the lounge."

After the briefest of hesitations, the two moved past him out the door into the hallway. He set the bag he'd brought on a chair, then went to Sophia and gave her a hug. "Are you alright?"

"I'm fine," she said.

"Okay. I'm going to talk to Callie. I'll be back in a few minutes."

She nodded, and even though Ryker wanted to stay and make sure she really was okay, he also needed to have a conversation with Callie and Lydia. That they were there, at the hospital, in Bryson's room, was both shocking and infuriating.

With anger coursing through him, Ryker stormed down to the lounge. He half-expected to get there and discover they'd both bailed. But no, there they were, huddled close together as if preparing for the verbal thrashing they knew was coming. Thankfully, other than the three of them, the room was empty.

"The fact that I found you in Bryson's room is wrong on *so* many levels," Ryker snapped. "And while I might have expected that of Callie, I would have thought for sure you would have known better, Lydia."

"We didn't do anything wrong," Callie said as she crossed her arms.

Ryker scoffed. "Oh yes you did! On a moral level, definitely, if not on a legal one. I'm pretty sure you didn't have Sophia's approval to visit Bryson's room." He crossed his arms, mimicking Callie's pose. "Please correct me if I'm wrong."

When they both remained silent, he asked, "What exactly are you doing here?"

The women exchanged glances before Callie spoke. "From things Mom has been saying, it sounded like you were getting pretty serious about this woman. So I thought we should come by and meet her."

"First of all, don't you think that if I wanted you to meet her, I would have invited you here to do that? And second, why would you think that Lydia needed to meet her?" Ryker shifted his gaze to his ex-fiancée. "You're not a part of my life any longer, so I'm not sure why you're here."

"She's not a good fit for a doctor," Lydia said, and Callie nodded.

Ryker was sure his incredulity at her reply was clear on his face. "I feel like I need to have this conversation in bullet points. Once again, I'm going to say: first of all, I'm not a doctor at the moment.

Second, who are you to decide she's not a good fit for a doctor when you don't even know her?"

"She's a single mom whose only job is as a babysitter," Callie said with a scoff. "Definitely not doctor wife material."

Ryker shifted, propping his fists on his hips. "Huh. Well, you know who knows best whether someone is perfect fit for a doctor? Here's a hint: not you."

Callie glared at him, her eyes flashing with temper.

"Oh, here's the answer. The doctor—whoever that might be—is the one who will know better than anyone else who is the best person for him."

"But you must have felt that way about Lydia since you proposed to her," Callie pointed out.

"Well, she definitely proved me wrong when she walked away from our engagement without a backward glance," Ryker said, flicking a glance in Lydia's direction. He might have felt sorry for being so direct in his responses except for the fact that she had agreed to come with Callie to ambush Sophia. "Not that it matters anymore because I'm a different man now. And the man I am now loves that woman in there, and I also love her son. Nothing you can do will change my mind about that."

"Surely you can't envision her helping your career," Lydia scoffed. "If you're starting out again after taking such a long break, you'll need someone to help you."

"Haven't you figured out yet that my career is not the be-all and end-all of my life? Whatever career I end up with, it will always come second to the people I love." He turned to Callie. "I would have thought that you'd already know that, given the example that Mom and Dad have set for us. If I decide to go back to pediatrics, I won't need Sophia's help to do that. Her support, yes, but if my abilities aren't enough to build my career, then I'm better off mowing grass and chopping down trees."

"You're just...ridiculous," Callie said. "It's like you have no motivation at all. I'm sure Mom and Dad regret all the money they dumped into your education."

"How about we each present our version of events as they've played out here this evening to them and see what they have to say?" Ryker suggested.

Callie's lips thinned as her expression tightened, but she didn't say anything.

"I don't understand either of you acting like you're so much better than Sophia." Frowning, he turned his attention to Lydia. "Is that why you didn't have any issues with what happened in Syria? You didn't connect with any of those people, did you?"

He waited for her response, but she didn't say anything.

"Why did you even go to Syria? It certainly doesn't seem like it was for the opportunity to serve others, if this is your attitude." He paused, feeling a bit sick that he'd ever thought he loved her. "You went because of what people would think of you, not because of what you could do to help those less fortunate than us."

Lydia crossed her arms. "I helped a lot of people while I was there. Probably more than you managed to while you were having an emotional breakdown."

Ryker fought the urge to let Lydia's words find a target within him. He knew that he wasn't the only one who had struggled with what had happened at the refugee camp, even if she hadn't.

"I don't understand why you even want to be with me now, Lydia," Ryker said with a shake of his head. "But it doesn't really matter because that's never going to happen. I don't know what else to say except that you need to leave Sophia and Bryson alone. Don't come around here again."

"You're blowing this all out of proportion," Callie said with a scowl.

"What exactly was your goal in coming here?"

The two women exchanged looks again, then Callie shrugged. "Just wanted to meet her."

"Well, you've met her, now stay away from her."

"You seem rather protective of this woman," Callie asked. "Isn't she strong enough to stand up for herself?"

Ryker stared at his sister, unable to understand why she was being so callous. They'd always had their differences, but at the end of the day, he loved her because she was his sister. Right then, however, he didn't like her at all, and he wasn't sure that he could forgive her for ambushing Sophia the way she had with Lydia.

"She's currently in the hospital with her son, who's recovering from a dangerous illness. I will absolutely stand between her and anyone who doesn't have her best interests at heart," he said. "And if that means I have to protect her from you, I will do that."

Callie gave a shake of her head. "I can't believe you're hung up on someone like her."

"Well, I can't believe that you two have this sort of attitude."

There was so much that Ryker wanted to say in response to that, but he knew it would just be a waste of breath. He did plan to tell his folks about the visit, though, because he figured they might be the only ones that would be able to get through to Callie.

"I'm going back to Sophia," he said, suddenly eager to be away from them.

Without waiting for a response, Ryker turned and left the lounge. As he walked toward Bryson's room, emotions swirled through him. Anger. Confusion. Sadness. They were emotions that he didn't want to have when he spent time with Sophia and Bryson.

Outside the door, he paused to take a couple of calming breaths. He had no idea what Callie or Lydia had said to Sophia, but if they had really upset her, he would have further words with Callie.

When he walked into the room, he immediately looked for Sophia and found her with Bryson on the small loveseat, a book her hands.

She glanced up as he approached them, a wary expression on her face. He hated seeing that look on her face, knowing it was the result of Callie and Lydia's appearance.

"Hey, Ryker," Bryson said with a smile.

He lifted his hand, making a small fist. Ryker lowered himself to his haunches and reached out to tap his fist to Bryson's. "How're you doing, buddy?"

"Good. Momma's helping me read."

"That sounds fun," Ryker said. "Can I read it with you?"

Bryson nodded but then frowned as he looked around. "There's no room for you."

"How about you sit on my lap?" Ryker suggested, and at Bryson's nod, he looked to Sophia for her permission.

He really wouldn't have blamed her if she'd shook her head, but instead, she also nodded. Ryker carefully lifted Bryson up, being mindful of the IV that was still in his hand.

The loveseat wasn't very big, so he and Sophia were pressed close together. After Bryson was settled on his lap, Ryker rested his arm on the seat behind Sophia.

He felt a surge of love as he smiled at her. "So, what are we reading?"

Slowly his emotions settled as he listened to Bryson and Sophia read, and the anger he'd felt after what had happened with Callie faded away. Contentment filled his heart, and he knew that he was exactly where he wanted to be. And he felt that it was also where God wanted him to be.

It had been so long since he'd felt such a sense of peace. He knew that there was plenty of work that needed to be done in his life, but for the first time since what had happened in Syria, he felt like he had direction.

They read through a few books before Bryson began to fade. Ryker felt the moment the little boy lost the battle to sleep. His body slumped back against Ryker, and his breathing evened out.

Sophia wrapped her arms around the small stack of books, holding them tight to her chest as she stared toward the door of the room. Ryker's heart hurt at the stoic expression that she wore. It was like she was bracing herself for the worst. Preparing herself to be hurt.

"Why don't we get Bryson into the bed?" he suggested.

Sophia nodded and set the books aside as he got up with Bryson in his arms. She helped maneuver the IV pole closer to the bed, and as he was laying Bryson onto the bed, the nurse appeared.

She helped them get Bryson settled, and thankfully, he didn't wake up. He was staying awake for longer periods of time now, but his body was still needing to heal, so Ryker was glad that the boy slept so soundly.

After the nurse was done, she left them alone. Sophia seemed uneasy as she walked over to the table and sat down. Ryker took the chair across from her. He reached out across the table, resting his hands, palm up, in front of her.

She stared at them for a moment before lifting her hands from her lap. As she looked up at him, her wariness was unmistakable in her gaze. Even though he didn't like seeing it, he understood completely why she was feeling that way right then.

With slow movements, she set her hands on his. He gently closed his fingers around hers.

"What did they say to you?" Ryker asked.

"Not much," she said. "They'd just introduced themselves right before you arrived."

"You looked upset."

"They were just very..." A frown flickered across her face. "I don't know the word to describe them."

"Well, I have a few, but I doubt they're what you are looking for." Ryker gave a huff of laughter. "I know that it's easy for me to say, but you need to just ignore them. I love my sister, but I didn't invite her here, and I certainly didn't invite Lydia."

"She said she's your fiancée," Sophia said, her fingers flexing lightly against his.

"She was, but she's not anymore. She might have been the one to make the decision to end the engagement, but I don't regret that she did."

"Does she want you back?"

"Apparently," Ryker said with a shrug. "Callie has been mentioning that she was interested in what was going on in my life lately. Today was the first time I've seen her in a long time."

"She's very beautiful."

Ryker thought about denying it, but the truth was that Lydia was beautiful in a very refined way. "Yes, she is, but then, so are you, and what makes you *more* beautiful than Lydia is that your beauty isn't only outward. You have a beautiful heart, which is something I really love about you."

Sophia's gaze dropped as her cheeks pinked. "But I'm not smart like her."

"I don't think the difference between you is smarts," Ryker said. "You just have different desires in life. I think if you'd wanted to be a doctor, you could have achieved that."

"I'm not sure about that," Sophia said with a soft laugh.

"It's not only geniuses who become doctors, you know. I'm definitely not a genius. I just wanted it bad enough that I was willing to work hard for it. The fact that you didn't want to be a doctor doesn't mean you're not smart."

"I just don't really get why you want to be around Bryson and me," she said. Her brow furrowed as she stared down at their hands.

"Oh. Well, that's easy enough to explain."

She looked up at him. "It is?"

Ryker shrugged. "I was first drawn to your devotion to Bryson. As I'm sure you've seen, I love children, so to see that in you too, felt a bit like I'd found a kindred spirit. I could see that you cared deeply about Bryson, doing what you could to help him. You exude a gentleness that I have to admit is quite attractive to me. When I'm with you, I feel calm and at ease. In a world that can be quite frenetic at times, I really appreciate that."

Sophia stared at him, her eyes wide and her mouth slightly open. "I don't know what to say."

"You don't have to say anything. Just know that I see you, Sophia. I see your heart in the way you love your son and Nana." Ryker tightened his hold on her hands. "I just hope that you might have room in your heart for me too."

She began to blink rapidly as moisture sparkled in her eyes. "Really? Even after everything I've told you about me, you still think I'm worth the trouble?"

"Did you not hear my story?" he asked. "None of us are perfect. What's most important is that we are honest about the things we're struggling with. I'm willing to do the hard work, both personally and together with you, if that's what you want too."

"I don't know how to do the work, to be honest. I know that Bryson needs counseling. I do as well, but it's expensive, and I don't even know where to go for it. I'm broken." She took a noticeably shaky breath and blew it out. "I feel like I'm broken, and that's not good for anyone."

"You're not broken, sweetheart. At least not any more broken than I am." He stopped talking, waiting for her to look up at him. "Do you trust me?"

Joy filled his heart when she nodded without hesitation.

"Can I talk to my mom about your situation?" he asked, certain that she was going to object. "She has connections that could be helpful. I know she'd want to help."

"You don't care if she knows about my past?"

"The best person to know about your past is my mom. She has experience with cult survivors. It's something she feels passionate about."

"I just feel so ashamed about it all," Sophia said, her head dipping again.

"It wasn't your fault. Most people don't expect that the person they're falling in love with will turn out to be a cult leader. The only person responsible for what happened is Ezekiel, and now that he's dead, he'll have been held accountable for his actions on this earth."

They sat in silence for a couple of minutes before Ryker said, "You know my story. Do you think less of me for how I responded to what happened in Syria?"

Her fingers jerked against his as she looked at him. "No. Of course not."

"We both ended up in bad situations," Ryker told her. "But we don't have to be defined by those situations. We can move beyond them and come out stronger on the other side, even using our experiences to help others. I want that for both of us. For all *three* of us. I want us all to get the help we need to become the people God wants us to be."

"I...I want that too." She bit her lip. "I just hope I'm making the right decision. I have a history of making...bad decisions."

"I don't want to force you into anything," Ryker said, seeing the worry on her face. "We can take it a day at a time. Just know that I'm going to be there each step of the way, sharing the ups and downs of my life with you and Bryson and hoping you'll do the same with me."

"So you're really going to be a pediatrician again?"

Ryker figured that might worry her, but he had to be honest with her. "Yes. I'm hoping that eventually, I'll be able to practice again. But not right away."

"And you would still want someone like me in your life?"

"I'm hoping that once I'm ready to step back into a practice, you'll be there to support me. I don't want to move away from New Hope, so my hope is that I can find a practice near by." He paused then said, "We don't have to have it all figured out right now. Just know that I want a future with you, Sophia."

"I just can't believe you want to take on the mess that Bryson and I are in addition to what you're already dealing with."

"Is that your way of saying that you don't want to take on the mess of my life in addition to your own?" Ryker hoped that it wasn't, but if it was, he'd certainly respect her wishes.

"No." Her hands gripped his more tightly. "It just seems that most people around us feel like it's too difficult to deal with everything in our lives right now."

Ryker knew that she was talking about some members of her family, and it made him a little angry to know that she didn't have the support she needed to recover from what she'd been through.

"I *want* to be a part of your and Bryson's life. I understand what I'm getting into, and I still want that."

He wished that they could have been in a different setting for their conversation. It would have been nice to take her on a date to discuss how he felt about her. But he understood that things would be different for them. Not just because Bryson was sick, but also because of the other issues he was dealing with.

It wasn't likely that the two of them would be able to go on a date without Bryson for the foreseeable future. Their relationship—if Sophia would give them a chance—would unfold differently than the one he'd had with Lydia, but he didn't mind that. If it meant they had a future together, he would happily work within the confines of the situation.

"So, what does this mean?" Sophia asked, uncertainty lacing her tone.

"For now, it means that I'll be here for you and Bryson."

Sophia didn't answer right away, but then she said, "I just don't want it all to be too much for you. You're already working so hard."

"I'm not here because I feel obliged to be," Ryker told her. "I'm here because this is where I want to be. At the end of the day, I like being able to spend time with the two of you."

A smile tipped up the corners of Sophia's mouth. "We like seeing you too."

"Then we continue on like we have been, which means I'll come here whenever I can."

She nodded then said, "As long as you promise not to overdo it. You're important to us, so you need to take care of yourself too."

Warmth spread through him at her words...at the care she was expressing for him. It was the type of care that his mom had for his dad and that Donna had for Silas. Why had he not realized that lack of care in his relationship with Lydia? Maybe he just hadn't been the right man to make Lydia want to give and receive that care.

It wasn't that he thought Lydia was incapable of caring for someone, but she'd seemed to expect each of them to take care of themselves. To be independent in their relationship. Looking back, he had no idea why he'd thought that was what he wanted. Maybe going through what he had in Syria had changed him...opened his eyes.

All he knew was that he saw a future with Sophia and Bryson that he'd never thought he'd want again. Others might look at the two of them and say that they weren't a good match, but he felt otherwise. He *knew* otherwise.

Being with her and Bryson had softened his heart. They'd reached beyond the walls he'd put in place after his experience in Syria. Because of his desire to be the best version of himself for them, he'd found himself willing to go back to therapy. But even more than that, he'd once again found himself turning to God and desiring to be the man God would have him be.

"When Bryson is home from the hospital, I'd like to take the two of you on a date," Ryker said.

Sophia's brows rose. "The two of us?"

"I know that for now, any dates we go on will need to include Bryson, and I'm okay with that."

For a moment, Sophia again looked like she was going to cry. "Thank you for being so understanding of him."

"I know he's important to you, sweetheart," Ryker said. "He's important to me too."

"I never imagined that I'd find a man who was willing to accept Bryson and care for him the way he needed to be cared for."

"I love him," Ryker said, then hesitated for a moment. "And I love you too."

His words seemed to take her by surprise, her eyes widening.

"I know that it seems like it might be too soon," he hurried to say. "And I understand that it might take you longer to trust what I feel for you and what you might feel for me. Just know that I will wait as long as it takes. You and Bryson are worth the wait."

Ryker knew that she might not believe him just yet, and that was okay. In the meantime, he was happy to shower her and Bryson with love whenever he could.

CHAPTER TWENTY-SIX

"He's here, Momma!" Bryson's yell brought a smile to Sophia's face as she took one last look in the mirror.

It wasn't often that she wore makeup. After five years of not using any sort of face products, she was surprised she still knew how to apply foundation and eye shadow. She could have gone for a while longer without using it, but what was happening that day seemed to call for makeup.

She was equal parts scared and excited about their evening—okay, maybe more scared than excited—so it had taken ages to decide what to wear and then to get ready.

They'd been home from the hospital for three weeks now, and Bryson was doing so much better. There were still a couple things that he struggled with. His energy levels were not completely back to where they'd been prior to him getting sick, and every once in a while, he'd forget words. Since it didn't happen all the time, she'd think it wasn't an issue anymore, only for him to stumble over or forget a word. She wasn't sure what it meant in the long-term, but Ryker had seemed to think it wasn't a huge concern.

"I'll open the door for him," Bryson called out as she walked down the hallway to the living room.

"Hiya, buddy," Ryker said as he exchanged fist bumps with Bryson. When she approached them, he looked up at her, his expression softening. "You look beautiful."

"Thank you."

Sophia's cheeks flushed as she looked down at herself. She hadn't had many options since her wardrobe was still pretty basic.

So when Ryker had told her that casual was okay, she'd settled on a pair of skinny jeans and a plain light pink shirt.

Thankfully, his outfit was pretty much the masculine version of hers—jeans and a green T-shirt. Bryson also wore jeans and a T-shirt. Only time would tell if the rest of the people there would be dressed as casually.

When Ryker had asked if she'd be willing to meet his family, she hadn't been sure. It was hard to imagine that his family really wanted to get to know her and Bryson, but apparently, they did. Sophia wasn't sure if that included Callie or not.

She moved closer to Ryker, anticipating the hug he always gave her when he showed up. He didn't disappoint, and as he wrapped his arms around her, she hugged him back. That she even wanted to be that close to a man again was a minor miracle, but Ryker made her feel safe in a way no man ever had.

"Ready to go?" he asked as he moved back to peer down at her.

"As I'll ever be." She took a deep breath and let it out. "Are you sure this is okay?"

"I'm very sure," Ryker said, understanding in his gaze. "They want to meet you, and I want you to meet them. I know you're worried about Callie, but you don't need to be."

He wasn't wrong about that worry, and though she usually trusted him completely, she wasn't sure when it came to this particular situation. Unfortunately, she had no choice but to accept what was to come because she'd already agreed to it.

"They're going to love you as much as I do," Ryker said, then paused, a smile taking over his whole face. "No. I take that back. I don't think anyone could love you as much as I do."

Sophia's heart felt like it was going to explode with emotion. He told her he loved her regularly. And not just her. He'd started telling Bryson too.

Each time, the words for what was in her heart were on the tip of her tongue. Why she hadn't been able to say them yet, she wasn't entirely sure.

She knew that Ryker wasn't Ezekiel. That he would never treat her the way Ezekiel had. Still, there was fear. She so wanted this to be a good decision. That after years of making bad or questionable decisions, this one would finally be the right one.

"They're still going to love you a lot." He always continued on to say something else after telling her he loved her. It was as if he didn't want her to feel forced to say the words because of an awkward silence following his own declaration.

"Are they gonna love me too, Ryker?" Bryson asked.

Ryker scooped him up with a smile. "They certainly are."

Sophia hoped that Ryker was correct in that regard. "Well, we'd better go so we're not late and make a bad impression right off the bat."

After she picked up her purse and a bag of toys and books she'd packed for Bryson, they left the house to climb into Ryker's truck. He'd gotten a car seat for Bryson, so they didn't have to always take her car whenever they went somewhere together.

It was almost an hour's drive to his parents' house, so she'd brought a few books for Bryson to look through. Since she wasn't sure that they'd have any toys for him, she'd also put in a coloring book and some crayons so he'd have something to keep him occupied. She was very glad that he was easily entertained, so she didn't have to worry about him getting bored.

As they drove, Sophia told him about her family's dinner earlier that day. It had been another fun and exciting episode in the Chloe and Natalie show.

"Is there anything they won't fight about?" Ryker asked.

"Not that I'm aware of. There have been times when I've wondered if Natalie was actually switched at birth. I mean, she's so unlike everyone else in the family."

"Really?"

"We're all pretty chill, for the most part. Natalie is the only one that we really get into heated arguments with. Well, I try my best not to, but others in the family will take her on. Like Chloe. It just seems like Natalie has to be right about everything, and even when she's clearly wrong, she still fights in defense of her opinion. Though some in the family don't mind the weekly sparring sessions, they just stress me out."

"Yeah, arguing is Callie's love language too, apparently. Silas won't even engage most of the time. I do on occasion simply because I find it hard to ignore some of the stuff she says. My dad will shut it all down if it happens at the dinner table, though because apparently, arguing gives him indigestion."

"So is that your way of warning me not to incite any arguments over dinner?"

Ryker chuckled. "Definitely. Most definitely. I mean, I'm so worried about you doing that."

After he pulled onto the highway, he reached over to take her hand. Sophia loved the feel of the rough skin of his hand against hers. It was a reminder that this man worked hard with his hands, and yet he was always so gentle with her and Bryson. She was grateful to be with someone who, even though he had the strength, didn't use it against those who were weaker than him.

Ezekiel had been the opposite. He'd rarely done any hard work around the compound, but he'd been quick to use his fists when he got upset with someone.

She blew out a quick breath, not wanting to let her thoughts go down that path. That was behind her. It was time to focus forward.

When Ryker pulled into the driveway of a huge home once they'd reached Seattle, Sophia could only stare in shock. Though he'd mentioned his parents' careers, she hadn't calculated what that might mean when it came to their income.

Ryker shifted in his seat, and when Sophia looked over at him, he was regarding her with a serious expression. "It's just a building."

She lifted her brows at his comment. "Isn't that kind of like saying the ark was just a boat?"

"Wasn't it?" he asked.

Sophia gave a huff of laughter, knowing he was trying to get her to relax. "Fine. It's just a house."

"Full of people who are going to love you both."

"How can you know that? They haven't even met me yet."

"They'll love you because they love me, and I love you."

Sophia knew the reason she was so uncertain about that pronouncement was because she wasn't so sure that she'd be able to say the same for her family. And it would have nothing to do with Ryker and everything to do with the fact that they wouldn't trust her judgment. Hopefully, once they actually got to know Ryker, they'd see he was a good man and come to love him.

"Okay. Let's go in." Sitting in the car wouldn't make things any easier.

"I promise it's going to be okay."

Sophia nodded as he gave her hand a squeeze before releasing it. Even though butterflies were beating up a storm in her stomach, she pulled on the handle to open the door. Ryker helped Bryson out of the back seat, then the three of them walked along the curved sidewalk to the front door.

Rather than knock on the door, Ryker opened it and led them inside. Almost immediately, an older couple appeared from an open doorway, smiles on their faces.

As they approached them, Ryker said, "Mom. Dad. This is Sophia and her son, Bryson."

Bryson pressed against her side, his hand tightening around hers.

"Sophia, these are my parents, Valerie and Robert."

348 · KIMBERLY RAE JORDAN

Valerie held out her hand with a warm smile. "It's an absolute pleasure to meet you, Sophia." Sophia shook her hand, then watched as the older woman's smile softened as she looked down at Bryson. "And look at you. Aren't you a handsome little boy?"

Bryson didn't say anything, just looked at Valerie with wide eyes. Sophia waited to see what Valerie would do. But rather than force Bryson to interact with her, she just stepped aside so that her husband could greet them.

"C'mon through to the dining room," Valerie said, waving them toward the door they'd come through.

Ryker rested his hand on her back as they made their way out of the foyer. When they walked into the dining room, Sophia's steps faltered. The room was decorated with a bunch of brightly colored balloons and streamers. The table was set with similarly colored paper plates and cups.

She glanced over at Ryker. Was this a party for one of them? Why hadn't he mentioned anything? Should she have brought a gift?

"Ryker told us that it was Bryson's birthday last week," Valerie said. "So we thought it might be nice to have a little party for him."

Sophia pressed a hand to her chest, tears stinging her eyes. "This is for Bryson?"

She had a hard time believing that these people who had never met Bryson before wanted to throw a party for him. Her mom had had a cake for him earlier that day, and there had been a few presents for him, but this looked a whole lot more like a party.

As her gaze swept the room, she took in the other people gathered there. There was a man who looked a bit like Ryker standing with a woman and a young boy and girl. Callie stood next to them as well. While the others had smiles, the woman didn't, but she didn't look angry either, so Sophia wasn't sure what to make of that.

"We heard that you're a big fan of pizza, Bryson," Valerie said.

Sophia glanced down at him in time to see him look up at her, his eyes wide. "Pizza?"

"Sounds like it, baby."

He grasped her hand in both of his, pressing his cheek to the back of her hand. "I love pizza."

"I'm so happy to hear that," Valerie said. "Jonah and Emery really like it too."

Ryker lowered himself down to Bryson's level, resting his hand on Bryson's back. With his other hand, he pointed to where the two children stood. "Jonah is my nephew, and Emery is my niece."

Sophia didn't know how much Ryker had told his family about Bryson, but she figured he must have told them something since they weren't rushing to invade Bryson's space in order to meet him. Ryker went on to introduce his brother, Silas, his sister-in-law, Donna, and of course, Callie.

"Why don't we sit down?" Valerie suggested as she gestured to the table.

She directed people to their seats, and when all was said and done, Sophia was seated next to Valerie, who was at the end of the table. Bryson was sandwiched between her and Ryker. Donna and the two kids were seated across from them. Silas and Callie were at the other end of the table with their dad.

After Robert said a prayer for the meal, Valerie and Donna got up and left the dining room, returning a few minutes later with a couple of large platters with pizza on them.

"Ryker said you liked cheese pizza, Bryson," Valerie said as she handed the platter to Sophia. "And Sophia, if you prefer something other than pizza, we have some non-pizza dishes as well."

"Daddy doesn't like pizza," Emery volunteered.

"And that's why we have other food for him," Valerie added.

"I'm not going to apologize for not liking pizza," Silas said.

"Just means more for us," Jonah said. "Right, Em?"

Emery nodded so vigorously that it set her curls dancing. "Lots of pizza for us."

As the meal progressed, Sophia felt the knot of tension she'd been carrying slowly unravel. The conversation was light, with Valerie and Donna doing most of the talking as if understanding that Sophia still wasn't entirely at ease.

Ryker checked in with her frequently, often reaching behind Bryson to rub her shoulder. Each time he did that, she would look over to find him gazing at her with so much love that she thought her heart was going to burst out of her chest.

After one such exchange, Sophia happened to glance over at Valerie. The older woman was watching them with an expression that could only be described as affectionate.

Valerie set her hand on Sophia's arm. "I'm so pleased that Ryker brought you and Bryson here today. I've been anxious to meet the woman he loves."

Heat swept up into her cheeks at the woman's words, and she wasn't sure what to say.

Thankfully, Ryker saved her from having to respond. "Mom! Don't you think she should have heard that from me first?"

"What?" Valerie's eyes widened as she glanced between them. "I..uh..."

After a moment of stunned silence around the table, Sophia couldn't hold back a giggle.

"Oh, you," Valerie said with an exasperated look and a wave of her hand at Ryker. "For that, I don't think you should get any cake. I'm going to give your piece to Bryson."

"I get two pieces of cake?" Bryson asked, a hopeful lilt to his voice.

"I think I might cry if I don't get some cake," Ryker said, a frown tugging down the corners of his mouth.

"Then maybe you should have thought twice before giving your mother a heart attack," Valerie huffed.

Bryson got up on his knees on his chair and patted Ryker's cheek. "Don't cry, Ryker. I'll share with you."

"Thanks, buddy. I love you."

As Sophia watched, her son cupped Ryker's other cheek and said, "I love you, too."

Emotion swelled inside her, and she knew that if her son could willingly give his love to this man, she could too.

"Oh, my," Valerie whispered as Ryker gathered Bryson in his arms. "My heart is full to bursting."

Sophia knew exactly how she felt.

As she glanced around the table, Sophia could see that she and Valerie weren't the only ones moved by Ryker and Bryson's exchange. Silas and his dad were smiling broadly, as was Donna. The kids were grinning, although they didn't seem to understand the significance of what had just happened.

The only person she couldn't see was Callie, who sat on the other side of Ryker, and Sophia found she was okay with that. Since she couldn't trust that the woman would be as happy about what was going on, Sophia didn't want to have the moment ruined.

"Do you want to help me put the candles on the cake, Emery?" Valerie asked.

"Yes!" The little girl scrambled off her chair while Donna got up and began to clear off the table.

Sophia also got to her feet and gathered up the paper plates they'd used.

"You don't have to do that," Valerie said when Sophia followed Donna into the spacious kitchen.

"I want to thank you for doing all of this for Bryson," Sophia said as she set the plates she carried on the counter.

"Oh, darling," Valerie said as she approached her with a smile. "It was our pleasure. We are just so happy that God brought you and Ryker together."

"Really?" Sophia couldn't help but ask. Had Ryker not told them about her past?

"Yes, really." She reached out to grasp Sophia's shoulders. "That expression on my son's face when he looks at you? I've never seen that on him before. But it's a look I know well because it's one I see on his father's face every day when he looks at me."

Sophia swallowed hard against the emotion that threatened to choke her. She lifted a shaking hand to brush away a tear that refused to be blinked away.

"After all Ryker's been through, I worried that he'd never open his heart to anyone again. But seeing how he is with you and knowing that even as he's opened his heart to you, he's opened it to God once again is such an answer to prayer." Valerie smiled at her. "Ryker's love of children and his desire to help them has always been a big part of who he was. That was why what happened in Syria hurt him so badly. The need had been so great, and he had felt helpless in the face of it.

"Seeing my son withdraw from something that had always given him great joy, and that I truly believe was a gift from God, was so hard. You didn't have to let him into your life, but I'm so glad that you did. Not just because it allowed him to get back in touch with an important part of himself, but because it brought you and Bryson into our lives as well."

"Ryker is a very special man," Sophia said. "I could see that from the moment he took the time to help Bryson when he could have said no."

"I'll never know why he said yes because he'd been so resistant to being around children, but I'm so grateful to God that he did." Valerie hesitated a moment then said, "I know about what happened with Callie and Lydia, and I just want to reassure you that you don't have to worry about any more of that. Callie knows that what she did was wrong, and I think after today, she'll truly understand what you and Ryker mean to each other."

"I didn't want to cause any problems."

"You didn't. She manages to cause problems all on her own. Now, enough about that," Valerie said with a smile. "Let's get this cake out to Bryson."

Sophia turned to look at the cake that sat on the counter. It was shaped like a book and had a plastic car on top of it.

"It's peanut butter and chocolate. I thought he might like the flavor combination."

"He will *love* it," Sophia assured her. "This is awesome."

With a broad smile, Valerie called for Emery. The little girl climbed up onto a stool at the counter and leaned over, eagerly taking the candles from her grandmother. With her guidance, she stuck them into the cake.

When they were all in place, Valerie lit the candles then had Sophia carry the cake into the dining room. Bryson's expression of utter joy at the sight made tears spill over again. She couldn't do anything but let them fall unchecked as she walked around the table to place it in front of him, where he now sat perched on Ryker's lap.

Silas stood on the other side of the table with an expensive-looking phone aimed at them. Valerie led everyone in a rousing rendition of *Happy Birthday,* then encouraged Bryson to blow the candles out.

When he looked around in confusion, Ryker showed him what to do, and Sophia had so much hope that Ryker would be there with her to guide Bryson through all the lessons of life that still lay ahead for her little boy.

Sitting down on Bryson's chair, Sophia leaned against Ryker, her cheek pressing against his shoulder. He looked down at her, and everyone around them seemed to fade away as she reached up to cup his cheek much like Bryson had.

She knew that she should maybe wait until it was just the two of them, but she just couldn't contain how she felt any longer. "I love you."

With all the noise, she wasn't sure he had heard her, but then his eyes widened. He moved his arm to slide it around her and pull her close. Turning his face away from his family, he pressed his cheek against hers. "I love you too, sweetheart. So very much."

When she heard him take a shaky breath, Sophia realized she wasn't the only emotional one right then. Why hadn't she told him sooner? He deserved to know what was in her heart...had been in her heart for awhile now.

"Momma?" Bryson said.

Sophia opened her eyes to see Bryson watching her and Ryker with concern. Ryker didn't move back to show Bryson that he was okay, so Sophia reached out to take Bryson's hand.

She felt Ryker take another shuddering breath and understood that he was reluctant to let Bryson see his emotions. Or maybe it was his family he was reluctant to show them to.

"We have presents for you, Bryson," Jonah said. "Do you want to open them?"

While Valerie moved the cake out of the way to cut it, Silas put a stack of presents in front of the chair where Valerie had been sitting. After a moment's hesitation, Bryson allowed Jonah to help him off Ryker's lap and up into Valerie's chair.

As soon as his lap was empty, Ryker wrapped both arms around Sophia. With her head tucked into his shoulder, she told him again how much she loved him.

"I didn't think I'd get this emotional," he said, his voice low and rough. "But you mean everything to me, Sophia. I hope you will always know that."

"You mean everything to me too. I'm sorry I didn't tell you sooner. Forgive me."

His arms tightened around briefly. "Nothing to forgive, sweetheart. I would have waited a lifetime for you to say those words."

Their whispered conversation was interrupted by Bryson's excited voice. "Momma! Ryker! I got books!"

Ryker chuckled, then took a deep breath. "Guess we'd better pay attention."

As he moved back from her, Sophia looked up to see that his cheeks were still damp with his tears. She reached up and wiped them away, then leaned forward to brush her lips across his. It should have felt wrong to share their first kiss in front of his family. But instead, it felt perfect because it was clear that these people loved Ryker, and without even knowing her and Bryson, they had opened their hearts to them as well.

Ryker seemed stunned by the kiss at first, then a smile spread across his face, his eyes shining. Sophia couldn't help but smile in return as joy and love welled up inside her and spilled out.

When Bryson called for their attention again, Sophia turned to face him, leaning back against Ryker as he wrapped his arms around her. She was glad for his embrace to anchor her because she honestly felt like she could float away on a cloud of happiness. It was as if releasing the fear that had kept her from sharing her love with Ryker had also released a weight that had tied her to the past.

At the thought, a verse came to mind. One that was an important reminder for her.

There is no fear in love; but perfect love casts out fear, because fear involves torment.

Fear no longer had a place in her heart. Ezekiel might have used love to manipulate her, but fear had replaced that when he'd begun to torment her. It was only through God working in her life as well as Ryker's love that she was able to finally let go of that fear and find healing for her heart. That healing had then allowed her to love Ryker.

She knew that she could trust that she'd made the right decision this time. That she didn't have to be scared about what her future with Ryker would hold because she knew he wouldn't hurt her. There was still a lot of work for them to do in their lives, both alone and together, but knowing that she wasn't on that journey alone meant everything to Sophia.

EPILOGUE

"We survived!" Bryson crowed as he grabbed onto Ryker's hand.

Ryker knew he shouldn't be grinning, letting alone laughing, at the boy's words, but he couldn't help it. As they hurried down the driveway to where his truck was parked, he glanced over at Sophia to see that she was trying not to smile too.

When they'd left Sophia's parents' home the first time, he'd made the mistake of commenting that they'd survived. Ever since then, Bryson had taken great delight in making the announcement each time they'd left a family dinner at his grandparents' house.

That first visit had been a bit stressful, especially for Sophia. He hadn't really cared what her family thought of him as long as she loved him, but it had really mattered to her. Of course, he'd known that it would go easier for all of them if they liked him.

In the end, though it had taken a while, they had eventually come around. Well, except for Natalie. She still eyed him with suspicion whenever she was around them. He could see now why Sophia thought the woman had been switched at birth. The first time Natalie had tried to pick a fight with him, he figured he'd been fully accepted by the whole family.

Once they were in the truck, Sophia let out a huff of laughter. "I shouldn't find that as funny as I do."

"Oh, I think it's fine," Ryker said, leaning toward her to give her a quick kiss. "Although surviving isn't the accomplishment it once was. Well, unless Natalie has been on the rampage."

Sophia laughed as he pulled away from the curb, then sighed. "I wish they'd been as quick to accept you as your family was to accept Bryson and me."

"It's okay, sweetheart," he said. "I understood that they were protective of you."

"I'm not sure about that. I think they were just being judgmental."

"Natalie was, for sure, but the rest just didn't want you to be hurt."

"After six months, hopefully, they know that's not going to happen."

The confidence of Sophia's words made Ryker smile. The fact that she trusted him enough to make that statement meant everything to him.

The past six months had been a period of incredible growth for them individually and as a couple. Bryson, too, had made great strides with the help of the child psychologist Ryker's mom had helped them find. The woman had been willing to see him without charging Sophia for their sessions, which had been a blessing.

Sophia had balked at that at first, but after meeting with the woman and understanding why she was willing to extend that generosity to them, she'd agreed. Getting her to accept free help for herself had been a bigger challenge. His mom had finally gotten involved, spending time with Sophia and helping her see how it was just as important for her to get the help as it was for Bryson. How it would help her parent him even better.

He'd continued to see Nick and felt like he was making progress. The biggest hurdle of the past six months had been telling Michael that he was a doctor. His friend had been shocked, to say the least, but he'd taken it in stride. Since his ultimate goal was to return to medicine, they'd had a long conversation about how to make that transition as easy as possible for Michael.

It was imperative that Michael have someone he trusted as his right-hand person, especially since Taylor, his sister, had bailed on him. Michael did an amazing job, considering he couldn't read hardly at all, but he still needed someone he could trust to help him out at times. At least Michael had Lani to support and help him, which would be even easier now that they were engaged.

"We're swinging by your place, right?" Ryker asked as he made a turn onto her street.

"Yes. I didn't want to leave the flowers in the truck through church and dinner."

That was something else that had changed for all three of them: going to church. It had been among the first things that had changed for him. Though instead of attending the church that had been his home for most of his life, he'd chosen to go to the one Michael, Lani, and Sophia's family attended in New Hope Falls.

Sophia and Bryson's attendance at church services had been a more recent occurrence. While he knew Sophia would have begun to attend much sooner—even before Ryker had—it was obvious that Bryson had too many negative memories of gatherings like that to be comfortable going.

Over the past month, she and Bryson had joined him for the morning services, though they sat in the very back in case they had to leave. The first Sunday, they'd taken turns staying with Bryson in the foyer. They could still hear what was going on, but Bryson seemed to do better without the crowd of people around him or the visual association of someone standing at the front and speaking to them.

This was the first Sunday that Bryson had managed to sit through the entire service, which was definitely cause for celebration. He'd colored and looked through Bible storybooks, which had helped to distract him, but at least he'd stayed.

Once they reached the house, Sophia got out and hurried inside. She reappeared a couple of minutes later with the beautiful floral arrangement that Lani had made for her to give Nana for Valentine's Day. They were going to drop them off a day early since the care home was having a special dinner the next day that Nana wanted to attend.

"Did you remember the chocolates, Momma?" Bryson asked as she opened the door.

Ryker leaned over to take the arrangement from her so she could get back into the truck.

"Yep. It's right here," Sophia said as she patted a bag she held. Grabbing the handle above the door, she pulled herself up into the seat, then took the arrangement back from Ryker.

"Those are her favorite chocolates," Bryson said. "So we can't forget them."

"I think you know she'll share with you, so you wanted to be sure I brought them," Sophia said with a laugh.

Bryson giggled but didn't bother to deny it. The sound of their laughter warmed Ryker and made him smile. It had only been in the past couple of months that their laughter had started to flow more easily and frequently.

After Ryker had parked, Bryson scrambled from the truck. He stood on the pavement, dancing from foot to foot in eagerness. Thankfully, it was no longer eagerness to quickly get inside the building. He'd slowly but surely—and with the therapist's help—come to terms with being outside for longer periods of time.

Of course, with it having been winter for the past few months, insects—wasps in particular—weren't as prevalent. The true test of his ability to endure being outside would come once warmer temperatures arrived in spring.

Ryker took the flower arrangement from Sophia and held it in the crook of his arm. Bryson reached out and took his hand, then grabbed on to Sophia's as they began to walk toward the care home.

When the nurse behind the welcome counter greeted them, Bryson gave her a friendly greeting in response. The woman smiled broadly at him, and Ryker knew it was because she had seen the changes in Bryson over the past few months.

Sophia stopped to chat with her for a minute, asking how her granddaughter was doing before they continued on to Nana's room.

"Nana, we brought you flowers and chocolate," Bryson announced as they walked into her room.

"Are you picking me up for a date?" Nana asked with a grin from her seat by the window.

Ryker chuckled as he waited for Bryson to figure out an answer for that. The boy had learned about dates since he'd been on plenty of them with Ryker and Sophia.

Bryson jumped up on a chair at the table across from Nana before looking over at him and Sophia. "Are we going on a date?"

"That wasn't the plan," Sophia said. "But it looks like maybe Nana has someone else who wants to take her on a date."

That was when Ryker noticed a massive bouquet of roses sitting on the windowsill. For a moment, he wondered if he should get his eyes checked since it had taken him more than two seconds to notice the abundance of roses in the room. It made him feel like perhaps the bouquet of roses he'd bought for Sophia for the next day was severely insufficient.

"Do you have a boyfriend, Nana?" Ryker asked as he walked over to set the flower arrangement on the table in front of her.

"Well, I don't know, Ryker. Does a man giving me flowers mean he's my boyfriend?" she asked. "Because if so, apparently you've just become my boyfriend."

"What's a boyfriend?" Bryson asked.

Sophia covered her eyes with her hand and sighed. "This was *not* the conversation I envisioned having this afternoon."

Ryker laughed as he slipped his arm around Sophia's waist. "I'm sorry that I can't be your boyfriend, Nana. I'm already spoken for."

"Well, I guess the best woman won," Nana said. "Though I'd say that the age thing was definitely a point in your favor, Sophia."

The three of them laughed while Bryson just looked confused.

"So what chocolate did you bring me, Bryson?" Nana asked.

"Your favorite!" Bryson exclaimed as he turned to take the small bag Sophia held. "Will you share them with me?"

"Bryson!" Sophia exclaimed. "You don't ask someone to share their gift with you."

Nana started to laugh again, and Ryker couldn't help but grin because he loved watching Sophia parent this more confident, outgoing version of Bryson. Though Bryson kept Sophia on her toes more, he knew she wouldn't trade how Bryson was now for anything.

After Nana looked in the bag and found the box of chocolates, she opened it and offered Bryson a piece, then she waved Sophia over.

"Thank you for the flowers and the candy, darling," she said as Sophia bent down to hug her. "And for stopping by."

"You're welcome." Sophia sat down in the chair beside Nana's wheelchair, so Ryker settled into the one next to Bryson.

"So, how's school going?" Nana asked. "What have you learned this week, Bryson?"

Bryson happily launched into what he and Sophia had worked on over the past week. Since school had started before he was physically well enough to attend, Sophia had decided to just school him at home for kindergarten. Plus, he still hadn't gotten to the point where he was okay with being separated from Sophia for longer than an hour or two, depending on who he was with.

Ryker knew that Sophia was hoping that he'd be ready to attend school by the start of grade one. The boy still wasn't keen to spend time with kids his own age, but over time he'd become comfortable with Jonah and Emery. Comfortable to the point where he would stay with them and Donna and Silas for a couple of hours at a time.

Which was good because that meant that he and Sophia had been able to go out on a few dates, just the two of them. After they were done visiting Nana, they were headed there to drop Bryson off so they could have a Valentine's dinner. Because he was working the next day, they'd decided to celebrate a day early, which worked out better for Silas and Donna too.

After spending an hour with Nana, they piled back into the truck and headed for Seattle. Bryson spent the trip playing a word game on his tablet. Sophia didn't mind him playing games on it as long as they were educational ones. So far, the little boy didn't seem to realize that there were any other kind. Jonah had been warned not to introduce him to any video games, even if they were age-appropriate.

It wasn't until they'd dropped Bryson off for a pizza party with Jonah and Emery that Ryker allowed himself to think about his own plans for the evening. He'd considered taking Sophia to a fancy restaurant, but he didn't think either of them would really enjoy that.

At one time, he would have automatically gone to an expensive restaurant to celebrate Valentine's Day, but that just wasn't who he was anymore. And he didn't think it was who Sophia was either.

Instead, he'd asked his mom to help him by packing a picnic basket. Before he'd left for church, he'd stuck a bag containing firewood in the back of the truck as well as a couple of blankets. He was just glad that even though there was a bit of chill in the air, it wasn't raining.

"We're going to your parents' place?" Sophia asked as he turned down their street.

"Nope. Well, yes, we are, but just to pick something up." He pulled to a stop in the driveway. "I'll be right back."

He hadn't wanted to linger too long, which was why he was just having Sophia wait in the truck. As soon as he stepped into the house, his mom asked where she was.

"We can't stick around, Mom," Ryker told her. "We'll come for a visit later this week."

"You'd better," she said as she handed him the basket.

"Thanks for making this for me," he said as he leaned down to give her a kiss. "Talk to you later."

"If you propose, you'd better call me tonight," she called after him as he headed for the front door.

Rather than respond, he just lifted his hand then left the house. He opened the rear door of the truck and set the basket on the floor.

"Is that a picnic basket?" Sophia asked when he slid behind the wheel.

"It is." He gave her a smile as he started the truck up. "Hope that doesn't disappoint you."

"Not at all. That actually sounds like fun."

Ryker was glad to hear that, as not every woman would have appreciated a Valentine's picnic instead of a meal in a nice restaurant. "Let's just pray there's no rain."

"Are you telling me you don't have a windbreaker or two in here somewhere? I'm not made of sugar," she added. "A little rain isn't going to melt me."

Ryker loved how she embraced things that not every woman would. He wasn't even sure his mom would have gone along with a wet picnic on the beach.

"We're going to the beach?" she asked a short time later as he drove past a sign for their destination.

"We are." He quickly found a parking spot, which wasn't too difficult since apparently the beach wasn't a destination for people that evening.

Once they got out, he handed her the blankets to carry, then grabbed the bag of wood and the picnic basket. Together, they made their way to the beach area where the fire pits were located. Though there were other people around, it wasn't so busy that there were no fire pits available.

They found one that was distanced from other people and began to set things up. Sophia helped him spread the blanket out then set the basket on it. He quickly set about starting the fire, since it chilly enough to warrant one.

"I love this," Sophia said as she sat down on the blanket, crossing her legs and zipping her jacket up to her chin.

Ryker smiled at her. "So do I."

Once the fire was started, he opened the basket and began to remove the food his mom had prepared for them. When he'd asked her if she'd be willing to prepare a picnic basket for them, she'd said yes, on the condition that he let her pick the menu. Since he trusted her—and really didn't want to try and prepare the picnic himself—he'd agreed.

They had some fun deciphering his mom's notes on heart-shaped post-its on top of the different containers. First up was an assortment of cheeses and crackers.

"I'm wondering if there might be peanut butter smeared on bananas somewhere in there," Sophia said as she picked up another cracker and a piece of cheese.

Ryker chuckled. "There better not be. She needs to save that piece de resistance for the one person who truly appreciates it."

They moved on to some chicken kabobs that his mom had wrapped in aluminum foil and packed with heat packs to keep them warm. Along with that were some potato wedges.

Since he'd been expecting sandwiches and potato chips, he was pleasantly surprised by the items in the basket. Everything was tasty, and it looked as though Sophia was enjoying it all as well.

Though he loved having Bryson with them, Ryker cherished the moments when it was just him and Sophia since it gave them the chance to converse more intimately. To share things about themselves that they just couldn't speak openly about when a five-year-old was around.

When it was just the two of them, they'd had conversations about their pasts, with Sophia sharing more about her time with Ezekiel. The therapy had helped her begin to come to terms with a lot of it, and Ryker was glad that was the case, particularly because it meant she was willing to talk more freely about it with him.

Ryker kept adding wood to the fire, but then began to allow the flames to die down a bit once they were done with their meal. At that point, he pulled the few remaining items from the basket.

"S'mores?" Sophia asked as she reached out to take the bag of marshmallows from his hand. "Did you bring sticks?"

Ryker chuckled as he reached into the wood bag. "Not just any old sticks. These are special telescoping sticks."

"I think that's cheating," Sophia informed him. "We had to use whatever sticks my dad could find on the trees that would reach the fire while still keeping us kids at a safe distance from it."

"Tonight," Ryker said, stretching out one of the sticks with a flourish. "You don't have to worry about getting burned. Well, unless you try and eat a marshmallow directly out of the flames."

Sophia moved to sit right next to him as she put marshmallows on the tips of the sticks. While he held them over the fire, she prepared the graham crackers with pieces of chocolate bars.

"First one up," Ryker said as he pulled back what he considered a perfectly cooked marshmallow.

Sophia held out the prepared graham crackers, sandwiching the marshmallow and gently pulling it off the stick. She put it on the clean plate he'd set on the blanket in front of him, then helped him with the second one.

As he took a bite, Ryker hummed his appreciation of the soft marshmallow and melting chocolate. "Best dessert ever."

"I can't argue with you there," Sophia agreed as she lifted her finger to lick the tip. "Thank you for this whole evening. It's all been wonderful."

Ryker put an arm around her shoulders. "You wouldn't have rather gone to a restaurant?"

"Definitely not," she said. "I love being here with you like this. Just the two of us without feeling like we need to hurry up and eat so they can give the table to someone else."

Ryker ate the last of his s'more then leaned his cheek against her head. He watched the flickering flames of the fire, cherishing Sophia's closeness. The butterflies were coming to life in his stomach as he considered what he wanted to say to her. To ask her.

"Have I told you today that I love you?" he asked her.

He felt her chuckle as she tipped her head back to look up at him. "Yes. You have, in fact. You do such a good job of making sure I know that. I love you too."

"You do a good job of making sure I know that too," he said, then kissed her lightly. "I'm very blessed to have you in my life, letting me see that the things I wasn't sure I'd ever want again, I do. But only with you."

Sophia shifted, facing him more directly. "I feel like I can say the same thing. I'd resigned myself to never loving a man again. But then you showed up and seemed to actually see me."

"I do see you." Ryker lifted his hand and cupped her cheek. "I see you, and I hear you. Of all the people in the world, you can always count on me for that."

"You don't know how much that means to me," she murmured.

"I think I do," he said. "Because you make me feel like who I am is important. Not *what* I am or what I can *do*, but just who I am."

She gave a soft huff of laughter as her head dipped forward. "Honestly, what you are and what you can do intimidated me at first. It was only because I had seen who you were before that that I was able to get past the intimidation."

"I'm so grateful that you did," he said. "And what I hope is that as I move into medicine again in the future, you won't let that intimidate you. Because if my choice is you or medicine, I'll gladly chop trees and mow lawns for the rest of my life."

Sophia shook her head as she gripped his hands tightly. "When Bryson was sick, I experienced how calming your presence was and saw how respected you were by the medical staff in that hospital. The world needs you." She smiled at him. "So no, you don't have to choose between me and medicine."

"Are you sure?" Ryker asked. "I don't want you to say that, but actually feel like you didn't have a choice."

"I'm absolutely positive. Just don't expect me to go to fancy dinners and hold conversations with super smart people."

"I wouldn't expect that because, to be honest, I have no desire to attend those dinners myself."

"Then we're good."

"Any chance you might want us to be better?" Ryker asked as he pulled the small box from his pants pocket. In the flickering light of the fire, he saw her eyes widen when she spotted what he held. "Before you say anything, let me explain."

He waited until she looked up at him and nodded before continuing.

"I know that this might be too soon. I know you might still need more time, but I wanted you to know where my heart is...what my hope is for us. I want to be your husband and Bryson's father one day. It doesn't have to be soon, but I wanted you to know that I'm completely committed to you and Bryson."

"Oh, Ryker," she whispered. "It's not too soon. People might think I'm crazy for agreeing to this when we haven't been dating for ages, given what happened to me before, but I'm not. I see how you are with the people around you. How you are with your family. How you are with Bryson, and how you treat me. You are a caring man. You are a *good* man. A truly godly man. I feel that, right down into the depths of my soul."

Ryker felt emotions swell up and choke him. This woman...from the moment he'd realized how he felt about her, she had never ceased to amaze him. He never wanted her to regret putting her trust in him.

"This can just be between us for now," Ryker said. "You can hide the ring in a sock drawer until you're ready for everyone to know. Although, my mom is a bit suspicious that I might be proposing tonight."

Sophia laughed, her face alight with happiness. "I'm not going to hide the ring."

"You haven't seen it yet." Ryker grinned. "Maybe I have the world's worst taste in engagement rings."

"I doubt that," Sophia said. "But even if you do, I will proudly wear your ring."

Ryker opened the ring box and slipped the thin band out. Shifting to one knee, he smiled at Sophia as he reached out and took her hand in his. "Sophia Haldorson, would you do me the honor of becoming my wife?"

"Yes." Sophia leaned forward, her grip on his hand tightening, and kissed him. "For always and forever...my heart belongs to you."

With a smile that he couldn't contain, Ryker slid the ring onto her finger, then drew her into his arms to hold her and kiss her again. He felt beyond blessed to have her in his life, and the fact that she also wanted to have him in hers filled him with an abundance of joy and hope for the future.

The healing he'd found over the past several months had been hard fought for, but it had brought him to the point where the hopelessness he'd felt following his time in Syria had faded away. He'd gotten back in contact with others who had been there at the time, and they'd formed a group chat where they could talk about what had happened and its impact on their lives. Finding out he hadn't been alone in the struggle with nightmares and guilt had been very freeing.

He was thankful that God had directed his journey over the past year. Having Bryson and Sophia show up in his life had been so unexpected, and though he'd resisted at first, he was glad that God had worked in his heart so that he was able to accept healing and a new direction in his life.

"I love you, Sophia," he said. "I hope you never have a moment of doubt over that because it will never change."

"I love you too." Sophia snuggled closer to him as they faced the flickering flames. "You've helped me see that there is hope beyond the hurt. I pray that we'll always remember that."

Ryker did too because he knew that moving ahead, God's will would always include healing, regardless of what caused the hurt. As long as they were both committed to God and each other, he knew they would be able to face life with determination and the promise that God would be their constant companion and guide.

~*~*~

ABOUT THE AUTHOR

Kimberly Rae Jordan is a USA Today bestselling author of Christian romances. Many years ago, her love of reading Christian romance morphed into a desire to write stories of love, faith, and family, and thus began a journey that would lead her to places Kimberly never imagined she'd go.

In addition to being a writer, she is also a wife and mother, which means Kimberly spends her days straddling the line between real life in a house on the prairies of Canada and the imaginary world her characters live in. Though caring for her husband and four kids and working on her stories takes up a large portion of her day, Kimberly also enjoys reading and looking at craft ideas that she will likely never attempt to make.

As she continues to pen heartwarming stories of love, faith, and family, Kimberly hopes that readers of all ages will enjoy the journeys her characters take in each book. She has no plan to stop writing the stories God places on her heart and looks forward to where her journey will take her in the years to come.